GODS OF MANHATTAN

SPIRITS
IN THE
PARK

SCOTT MEBUS

GODS OF MANHATTAN

SPIRITS IN THE PARK

DUTTON CHILDREN'S BOOKS

DUTTON CHILDREN'S BOOKS

A division of Penguin Young Readers Group

PUBLISHED BY THE PENGUIN GROUP

Penguin Group (USA) Inc., 375 Hudson Street, New York, New York 10014, U.S.A. • Penguin Group (Canada), 90 Eglinton Avenue East, Toronto, Ontario M4P 2Y3, Canada (a division of Pearson Penguin Canada Inc.) • Penguin Books Ltd, 80 Strand, London WC2R 0RL, England • Penguin Ireland, 25 St Stephen's Green, Dublin 2, Ireland (a division of Penguin Books Ltd) • Penguin Group (Australia), 250 Camberwell Road, Camberwell, Victoria 3124, Australia (a division of Pearson Australia Group Pty Ltd) • Penguin Books India Pvt Ltd, 11 Community Centre, Panchsheel Park, New Delhi - 110 017, India • Penguin Group (NZ), 67 Apollo Drive, Rosedale, North Shore 0632, New Zealand (a division of Pearson New Zealand Ltd) • Penguin Books (South Africa) (Pty) Ltd, 24 Sturdee Avenue, Rosebank, Johannesburg 2196, South Africa • Penguin Books Ltd, Registered Offices: 80 Strand, London WC2R 0RL, England

The publisher does not have any control over and does not assume any responsibility for author or third-party websites or their content.

Library of Congress Cataloging-in-Publication Data
Mebus, Scott.
Gods of Manhattan: spirits in the park / Scott Mebus.—1st ed.
p. cm.
Summary: As thirteen-year-old Rory continues his mission in Mannahatta, a spirit realm that co-exists alongside modern-day New York City, filled with fantastical creatures and people from the city's colorful past, he discovers that his father, whom he never wants to see again, is the only hope for peace.
ISBN 978-0-525-42148-1
[1. Fantasy. 2. Space and time—Fiction. 3. Gods—Fiction. 4. Goddesses—Fiction. 5. Spirits—Fiction. 6. Adventure and adventurers—Fiction. 7. New York (N.Y.)—Fiction. 8. New York (N.Y.)—History—Fiction.] I. Title.
PZ7.M512675Gv 2009
[Fic]—dc22   2008034229

Published in the United States by Dutton Children's Books, a division of Penguin Young Readers Group
345 Hudson Street, New York, New York 10014 • www.penguin.com/youngreaders

Designed by Jason Henry
Printed in USA • First Edition
1 3 5 7 9 10 2 6 4 2

To Dave Dunton, for your unwavering belief

·CONTENTS·

CAST OF CHARACTERS

Rory Hennessy—*A thirteen-year-old boy; the last Light in New York City*

Bridget Hennessy—*Younger sister to Rory Hennessy*

Lillian Hennessy—*Mother to Rory and Bridget Hennessy*

Peter Hennessy—*Rory and Bridget's father; missing for past ten years*

Tucket—*A spirit dog*

Toy—*A papier-mâché boy*

Olathe—*Owner of mysterious wampum necklace*

Harry Meester—*A murderer*

· THE RATTLE WATCH ·

Nicholas Stuyvesant—*Son of Peter Stuyvesant*

Alexa van der Donck—*Daughter of Adriaen van der Donck*

Simon Astor—*Son of John Jacob Astor*

Lincoln Douglass—*Son of Frederick Douglass*

· THE M'GAROTH CLAN ·

Fritz M'Garoth—*Lieutenant-Captain and Rat Rider of M'Garoth Clan*

Hans—*Member of M'Garoth Patrol*

Sergeant Kiffer—*Member of M'Garoth Patrol*

· GODS OF MANHATTAN ·

Mayor Alexander Hamilton—*God of Finance; Mayor of the Gods of Manhattan*

Willem Kieft—*First Adviser to Mayor*

Peter Stuyvesant—*God of Things Were Better in the Old Days*

Caesar Prince—*God of Under the Streets*

T. R. Tobias—*God of Banking*

Walt Whitman—*God of Optimism*

Boss Tweed—*God of Rabble Politics and Back Alley Deals*

Captain Kidd—*God of Pirates*

Alfred Beach—*God of Subway Trains*

Giovanni da Verrazano—*God of Unappreciated Explorers*

Mrs. Astor—*Goddess of Society*

Jimmy Walker—*God of Leaders Who Look the Other Way*

Washington Irving—*God of Tall Tales*

Langston Hughes—*God of Poetry*

Billie Holiday—*Goddess of the Blues*

George Gershwin—*God of Snappy Tunes*

Aaron Burr—*A fallen god*

· MUNSEES ·

Wampage—*Only Munsee to escape the Trap*

Penhawitz—*Sachem of the Munsees*

Tackapausha—*Son of Penhawitz*

Sooleawa—*Daughter of Penhawitz; sister of Tackapausha; Medicine Woman*

Sokanen (Soka for short)—*Daughter of Sooleawa; Sister of Tammand*

Tammand—*Son of Sooleawa; Brother of Soka*

Askook—*A magician*

Chogan—*A tanner*

Buckongahelas—*Murdered son of Tackapausha*

· IN THE PARK ·

Pierre Duchamp—*A trapper*

Finn Lee—*Grandson of Pierre Duchamp*

· OTHER SPIRITS OF NOTE ·

William "Bill the Butcher" Poole—*A convict*

Mary "Typhoid Mary" Mallon—*A convict*

The Abbess—*Founder of the convent on Swinburne Island*

Sly Jimmy—*Member of the B'wry Boys*

IMPORTANT TERMS

Blood (Bronx, Manhattan, Brooklyn, etc.)—*The restriction of a divine being to the boroughs where his or her mortal self was known to dwell. For example, a god whose mortal self lived on a farm in the Bronx possesses "Bronx blood."*

Sachem—*Munsee word meaning "chief"*

Shell Pit—*Place of power for the Munsees*

The Sachem's Belt—*Belt of powerful wampum*

The Trap—*Barrier erected around Central Park to keep the Munsees in, and New York spirits and gods out*

Wampum—*Jewelry made from seashells; common source of Munsee magic*

GODS OF MANHATTAN

SPIRITS
IN THE
PARK

PROLOGUE

The boy walked slowly down the city sidewalk bouncing a dusty basketball. Sweat sent dirty streaks down his forehead; he wiped his face with the back of his free hand, blinking furiously when he missed a drop before it could dive-bomb his eyes with its saltwater sting.

The city was hot, too hot, and had been for weeks now. 101, 102, 103: the city was running a fever and no one seemed to know when it would break. The asphalt sizzled under the burning sun, causing the thick, heavy air to shimmer above the sidewalks as if all of Manhattan were one huge mirage. The trees that lined the city blocks wilted under the assault. Those with the pocketbooks fled to the countryside, desperately seeking the sandy beaches of Long Island or the Jersey Shore. Those without hid inside their cool apartments, huddled around overworked, sputtering air conditioners.

The streets of Manhattan were eerily quiet, and so the *thwack* of the basketball hitting the sidewalk rang much louder than it should have, breaking a silence usually unknown in the great city. Except for the tawny dog trotting gamely at his side, the boy could have been all alone in an empty metropolis. But he was most definitely not alone.

The jerm kept its distance, gliding along the hot sidewalk a couple of car lengths behind its prey. It knew it would have to strike quickly when the time came, for the dog at the boy's side would not be affected by the jerm's poison, and the golden beast would have the would-be attacker in its jaws in a moment if alerted to its presence. The jerm was not a bright creature, but it knew how to adapt to the situation. Just yesterday it had been going about its usual business—the business of all jerms, running its sluglike, mucus-covered body over public phones and doorknobs, leaving behind a film of sickness for the mortals who touched it to contract. Nothing too deadly, just a summer flu. But enough to put whoever caught the bug out of commission for a while. Then it had felt the call, sending it on this mission that ultimately led to the boy walking just ahead.

The boy stopped for a second to tie his shoe and the jerm held back. Most mortals could never have seen the creature. But this boy was different. He was a Light. He could see Mannahatta, the spirit city that overlapped Manhattan. If the boy glanced in the jerm's direction, he would be able to see the glistening slug the size of a football pulsating on the sidewalk, a long line of green slime extending into the distance, marking its trail. If that happened, then the jerm would have to move fast. It had been saving up its secretions, the excess mucus puffing it up to twice its normal size. When the mucus found its way into the boy's skin, he would contract a flu so powerful he should be dead within hours.

The boy fiddled with his shoelace without looking in the jerm's direction, but the dog was sniffing the air. The longer the jerm waited, the more likely it became that the dog would pick up its scent. It would never have a better chance than now, it decided, with the boy distracted by his shoe and unable to move quickly. Seizing the moment, the jerm slid forward, picking up speed, ready to launch itself past the dog and onto its quarry to finish the job.

A searing pain suddenly exploded in the jerm's side and it found itself yanked sideways under a parked car. It struggled to move forward, but something was holding it back, tearing at its insides every time it tried to escape. From under the front of the car, the jerm watched helplessly as the boy straightened up and proceeded to stroll on down the street, getting farther and farther away as the *thwack* of the basketball echoed through the still air, the sound growing fainter with each bounce. Then something stepped in front of its eyes to obscure its vision, something much smaller than itself. The jerm gave a last desperate heave and felt something tear free, sending its hard-saved mucus squirting out in every direction. It rushed forward, blinded by pain, intent on covering its attacker with sickness before it died. But the small creature in front of it calmly lifted its arms, a long knife jutting out from each wrist. The jerm tried to pull up, but its own slime slid it helplessly forward until it impaled itself on the long knives. Mucus exploded everywhere, covering its dispatcher. The jerm could only hope that the sickness would take down its attacker and serve as its revenge. With that last wish still echoing through its fading brain, the jerm shuddered, once, and then knew no more . . .

"This is so disgusting!"

Fritz M'Garoth, battle roach and rat-rider for the M'Garoth clan, stood stiffly, covered in green goo. He flicked his arms, sending waves of mucus out in each direction. He would scrub and scrub, but something told him he might never get the smell off his poor knives.

He turned to his companion, a battle roach four times his size.

"Are you okay, Sergeant Kiffer?" he asked the roach.

"This is worse than the time I got swallowed by the German shepherd," Sergeant Kiffer complained sourly, and Fritz had to stifle a laugh. The huge roach had definitely received the worst of it; not one inch of his armor had escaped the rain of goo. Sergeant Kiffer dropped the wire he was holding, the other end of which led to the hook that had dragged the jerm under the car, and reached up to take off his helmet.

"Wait! Don't do that!" A third battle roach, this one smaller than the other two, ran up, narrowly missing skidding into the dead slug. "You're covered in liquid flu!"

"I see you somehow managed to stay clean, Hans," Sergeant Kiffer muttered as he dropped his hands down to his side. It was true; Hans's armor was almost spotless. He shrugged.

"The wheel of the car took most of the slime sent in my direction," Hans said breezily. Sergeant Kiffer took an irritated step forward as if to say something and Fritz decided to cut in.

"It doesn't matter," he said. " Everyone did a good job.

Hans, you're going to have to run after Rory. You're the only one who's still clean."

"That's easily remedied!" Hans said brightly. He lifted an arm and sent a strong stream of water toward Fritz, dousing the roach's slimy armor with its cool spray. A moment later, Fritz was clean.

"Where did that come from?" Fritz asked, astonished.

"Just something I was working on," Hans replied. "You never know when you need to wash!" He sent a spray out to Sergeant Kiffer, scouring the slime from the large roach's armor in a matter of seconds.

"Well done!" Fritz was impressed. "I guess we can all go after Rory."

"They're getting closer to the kid, boss," Sergeant Kiffer said as he carefully gathered up his wire. Fritz sighed, his heart heavy.

"This is more than closer, Kiffer," he said. "This time, Kieft almost got him. Next time . . ." He trailed off, unwilling to finish the sentence.

"Why don't we just tell Rory what's been going on for the past month?" Hans asked. "We can't protect him forever."

"I know," Fritz said, staring down the sidewalk where Rory had disappeared. "It's just . . . he had a rough time for a while there and I wanted to give him—I don't know—some peace. Just for a little while."

"You do him no favors coddlin' him like that," Sergeant Kiffer muttered.

"You're probably right," Fritz said. "Looks like we're out of time, anyway. The days of hiding are almost over."

"Ew!" Hans jumped back suddenly, clutching at his helmet. *"Ew, ew, ew, ew, ew, EW!"*

He ripped off his insect head, exposing the pink humanoid face underneath.

"What's wrong with you, Private!" Kiffer roared.

"It's *on* me!" Hans shouted, shuddering. Sure enough, a small drop of goo was sliding down his cheek.

"You never attach your helmet right!" Kiffer scolded him. "You're a horrible soldier!"

Hans didn't answer; he was too busy shooting water up onto his own face.

"Is it gone?" he asked finally, his eyes wide with fear.

"You're not a human," Kiffer said scornfully. "It won't kill you like it would one of them. It'll just be pretty darn unpleasant for a few days. So roach up, soldier!"

"But . . . I hate getting sick!"

"Come on." Fritz took Hans's shoulder. "I'll take you up to the village. You'll be fine. Kiffer, look after Rory, would you?" The large roach nodded, saluting sharply before setting out down the sidewalk after Rory. Fritz watched him go before glancing down at the dead jerm. That was too close. It looked like the days of Rory's safe hiding were just about over . . .

THE NECKLACE

ory Hennessy stepped across the threshold into Central Park, half hoping that this time he would feel something as he passed through the barrier that kept the gods and spirits of Mannahatta out, and the Munsee Indians in. He sighed. *Nothing.* He'd been sneaking away to the park almost every other day for the past month, but he never felt so much as a tingle as he crossed over. For something so monumental, so overwhelmingly evil, he should at least get a zap or a shock or a tickle or *something.* It just didn't seem right to feel nothing at all.

He glanced back to the other side, spying Tucket lying forlornly by the break in the wall. Rory felt a flash of guilt. Though Wampage had told him that Tucket could follow his new master anywhere, he had quickly discovered that the tawny dog refused to enter the park. Wampage explained that because of the nature of the Trap, Tucket couldn't feel the island, the *land,* while inside the park, which was why he would not go in. Wampage warned Rory not to leave the dog, his protector, behind for any reason. But though Rory had grown fond of the fun-loving pooch, Tucket had never protected him from anything, as far as he could tell. So the lure of the park won out in the end.

Rory breathed deeply. The shady trees and soft grass calmed him, helping him forget that he lived under the constant fear of discovery and death. They couldn't get to him here, he told himself. He was safe.

Dribbling his basketball, Rory set off down the path toward the courts. Above him, a flock of unfamiliar birds filled the sky, heading north. He wondered if anyone else could see them; he had a hunch they were extinct. It seemed like he couldn't walk five feet anymore without stumbling across the impossible. One afternoon he'd almost been run over by a huge herd of pigs stampeding down East 4th Street—pigs invisible to everyone but him. He must have looked like a crazy person, jumping around to keep from getting trampled by the hogs only he could see. Another evening, as he walked toward the subway station, a smoky locomotive had roared over his head, flying through the air along Ninth Avenue. It was the memory of the old El train, Fritz later told him, still running along elevated tracks that had long since been taken down. Rory came across these impossibilities everywhere: little farms where everyone else saw apartment buildings; horse-drawn carts trotting unseen beside the taxis and buses; costumed people long dead, gathered on street corners for reasons he never discovered; old, forgotten buildings peeking out from inside the doorways and side alleys of newer skyscrapers; not to mention a whole slew of strange creatures the likes of which he hoped never to see again. Sure, it all sounded like a never-ending adventure, or so his younger sister, Bridget, argued. But, in truth, these wonders only made him feel more alone.

For Rory was a Light, and a Light didn't just see the hidden city of Mannahatta. A Light could also reveal that world to others. But opening people's eyes was dangerous, as he discovered when Bridget had her mortal body stolen by the evil magician Hex—all because Rory opened her eyes to Mannahatta. Rory would never expose a mortal to that danger again, if he could help it. So as he walked the streets of New York, he refused to acknowledge the wonders around him for fear of dragging someone else into a world they never asked to see, holding him forever apart from the people around him.

His mind elsewhere as he dribbled, Rory accidentally hit the side of his shoe with the ball. It bounced away, disappearing into the trees.

"Crap!" he cursed to himself. Annoyed, he ran after the ball, diving into the brush. The greenery grew particularly dense along the path, and at first Rory couldn't even see his basketball for all the branches and leaves in his way. Finally, he spied orange through the green; there was his basketball, resting against the trunk of a huge elm tree. He reached down to pick it up when suddenly his wrist blazed fire.

"Ow!" he cried, falling back. What was that? He checked his wrist to see if he'd been stung by something. It looked perfectly fine; the skin was unbroken and the small bracelet of purple beads he always wore appeared unharmed . . . *Wait a minute*. The *bracelet*. How could he have forgotten?

These were no ordinary beads, of course. The bracelet was made of pure wampum: the Native American mystic shells that not only made beautiful jewelry, but also, according to Wampage, held a variety of magical powers. Among this bracelet's properties was the tendency to grow warm when other wampum was near. But he had never felt it blaze so hot as it did now. What was setting it off?

Curious, Rory moved his arm over the dirt at the base of the tree until he found the spot where the bracelet burned hottest. Then he dropped to his knees and began to dig.

A small pile of dirt formed by his side as he shoveled deeper into the ground at the base of the elm. Finally, after lifting up a particularly large clump of earth, he spied something poking out of the bottom of the elbow-deep hole he'd dug. His wrist was on fire as he reached down to pick up what appeared to be a dull black bead. But bead after bead followed, until a long loop of wampum dangled from his fingers. He brushed off the dirt and took a good look at what he'd found.

It appeared to be a necklace, fashioned out of a single string of beads. The beads themselves alternated between black and purple all the way around. He couldn't begin to guess how old it was. But even though it was dirty, he could tell it was beautiful.

He couldn't explain what happened next. He was always the last person to do anything rash. But for some reason, despite his better judgment, he found himself lifting the necklace up over his head, letting the wampum beads fall gently around his neck.

A roaring sounded in his ears as the world around him began to blur. The noise grew louder and louder, threatening to burst his eardrums, as if a fierce wind were battering him senseless. He felt himself blown back, but not through the air; rather a hurricane thrust him somewhere inside, with such force he closed his eyes in fear. When he opened them again, he was somewhere, and some*one*, else entirely . . .

She sits anxiously by the newly lit fire, concentrating closely on the beads in her delicate, white hand. The soft light of sunset bathes the purple-and-black wampum in a golden glow, as if to reassure her that the magic is working. It hadn't been easy to learn how to bend the wampum to her will, and if not for her new husband's father sitting across the fire giving her encouragement and wisdom, she would have long since given up. Even now, she fears the beautifully worked beads will reject her unskilled mind and refuse to hold her command. She teeters on the edge, a moment from giving up all together.

"Do not waver," her father-in-law encourages her. He seems so young with his long black hair bound up with eagle feathers and unlined face bare of the tattoos many of his people wear to display their inner selves to the world, but his eyes are as old as stone. "Olathe, it is almost done."

Olathe. That is her name now, here among her new family. She will not go back to the girl she had been. Her own father has made certain of that. She is a Munsee now and her old name is as dead as her past.

Determined, she bears down harder, willing the wampum to accept her. Finally, with a soft sigh, she feels something give and the beads open like tiny flowers in her mind. She looks up in joy, pride bursting from her lips.

"I did it!"

"You did, indeed, daughter of my heart," he agrees, grin-

ning hugely. He radiates the same wisdom and strength as his son, her husband. If only her own father had been so wise and good, she would not have been forced to make the wrenching choice between her old family and her new one. Her father-in-law reaches over to pat her hand. "Buckongahelas will be proud of his young bride. You have learned one of our oldest skills so quickly, even though you are only newly among us. It is as if you were listening at Sooleawa's feet since birth."

"When can I begin giving it memories?" she asks, eyes shining at at his praise.

"You can begin now, if you wish," her father-in-law informs her. "You have opened the beads, and they will fill whenever you hold them and concentrate. But be careful. They will overflow before you know it. There is room for maybe three true memories inside the necklace, so choose them wisely."

Only three . . . so few. She glances around the bustling camp, where the entire Munsee nation had set up temporary quarters earlier that day. All around her, newly planted trees and weak patches of thin grass remind her of the newness of this man-made wilderness in the center of Manhattan Island. The Munsees have been invited here, to live in peace with the gods, but apart in a land all their own. Hope shines upon every face as the Munsees put aside their centuries old struggle for the island in the name of a future free of war. Even Buck felt it; he'd traveled to the house of her father that very morning to beg him to consider a reconciliation. She holds out little hope for that, however. Her father is not a bad man, but he can be hard. She will survive without him. She has a new family now, one that loves her. Clutching the necklace in her hand and filling it

with its first true memory, she smiles at her father-in-law, who
winks back. How she was so lucky as to find a husband as good
as Buckongahelas and a new father as openhearted and kind as
Tackapausha, she will never know . . .

The roaring overtook Rory, blowing him from one memory to
the next as he closed his eyes beneath the pressure. *That man*
was Tackapausha? he thought. *But he seemed so peaceful . . .* Then
his eyes opened again, and he was elsewhere . . .

She pushes through the brush, Tackapausha at her side, worry
tearing at her heart. Buck had not returned the night before
from his visit to her father and she does not know what to think.
Her father-in-law's face does not appear disturbed, but judging
by the speed with which he leads her on, he feels something is
wrong. Buck should have been back by now. What has hap-
pened to her beloved?

    She stumbles; she'd been up almost the entire night. Last
night, she'd been unable to sleep and had decided to travel to-
ward the edge of the park by starlight to meet her husband on
his way home. But instead of finding him, she'd happened upon
a very strange procession moving through the trees, led by a
familiar face that sent her ducking for cover behind some thick
bushes. Willem Kieft, the black-eyed first adviser, guided a party
of spirits into the park under the cover of night, some holding
torches while the others bore shrouded boxes upon their backs.
Recklessness overpowered her better sense. She and Buck had
often wondered about Kieft; she would not let the chance to dis-
cover one of his secrets slip away. So she followed alongside them

unseen, all night, as they traveled north through the new wilderness. Kieft set magical snares as he walked to punish pursuers, but she stayed close enough to spy where he placed them and thus avoided them easily. Even still, she lost the party at the base of the Great Hill, and when Kieft finally reappeared, he was alone. What had he been doing? What was hidden up in the treacherous mountain passes of the Great Hill? Not foolish enough to tackle the climb alone, she had raced home to tell Buck all about it as the night sky brightened into early dawn. But he had never come home. So all thoughts of Kieft and his secrets flew from her mind as she and Tackapausha set out to find what had become of her husband. Which led them here . . .

They step out of a small copse of trees. Before them looms the wide circle that forms the southwest corner of the park. Well-dressed mortals in their horse-drawn carriages rattle around the circle as they make their way downtown, completely unaware of the spirits emerging from the park into their midst. Suddenly she gasps as her husband bursts into view, racing across the circle while dodging the trotting horses and fine carriages, a look of desperate horror on his face.

"Beware!" Buckongahelas yells as he approaches them. "It is a trap! They have betrayed us!"

"I don't understand," Tackapausha says haltingly at her side as a wave of horror washes over her. "Who has betrayed us?"

"Hamilton!" Buck calls back, crossing the last bit of road to join them. Olathe reels as if struck. "We must hurry! He has betrayed us all . . ."

A shot rings out, overpowering all other sound. Buck stumbles, his face startled. The white shirt he had donned to curry favor with her father suddenly blossoms red as her husband, her

*heart, sinks to his knees, mouth opening in pain, before falling
over to land face-first in the dirt. There, he lies still.*

*The world slows around her as her beloved bleeds into the
ground before her. In the center of the busy traffic circle stands a
man with a pistol in his hand, the horse-drawn carriages passing
in front of him, hiding, then revealing him, over and over again.
The smoke from the gun obscures his face, but something about
the way he carries himself is familiar to her.*

*"Meester," Tackapausha whipsers next to her, his fierce voice
promising murder or worse, and she realizes that the man behind the pistol smoke must be Harry Meester, who had always
been her friend. So many betrayals, it tears at her heart . . . but
at the moment she cannot think about the man with the pistol.
She needs to get to her husband. But before they can cover two
feet, a brilliant blue light shoots up before them, cutting off
their view of the city. They bounce right off it as if it were stone.
Throwing themselves against the barrier, she and Tackapausha
hammer and shout, but they cannot break through. The trap
has been sprung and she is caught in its snare. She drops to her
knees, reaching up to clutch at her wampum necklace as the
tears begin to fall unchecked . . .*

The roaring returned, drowning out that heartbreaking sight
as Rory was pushed onward. In the midst of his sorrow at the
murder of Olathe's beloved, a glimmer of recognition beck-
oned. He'd heard of Kieft's midnight trek into the park before;
the magician Hex had tried to trick Rory into opening the Trap
just to get at that same secret. And this woman knew where it
was hidden! But he barely had time to dwell on his discovery
before he tumbled into the final memory . . .

She runs through the woods, the necklace dangling from her hands. The man chasing her is near; she can hear the disturbance in the brush behind her. She does not have much time. She knows it will be her death if he catches her. She has uncovered Kieft's secrets and her life is forfeit. If only she had understood what she had seen up there on the mountain. She thinks of the sheet of parchment she took from the cave, the one treasure she had recognized. Before the man chasing her gets too close, she can use the magic it teaches to protect herself. But the price is steep and she might not even survive the invocation. Yet she can think of no other way out.

She never should have set out from the Munsee camp alone. But she couldn't stay there. No one seemed to blame her, but they couldn't look at her, either, and she understands why. Tackapausha had sunk into a deep depression; the death of his son and the betrayal by his friend hit him hard. He had begun to speak bitterly about revenge, which made Olathe unbearably sad. Through the gods' treachery, the wars between Munsee and Newcomer will come again, laying waste to Mannahatta. Maybe Kieft's secret hidden in the high reaches of the Great Hill, incomprehensible as it may be to her, would be the key to averting catastrophe. After all, it seems a bit too coincidental to her: Kieft hides his boxes of strange items in the cave the night before all of Central Park is encased in an impassable barrier? Far too convienent for her liking.

But the frightening truth is that there is no one left for her to tell about what she'd seen up on the mountain. She is all alone now. She grasps at one slim hope, the last resort of last resorts before she turns to the parchment in her hand. She will leave a trail behind for the one person she swore never to talk to again:

her father. Perhaps when the Trap is opened, whenever that may be, he will come looking for her. It is unlikely, given how the two of them left matters, but it is all she has to hold on to. After everything, she still loves him; maybe he still loves her as well. It isn't much, but she knows no other option with her pursuer so close behind.

She closes her eyes to concentrate, setting a charm onto the necklace that will call to her father if he comes within fifty paces, a trick Sooleawa the medicine woman herself taught her. Then he will wear the necklace, learn of her fate, and, hopefully, follow her trail, starting at the cave atop the Great Hill. She checks the half a token she keeps in her pocket to make sure it is safe. She'd left its other half in the cave—its magic called out to its brother in her possession, serving as a beacon that was to lead her back to Kieft's hidden treasure room up on the mountain. But with her pursuer almost upon her, her plans must change. Now she must hope that her necklace leads her father to that cave, where the half token she'd left behind waits to guide him to her, wherever she might be. If she lives, he will find her. If not . . . she pushes away the fear and lays her necklace down, beneath a newly planted elm, and begins to cover it with leaves, all the while checking over her shoulder for signs of he who pursues her. Come quickly, Father, she prays. Come quickly . . .

The hazy world of the distant past fell away as Rory lifted the necklace from around his neck. His eyes remained unfocused as he shook his head to clear it; the feelings of sadness and fear didn't lift away as easily as the necklace. He blinked, then started in shock. Someone was kneeling down right in front of him, inches from his face!

"Tell me you are really not this stupid, Rory Hennessy," the figure said sharply. Rory relaxed as he recognized those playful, mocking eyes.

"Soka?" he whispered. Actually, her eyes didn't seem so playful right then. In fact, the Indian girl looked ready to smack him.

"My mother told you not to enter the park until she calls you." Soka's voice was tight with fury. "And yet here you are. That is bad enough. But this . . . !" She grabbed the necklace from his hand. "This seems like a wish for death. Wearing unknown wampum? You could have died, or your mind could have been taken over by some evil spirit residing in the necklace, or a million other things I do not wish to think about! Did someone hit you on the head recently? Have you eaten any strange berries? There must be some explanation, because otherwise I have to believe you are really that dumb. And then we're all in trouble, because that means my people's fate rests in the hands of a nitwit!"

Soka finished her tirade, sitting back to catch her breath as she glared at him. He couldn't help noticing how pretty she looked as her fingers tugged at her single braid in frustration. The last time they'd met, she had told him he had a nice nose, moments before her brother, Tammand, started shooting arrows at him. Now here they were, together again, with her brother nowhere to be found, and his heart leaped at the opportunity to talk to her without the fear of becoming a human pincushion. Perhaps the love Olathe felt for her husband still coarsed through him, which was why he opened his mouth and said something dumb.

"Your hair looks nice."

Soka blinked, thrown. Rory started to scream at himself inside, aghast at his own stupidity. He really shouldn't be allowed to talk to girls. But then, finally, Soka's frown melted away and she began to laugh.

"You . . ." she began, shaking her head. "Pretty Nose . . . you know you could have died."

"I don't know why I did it," he protested. "It just seemed like the right thing to do."

She nodded, begrudgingly.

"Well, you are *Sabbeleu,* and that means you see the true nature of things; this wampum is meant to be worn and you must have felt that." Soka lifted the necklace to take another look, running her fingers across the beads. "What did you see when you wore this?"

Rory described Olathe and her sad story. Soka looked thoughtful.

"We all know how Buckongahelas died," she said. "Though it happened before I was born. Tackapausha will not let us forget it."

"Do you know what happened to Olathe?"

"No one has ever mentioned her," Soka admitted. "I will ask my mother; after all, apparently this Olathe learned our magic from her. Of course my mother will wonder why you ignore her warnings and risk your life by coming here. This park is filled with many dangers. We Munsees are not the only inhabitants of this park, you know. You are lucky I was the one who found you, and not someone, or some*thing,* else."

Rory took a deep breath to steady his nerves. Being chased

by assassins was nothing compared to trying to talk to the girl he liked. "You know I'd hoped I would see you again . . ."

Suddenly Soka shushed him, glancing around furtively. "Put the necklace away," she whispered. "I think I heard something . . ."

Rory stuffed the wampum in his pocket. He joined Soka in scanning the trees around them. A rustle in the bushes made him jump and he prepared himself to protect Soka from whatever was coming. The sound came closer and closer until the bush right before him began to move . . .

A squirrel ran up to them, chattering. Rory relaxed, laughing at his foolishness.

"Look at us, all worried," he said, nudging her. "It's just a squirrel."

But Soka wasn't looking at the squirrel. She was staring past it at the man stepping through the brush into the clearing. Rory's stomach dropped.

"Hello, Tammand," Soka said, taking a small step in front of Rory as she greeted her brother.

"Soka," he greeted her stiffly. "Chepi, here, told me you'd been sneaking off." He held out his arm as the squirrel ran up the elm and leaped onto it. "I wanted to see for myself. And look what I find."

"Hey, we're just talking, that's it," Rory said, not wanting Tammand to get the wrong idea. Soka's brother was an impressive fellow. He stood straight and tall, lanky and muscular. The Munsee's hair was greased into a Mohawk, with a slight ponytail interwoven with feathers hanging down his back. But it was Tammand's face that sent shivers down Rory's spine. A tattoo of a snarling dog adorned each cheek, so lifelike they threatened to leap off Tammand's face and chase Rory down the path. Soka's big brother was no one to be trifled with.

"Are you following me?" Soka demanded.

"I simply set Chepi on your trail, for your own good," Tammand replied sternly. "And I am glad I did. This is a great prize."

"I was just telling him to leave!" Soka told him. Tammand shook his head emphatically.

"Not when the fate of our people rests on his scrawny shoulders." He reached for Rory. "No, you must come with me, *Sabbeleu*."

Shocked, Rory pulled away. "I'm not going with you."

"You are too important to let loose like a wild turkey," Tammand insisted, irritated. "I will take you back to Tackapausha and he will decide what to do. Do not worry. I know what Mother thinks, but her fears are groundless. Tackapausha does not want to start up the war. He only wishes to make Mayor Hamilton pay for his crimes. He and the murderer Harry Meester. They were the ones who wronged us. Tackapausha knows this; he is not reckless. He only wants justice."

"No!" Soka replied. "Mother told us not to trust Tackapausha, especially with Rory." She grabbed Rory's arm protectively, sending a shiver down his spine.

"Well, she is wrong," Tammand insisted. "And I will not bow to family over my sachem any longer. You are coming with me, *Sabbeleu*."

Despite Soka's grip on his arm, Rory had no illusions about her protection. Tammand was bigger and stonger than he was, and Rory knew he was in a lot of trouble. He should have listened to Sooleawa's warning, he thought as Tammand reached out to grab his other arm. She'd been right after all.

And that was when the ground began to shake.

Rory fell backward, wrenching out of the grip of both Munsees as he fell to the ground. Out of the corner of his eye, he saw the two siblings stumble as well, reaching for the elm to steady themselves as the ground vibrated like the floor of a fun house. Screams floated by from elsewhere in the park as the world continued to move. A crack and a crash sounded behind him, but Rory didn't turn to look. He gritted his teeth and waited for the shaking to pass.

And pass it did, finally, leaving Rory shaken but unhurt. Glancing around, he caught sight of the origin of the crash; the large elm had toppled to the ground. If it had tilted in a different direction, he realized with a shudder, it would have landed right on top of him. Rory pushed himself to his feet and staggered over to Soka, who remained kneeling where she fell. Tammand lay nearby, stunned.

"Are you all right?" Rory asked, still trying to catch his breath. Looking up with wild eyes, Soka climbed unsteadily to her feet, clinging to him for balance.

"Go!" she hissed in his ear. "You must! Before Tammand gets his wits about him again." Her lips were so close it almost felt like a kiss. Rory glanced guiltily over at Tammand; the older boy was staggering to his feet, slowly regaining his balance. Rory touched the cheek where her breath had caressed him, imagining that the skin felt warmer there. Then he shook himself out of his stupor.

"Good-bye," he said, backing away. Soka watched him retreat, already regaining her composure as she waved a hand in farewell, while her brother finally found his footing. Seizing the last of his moment, Rory turned before Tammand could stop him and dove through the brush, trying to get away as fast as he could.

McCool's

The man in the fedora climbed up out of the manhole, brushing the dirt off his nicely tailored suit. The earthquake had surprised even him, but he knew what it meant. They were just about out of time. He'd designed the Trap to be opened, and opened it must be. What happened after, *that* was the worry now. He had hoped to avoid resorting to drastic measures, but circumstances pushed him. He'd wanted to spare Rory; they all did. But he no longer had a choice.

The man in the fedora began to stroll down the street, surrounded by the confusion left in the earthquake's wake. He prayed the Light was strong enough for what was to come. He could only hope that one day Rory would find it in his heart to forgive him for what he was about to do.

I'm sorry, kiddo, he thought, then pushed the regret out of his head. He had work to do, and little time to do it.

Rory burst out onto the path, running full speed toward the street entrance. Leaves covered the walkway, and fallen branches blocked his path as he ran. Finally, the exit came into view. Breathing a sigh of relief, he swept through the opening in the wall and out onto the street. But that relief was short-lived as he took in the crazy scene around him.

Cars had run up onto the sidewalks all along Central Park West, slamming into street signs and lampposts, and one another. Smoke rose steadily from their ruined, still-sputtering engines. People were pouring out of the buildings, looking bewildered and frightened. Tree branches lay strewn all over the sidewalks, as did pieces of stone fallen from the buildings lining the street. Everywhere Rory looked confusion reigned. Big earthquakes were supposed to happen to Los Angeles and San Francisco, not New York City.

A loud bark warned him to brace himself before Tucket barreled into him, jumping up to try to lick his face. Then the tawny dog noticed something near Rory's feet and his tail began to wag at supersonic speed.

"Keep that monster away from me!" a voice cried. Glancing down, Rory spied a gigantic cockroach by his feet, trying to hide behind his ankle. A shiver ran down his spine, even as he recognized the battle roach. A huge insect will do that to you.

"Sergeant Kiffer?" Rory bent over to give the battle roach a hand to escape into. He had to resist his instinctual urge to fling the roach into the bushes. Tucket tried to leap up and lick the roach, and Rory had to fight to keep the spirit dog down. "Have you been following me?"

"What did you think, we'd let the last Light on Manhattan

Island run around willy-nilly?" The roach's voice dripped with disdain. "What kind of protectors of the future of Mannahatta would we be if did that? We know that you've been hiding in Central Park. I don't know why Fritz allows it. I tell him over and over that you'll be a spoiled brat with no discipline if he keeps babying you like this. But he never listens . . ."

"Babying me?" Rory didn't know what the large roach was talking about. He'd met Sergeant Kiffer and the other members of Fritz's patrol a few times over the last month, but he didn't know any of them particularly well. "What do you mean?"

"Look, once you're safe, then we can gab all night long like two schoolgirls if you want," Kiffer said. "But right now I'm gonna take you to McCool's."

Rory shook his head. "No, I've got to go home and check on my sister and my mom."

"And how will you get home? The subways must be closed. And look at the streets. No bus or cab will be running for a while, trust me."

"Then I'll walk."

"It's too dangerous. We have to get you off the streets and MacCool's is the closest friendly place. I don't know why the world almost shook itself to death, but chances are it has something to do with you, and I won't be the roach who lets you get killed on his watch, you hear me? We need to get you to a safe place, *right now*."

"I know they're looking for me," Rory said. "But is it really that bad? They haven't gotten close yet, right?"

"We've taken down at least ten assassins in the past month," Sergeant Kiffer replied. "The last few came a hairbreadth from doing their jobs. If not for the M'Garoth patrol boys, you'd be dead right now."

Rory was shocked. He'd really been that close to death? And he'd thought he was so clever, hiding in the park. He was shaken, badly, and Sergeant Kiffer seemed to notice.

"Come on, kid," Kiffer said, softer this time. "Let's get you inside."

The earthquake shocked Manhattan from its heat-induced daze. Frightened people wandered the streets, taking in the fallen masonry and downed lampposts with bewilderment. Sirens rang throughout the streets as fires sprang up all over the city. There were people pinned under fallen rubble and people trapped in unstable old buildings and people just terrified because the shifting ground had destroyed the illusion of permanence they'd enjoyed all their lives.

On one street corner, a five-car pileup had attracted a large, frightened crowd. The fire trucks were on their way, the people were told, though the damage across the city had spread the firefighters far too thin to rely on them for a prompt response. Most of the victims had been pulled away from the crash, but the car on the bottom was compressed so much that no one could get the doors open. A woman and her young child pressed against the car window, frantically beating against their jammed door, desperate for rescue. The people around the car tried to help, but they were running out of time; it would take only one spark to light the gas currently dripping from four gas tanks. A small fire had already sprung up; it was only a matter of time before the pool of gas forming beneath lit up like a Roman candle.

And then the figure appeared, shrouded in a hooded sweat-shirt, leaping through the crowd to dive into the fire.

Through the smoke, onlookers could see the figure yank-ing at the door to the car that held the mother and daughter prisoner. They peered in intently, trying to catch a glimpse of a face. But the smoke was too thick, enveloping the figure in secrecy.

Suddenly, to everyone's shock, the figure somehow tore the car door off its hinges entirely. Reaching in, the figure helped pull the mother and daughter out of the car, carrying them through the fire to safety, where they collapsed into each other's arms. Then the figure was gone, disappearing into the cloud of smoke. No one had caught a good look at the rescuer; but some of the folks on the edges of the crowd thought they heard a voice as the figure raced by.

"I'd like to see Barbie do that!"

McCool's proved to be a small wooden structure nestled in the midst of towering skyscrapers. Smoke wafted from a rusted iron pipe in the roof, and the sound of animated conversa-tion drifted out from inside. Rory had just reached his relieved mother on her cell via pay phone and he'd promised to meet her at home; she was slowly making her way up Broadway and he'd much rather be walking north with her than entering into this broken-down shack. But acknowledging that he did not know everything that was going on, he bit his tongue and fol-lowed Sergeant Kiffer inside.

The interior made good on the exterior's promises; this place was a dive. Dimly lit by oil lamps on the wall, the old tavern was filled with shoddy, broken-down tables and chairs and dominated by one long bar that looked as if it hadn't been cleaned since the War of 1812. Behind the bar, manned by a large fellow with red hair and redder cheeks, sat barrels of whiskey with tubes coming out of the spigots. These tubes carried the whiskey directly into the mouths of the customers at the bar. Why waste money on glasses, Sergeant Kiffer explained, when they'd only get thrown at the bartender anyway.

Every seat in the place was filled, and then some, by the most disreputable spirits in all of Mannahatta. Nineteenth-century gang members in top hats and dirty jackets, members of the fire brigades of two centuries earlier, notorious for fighting among themselves for the right to fight the fire, while the buildings in jeapordy merrily burned down around them, and shady sailors on shore leave from the clippers that sailed into the mist beyond the harbor. They all turned to watch as Rory entered, throwing him evil, calculating looks before returning to their conversations.

"Friendly place?" Rory muttered to Kiffer. "This place couldn't be any seedier if it sold orphans."

"What are you talking about?" Sergeant Kiffer scoffed. "These are my boys! Big Mickey!"

The bartender, whom Kiffer introduced as Big Mickey Connolly, owner of McCool's, gave Kiffer a nod of welcome.

"Need anything, just holler," Big Mickey told Rory before moving down the bar to tend to his customers. He stopped to speak to a group of brightly dressed sailors led by a short man whose deep brown skin was covered in colorful tattoos. The tattooed man noticed Rory watching him and gave him a know-ing wink and a smile. Rory quickly looked away, disturbed.

"I think we should go," Rory whispered to Kiffer.

"I already sent word to Fritz that we'd wait here, so we're gonna sit tight till he shows up," Kiffer said, yanking on his helmet. "Stupid helmet must have been dented in the fight this morning. Ah! There we are!"

Sergeant Kiffer finally managed to free his helmet, lifting it off with a relieved sigh. Rory had seen this before, but he still had to stifle a laugh. Though Kiffer's armor was giant, the roach inside was actually no bigger than any other battle roach. The small human head on the huge body gave the effect of two very different-size action figures glued together by a sadistic third grader. Rory tried to be subtle.

"Is this what you would call regulation-size armor?"

"Hans made it for me," Sergeant Kiffer explained stiffly. "This way, people know I'm not some scrawny runt with eight hulking brothers. I am a roach to be reckoned with!"

"I bet you get stepped on a lot," Rory said.

"And it never even cracks!" Sergeant Kiffer said proudly, rapping his armor with one fist. He spied a small bowl on the bar and his face lit up. "I think I'll have a nut!"

The roach munched on nuts as big as his helmet while Rory sat back to wait for Fritz. Gradually, snippets of the conversa-tions around him floated by. Everyone seemed to be talking about the earthquake, and they didn't appear to know any more than Rory did. Though it didn't stop them from speculation.

"The island tore free of its moorings and is floating out to sea!" a sailor maintained with utmost certainty. He didn't seem too alarmed, however, as he made no move to leave his drink.

"It's a weapon, a gun going off in one of the big boys' faces, and we're next!" a gang member said, spinning his knife in his palm nervously. His friends laughed at him, though some looked worried at the thought.

"It was Caesar Prince, doing one of his experiments again," one fireman asserted. Rory had met the God Under the Streets and he wouldn't put it past him.

"It's the Munsees, I tell you," someone said loudly. "They're trying to break out of their prison and wreak their revenge on us all!"

Disturbed by that last declaration, Rory scanned the room for the source of the comment.

"Yer crazy!" Big Mickey shot back from behind the bar. "The Munsees been locked away, good and tight, fer years and years. Always will be, too."

"Really?" the first voice said. Rory could tell it came from a table in the corner, but he couldn't see past the sailors. "That's not what I heard. I heard there's a Munsee loose outside the Trap right now!"

This caught everyone's attention. Rory's heart skipped a beat and he exchanged a worried look with Sergeant Kiffer. Could the man be talking about Wampage? How did he know? Rory moved over, straining to see past the sailors into the corner.

"Now yer just talkin' nonsense!" Big Mickey scoffed, and many of his patrons agreed. But not all. Some of the firemen looked worried, while the tattooed sailor appeared thoughtful.

"Maybe I am, maybe I am," the voice continued. Rory leaned over the bar, trying to peer into the dark corner. "But listen to me now. No one can kill a god, correct? Yet Adriaen van der Donck was murdered last month, as was Jenny Fingers and Hiram Greenbaum and who knows who else. So who killed them? And how? Well, you know who can kill a god, don't you? A Munsee, that's who. So chew on that, my friends. Chew on that."

Indignation ran through Rory at the bald-faced lie. Albert Fish, former member of the Rattle Watch, had murdered those gods at Kieft's order. He wanted to call out the falsehood, but he knew he shouldn't attract any attention. Muttering rippled through the crowd and the sailors leaned in to listen, finally giving Rory a clean look at the gossip. One glance at the tall, thin man in the corner and Rory quickly dropped back into his seat, his face white.

"I know him," he whispered to Sergeant Kiffer, his heart pounding. "His name is James!" The last time Rory had seen James had been in the vault of T. R. Tobias's bank, standing behind Tobias himself. This man spreading lies worked for Tobias. And he knew what Rory looked like. "I need to get out of here," Rory told the battle roach. "Now."

"You'll never make it to the entrance without him seein' you," Kiffer whispered back. Rory didn't know what to do; he moved around the bar to duck down behind it. Big Mickey noticed and stepped over to him.

"Friend of yours?" he asked, nodding toward the corner. "Would ye be lookin' to stay out a sight?"

"I wouldn't mind it," Rory answered, crouching down.

Big Mickey winked. "If ye want, I got a room in back where ye can wait fer yer friend in private. It's where I stay when I don't want to go home to the missus. Interested?"

Rory didn't want to say yes. But it was only a matter of time before James spotted him and then it was all over. Safer to wait in this back room until Fritz arrived.

"I'll take it," he said. Big Mickey smiled.

"Yer a customer a' mine, and I always treat me customers right."

"Mark my words!" James was saying as Rory began to creep toward the back. "It's only a matter of time before that Munsee killer helps his murderous friends escape and take their revenge on us all!"

The room exploded in argument, and under cover of the din, Big Mickey led Rory and Kiffer quietly behind the bar to a door in the back. Opening it, he stood aside to let them pass. Rory took one last look at James, who stared around the agitated tavern with a satisfied smile before slipping into sanctuary, Tucket by his side. Kiffer held up behind him.

"I'll wait out here for Fritz," he told Rory. "And to make sure no one comes back here to bother you. Don't worry, you'll be safe and Fritz will be here soon."

Rory nodded with a smile he did not feel, and stepped back, letting the door close behind him as he turned to take in his new surroundings.

Suprisingly, it seemed like a normal little bedroom, complete with a large red bed sitting in the center, inviting any and all to take a load off and rest for a while. It seemed so comfortable that Rory sat on the edge, intending to test the springs and such while he waited. Gradually his worry faded as, lulled by the soft bedspread, Rory leaned back to enjoy its comforts. He fiddled with the necklace in his pocket, thinking about the woman who made it. What had happened to her? Maybe Soka would find out. Would he ever see Soka again?

He smiled at the thought of the Indian girl's mocking eyes. He *would* see her again, he told himself. After the Trap came down, Soka would be so impressed with how he saved the day that she'd go out with him, maybe on a Circle Line cruise or something. She'd never actually been to New York, even though she'd lived her whole life in Central Park, so she'd probably want to do all the touristy things, like the Statue of Liberty and Katz's Deli. Finally they'd go for a walk along the West Side by the water, holding hands as they gazed across the Hudson at the bright lights of Jersey City. Beyond that, Rory's imagination dared not go.

Rory grew sleepy as he daydreamed in the big comfy bed. Maybe he'd catch a little shut-eye until Fritz came to get him. It had been a trying day, after all. A little nap wouldn't hurt. He slowly closed his eyes, surrendering to the power of the plush mattress and luxurious bedspread.

And then whole world went crazy.

First he heard a loud click, which cut through the air like a gunshot. Before he could react, the entire bed dropped down beneath him, sending him tumbling into a dark hole. He plummeted for what felt like years, until he landed roughly on the ground somewhere in the dark. Before he could get his bearings, hands grabbed at him, pulling at him.

"Get 'im, lads," a rough voice sounded near his ear. "This'll fetch a nice reward from the captain."

Rory pulled away, ready to fight. By the dim light streaming in from the trapdoor above, he could make out a small group of sailors, the very ones who had been speaking with Big Mickey at the bar. At their head was the short man with the tattoos, only this time he wasn't smiling. Before Rory could decide what to do, another pair of arms wrapped around him from behind, pinning his arms to his side. He struggled, but try as he might, he couldn't break free of the guy's grip. But just when he thought he was a goner, a bark and howl heralded Tucket's arrival, leaping into the hole after his master. Sly chuckles were replaced by shrieks and curses as Tucket launched into the group of attackers, scattering them.

"What *is* that thing?" one of the sailors cried.

"Kill it!" another yelled.

At first Rory feared for the dog, but then he noticed something extremely strange. Tucket had somehow grown, dramatically. At first he thought it was a trick of the light, but as Tucket held the sailors at bay with his snapping jaws, it became apparent that the dog had expanded to the size of a small bear. Almost instantly, the doofus dog had transformed into a fearsome protector. The grip holding Rory prisoner disappeared as Tucket fought off the attackers, snarling like a wild animal, and Rory tumbled to the ground. Finally, the sailors cut their losses and ran down the tunnel, disappearing into the dark. Tucket padded over to Rory to check on him, and Rory sat up to give the huge beast a hug.

"Good dog," he muttered. Already Tucket was beginning to shrink again. "That's a nice little talent you have there. I'm sorry I ever called you a doofus. Forgive me?"

Tucket licked Rory's face and he laughed, shaking his head ruefully. "This has been one of my crazier mornings, Tucket. And considering the month I've had, that's really saying something."

Rory glanced up at the hole he had fallen through; it was too far above him to reach. He'd have to find another way to the surface.

Rory climbed to his feet, gazing both ways down the tunnel he'd fallen into as he mused aloud. "There has to be a manhole around here somewhere. I didn't fall that far. And those sailors have to know an easy way down to get here so fast. I don't want to wait here like a sitting duck. So I guess I'll follow where they went. Just don't forget to supersize if we run into them again!" Tucket stared up at him, his face happily blank as his tail wagged back and forth. Rory said a little prayer to whichever god was listening and began to walk into the darkness.

HITCHING A RIDE

Nicholas Stuyvesant gazed down the long alley of lodging houses, shaking his head at the mess in front of him. Built close to the main docks on Pearl Street, near the South Street Seaport, these poorly constructed wooden structures had been thrown up to house the spirits of the sailors on shore leave. So poorly constructed, in fact, that the earthquake had shaken many of them to pieces. Spirits wandered the alley, suddenly homeless, and Nicholas could hear them muttering among themselves at the unfairness of it all. More than once, in defiance of all reason, he heard the Munsees being blamed. Not good.

"What a fiasco." Alexa van der Donck sighed next to him, her tightly pinned brown hair dusted with white mortar she couldn't be bothered to brush off. "Each place we visit is worse than the last. I think Mannahatta was hit far harder than Manhattan."

"Dad was right to be worried," Nicholas replied heavily. "You just can't trust everyone on the council." Peter Stuyvesant, God of Things Were Better in the Old Days, sat on the

Council of Twelve, the elected rulers of Mannahatta. Some of the council members maintained that nothing was wrong, that the earthquake had been a minor blip in the life of the city. But Peter decided to send out the Rattle Watch, that band of the children of the gods assembled by Alexa's late father, Adriaen van der Donck; Peter charged them to see the aftermath for themselves and report back. Nicholas and Alexa headed south, and everywhere they went, they came across angry spirits throwing the blame for the earthquake squarely on the Munsees. Nicholas didn't need to visit the fortune-teller to know that Kieft likely stood behind the rumors. But why?

"He's riling them up, that's what he's doing," Alexa said, obviously thinking the same thing. "Reminding everyone about their hate. Of course, it could be the Mayor. He's the one who really hates the Munsees."

"I never understood what happened to the Mayor all those years ago," Nicholas said. "One day Hamilton is best friends with Tackapausha. The next"—he slammed his hands together—"he's condemning them all to eternity in prison. I never got it."

"Breaks your heart," a voice from behind them slurred, startling the two Rattle Watchers. Nicholas and Alexa whirled to see a spirit leaning against the wall of one of the few buildings still standing on the block. He swayed as he fought to keep his balance. Alexa raised an eyebrow at Nicholas; the stink of booze coming off the sailor threatened to asphyxiate them both.

"It sure does, friend," Nicholas replied. "You been drinking?"

"Oh yeah," the drunken man said with a sloppy smile. "I've

been drunk now, oh, I don't know. Hundred years? Something like that."

"Sorry to hear that," Alexa said, giving Nicholas a look that begged him to move on.

"It's a shame they all talking about the Munsees this way," the man continued, his eyes gazing into the distance. "It is disrespectful. It's not the Munsees' fault, anyone with brains should see that. Even the Mayor should see that. 'Course, the Mayor never did think clear when it came to the Munsees. Someone should ask Harry Meester; he'd set them straight."

"Is that you?" Nicholas asked, humoring the drunk. He was surprised to see the man throw up his hands in fright.

"Oh no! Not me! Don't go tellin' people I'm Harry Meester! Harry's problems are his own and I won't stand you making them mine!"

"Sorry," Alexa said, calming the drunk down. "It's okay. You're not Harry Meester, don't worry. Nobody thinks that. In fact . . . that name sounds familiar . . ." She stared off into space, trying to remember.

"You're humoring me," the man said, closing his eyes wearily. "You think Alberto is just a harmless drunk. But I know things. I've been following you for two hours trying to work up the courage to tell you what I know. If the world's shaking itself to pieces, somebody's gotta say something to make it right."

"Like what, Alberto?" Alexa asked gently.

"I already said! If you want to know the truth about the Trap, the real truth, you gotta ask Harry Meester."

A crash sounded behind them, and Nicholas and Alexa spun to see one of the last standing lodging houses collapse in on itself, sending up a shower of dust and mortar. When they turned back to Aberto, he was gone. And try as they might, they couldn't find the drunken man again.

It didn't take long for Rory to realize that he'd made a bad decision. The light from the trapdoor faded behind him and soon he couldn't really see at all. If there was a manhole, he could easily have passed by it unknowing. Somehow, he kept from bouncing into the invisible walls, but who knew how long that would last. The farther he walked the closer he came to becoming truly lost, but onward he trudged, telling himself that the way up was practically in front of him. But soon the truth could be denied no longer and Rory had to admit he was lost.

He should have waited by the open trapdoor, he chastised himself. He should turn around now, before he was lost for good, doomed to wander beneath the streets of Manhattan forever. He had to turn back, he decided, and spun in place to do just that. But before he could move, he felt a rumble in the air. Something was coming, something big.

Gradually he noticed that the dark had lightened and he could see where he was. He stood in a long tunnel, lined with metal and rock. Rails ran along the ground on either side of him down the length of the tunnel, though no third rail as far as he could tell. How old were these rails? The light brightened further and Rory realized with a sinking stomach the source of the rumbling. A train was coming, and he had nowhere to go.

Tucket began to bark as Rory spun in a panic looking for a place where he could wedge himself, but there wasn't enough room on either side to hold him while the train passed. He had no place to hide. Tucket jumped in front of him, barking at the oncoming train. Out of time, Rory braced himself, throwing it up to higher powers as the wheels began to shriek as if someone had pulled the emergency lever and the subway train was fighting itself to come to a stop. It slid along the rails, sending bright sparks in every direction as it headed right at them, its headlights growing brighter and brighter until Rory was blinded. The squeal of metal on metal coupled with Tucket's barking blended into a deafening racket, until he could neither see nor hear. This was it, he thought. It ended here.

And then the squealing cut off, leaving only Tucket's barking. The lights of the train had stopped maybe two feet away. Rory let out a long breath of air.

"Hello, there!" a voice called out. "Are you dead? If so . . . well . . . sorry!"

Rory cleared his throat, putting a hand on Tucket's neck to calm him; the dog quieted, though a growl still rattled his jaws.

"I'm not dead, thanks," Rory said.

"Excellent!" the voice returned. "Then we owe you a ride!"

Rory stepped to the side to get out of the reach of those blinding lights and took a good look at the train that had almost killed him. Oddly enough, there seemed to be only one car; Rory had never heard of a subway train so short. It was tough to tell in the darkness of the tunnel, but the train appeared to be built from wood and riveted steel with a rounded roof that made it seem more like an old trolley than one of the subway trains Rory knew. A small terrace, enclosed by a metal railing, jutted out from the front. On the terrace stood an unassuming man in a nineteenth-century suit and top hat, a small mustache resting impishly atop his thin mouth. His open face appeared delighted to find Rory in front of him. He smiled.

"Why, you're just a boy!" he exclaimed. "Please, come aboard. It's the least we can do."

"Who is 'we'?" Rory asked warily.

"We are losing precious minutes, Alfred!" a heavily accented voice yelled out form within the car. "Either bring the boy aboard or run him over, but we have a schedule to keep!"

Alfred shrugged apologetically with a little smile. "I bet I can guess which you'd rather."

Rory didn't wait to take the bet. He climbed aboard, lifting Tucket up behind him. The man held out his hand for Rory to shake, which Rory did.

"Alfred Beach," the man said, pumping Rory's arm with enthusiasm.

"Rory," Rory replied, than winced inwardly. So much for secrecy.

"Wonderful to meet you, Rory," Alfred said warmly. "Welcome aboard!"

Alfred opened the door for Rory and Tucket, inviting them into the train. Rory let his dog in before following, still distracted by his near-death experience. Once inside, however, he couldn't keep his eyes from widening as he gazed around in wonder.

It was as if he'd stepped back a century. The seats were made of wicker and they smelled like musty lawn furniture left under a house all winter long. Everything was wood: the doors at either end of the car, the trim that lined the walls, even the frames surrounding the windows, windows that easily lifted

open as if they looked out on someone's backyard rather than
the pitch black of a tunnel deep underground. Straps made of
cloth hung in loops from the ceiling, ready to give commuters
something to cling to as the train roughly rattled its way along
the rails. Advertisements lined the panels between the windows
and the ceiling, touting strange products from another age:
long-forgotten soda pop and hair-restoring ointment and ancient cameras sold for ridiculously cheap prices.

"Is this the first subway car ever built or something?" Rory
guessed. "It's beautiful."

"Not quite the first," Alfred replied, pleased at his reaction.
"Someday you will have to see the first subway car I built. If
you think this is something, then that beauty will knock your
socks off."

"What are you two yammering about?" the heavily accented
voice demanded. A man detached himself from the corner
of the subway car, striding over to meet Rory. This man was
dressed completely differently from Alfred Beach; in fact, he
appeared to be wearing a light suit of armor, which clanged as
he walked. His bushy beard hid most of his face, but his large
nose stuck out prominently and his eyes were fierce. "We're
wasting time."

"Giovanni, this is Rory," Alfred said to the man in armor
before turning back to Rory. "Rory, you have the extreme good
fortune to be in the presence of the famed Giovanni da Verrazano, explorer and adventurer . . ."

"I go where no man has gone before!" Gionanni exclaimed
proudly. Rory snorted at the *Star Trek* reference, but judging
from his face, the explorer meant what he said.

"Nice to meet you," Rory said. "Thanks for picking me up."

"It was not my idea!" Giovanni told him. "We are on a schedule! But Grace must have heard the barking of your dog, so you owe your life to her."

"Who's Grace?" Rory asked, glancing around. "Your conductor?"

Alfred laughed. "You could say that. Have a seat, you don't want to fall. Grace, shall we?"

The train lurched forward and Rory stumbled, dropping into a wicker seat. Tucket curled up beneath his feet, apparently certain that the threat of imminent death was over for the time being. Alfred and Giovanni sat across from him, the former smiling at him while the latter glared.

"I'm sorry I knocked you off schedule," Rory said, hoping to appease the angry Italian in front of him.

Alfred chuckled. "I wouldn't call it a schedule. We're simply exploring some new tunnels, trying to find our way down."

"There is indeed a schedule!" Giovanni insisted. "Soon the other explorers will tire of the ocean and the sky and they will come down here in search of new discoveries. Our window is short to find new lands and give them names that will last forever. You are the train man, Alfred. Leave the exploring to me."

"Of course," Alfred said, placating him. "But we can't take this poor boy down into the depths with us. We have time for one stop before we forge ahead with our journey down."

Giovanni reluctantly grunted his assent. Alfred gestured for Rory to take a seat, which he did, and the subway car gradually picked up speed as it raced into the dark.

Alfred made small talk as they traveled, but soon Rory noticed that Giovanni was giving him a strange look. Finally, the explorer leaned forward, his eyes searching. "Do I know you, boy? Have we met?"

"No, I'd remember," Rory answered, suddenly uncomfortable. He had no clue if either of these men could be trusted.

"So familiar," Giovanni repeated. "You never sailed with me?"

"Definitely not," Rory answered. He didn't like where this line of questioning was leading, so he quickly steered the conversation away from his identity. "You were a sailor?" he asked.

"Sailor?" Giovanni scoffed, taking the bait. "I was a great captain! In my mortal days, five centuries ago, I guided my ship across the great sea, traveling up and down the coast of the New World, claiming huge tracts of land for France!"

"France? I thought you were Italian," Rory said.

"France paid me a great deal of money to be French, so, for that voyage, I was French. It was I who discovered the untamed shores of Francesca!"

"Where's Francesca?" Rory asked, confused.

"His name for North America," Alfred cut in, winking slyly. "It didn't quite take."

"America has such a pedestrian sound to it," Giovanni complained. "Now, Francesca, that is the name of a great land!"

"It's a done deal, Giovanni," Alfred told him, his tired tone making it obvious that this argument came up a lot. "Francesca just isn't going to happen."

"No respect for the man who discovered the isle of Manhattan!" Giovanni announced, his voice ringing with centuries of resentment.

"But I thought Henry Hudson discovered New York," Rory said. "Did you sail with him?"

"Oh boy," Alfred muttered, putting his head in his hands. "Now you've done it."

"How dare you!" Giovanni exclaimed, his voice quavering with indignation. "As if that bumbling nincompoop of an Englishman were even fit to lick my boots! *Henry Hudson.*" The name came out drenched in disdain. "He followed in my footsteps almost a century later. A *century*! So why does his name go on all the good stuff? Just because he decided to sail up the river, while I, who was very busy, remember, discovering *everything* for the first time, stayed out by Staten Island—just because of that, he gets the Hudson River, the Hudson Valley, the Hudson everything! It should be the Verrazano River! The Verrazano Valley! I was here first! All I get is a stupid bridge!"

"Easy, Giovanni," Alfred soothed his cohort. Indeed what little of the Italian explorer's face that showed through the beard had turned bright red. "You don't want to pass out again."

Pouting like a kid who lost at Candyland, Giovanni crossed his metal-encased arms with a frown. "That is exactly why I gave up on discovering new lands beyond the mists. Everyone is trying it. The true discoveries await belowground! So I recruited Alfred here to help me explore the depths of the island. My only competition down here is Caesar Prince, and who knows what that man is looking for . . ."

"So you'll be kind of an underground Columbus?" Rory asked.

"*Columbus!*" Giovanni spat. "Let me tell you about that imbecile Columbus . . ."

Giovanni raged on as the train sped through the dark tunnel, Alfred Beach shaking his head the entire time. Finally, light streamed through the windows as the subway car pulled into the familiar 207th Street station, the end of the line.

"Here you go, Rory," Alfred said, gesturing outside. Glancing out the window, Rory wasn't surprised to see that no one even looked in their direction. He thanked his benefactors and stepped off the train, helping Tucket down onto the platform. He gave a wave as the train began to pull out of the station, on its way back to exploring the depths of the island. Then, with a screech, the car shuddered to a halt. One of the windows flew open and Giovanni stuck his head out, his beard hanging over the sill.

"Two's Boys!" he yelled.

"What?" Rory asked, thoroughly confused.

"That's where I know you from! It finally came to me. You look like one of Two's Boys! You sailed with me into the mists a few times, including that last voyage to Fletcher's Island. Don't you remember? It was about seventy-five years ago."

"He's a mortal, Giovanni," Alfred said from inside the train. "He never sailed with you anywhere."

"What are you talking about?" Rory asked, feeling bombarded. Giovanni squinted at him, sticking his head farther out the window as he peered at Rory intently.

"Maybe you're not him," he admitted. "You look like him, especially around the cheeks and chin, but you don't have his eyes. Two's Boys all have those eyes that never smile. You can't mistake it. Strange. That man could have been your brother."

A shock ran through Rory.

"Or my father?" he asked softly. Giovanni nodded thoughtfully.

"Definitely," Giovanni agreed. "Was your father a sailor?"

A memory popped up in Rory's head, of a man who looked just like his father on the deck of the ghost ship *Half Moon*. He'd doubted he really saw it. But could it be true . . . ?

"Oh well," Giovanni said, pulling back into the train. "We've got a schedule to keep."

"Wait!" Rory called, running up to the train. "What are Two's Boys? Did you know him? When did you see him last? Was his name Peter Hennessy?"

"Peter who?" Giovanni replied. "Never heard of him. Grace, forward! Schedules must be met or everything falls apart!"

Alfred shrugged apologetically from inside the train as the subway car began to move. It picked up speed as it headed out of the station, disappearing into the darkness of the tunnel. And all Rory could do was watch, unanswered questions racing through his brain in endless circles.

Who were these Two's Boys? If his father was one of them, then had he really been sailing on ghost ships, voyaging out into these mists Giovanni spoke of? Is that where he'd been all this time? Was he really that old?

Just who was Peter Hennessy, anyway?

HOME AGAIN

Down on the southern tip of the island, not far from the South Street Seaport, stood the oldest fine dining restaurant in the United States. Its rounded entrance looked out proudly onto the corner of Beaver and South William streets, guarded by a pair of stone pillars imported from the doomed city of Pompeii by the two brothers who had opened the establishment back in 1837. The sign above the door still boasted their famous last name, which had come to be synonymous with culinary greatness: DELMONICO'S.

Little besides the name connected the Delmonico's that occupied the building in the present to its famous namesake. The restaurant had passed out of the family's control during Prohibition, when the inability to cook with wine or serve spirits of any kind doomed the New York institution to closure. But the pillars from Pompeii remained, as did the name above the door; more importantly, the memory of the great restaurant that had so dominated nineteenth-century New York endured. And upstairs, unreachable by any mortal, a very different Delmonico's from the pale imitation below lived on. Delmonico's the way it was in its heyday a century before. Delmonico's the way it was always meant to be.

Gods and spirits occupied almost all the tables in the large, candlelit room, drinking the memories of wine and diving into fond recollections of Delmonico's renowned steak. Lorenzo Delmonico himself, the famous nephew of the founders whose sure hand had catapulted the establishment into the annals of history, manned the host station, seating the otherworldly guests as they arrived. Now the God of Fine Dining, Lorenzo prided himself on his attention to his diners' every need. He had stopped by Diamond Jim Brady's table at least ten times already in his vain attempt to somehow fill the man's gigantic belly. Diamond Jim had been a millionare during his life, but it was his legendary love of food and stomach eight times normal size that had earned him the title of God of Overeating. But tonight even Diamond Jim's jolly belly laughs sounded forced under the suffocating presence of the black-eyed man, who sat barely eating in the darkest corner of the room. He was joined at his table by a man whose girth challenged Jim's own, a man who was also not a god to trifle with: T. R. Tobias.

The entire room quivered on edge as everyone avoided looking in the direction of the two gods' table. Lorenzo knew he should see if their cups needed refilling, or if their meal was satisfactory. But he couldn't bring himself to walk over to the black-eyed man's table again. Each previous time, those eyes had rested upon him, marked him, remembered him. The last thing Lorenzo (or anyone in Mannahatta for that matter) wanted was to be noticed by Willem Kieft.

"What's he doing here?" Diamond Jim muttered as Lorenzo refilled his wine.

"I believe he's showing us that everything is fine," Lorenzo replied. "He doesn't want a panic."

"If he doesn't want a panic, then he shouldn't come 'round ruining our dinner." Diamond Jim's scowl suggested there could be no greater sin.

Lorenzo said nothing, noting that both Kieft and Tobias had drained their glasses. Kieft drank only wine and barely touched his plate of vegetables, while Tobias was well into his fifth course. Lorenzo sighed, and gestured to a waiter nearby. He handed the luckless waiter a bottle of wine and sent the protesting spirit toward Kieft's table. No need to risk himself, he thought, returning with a sigh to the host's station. He had a restaurant to run.

The waiter had been one of the restaurant's prize servers in his day; he'd seen no reason to stop after death. But right then he regretted not letting oblivion take him; anything to avoid the black-eyed man. As he timidly approached Kieft's table, the waiter heard snippets of his conversation with Tobias; they seemed to be discussing a new play. But then something strange happened; the waiter stepped through some sort of invisible barrier and suddenly Kieft and Tobias were discussing something else entirely, and apparently had been the whole time. He froze, wine bottle in hand, terrified they'd realize that he'd broken their ward. They hadn't noticed him yet, giving him time to make his escape, but he couldn't make his legs work. Fear held him captive as their conversation drifted by.

"The rumors are flying all over the island," Tobias was saying, waving his heavily laden fork about before taking a bite.

"They may not all believe the Munsees are responsible, but it's on everyone's mind."

"Good," Kieft said, running a finger along the rim of his empty glass. The waiter prayed Kieft didn't turn to ask for more wine. "I did not think it would take much pushing to remind the sheep why they feared the wolves."

Tobias leaned back, his face looking bored with the entire conversation. "I still don't understand the point."

"Things are changing," Kieft replied. "And we must change as well. Today's earthquake will not be the last natural disaster to assail us. The island tries to throw off its shackles, and each attempt will be more violent than the last, until at last everything will lie in rubble at our feet."

"That's depressing," Tobias replied, taking a small bite of a carrot before making a face and throwing it over his shoulder onto the floor. He picked up a potato and took a big bite with a satisfied sigh.

"Do you care for nothing but your next meal, you gluttonous fool?" Kieft said, his voice a whip across the God of Banking's face. Tobias's bored mask dropped for a moment and the waiter noted a real fear in the god's eyes before the mask returned so quickly he doubted seeing it in the first place.

"Money and fine dining, is there anything else?" Tobias said glibly. "I will miss them both if the island falls apart around our ears."

"That is why the Trap must come down," Kieft said. "The island will no longer tolerate it."

"This is . . . unexpected," Tobias replied, putting down his fork. "Are you sure?"

"I assumed it would last forever, but that has proved optimistic of me. The Trap must fall or I will rule over a dead city. But once it falls . . . that is when we must act. Our secrets will be exposed, which must be handled swiftly, and with care. And then there are the Munsees. They are a threat to us and they must be eliminated. That is why I sow the rumors and the insinuations . . . we must ready the people for a desperate battle to the death with their ancient enemies. That is the only way to protect ourselves as we reach for what we ultimately desire."

"What about the boy?" Tobias asked. "He has proven hard to kill."

"We cannot kill him anymore, not if we want the Trap opened." Kieft picked up his glass and stared at the empty bottom. "We must capture him and hold him until the city is ready for war. Then he will release the enemy and the games will begin. Of course it helps that after using every last trick I've learned over the past four hundred years, I have finally divined his own lost Light's name . . . waiter!"

Kieft had turned to call for wine, when his gaze fell on the waiter standing near. His eyes widened, then glinted in the soft lamplight. "I see you anticipate my needs," he said, in a voice that made the waiter's bowels turn to water. "I fear I require you to stay close from now on. We have much to discuss, now, don't we?"

The waiter couldn't move as Kieft held him fast with those deep, black eyes. He knew he'd never repeat anything he just heard. He would never get the chance . . .

By the time Rory reached his family's stoop on 218th Street, Tucket padding dutifully behind, the afternoon sun was beginning to dip behind the apartment buildings. The Hennessys lived in Inwood, the northernmost neighborhood in Manhattan, on the last street before the river. As Rory walked up his street, many of his neighbors were out on the sidewalks, picking up rubble and clearing the stoops and driveways of debris. Rory had no idea how powerful the quake had been, but the people of Inwood seemed to have weathered it all right; many of them were already smiling and joking as they worked. Lightning-fast Spanish darted back and forth through the air as the mostly Dominican and Puerto Rican families slowly relaxed after the ordeal of the day. Even though the ethnic makeup of Inwood had changed over the years, Rory's mother fit in among her Hispanic neighbors as well as her mother had with the Irish who used to make up most of Inwood. Mrs. Hennessy had made it a point to learn the language, though she constantly apologized for her thick accent. Bridget, for her part, loved speaking Spanish (especially the cursing, to their mother's mortification). It made Bridget feel like a great adventurer, able to speak many tongues. Rory had picked up some through osmosis, though not much. Enough to ask someone to throw him his ball on the basketball courts when it rolled away.

Even though thoughts of his father ran circles around his brain, Rory was still worried about his sister, and he raced up the steps to their second-floor apartment to make certain she'd made it home all right.

"Hello!" he called as he walked in the front door, Tucket trotting in behind him. "Is everyone okay?"

A loud squeal rang through the apartment. A figure ran across the living room and dove into the next room, slamming the door behind it.

"Bridget?" Rory called out, bemused. "Is that you?"

A muffled voice drifted through the door.

"Hold on! Jeez! Can't I have a minute to myself? I am nine, you know. I'm not a baby!"

Rory rolled his eyes at Tucket, who, unsurprisingly, did not return the gesture.

"I just wanted to know that you weren't dead or bleeding on the carpet."

"Can't I have some privacy?" Bridget shouted through the wood.

"Sure. It was just an earthquake. Nothing too important. By all means, enjoy your privacy. Did Mom come home yet?"

"She called to say that she's *still* walking. So give me a second, already!"

Rory plopped down on the sofa as Tucket lay at his feet. The TV was on, a newscaster giving a solemn report in front of a couple of crashed cars.

". . . out of nowhere," she was saying. "No one got a good look at the figure's face as it pulled the woman and her child from inside the car that had been almost completely crushed."

A young woman appeared on-screen, being interviewed by the reporter.

"Whoever he was, I'm thankful. We would have been goners without him. Thank you, stranger! Thank you!"

The door to Bridget's room opened behind him and his younger sister ran in and gave a quick twirl.

"I'm great!" she cried. "See! How are you? Hey, Tucket! Here doggy!"

Tucket bounded up to Bridget and leaped up on her, licking at her face. Besides Rory, she was the only mortal who could see the dog, and she loved him to death (which, judging from the mauling she put the poor beast through when they played, wasn't so far-fetched a concept). Rory gazed past her to her bedroom door, which was closed. Lately, Bridget was closing her door a lot. It was unlike her, and at first he had been worried she was using her papier-mâché body again—which he'd only allowed her to keep as a souvenir if she promised to never actually enter it—so he took an old bike chain and chained the empty paper shell to an ancient pipe in the back of her closet. He hid the key in the back of his own closet, in a shoe box under some old baseball cards, where he knew she'd never find it. And sure enough, the body remained locked up, undisturbed. But Bridget continued hiding away in her bedroom, so Rory decided it must be some sort of girl phase. He was a boy, so he couldn't understand what she was doing in there all the time. But he knew enough not to get involved.

"I'm okay," he said. "Where were you when the quake hit?"

"We were just finishing a basketball game, and I was killing them all," Bridget exclaimed, waving her arms around her head, making Tucket chase her hands. "And then everything went crazy! The ground jumped around and everyone fell down except me. I was ready to fight whatever creature was coming to kill us, because I was sure it was something bad, like a giant hedgehog or something, but nothing showed up! It was just a stupid earthquake. All the girls were crying, but not me. I've beaten up big green monsters! I was like '*Ooo*, the ground moved! Scary!' and the counselor told me to stop being sarcastic. It's not my fault I'm not easy to scare!"

As usual, Rory felt exhausted after one of Bridget's monologues.

"I'm glad you're all right," he said.

"Right back at ya!" Bridget exclaimed. "I was worried!"

"She's not the only one," a new voice said.

Rory twirled around to see a rat scamper into the living room. Upon its back, holding a pair of reins like a medieval knight, sat a cockroach. Fritz M'Garoth, battle roach and rat-rider, took off his roach helmet to reveal his pink human face.

"Someone has something to say to you," Fritz said, nodding behind him. Sergeant Kiffer trudged in, head hung low, holding his helmet between his top hands.

"Kiffer, what do you say?" Fritz prompted him.

"I'm sorry I almost got you kidnapped by pirates," Kiffer recited, looking miserable.

"It's okay, I got away," Rory said. Fritz shook his head violently.

"It's not okay. We have to be careful who we trust, and Kiffer was definetly not careful. At least Big Mickey wasn't working for Kieft, or you'd probably be dead."

"Who was he working for, then?" Rory asked.

"He has a deal with the sailors," Fritz explained. "It used to happen a lot around the time of the Civil War. Bar owners built those trapdoors into their back rooms in order to hijack a young guy newly arrived in the city. They'd get him drunk, put him in that room to sleep it off, pull the trapdoor, and let an unscrupulous captain's men take him away to their ship, where he'd be wake up so far out to sea he'd have no choice but to work as a sailor. You came *this* close to waking up on a boat in the middle of the ocean." He glared at Kiffer, who looked like he wanted to die.

"Well, I'm fine, Fritz," Rory said, feeling bad for the huge roach. "Oh, stop that!" This last sentence was directed at Tucket, who was whining and trying to hide behind Rory at the sight of Clarence, Fritz's rat. The first time Tucket met Clarence, he tried to play with the rat like a chew toy. One well-timed swipe at his snout had quickly taught the dog to leave a trained fighting rat alone. "Maybe I was meant to end up at sea. Apparently being a sailor runs in the family."

"What are you talking about?" Bridget asked. "Granddad sold insurance."

So he told them what he'd learned about his father from Giovanni da Verrazano.

"Do you know who these Two's Boys are?" he asked Fritz.

"Never heard of them," the battle roach said. "If they were sailors, perhaps the docks are the best place to look."

Bridget's face had lit up, as Rory feared it would.

"I knew it." Her eyes were shining. "He's probably lost at sea. We have to go find him!"

"Bridge, we're not running after him just because he's a sailor," Rory explained, determined to nip his sister's romantic dream in the bud. "It doesn't change anything. Who cares if he's in Mannahatta or Madagascar? He still left us. We have too many other worries. The city is falling to pieces around us."

"You never want to see him again!" Bridget shouted, stamping her foot in anger. "You think he's as bad as Kieft! Well, you don't know any more about him than I do. At least I want to find out. You stick your head in the sand like a stupid emu!"

"Ostrich," Rory corrected her. She balled her hands into fists and shook them in frustration as her eyes teared up.

"You're such a know-it-all! You don't know anything!"

"Children, children, enough," Fritz scolded them. "Look,

we'll do some digging, see what we can find out about these Two's Boys down at the port. We won't ignore it, Bridget, I promise. But Rory's got a point: right now we've got bigger problems than your dad. This earthquake may just be the beginning of something really, really bad. I need you both to meet us down at the Dyckman farmhouse tonight. Can you do that?"

They both nodded, not looking at each other. Sergeant Kiffer snorted.

"Try not to kill each other on the walk over." He smirked.

"Kiffer, shush," Fritz said, giving him a warning look before turning back to the Hessessy children. "So meet us at midnight . . ."

Suddenly the television flicked off, along with every light in the room. The air conditioner, which had sputtered along in the background all summer long, cut out, covering the room in an eerie blanket of silence. Rory ran to the window and saw that the streetlamps, which should have been turning on with the onset of evening, were all dark. It could only mean one thing . . . a blackout.

Fritz sighed.

". . . and bring a flashlight."

DADDY ISSUES

*E*verything about William "Boss" Tweed was big. At more than six feet tall, he towered over most of the men of his day. His belly was round, his nose was bulbous, his beard grew long and thick. And then there were his deeds: Boss Tweed lived as big as he looked. At one point, he ran all of nineteenth-century Manhattan as the head of one of the most corrupt political machines in history: Tammany Hall. And no one in Tammany Hall was more corrupt than Boss Tweed. He stole money right from under the noses of the citizens of New York, throwing it around on mansions and extravagant vacations as if daring anyone to catch him. But catch him they did, sending him to prison, where he died, penniless.

So it is understandable that Tweed did not enjoy making his way down the dark corridors of another prison: the infamous Tombs. He cursed as he stumbled along the tiny black hallway, scrunching his big body up to keep from bumping his head on the ceiling or touching the dirty walls as he headed toward the area where the Council of Twelve housed the most dangerous criminals. He wished to be at home in his beautiful mansion, where every comfort awaited him. He was a god, Tweed thought peevishly. The God of Rabble Politics. He sat on the Council of Twelve! He was no errand boy for Kieft to order around. But the First Adviser was hard to refuse; he made it very clear whose side you wanted to be on. Tweed knew the benefits of backing the right horse; he'd made a career of *being* the right horse. So when one of Kieft's possessed spirits showed up at his office in Five Points, eyes rolling around in terror as the rest of its body did what Kieft told it to, Tweed listened. The spirit, a waiter of some kind by his outfit, had sent him here, to the most notorious prison in the history of New York, and now Tweed hurried past the dank cells holding their forgotten prisoners, hoping to fulfill his task quickly and be home for supper.

Finally, he stopped in front of a cell door, a large slab of iron with a single slit cut out at the height of a man's eyes. Peering in, Tweed spied a dark shape in the corner. He'd have to be careful; he knew this spirit from before, knew what the murdering madman was capable of, and the moment he let his guard down he would regret it. *I could be smoking a cigar right now*, Tweed thought ruefully, *resting in my comfortable den, instead of standing ankle-deep in dirty water about to let a madman loose on the city*. The things he did for his "friends" . . .

"Who's out there?" a voice rasped from the corner of the cell. "Declare yourself or I'll rip out yer eyeballs, so help me."

"As charming as ever, Bill," Tweed answered drily.

"Tweed? That you?" The dark form stirred, unfolding into a tall figure. "Come to gloat, you fat bastard?"

"Come now, be civil, Bill. I am your friend, and as your

friend, I resent that you would believe that of me. I'm here to help."

"Help me?" The figure's voice was incredulous. "Where was you a hundred years ago, when they buried me down here? Where was you then?"

"Now, Bill, you were caught red-handed cutting the throats of a pair of harmless house spirits." Tweed shuddered to remember it. Not a pretty sight, what Bill did to those poor things.

"So what?" Bill answered belligerently from the shadows. "They was a pair a' dirty immigrants, not fit to breathe the American air. I was takin' back the city for the true natives!"

You mean the Indians? Tweed thought with a smirk, but he didn't say a word. William Poole's hatred of non-Anglo-Saxon Americans was legendary and not to be trifled with.

"What do you want, anyhow?" Bill continued.

"I have a job for you," Tweed answered. "In return I'll give you your freedom. Deal?"

"What's the job?" Bill asked suspiciously.

"There's a boy, a special boy. His name is Rory Hennessy. The First Adviser wants the boy kidnapped and brought to him."

"Can I have my cleavers?" Bill asked hungrily.

"You're not to kill him, Bill!" Tweed admonished. "I won't have you slitting any unauthorized throats, hear me?"

"I won't harm a hair on his Irish head," Bill promised, though his rough voice didn't sound convincing. "He is Irish, right? Hennessy? Sure sounds it . . ."

"No killing! Just kidnapping. Anyone in his presence, however . . . with them you may have all the fun you wish."

"Then you'll give me my cleavers, yeah?" Bill stepped eagerly into the light, his gaunt face practically skeletal beneath his large, greased mustache. "I can't do the job without 'em."

"I have them right here for you," Tweed promised, though his stomach tightened at the thought of loosing Bill the Butcher onto the city with his cleavers and no one to hold him back. But he'd been told to free William Poole, so free him Tweed would. He could only hope Kieft knew what he was doing.

Tweed unlocked the cell, and Bill stumbled out. Tweed reluctantly handed over several rusty old cleavers, which Bill loving caressed, his greedy eyes shining in the torchlight. Then Tweed stepped aside as Bill swept by him to disappear into the shadows of the tunnel leading to the exit. Tweed watched him go with a heavy heart before turning to walk deeper into the prison. He had one more stop to make before his night was through.

The area of the Tombs he moved through now was even dingier than the rest of the prison, if that were possible. The narrowing passage worried him; what if he reached a point where he could not go farther? Dare he go back to Kieft with only part of his duty discharged? He could not turn back, he knew. Not now.

He finally came upon another iron door. This one sported no eye slit, however. He could not see inside without opening the cell. He hesitated; he feared what lay behind this door far more than he feared Bill the Butcher. Bill's brand of violence was common and familiar. Behind this door . . . the thought of it made him shudder in his boots. But there was no going back now.

"Hello?" he called through the door.

"Who is it?" a sullen, scratchy female voice answered him.

"A friend, Mary," Tweed replied.

"I didn't do nothing. It was all a setup, I swear to ye."

"I know it was," Tweed said, as he'd been coached. "They framed you. If you help me, I'll clear your name."

Tweed lifted the latch and pushed on the rusty door, which creaked loudly as it was wrenched open. From within, a thin, middle-aged woman stepped tentatively into the light of Kieft's lantern.

"Who are you?" she asked, shielding her tender eyes from the harsh light.

"I am your new friend, Typhoid Mary," Tweed answered her, even as he backed away.

"Don't call me that awful name," Mary said, frowning. "It's not true, I told ye. I'm just Mary Mallon. Just a simple cook. I'm innocent."

"Of course you are," Tweed said. Typhoid Mary had long maintained her innocence, even as everyone she cooked for died horribly of disease. "I only want you to do what you do best. I want you to cook—for some special people. Can you do that?"

"What special people?" she asked.

Tweed began to explain, ignoring his unease over what he was unleashing on the city. Ah well, he'd crossed the line before and he'd cross it again. It was what you did in order to hold power. In the end, it was an easy choice to make.

Mrs. Hennessy had rushed in soon after Fritz and Sergeant Kiffer left, gathering up her children in an outpouring of relief. It had taken her the better part of the afternoon to reach the apartment, since, with the roads closed to traffic, she'd had to walk the length of the island. Mrs. Hennessy was nervous about the heat harming some of the older people in the building with their air conditioners not able to function, so she, Rory, and Bridget paid visits to the Brignolles downstairs and Mr. Little on the third floor. They made certain that windows were open and everyone had candles to burn. As they hunted for matches in his cluttered apartment, Mr. Little launched into one of his stories about the great blackout of '77, when the city crumbled into riots and looting. Rory hoped the past wouldn't repeat itself this summer.

Mrs. Hennessy sent her children downstairs to clean up while she made Mr. Little some dinner. Rory was happy to wash off the trying day, leaving his clothes strewn about behind him in his hurry to take a cool shower. Afterward, he rummaged through his dresser to find some new clothes. In the process, he stopped to pull out a small box he'd hidden in the back of his sock drawer. Once he finished dressing, he flopped down on his bed and opened it up.

Inside lay three items. The first was a rusty old padlock, its mundane appearance belying the fact that it was one of the magic items needed to open the Trap. Beside it lay another piece of the puzzle: a key made of white wampum dangling from a piece of string. The key fit the lock, and he'd almost turned it that day in Hex's office, before Toy tore it from his hands and escaped out the window. Rory had feared he'd never find the paper boy—or the key—again. But to his surprise, he'd woken up one morning less than a week later to find the key lying on his windowsill. Toy must have left it for him during the night, evidently deciding to trust Rory not to use it thoughtlessly. Rory had no idea where Toy was now, but he hoped the poor paper boy had found some form of comfort out in the world. He deserved it after all he'd been through.

The final item in the box wasn't what some might have expected; there was no Sachem's Belt here. That third piece to opening the Trap lay hidden in Wampage's cave. Its powers stretched beyond freeing the Munsees, and Rory felt more comfortable knowing the Indian warrior guarded it. No, the last item in the box was an old photograph, creased at two corners. Rory didn't quite know why he'd hidden it with these magic objects, but ever since that day the *Half Moon* sailed by, he'd felt it belonged here. He reached down and carefully lifted it out.

His father stared out at him, holding baby Bridget in his arms and smiling. Rory had long ago noticed that the smile didn't reach his father's eyes, and as he stared at the picture, his father's smile seemed more and more forced, becoming a simple baring of the teeth for the benefit of the camera. *What was he thinking?* Rory wondered. Was he already planning to leave? Did the thought of Mannahatta dance in his head, calling to him, turning the time spent with his family into a horrible chore? If so, why had he settled down in the first place? So many questions, and no one to answer them.

His father really did look like him, Rory noticed. He'd never wanted to see that before. It must kill his mother to see her lost husband in her son, every day. Maybe that was why she was so sad all the time. Rory hoped not, with all his heart.

Rory was overcome with a sudden urge to seek out his father, to talk to him and discover all his secrets, despite what he'd said to Bridget. He didn't want to feel like this, he wished he could just walk away, but this unknowable man in the picture tugged at him.

One day I'll find you, Rory told the virtual stranger in the photo. *When this is all over. And we'll have a long, long talk . . .*

A loud gasp coming from the next room interrupted his reverie. Startled, Rory leaped to his feet, sticking the photo in his
pocket and rushing out into the hall. His clothes still formed a
path to the bathroom, and he stomped over them as he raced
to Bridget's room.

"Bridge? You okay?" he called, pushing open her door. She
lay on her bed, eyes staring blankly at the ceiling, tears running
down her cheeks. Rory's shorts lay at the foot of her bed, and
a familiar necklace of purple and black hung limply around
her neck.

"Bridget!"

Rory rushed forward, lifting her up and yanking off the necklace so hard it almost broke. With a sob, Bridget came to.

"So sad . . . that poor lady."

Rory had to refrain from shaking her.

"What were you thinking!" he yelled at her. She trained her
eyes on him, wiping the tears away with her blanket.

"I saw the necklace poking out of your pants, and I thought
it looked pretty, so I tried it on. I felt so bad for her! I even
felt bad for Tackapausha! I think I stained my pillow from crying. And to think her father never came for her. She must be
so scared!"

Sighing, Rory tried to be delicate.

"Bridget, she's not . . . she's not really alive anymore."

"You don't know that!" Bridget angrily crossed her arms.
"You're being Captain Poop-Face again. I bet she got away and
went into hiding. So now she's waiting for her father to come,
but he can't because of the Trap. I bet she's built a house at
the top of a tree or something and every day she looks down at
the ground waiting for her father to look back up at her. It's

the saddest thing ever! You know what?" Bridget snapped her fingers excitedly. "I bet she's a princess!"

Rory groaned. "I thought you hated princesses," he said, bemused.

"I hate stupid, wimpy cartoon princesses with upside-down ice-cream cones on their heads, waiting around all day for some jock to make out with them. Olathe's not one of those dorks, I can tell. She's a warrior princess, like me. She's living in her tree house, fighting off evil woodland creatures, hunting deer with only her teeth, staying alive until her dad can come and get her. And if her dad can't make it, then we have to."

"Even if she were still alive and up in a tree, we have no idea where to find her—or her long-lost father."

"We could go to that Great Hill she talked about," Bridget replied, giving the necklace a good once-over. Rory pulled it away, stuffing it into his pocket for safekeeping. "Rory, don't you wanna know what Kieft hid there, at least?"

"One thing at a time, Bridget," Rory said. "We have to deal with the Trap before we worry about strange princesses and old secrets."

"Come on, Rory," Bridget said, clearly not convinced. "Don't you know that in every story, princesses always end up being pretty important?"

An hour had passed, and Rory lay on his bed, waiting for his mother to fall asleep in the next room. His eyes fluttered, heavy after the long day. Before he knew it, they drifted shut and he fell into a fitful slumber.

He knew it was a dream because he was flying. The city

below was dark. The blackout covered all of Manhattan, as if someone had put the island in a closet and shut the door. Rory sailed forward over the shadowed city toward Inwood Hill Park, heading for the ancient trees. The bridge to the mainland was a dark shape against the sky, with small lights like fireflies running along the top; headlights, Rory realized, from the cars crossing the river. He dipped down toward the hill, which was covered in thick forest. The trees were old, far older than anything else on the island. Rory felt like an intruder as he soared up to them, dipping down to slip under the branches and into the forest.

Rory darted between the twisted branches deeper into the woods. Bursting into a clearing, he sailed over Wampage's camp with its round pit of white wampum glowing softly, and he thought for a moment that this was his destination, but he did not slow. Instead he continued on until he reached a small stream. Dogs, many dogs, gathered upon the bank of the water and they barked as he flew into view. Floating in the middle of the stream was a canoe, heavily laden with supplies as if for a long journey, and standing knee-deep in the water beside the boat, holding it steady, waited Wampage. He glanced up and smiled at Rory floating above.

"I am glad you could come," he said. "I wished to say good-bye before I left and this was the only way I could accomplish that."

"Where are you going?" Rory asked, worried.

Wampage pointed down the stream, which disappeared around the bend.

"This stream empties into the river, which empties into the ocean that leads into the mist. Long ago, when my people alone walked Mannahatta, we were ruled by Kishelamakank, the first Sachem. When the newcomers arrived from over the sea, there was a struggle over Mannahatta. For the longest time, we were winning and the newcomers were fading. But they somehow found a way to get the land to accept them as it had long ago accepted my people. Once this happened, everything changed as the balance of power shifted. The mortal Munsees were driven out by your ancestors, until none remained. Soon, many of the Munsee gods passed on without a mortal people to strengthen them, until only the oldest and newest endured. The newest swore to stay, even after our people had left. But the oldest had no stomach for it. One after another, they left us, until only Kishelamakank, the greatest of us, remained. One day, he called us all together, and declared that he could no longer fight. He was old and weary of the struggle. He passed on his mantle to Penhawitz, who had only recently gained his godhood. Then our oldest, greatest leader took to his canoe and paddled out into the mist, never to be seen again.

"Not too long after, my people fell for the great Trap, which only I escaped, and now here we are. This quaking of the earth today, it will not be the last of the terrors to strike our island if we do not bring down the Trap. Something else comes, something that will blow us all apart. But we cannot tear down the Trap, not yet. Not while our two peoples are still so far apart. We must bring them together, you and I, or you will be faced with a choice that will hurt us all either way."

"But how do we do that?" Rory asked.

"I must find Kishelamakank. I am lost and he will help me find my way. You . . . you have already started down your path, though you might not realize it. But you are not alone. Trust in your sister, and in your friends. And I see glimpses from your memories that you learned how useful a spirit dog can be; he senses the danger surrounding you and grows accordingly. He is your spirit guide, and that is partly how he protects you."

"Don't go, Wampage," Rory begged, one last time. Wampage gave him a look of infinite compassion before climbing into the canoe.

"The dogs will remain here, until I come back," he said. "They will protect the Sachem's belt until you need it. I will return soon. Good-bye, Rory."

Wampage waved once and pushed off down the stream. His paddle dipped into one side, then the other, as his boat gathered speed. The dogs let out a cacophony of howling as their master paddled away from them and Rory wanted to join in. The canoe disappeared around the bend into the darkness and Wampage was gone.

Rory floated back up into the air, rising out of the trees of Inwood Hill Park. He began to float back toward his body, but he felt a tugging at his chest, pulling him downtown. Following the feeling south, he soared over the darkened city, darting around the tall black buildings with airy ease. He approached Central Park, which shone blue as he neared it. With a gasp he hit the barrier, and pressure bore down on him as he passed through. Sighing with relief he burst out the other side and quickly flew into the center of the park, where a familiar form sat cross-legged around a fire.

"Soka!" he cried. The young girl looked up at him, her eyes heavy and tired.

"I do not have much time and it takes all of my will to call you like this," Soka said quckly. "So listen carefully. I have looked into this Olathe from the necklace, and it is very interesting what I found! My mother was not the only one who remembered the poor girl; many knew her story, though not how it ended. But the truly fascinating thing I learned was who she used to be before she married Buckongahelas . . ."

Suddenly Soka began to choke. Her mouth opened and closed soundlessly, her hand clutching frantically at her throat. She bent over, as if she were trying to throw up, and then looked up in a panic. Rory was shocked to see something forcing its way out of her mouth, something covered in scales. It was a snake, forked tongue flicking lazily about. With a slither the snake burst free, flying through the air toward Rory's neck, its venom-drenched fangs bared. He screamed, willing himself away from this horrible nightmare before it could suck him dry . . .

Rory woke up with a whimper, sitting straight up. The apartment was quiet and dark. He collapsed back into his bed, sweat covering him, overwhelmed by his dream that wasn't a dream. Not only was Wampage gone, but Soka had been silenced by that *reptile* before she could tell him Olathe's identity. He hoped she was all right. Fritz would send in a rat to check up on her, he reassured himself. He would never forgive himself if Soka was harmed because of him. He shuddered. The image of that snake straining to sink its fangs into his neck would not fade. He wanted to crawl into bed with his mother and let her chase away the nightmare like she used to do when he was small. But people depended on him now, and he couldn't hide from that. His heart continued to pound in his ears as he forced himself upright and readied himself to face the night.

THE DYCKMAN HOUSE

With Tucket in tow, Rory and Bridget hurried down a deserted Broadway toward Dyckman Street, past the dark storefronts that lined the usually busy main drag. The occasional police car passed by, slowly traveling down the shadowed street, but the sidewalks were empty. In the distance, Rory could hear the sounds of some of the younger inhabitants of Inwood throwing a blackout party. But the revelers were far from Broadway and Dyckman.

Rory was still shaken by his dream of the snake, but it soothed his fears to think that soon he'd be among friends. Up ahead he spied their destination: the Dyckman farmhouse. One of the oldest buildings in New York, the farmhouse had been a fixture of the Hennessys' childhoods. Set up on a hill overlooking Broadway, the old wooden-frame house seemed almost like a mirage, frozen in time amid the rising apartment buildings of modern New York. As they were growing up, their mother used to tell Rory and Bridget ghost stories about the place, about how the spirits of old man Dyckman and his wife still haunted the rooms and grounds of the house, stomping about in anger at how the rest of their once-sprawling farm had been overtaken by buildings and pavement and cars and people. Rory had always dismissed these tales as superstition. He snorted; he was the one eating his words now.

Tonight, the old house was ablaze with light, in direct contrast to the dark neighborhood around it. Lanterns hung outside the front door and flickering yellow hues shimmering in the window spoke of a blazing fire within. The house called to Rory, so warm and cozy, like a tiny cottage in the middle of the forest. He and Bridget had met the Rattle Watch here twice during the past month to discuss their progess in discovering a way to topple Kieft and free the Munsees; he had been sorry to leave both times.

They climbed the stairs up the hill to the house, whose front door was already opening. Mr. Dyckman stood there, nodding at him grimly.

"Come in, come in," he said. "The rest of them are around the fire."

"Thanks," Rory said as they followed Dyckman inside, nodding politely to Mrs. Dyckman, who stood tensely nearby. Old friends of Nicholas Stuyvesant and his father, the owners of the house were normally quite welcoming and talkative, but tonight they looked pensive. The couple stayed by the door to keep watch for unwanted company as Rory and Bridget stepped into the living room, where around the crackling fire sat the only people Rory ever considered calling friends: the Rattle Watch.

Nicholas Stuyvesant, leader of the watch, stood up to greet

them with a smile. The lanky boy appeared to be no more than eighteen, but Rory knew he was, in fact, over four hundred years old. Seated beside Nicholas was Alexa van der Donck, who gave them a tired grin. A hard worker, she didn't have Nicholas's flash, but she was smart, brave, and steady as a rock. Across from her, Lincoln Douglass bounded up from his seat to say hello, shaking Rory's hand vigorously. The son of Frederick Douglass, God of Freedom, Lincoln always seemed to be in motion, hopping up and down through the world like a pogo stick. A languid wave fom the seated final member of the Rattle Watch, Simon Astor, was all the Hennessy children could hope for from the lazy boy. The hapless son of the exiled God of Excess, John Jacob Astor, was wearing an inhumanly loud pink-and-yellow shirt; he probably didn't want to mess up the effect by moving.

There were happy greetings all around as the Rattle Watch welcomed Rory and Bridget. The Hennessy kids had been made members of the watch following their last adventure. But aside from those two times they had all met in this farmhouse, the watch had disappeared from the Hennessys' lives. At first Rory resented their absence, but soon he came to realize they were protecting him. Kieft still didn't know who he was, but the First Adviser knew Nicholas, Alexa, Lincoln, and Simon. Even this little excursion was a risk, but some things were worth the danger.

As the welcomes wound down, Fritz rode into the room on the back of Clarence, his rat, followed by Hans and Sergeant Kiffer.

"Was anyone followed?" he asked brusquely.

"I was!" Simon replied, raising his hand with a smirk. "I

swear this one bee would not leave me alone the whole way up here. So annoying."

"It probably thought you were some strange new flower and couldn't wait to pollinate," Alexa said, nodding slyly at his crazy shirt. Simon stuck his tongue out at her as Nicholas and Lincoln snorted. Fritz gave all of them a stern look.

"This isn't a joke," he said. "Kieft is right on our tail. He's practically knocking at the door."

"He's all over these days," Nicholas said. "I mean, I don't think all this talk about the Munsees breaking free and killing everyone came from nowhere."

"We heard that, too!" Lincoln cried. "They even think the assassin was a Munsee!"

"Then who stabbed me in the hand—my mother?" Simon asked wryly, lifting the recently healed appendage that had been so brutally run through by the traitor Albert Fish.

"It doesn't matter," Fritz replied. "It's a better story, and frightening enough to be taken seriously whether everyone believes it or not."

"So what do we do?" Hans asked.

"Well, one name did come up today," Nicholas said, glancing at Alexa. "Harry Meester. Mean anything to anyone?"

"It tugs at me, but I just can't place it," Alexa admitted. Rory frowned. Where had he heard that name? Thankfully, his sister had a better memory than he did; Bridget was hopping up and down with excitement, waving her hand in the air. "I know! I know! He's the guy who shot Bucky!"

Rory whistled. Of course . . . The Rattle Watch, however, gave Bridget an assortment of confused looks. "What are you talking about?" Fritz asked.

Rory jumped in, explaining about the necklace and the story it contained. He pulled it out and everyone took a good look at the wampum.

"We should all take turns putting this on before we leave tonight," Nicholas said to the rest of the Rattle Watch.

"I wonder what Olathe's name used to be," Alexa said, her eyes distant. "I wonder if I knew her."

"Soka almost told me," Rory said. He told them about his dream. Fritz pursed his lips.

"I'll send someone in to make sure your friend Soka is all right," he said. "Maybe she can tell him Olathe's original identity."

"Finding this broad is not going to make everyone suddenly like the Munsees again, will it?" Sergeant Kiffer opined. "Sounds more like a wild-goose chase to me."

"Hey, watch it peahead . . ." Bridget began, indignant.

"Let's focus here," Nicholas put in, cutting off the argument before it could begin. "We can't go around making everyone love the Munsees overnight. And the mortals may be able to enter the park, but the rest of us can't, so searching for Olathe is just too dangerous. But if the name Harry Meester keeps popping up, maybe there really is something he can tell us that might change things. We need to find out what it is. Which means finding Harry Meester. Agreed?"

A tinkling crash came from the direction of the door. If sounded as if someone had dropped something. They all froze at the sound, nerves on edge.

"Mr. Dyckman? Mrs. Dyckman?" Nicholas called. "Are you all right?"

No one answered. Tucket began to growl as the watch warily rose to their feet. Fritz turned to Rory.

"If anything happens, you run. Both of you," he quietly ordered the Hennessys. "No being a hero. Got it?"

Rory reluctantly nodded as he stepped in front of Bridget, giving her a look to let her know that if she didn't follow orders he'd throw her out the window himself. She gave him her best annoyed "all right!" face and stayed behind him. Tucket stepped forward, teeth bared. The dog was noticeably larger now, the sight of which made Rory's stomach drop. Something was coming . . .

"Okay, everyone, be ready for anything," Nicholas whispered. "The important thing is to stay together—"

His order was cut off suddenly by a whistle through the air, followed by a thud. Nicholas stared down in shock at the rusty cleaver sticking out of his stomach. Unable to speak, his eyes widened in pain as he fell to the ground.

For a moment they all stood frozen at the sight of their wounded leader. Then Bridget screamed, breaking the silence.

"Scatter!" Fritz shouted, and the Rattle Watch ran for cover just as the windows exploded and blue-jacketed men burst into the room.

"Hessians!" Alexa cried, and Rory's stomach rolled with fear. The Hessians were German soldiers hired by the British to fight in the Revolution. A band of them still lived in Inwood, in a camp down by the Harlem River, where they'd been stationed during the war. Rory had always made certain to avoid them, but there was nowhere to hide now.

"Run!" Fritz shouted up at Rory before urging Clarence into the fray. Rory backed into a corner, frozen, as the Hessians struggled with his friends. Lincoln, fearless, wasted no time fighting back, wrestling with a determined soldier trying to spear him with a bayonet. The long knife was affixed to the barrel of a musket. Rory wondered why the Hessians weren't shooting. But then one of them took aim directly at him and fired. Rory closed his eyes, certain that his number was up.

But no flash of pain hit him and he opened his eyes. Feathers floated through the air and he realized that the musket ball had hit a pillow on the seat beside him. Of course! Now he remembered his history teacher teaching the class about how unreliable a musket's aim could be. No wonder they stuck knives on the end.

Rory glanced around to check on Bridget. To his surprise she was already pulling herself through the window. She quickly dropped out of sight. He didn't know what to make of his sister's quick exit; she never ran from a fight. Oh well, at least she was safely on her way home. He heard a growl and turned back to the action to see what was happening.

Tucket had launched himself at a group of Hessians, snapping at them with his great jaws. He'd grown to three times his size so far, and the Hessians seemed shaken by the sight of this huge beast. They tried to stab at the dog, but Tucket simply grabbed the guns out of their hands with his mouth and bit them in two. Rory was impressed; that was one badass puppy.

The falling feathers were making it hard to see; Rory could barely make out the flashes of Hessian blue through the downy white as the intruders struggled with his friends. One of them trapped Alexa in the corner, raising his bayonet to stab her. Rory could stand by no longer; with a yell he launched through the feather-filled air and landed on the Hessian's back. The force of the impact threw off the Hessian's aim, sending the bayonet deep into the wall to Alexa's right. The soldier struggled to free his weapon, giving Alexa just enough time to grab a fireplace iron and whack him into oblivion. She turned to Rory, who waited for the inevitable grateful thanks.

"What are you still doing here?" she scolded him instead. "Run!"

Rory glanced around, frozen with indecision. Tucket was keeping a group of terrified attackers at bay across the room. Lincoln's leg was bleeding profusely, but he fought on with a stolen bayonet, slashing at a pair of Hessians. Fritz was riding to and fro, tossing firecrackers at the Hessians' feet to disable them. Hans and Kiffer were at his side. Simon had ripped off part of his gaudy shirt and wrapped it around Nicholas's stomach, in an attempt to stanch the bleeding. Rory had to stifle a cry as blotches of red seeped into the yellow and pink. Alexa grabbed Rory by the arm and led him to the ruined window.

"Please, we'll be all right," she promised. "You have to get out of here."

Reluctantly, Rory reached up and pulled himself through the window, dropping down into the dirt behind the house. The sounds of fighting drifted through the window, and fear ran through him as he hoped fervently that everyone came out okay. Alexa's face appeared in the window and she mouthed the word *go* one last time before disappearing again. But go where?

Then he remembered that the M'Garoth village lay under the Dyckman playground, just across the street. He'd go there for help. Liv, the captain of the patrol and Fritz's wife, would come running to save her husband, he was sure of it. He turned to race across the backyard toward the street.

An arm snaked over his neck, choking him. Another hand appeared, holding a rusty old cleaver to his throat, the twin of the one buried in Nicholas's stomach. A harsh voice whispered in his ear.

"Got ya!"

BILL THE BUTCHER

Rory's kidnapper dragged him down a side street toward the Harlem River. With his top hat, waistcoat, and large mustache, the man looked like he'd stepped right out of the nineteenth century. But Rory wasn't so keen on figuring out what century his abductor hailed from as he was on planning an escape. The man's grip was steel and Rory couldn't shake it. The first time he tried to pull away, the man calmly backhanded him right across the face. His lip bleeding, Rory pretended to have all the fight knocked out of him, but all the while he searched for ways to get free.

"Where are you taking me?" he asked, digging for information.

"You're Irish, ain't ya?" the man asked instead.

"Yeah," Rory replied hesitantly.

"That's good," the man said. "I'd feel worse about handing you over to the big guy if you weren't a dirty Irishman."

Wonderful. He was in the hands of an old-school bigot.

"Who's the big guy?" Rory asked, undeterred. "Kieft?"

The man stopped, spinning Rory around to face him. Rory recoiled; the man seemed to look right through him.

"Don't be playing games with me, Rory Hennessy," the man said. "I promised I wouldn't kill you, but it gnaws at me to have a Paddy by the neck and let him live. So, I may not kill you, but I will knock you around, hear me? So don't test me. You get me?"

Scared, Rory nodded. The man knew his name and had known where to find him. His luck truly had run out. The man resumed dragging Rory toward the river, muttering to himself.

"This whole city makes my skin crawl," the man said, disgust coloring his voice. "In my day you had the micks and the krauts and the Chinks and the darkies. And that was bad enough. But I been out of the Tombs a half a day and already I've crossed paths with more dirty immigrants than I ever saw in my life. So many colors and accents and the like, it makes me sick. My family stretches back generations! They built this country! They didn't slink off the boat like a rat in the night.

"I even had to hire kraut Hessians to be my distraction; I'll be bathing for weeks to get their stench off me. Let me tell you, once I've handed you over, I got some real work to do. This city needs cleaning up and me and my cleavers have to rise to the challenge. I gotta take it back from the hebes and wops and micks like you. Dirty little micks like you . . ."

Suddenly Bill pulled up, roughly spinning Rory to face him. The kidnapper's cheek twitched as his eyes stared right through his captive. A shiver ran through Rory as he realized that madness had taken over his kidnapper. Bill's promise to refrain from murdering Rory teetered on the edge, as Bill's hands reached, grasping for the handle of his rusty cleaver . . .

Just then a blur shot through the air in front of them, crashing into Bill and knocking him to the ground. Rory staggered backward as his captor's hand was wrenched from his arm. Bill struggled to rise, but someone in a hooded sweatshirt was jumping up and down on his chest. Bill reached into his belt and pulled out the cleaver. Rory let loose a cry, but not in time, as Bill swung his arm around and buried the cleaver in the shoulder of Rory's rescuer.

"Hey! This is a new hoodie!" Rory's growing suspicions were proven true as the hood fell back to reveal a rough paper face. It was, of course, Bridget. Relief and anger warred inside Rory—and anger won.

"Why are you in that papier-mâché body!" Rory cried. "I told you not to wear it, it's too dangerous!"

"You're welcome!" Bridget replied as she struggled to hold Bill down. "I'm so sorry I ran all the way home to get it so I could stop this maniac from murdering and eating you. You're too ungrateful to be saved."

"You're not by yourself, right?" Rory looked around for the cavalry. The streets were empty.

"I ran into Tucket when I was running back," she said before head-butting Bill in the face. "He was already on your trail and I followed him."

"Where is he, then?"

"I sent him back to get the others!"

"Why didn't you send Tucket to me while you went back and got the others?"

Bridget paused, glancing back at her brother.

"I didn't think of that," she admitted, shrugging sheepishly. Sensing an opening, Bill thrust her off him, sending her skidding across the road.

"I don't know what you are," he said, pushing himself to his feet. "But anything can be carved up with enough swings of the cleaver." He reached into his belt to pull out another wicked knife. Rory ran over to his sister's side and pulled her to her feet.

"We gotta run for it," he whispered urgently.

"But the reinforcements are coming . . ." she answered. Rory glanced back at Bill, who was advancing warily, cleaver in hand.

"By the time they get here, I'll be cut into steaks and you'll be the plates he serves me on."

"Okay, fine." Bridget pouted. She reached up and yanked the cleaver from her shoulder, making Rory wince. "Ready," she whispered, holding the weapon loosely in her hand.

"Now!" Rory shouted, and Bridget threw the cleaver right at Bill's face. The kidnapper barely got his other cleaver up in time to deflect the blow, and in that moment of confusion, Rory grabbed Bridget's hand and took off.

The siblings raced down the side street toward Broadway. They could barely see where they were going in the darkness of the blackout, but they could hear Bill's curses as he chased them. Rory hoped that they'd run into the Rattle Watch, coming to rescue them, but the streets remained deserted. And by the sound of it, Bill wasn't too far behind.

Broadway seemed impossibly far. Rory realized they had to try something different if they were to escape. They had to use the darkness to their advantage. Rory spied an alley up ahead and decided to chance a right turn. He pulled Bridget toward the passage as a gust of air kissed his ear, followed by the thwack of a cleaver landing right in the center of Bridget's back.

"What is with this guy!" Bridget cried, trying to look behind her at the weapon sticking out from between her shoulder blades. "Who throws cleavers? Honestly!"

Rory shushed her as he pulled her into the alley. They didn't stop running, sprinting down the narrow space between the buildings. The siblings could barely see in front of them, and Rory almost fell as he stumbled over some cans. A muffled curse behind them told them that they weren't alone in their difficult maneuvering through the dark. Rory had the sinking sensation that entering the alley hadn't been the best move. It slowed them all up, but Bill was just a cleaver's throw away from ending this chase for good.

Rory quickly glanced around for some other escape route, but he couldn't find any. He spied a Dumpster and he pulled Bridget behind it, crouching down in the hope the kidnapper would pass.

Footsteps approached, deliberate, sending loud echoes through the alley. Rory bent over to peer beneath the slightly raised Dumpster; he spied two black boots passing right by them. He held his breath, hoping Bill would keep walking. Bridget rustled behind him and the boots slowed. His heart in this throat, Rory turned to keep Bridget quiet. She was tugging at the cleaver in her back, finally yanking it free with a light grunt. Rory made a fierce face at her, willing her to be quiet. He returned to peering at his kidnapper from beneath the Dumpster.

The boots had stopped moving entirely, and the toe of the right shoe turned toward them. Bill had heard, and he was coming right for them. Rory took a deep breath; maybe the element of surprise would help him. He braced himself, about to rise, but before he could, Bridget was already standing.

"Hey, bozo!" she called out, and ran forward. Rory heard a thud and a cry. He leaped to his feet and raced out from behind the Dumpster. To his considerable surprise, Bill lay prone at Bridget's feet, a huge red mark square in the center of his forehead. Bridget shrugged, lifting the cleaver in her hand.

"I whacked him with the blunt end," she said proudly. "He sure didn't see it coming!"

Rory took a second to breathe before hitting his sister in the shoulder, hard.

"When we get home, I'm going to kill you," he said crossly. "Come on, we've got to get moving before he wakes up."

He started to jog away. Bridget ran after him.

"No 'thank you, Bridget'?" She pouted. "No 'You're the best sister ever'? You are an ungrateful brother, Rory Hennessy." They reached the end of the alley and turned the corner. As they rushed back toward Broadway, Rory glanced angrily at Bridget's paper body.

"I thought I locked that body up!"

"Come on, the apartment's only so big," Bridget shot back. "Behind the baseball cards was, like, the third place I looked."

"How many times have you gone out in that thing anyway?" he asked, frowning.

"This is the first time—" Bridget began to say, but Rory was sniffing the air.

"Is that smoke?" he asked, cutting her off. "Have you been around a fire or something?" A memory tickled him from earlier that day. "Wait a second! That burning car, with the mystery person saving the baby . . ."

"No one knew it was me," she protested. "I had to do something! I saved your life, too, remember!"

"Being a hero is too dangerous, Bridget," he scolded her. "You'll get yourself hurt or killed, paper body or no paper body. Remember what Flavio said about the body being temporary? Every little tear in the papier-mâché could be very dangerous, in ways we don't know anything about! When we get home, we're throwing that thing out!"

Bridget lapsed into silence, still pouting. The dark streets around them seemed deserted. Rory had no idea what to do next. Should they head back to Dyckman's farmhouse? For all he knew, Nicholas was dead. So what should he do now? Thankfully, before he had too much time to worry, a bark cut through the quiet air.

Tucket bolted out of the shadows, racing right for them. Close on his heels came Alexa, disheveled and bleeding—but alive. Relief erupted on her face when she saw them.

"Thank the gods!" she cried, pulling both of them into a rough embrace. "We thought you were dead, Rory."

"Not yet," Rory said, peering around for the other members of the watch while trying to keep Tucket from mauling him with his big tongue. "Where is everyone else? How is . . . is he okay?"

Alexa's eyes looked tired and heavy.

"We're not sure yet. That cleaver got him good, right in the midsection. We beat the Hessians off; or at least we think we did. They probably rereated once you were taken. Fritz called the gypsy cab and paid for it himself to bring Nicholas down to his father's farm. Simon's helping him. Lincoln's with them, too. He was hurt pretty bad in his leg, but I think he'll be okay."

"How did you find us?" Bridget wanted to know. Alexa nodded toward Tucket, who was happily hopping around at their feet.

"I just followed the dog," she said. "He took me right to you."

Rory gave Tucket a rough hug. "Thank you, Tucket." He glanced up at Bridget. "And thank you, Bridget. You're the best sister ever."

"You bet your booty I am," Bridget replied, fighting a smile and failing.

"You need to go underground," Alexa said. "Both of you. They knew just where to find us and the only one they could have followed was you, Rory. They know who you are."

"Are you sure?" Rory asked, his stomach roiling.

"Sure enough. We need to get you into hiding, right away. And since the kidnapper now knows who you are as well, Bridget, it's probably best if you go, too."

"What about Mom?" Bridget asked, choking up. "We can't leave her."

"She'll be safer if you're not there," Alexa assured her. "And we'll make certain she never knows you're gone."

Not long after, they stood in Rory's bedroom, staring at the apparition curled up under the covers. A similar ghostly figure lay in Bridget's bed next door. Alexa explained quietly, taking care not to wake up their mother.

"My father used to use this trick when he was traveling and didn't want his enemies to know he was gone. It's a memory I grabbed from your own heads, of you being sick and unhappy, and I gave it form and placed it in your bed."

Bridget nudged the ghostly form carefully, seeing if she could wake him up.

"Go 'way," fake Rory murmured, turning over under the covers. "I don't feel good."

"But it looks so . . . soft," Rory said by her side. "Not completely there, I mean."

"Well, you can tell what's true, Rory, so it won't fool you," Alexa explained. "And I made it deliberately easy for someone from Mannahatta to see through, so Kieft's people will know you're not here and that your mother had to be fooled so she knows nothing. But to anyone mortal, this would appear to be you. I plucked it right from your memory. Hopefully, this will last us a few days, which should be enough time to figure everything out."

Nodding, Rory desperately hoped this worked. But he still felt like he was leaving his mother behind to take the heat. If anything happened to her . . . he fought tears as he thought of his mother, all alone though she didn't know it, looking after her two sick phantom children. It wasn't right, but what could he do? It was the only way to protect her. Rory just hoped that he found his answers before anything found his mother. No, no hoping. He would do it. Any other outcome was unthinkable.

AN UNEXPECTED VISIT

Walt Whitman, God of Optimism, sat in his study reading the papers. The New York *Tribune* and the New York *Herald* lay spread out in front of him. Both papers had once been the preeminent news rags of their day, run by archrivals Horace Greeley and James Bennett respectively. Now those two bitter enemies were the co-Gods of Newspapermen—there are two sides to every story, after all—and their papers, long gone from mortal New York, lived on in Mannahatta, continuing their editors' feud. Each paper reported the news of the earthquake from the exact opposite point of view. Bennett's *Herald* was certain the quake was the result of natural forces, while Greeley's *Tribune* implicated the Munsee menace as the hidden cause. It was an open secret that Greeley had long been in Kieft's pocket, but it didn't matter. His more sensationalist *Tribune* was more widely read among the spirits of Mannahatta, due to its lurid details and wild speculations. People just want to be shocked, Whitman's old friend Adriaen would say.

Whitman sighed. He missed Adriaen. He'd have known what to do in this crisis. Instead, they seemed to be headed toward disaster. It was important that the Council of Twelve stick together and be strong—those not on Kieft's side, anyway—so it was up to Peter Stuyvesant, Dorothy Parker, Bennett, Zelda Fitzgerald, himself, and even the wishy-washy Babe Ruth to lead the way. Adriaen wouldn't have hesitated to accept the challenge. If Whitman could prove himself to be half the man his old friend had been . . .

A knock at the door disturbed his reverie. Not expecting anyone, he approached his front door with suspicion, picking up a fireplace rod along the way.

"Who is it?" he called through the door.

"I'm sorry, sir, to bother you so late," a woman's voice called back. "I have a package from Ms. Russell. Just a little somethin' to brighten your evenin', she said, sir."

Whitman had to smile. He'd begun to spend a lot of time recently with the Goddess of Overacting, as she was the only one who could match him exclamation point for exclamation point. And it certainly was flattering that the once-world-famous actress Lillian Russell was interested in him. His friends warned him that Lillian was known to grow easily bored with her men once the initial romantic drama fizzled, but, as always, Whitman was optimistic.

Whitman carefully opened the door. A middle-aged woman, rail thin and tired, stood on his stoop, holding a covered plate.

"What is it?" he asked.

"Shortbread, sir. Sorry, I looked."

His favorite! Grinning, he reached out to take the plate.

"I'm sorry I'm acting so suspicious," he told the woman. "These are dangerous times. Thank you, Mrs. . . . ?"

"Mallon," she answered, handing over the plate and nodding her good-bye. "But you can call me Mary. Have a nice evening."

"You as well," he called after the retreating woman. He lifted the cover off the plate and took in the delicious smell of shortbread. The scent took him back a hundred years or more. He lifted a piece and took a bite, enjoying the dessert immensely. He contentedly backed into his home, closing the door behind him, devouring the shortbread until not even the crumbs remained.

The sun had risen high in the midmorning sky as Rory and Bridget gazed up at the roof of the brownstone at the corner of Stuyvesant Street and East 10th Street, hope blooming in their hearts.

"We're staying at the farm?" Rory asked.

"Sorry," Alexa answered, leading them to a small alley next to the brownstone. "We're only stopping here to check on the boys and figure out our next move. The Stuyvesant farm will be one of the first places Kieft will look when he realizes you've disappeared."

Rory and Bridget sighed with disappointment. The farm was one of the more idyllic spots on the island. But staying there was probably too much to ask for in the middle of a crisis.

They reached the alley and began climbing a staircase that led to the roof. Bridget struggled a bit, carrying her papier-mâché body clumsily in her arms. Rory had argued to throw it out, but Alexa reminded him how dangerous the next few days could be. Bridget might very well need the body, outweighing the risk of using it. So in a moment of pure pettiness at being overruled, Rory made Bridget carry the thing. She didn't complain, though she stuck her tongue out at him when she thought he wasn't looking.

As they climbed the stairs, the top of the brownstone slowly came into view, and the Hennessy children's hearts warmed at the sight. Instead of a typical tarred New York City roof, lush green grass covered the entire top of the building, leading up to an old Dutch farmhouse. Tucket barked happily and raced up the last of the stairs, running madly through the greenery. On the surrounding roofs, crops grew in neat rows: corn, beans, tomatoes, squash, and potatoes. Down the street, a big barn sat atop a group of prewar buildings. Inside, Rory knew, the horses were stabled, including Nicholas's stallion, Revolution. Two unfamiliar figures leaned against the barn door; farmhands, perhaps, resting before a long day in the fields. But was that a musket leaning against the door behind them?

"Are those guards?" he asked Alexa. She shot him a warning look, her eyes asking him to keep his questions to himself. He swallowed his curiosity for the time being, dutifully following Alexa and Bridget as they made their way up the path to the front porch of the Stuyvesant farmhouse. But the thought of what might be in the barn stayed in the back of his head.

No one came to greet them as they pushed through the front door. But once Alexa called out a hello, a familiar maternal figure came barreling down the steps.

"Rory! Bridget! You're all right! We were worried sick!"

Mrs. Stuyvesant hugged the Hennessy children, clutching the two of them to her ample bosom. Tucket jumped up on Rory's back, wanting in on the love.

"How is he?" Alexa asked. Mrs. Stuyvesant stepped back, worry plain on her face.

"He's very tired. Peter wore him out this morning, shouting about how Kieft will pay. I don't care if my husband is on the council now, you have to watch yourself with such talk! Kieft is a powerful man! Peter's up at Walt Whitman's house now; apparently Walt has come down with some sort of illness."

"I didn't know gods could get sick," Bridget said.

"Neither did I," Alexa replied, worried.

"I'm sure it's nothing," Mrs. Stuyvesant said, though she didn't seem convinced. "Nicholas needs to sleep, but you can have five minutes."

They followed her upstairs toward Nicholas's room. Mrs. Stuyvesant waved them inside.

"Visitors, Nicholas," she announced. Rory gasped as he stepped through the door, and judging from the startled cry beside him, Bridget was equally dismayed by the sight of a gray, weak Nicholas Stuyvesant lying on his bed, barely able to raise his head. Another bed had been pulled up beside him, and Lincoln lay there, his leg in a splint, but otherwise no worse for the wear. Simon sat in the corner, playing with something in his pocket. Rory thought he saw a flash of gold; probably a watch or something, he guessed. Fritz and Hans stood atop one of the side tables; everyone looked up as they entered.

Rory felt his lip quiver, but surprisingly, Alexa broke first. Tears poured down her cheeks as she ran over to cradle Nicholas's head in her arms.

"I'm okay, I'm okay," Nicholas said, patting her arm gently. His voice had barely any strength to it. "You did the important thing; finding Rory and bringing him back."

"I'm just glad you're all right." She sniffed, regaining her composure.

"I'm okay, too, in case you were wondering," Lincoln called over from his bed. "I appreciate the concern!"

"Fritz was just telling us about his morning," Nicholas whispered, his voice so soft they had to strain to hear. Fritz glanced over at him with pain in his eyes, but he shook it off to speak.

"I've been sending the boys out to see if anyone has heard of Harry Meester. A few seem to recognize the name, but so far no one knows anything definite. This is going to be harder than I'd hoped."

Nicholas nodded and tried to speak, but he began to cough instead. Alexa ran over to give him water before turning to the rest of them.

"Then we keep looking," she said. "And I'll keep trying to remember where I've heard that name before . . ." She gazed off into space, shaking her head.

"I also sent Hans into the park to check on Soka," Fritz continued, glancing at Rory, "but he couldn't seem to find any trace of the Munsees. Their village is supposed to be deep in the Ramble, but he just got lost in all those trees. I'm sorry, Rory. We'll try again, I promise."

Rory felt like he had elephants on his chest, weighing on his heart. Was Soka okay? He wanted to rush into the park and find her, but Soka had expressly told him to stay away. It made him so angry that there was nothing he could do . . .

A commotion in the hall outside caught everyone's attention.

An Unexpected Visit · 99

"You can't come up, he's resting!" Mrs. Stuyvesant's voice called out. A flurry of footsteps raced down the hall and suddenly Mrs. Stuyvesant stuck her head into the room, her face frightened.

"Rory, Bridget! Hide! Now! You too, roaches!" She pulled back into the hall, closing the door behind her.

Rory started, leaping to his feet. Glancing around, he spied a large armoire in the corner. Following his gaze, Simon reached out and flung it open without even getting up, and Rory hopped inside, slipping behind some old coats. Simon closed the door again, leaving a sliver of light down the middle. Rory pushed an eyeball up to the opening just in time to see Bridget scurry under the bed. The nightstand by Nicholas was now empty as well; the M'Garoths must have found some hidey-hole. Then the door opened to admit Nicholas's new visitors.

A group of slick, well-dressed men in matching black suits glided into the room. Their pasty-white skin practically glowed, and Rory thought he saw a flash of pointed canine. He stifled a shudder; Fritz had told him about these men. They were the Mayor's Lawyers, feared throught the city not only for their legal know-how, but also because they were vampires. They could suck you dry in every sense.

Behind the Lawyers strolled a dapper gentleman with a twinkle in his eyes. He wore a crisp, overlarge fedora and puffed away on a cigarette stuck on the end of a long holder. Alexa crossed her arms, unimpressed by his airs.

"Jimmy Walker," she spat. "Has the Mayor's right-hand man come down to see why Nicholas didn't die outright?" Rory recognized the name from one of the many New York history books he'd begun reading ever since he'd been introduced to Mannahatta. Jimmy Walker had been a corrupt mayor during the 1920s, famous more for his partying, womanizing, and celebrity hobnobbing than for any political expertise. Now he was the God of Leaders Who Look the Other Way.

"Calm down, baby," Walker said, his voice oozing insincerity. "I heard about the attack and wanted to check up on our brave boys. Look at the two of you, you sick puppies! You look terrible! You boys need a night out, or a dance with a pretty lady, or something! You come to me, you ask me, and I'll set it right up. Anything for such brave, noble boys!"

The Lawyers stood slightly behind the short, smiling god, saying nothing as they stared at the Rattle Watchers hungrily.

"What do you want, Jimmy?" Simon asked from his chair. "I haven't owed you money in fifty years."

"It's not what *I* want," Walker said, smiling like a used-car salesman. "I'm just here to make sure you're awake and in a good mood. You in a good mood?"

"I'm tap-dancing, Jimmy," Nicholas breathed, his voice barely audible.

"Good, good. Then he'll only be a minute. Sir?"

Walker moved to the side to let in a new visitor, and Rory realized why Mrs. Stuyvesant had been such a mess.

"Nicholas, Lincoln, I'm glad to see you're healing nicely," Mayor Alexander Hamilton said, striding into the room. Rory recognized him from the ten-dollar bill; it looked just like him. A strikingly handsome man in stylish, late-eighteenth-century jacket and hose, Hamilton filled the room with the force of his charisma and personality. Though Kieft might have eroded his power over the decades, in person Hamilton still packed a punch.

This didn't stop Lincoln from speaking his mind.

"Hey, sorry to see we're not dead yet?" he asked loudly. "You'll have to try harder than that to stamp out the Rattle Watch!" Inside the armoire, Rory almost snorted in disbelief; that kid just didn't know when to shut up.

Alexa sighed. "Cool it, Lincoln. I doubt they're here to gloat." She turned to the Mayor. "Why *are* you here? If Peter knew you were on the premises, he'd probably release the hounds."

"Just seeing how our two injured friends are convalescing," Hamilton said. "It was quite the vicious attack, from what I heard. Rest assured, the culprits will be tracked down and dealt with."

"That's awful nice of you," Alexa said sarcastically. "To come all the way here just to check up on us."

"I am a nice person, Ms. Van der Donck, you should know that by now," Hamilton replied. He turned as if to leave, then stopped. "One other, little thing. I've received word of some questions floating around the city this morning. About a certain gentleman long gone from Mannahatta, a Mr. Meester. I think it is in everyone's best interest if those questions were to cease. Nothing good can come of dredging up the past. No one can change it; to revisit it can only cause us . . . discomfort." Here Hamilton glanced away and Rory could have sworn he saw a flash of pain cross the Mayor's face. Just as quickly, it was gone. "Can we agree?"

"Wow," Simon said drily. "Ask a few questions on the street and have the man in charge in your bedroom in an hour. Now, that's service."

Hamilton pursed his lips in annoyance and gestured; in

a flash, one of the Lawyers had Simon by the throat. Alexa sprang to her feet, but a strong look from Nicholas sent her back down into her chair as Simon sat frozen in the vampire's grasp. Hamilton sighed. "Everyone worries about Kieft, and no one worries about me. It is a tragedy. Well, on this subject, Kieft and I are one. I have a large legal team, you can see." He gestured toward the Lawyers, who exposed their teeth en masse. "And they love to sue. They will drain you if you continue with your questions. Understand me?"

He stared at Simon until the boy nodded. The Lawyer released him, sending Simon gasping and rubbing his throat.

"Hey, you can't just—" Lincoln began to say, but Nicholas stopped him.

"We understand you," he whispered. Hamilton gave him a piercing look before nodding once and abruptly turning to stride out of the room. The Lawyers followed, gliding across the floor like ghosts. Last of all went Jimmy Walker, who turned at the door.

"He ain't kiddin', boys," Walker said. "I could have told you all of this, but he insisted on coming down here himself. I'd hate to see you lose everything in a lawsuit. *Everything.* Toodles!" With that, he turned and disappeared out the door.

Rory waited to move, not willing to risk stepping out of the closet just yet. As he waited for the footsteps to fade down the hall, he knew that one thing was now certain: finding this Meester person was more important than ever. They'd just have to be more careful from now on. But anything that brought the Mayor to their door so quickly was worth pursuing, no matter what.

AN OLD FRIEND

Fritz led Rory across the fields atop the brownstones that held up the Stuyvesant farm, bouncing gently on Clarence's back as he trotted through the grass. Rory had convinced the battle roach to slip away with him for a moment before the Hennessy kids were taken to a safe house. This was after Fritz had taken Rory aside to quietly give him the rest of the news he'd gathered that morning.

"First off, Giovanni wasn't saying Two's Boys, like the number," Fritz had told him as Rory listened, captivated. "It's Tew, as in the pirate Thomas Tew. From what I gathered from the sailors down at the docks, for centuries the spirits of the two worst pirates in New York history, Captain Kidd and Thomas Tew, were the scourge of the ocean, making life miserable for anyone sailing into the mists. The two of them were constantly at war with each other as well, always fighting over who got to attack which rich merchant ghost ship. Finally, Kidd tired of the competition and apparently ambushed Tew, stranding him on some island far out to sea. Most of the crew perished, but a few survived after floating on the ocean for months on a make-shift raft of planks. Ever since, they've been bound together by a terrible secret, or so I heard. This was a century ago. Ever since, Tew's Boys, as they're called, have floated around from ship to ship, always for hire. And you could always tell one of Tew's Boys from the haunted look in their eyes."

"And Verrazano thought my father was one of them," Rory had said quietly.

"Who knows what that old god thinks?" Fritz had replied. "He's always been a little batty."

Rory had simply stared back at him for a moment before suggesting that the roach take a walk with him to the barn, to see an old friend.

"How did you know he was here?" Fritz asked Rory as they approached the barn.

"Who else would you be guarding like that? Why is he here, anyway? Shouldn't he be in the Tombs?"

"Too dangerous," Fritz replied. "Kieft would have him killed in a heartbeat. It's taken the combined skills of all our friends on the council to protect him as it is. None of us want another Albert situation. Kieft will find him eventually, of course, but maybe we'll learn something useful before that happens. I hope so. Here we are."

They reached the barn and Fritz nodded at the guards. They moved aside, opening one of the barn doors to admit the boy and roach, with Tucket following close behind. Once they passed through, the door was shut behind them with a clang that made Rory jump.

It took a moment for Rory's eyes to adjust to the inside of the barn. Finally, he was able to make out the high arcing ceiling, which let in thin slivers of golden light that sliced through the black interior of the barn. Most of the barn was empty; the horses no longer resided in the stables. But the barn was not completely barren. A disheveled man sat on a bale of hay, a long chain running from the irons wrapped around his ankles to a thick post rising up from the floor to the ceiling of the barn. He smirked as he recognized his visitor.

"Hello, Rory," the man said. "You're looking well. Kieft hasn't killed you yet, I gather. Ah well, he still has plenty of time."

"Hello, Hex," Rory replied, forcing himself not to react to the prisoner's gibes. "You're lucky Kieft hasn't killed you, either."

Hex shrugged, patting his chains.

"I'm the luckiest guy in the world."

Rory could understand his bitterness. After all, Hex had once been Aaron Burr, a great and influential man and god. But then he'd fallen, resorting to petty thievery in an effort to win back power and exact revenge on his old ally, and eventual betrayer, Willem Kieft. Bridget had been caught in the cross fire—literally—for which Rory would never forgive the traitorious ex-god.

"You should ask your question so we can get out of here," Frtiz whispered.

"Yes, yes, please, ask away," Hex said sardonically, overhearing. "I'm very busy." He picked up a piece of hay. "I'm teaching myself how to weave a basket. It's very fulfilling."

"You did this to yourself," Rory reminded him. Hex shrugged.

"Not at all. You did this to me. If I had my way, the Munsees would be free, no one would be chasing you around trying to kill you, and I'd have the secret Kieft hid in the park. So don't blame this on me."

"That's not true!" Rory was shouting. "You knew what would happen!" Tucket began to bark, picking up on his master's dismay.

"Calm down, Rory," Fritz soothed him. "Maybe it was a mistake to bring you here."

Hex laughed softly. "Come to see if you, and only you, can get me to talk, eh, Rory? Let me save you the breath. As I told Peter, I've heard the name Harry Meester, but only as a name. He could be anyone from those days when we sprung the Trap. Anyone at all. And I sure don't know where he is now. Sorry to waste your time."

Rory hesitated. Something about Hex's nonchalant answer seemed . . . off. Hex knew something, all right, Rory could feel it. But he knew he wasn't the one to get to the bottom of it; he'd leave that to Nicholas's dad. No, Rory had come to ask a different question entirely. He pulled the photo out of his pocket, glancing down at that smiling face. He might never get another chance; he had to know for sure. He gritted his teeth and spit it out. "I wanted to ask you about my father."

"So *that's* what this is about," Hex said, his eyes darkly amused. He leaned back against his bale of hay, putting his hands lazily behind his head. "I told you the last time you asked, I don't know any more than you do. When I worked that invisibility spell on you, I caught a brief whisper inside your head—you believed you'd seen him on that ghost ship as it sailed past. Beyond that, your guess is as good as mine."

"What about Tew's Boys?" Rory asked, even as his heart sank. "Do you know anything about them?"

"Not a thing," Hex replied, leaning forward to rest his chin on his arched fingers. "If you want to know more about your dad, ask your mom, that's my advice. I thought you were smarter than this."

"I needed to make sure," Rory mumbled. Why did he keep chasing his dad when he knew he should just leave him be? It only left him feeling foolish, like he did right now.

"Are you sure yet?" Hex said, smirking. "Maybe you should worry about real things, like the earthquake that almost buried me under this cursed barn. Did I not say it from the beginning, Rory? Did I not say the Trap had to be opened or we would all suffer?"

"You haven't been particularly helpful since then," Fritz said. "You haven't answered a single question about what happened during the making of the Trap."

"Nor will I," Hex replied.

"But people will be hurt," Rory pleaded with him.

"People like your mother?" Hex stared at him intently. "Your sister? Or does she still run around in that paper shell? I hope you warned her of the dangers. I'd hate for her to go mad."

"Like Toy went mad?" Rory shot back. Hex locked eyes with him for a moment before nodding.

"Yes, like Jason," he said quietly. "You had your chance, Rory. You let it slip through your fingers. There is nothing more I can, or will, say to help you."

"But the island . . ." Fritz said.

"All of Manhattan can shake itself to pieces for all I care," Hex shouted, disturbing some birds in the rafters.

The barn gradually settled back into silence. Sighing, Fritz turned to Rory and shook his head.

"I think we're done here," the battle roach said. Rory nodded, his heart heavy, and glanced down at the photo. His father looked back at him, as inscrutable as ever. Sighing, he turned to go.

"Can I see it?" Hex called after him. "The photo in your hand?"

Rory ignored him, heading for the door.

"Hey, city killer!" Hex yelled. "Can I see the picture of the famous man who left his family to fend for itself? Just out of curiosity."

Rory turned back to face him.

"Didn't you see him in my mind?"

"I didn't see an image. I only picked up that you'd thought you'd seen him. I wouldn't mind taking a look at this guy, if I could."

"One might think you don't want to be left alone again," Fritz said, giving the prisoner a knowing glance.

"I'm just curious," Hex answered innocently.

Fritz shrugged, not sure what to say. So Rory walked back and handed the photo to Hex, who took one look and froze. He leaned in, gazing intently at the picture in front of him. And then, softly, he began to laugh.

"What . . . ?" Rory said, confused. "Why are you laughing? Do you recognize him or something?"

Hex laughed louder, until tears came to his eyes, gazing down at the picture of the elder Hennessy.

"STOP LAUGHING!" Rory shouted. Hex wiped his streaming eyes. He looked up at Rory, still grinning, and began to speak.

"I'm afraid I haven't been entirely up front with you, Rory," he said, his eyes dancing with joy. "Let me make it up to you with a little story. I'm sure you've heard that Mayor Alexander Hamilton used to be the best friend the Munsees ever had. It's true. There was no one the Munsees trusted more. Especially Tackapausha. Those two were like peas in a pod. We all believed our struggles would be worked out with the two of them tackling the problem. And who knows what might have happened. Maybe the Munsees would be as much a part of Mannahatta, and Manhattan, as the rest of us. But then, one night, Mayor Hamilton went into a room with two men. When he emerged, he was livid, and he gave Kieft the authority to immediately commission the Trap. I worked out all the details, though the nuts and bolts of how the thing actually operated came from Caesar Prince—"

"What!" Rory blurted out.

"Oh yes," Hex said. "Caesar is as much responsible for that Trap as I. My idea, his execution. And the rest is history. Hamilton went from being the Munsees' best friend to their worst enemy, overnight. It's often run through my mind. What happened in that room that night? No one knows but Hamilton and those two men. One was Willem Kieft, of course. And the other was someone I had seen before, but knew little about. He did odd jobs for some of the gods. He also spent a lot of time with the Indians, though I don't think anyone, us or them, really knew much about him. And soon after that meeting, he disappeared. His name was Harry Meester."

"What!" Fritz cried. "You filthy liar, you said you never knew anything about him."

"I know what I said," Hex replied, still smiling. "But I've changed my mind. The truth is just too delicious to lie about anymore. See, after that night, I never saw him again . . . until now. I'm looking at him in this photo here. That man was your father."

Rory's jaw dropped as Fritz gasped. Hex smiled at the reaction his pronouncement had received.

"It would seem, Rory," Hex continued, his eyes glinting yellow in the darkness of the barn, "that you *really* don't know who your daddy is at all, do you?"

10

GOING UNDERGROUND

The news spread throughout Mannahatta; Walt Whitman was ill, *deathly* ill one would say if there were any worry of him dying. He slipped in and out of consciousness, hardly lucid at all. And if that wasn't bad enough, the same affliction had struck Mrs. Parker, Hamilton Fish, Frederick Douglass, James Bennett, Zelda Fitzgerald; the list went on and on. The pillars of the community were being struck down, people whispered. Was this the next stage in the Munsees' plan? they asked. After all, it couldn't be a coincidence so soon after the earthquake . . .

Tweed worked overtime to make sure no one believed it *could* be coincidence, sending whispers up and down the taverns and halls of the spirit city. The rumors were a rousing success, pushing Mannahatta to the brink of hysteria. Only two blights marred his work. For one, Peter Stuyvesant remained hale and hearty. The paranoid old fool wouldn't eat anything not prepared by his own wife. Such a lack of trust was a crying shame. Tweed would have to try harder to get some of Mary's home cooking to the god's lips.

The other worry on his mind was the whereabouts of Bill the Butcher. The criminal had failed in his duty to kidnap the Light, and now he'd gone missing. Both the killer and the boy had disappeared off the face of the island.

Ow!"

Bridget banged her head on the ceiling of the cramped space she and Rory, along with a heavily panting Tucket and her papier-mâché body, were stashed inside. She felt like one of the dice in a Yahtzee cup right before the toss as she rattled around the inside of the secret compartment. Their ceiling, she knew, was actually the false floor of a wagon Nicholas's dad used around his farm. They'd lain down into the secret space, the floor had been closed on top of them, and then, voilà! The Hennessy kids had disappeared from the face of the earth, like magic.

The wagon itself was ancient; typical of the early eighteenth century, Alexa had explained, and it was drawn by a really smelly horse. Horses were overrated, she decided. She didn't know why all her friends at school gushed over them (probably brainwashing or mercury poisoning or tumors). A Stuyvesant farmhand named Diedrich drove the wagon to wherever they were going; no one had seen fit to tell her where they'd be hiding. It burned Bridget to be kept in the dark, about anything, and the painful way the wagon bounced along only made her more PO'd. When she complained to Rory about the roughness of the ride, he explained absently about how they didn't have rubber tires back in the old days. She scoffed; people in olden times were not the brightest, she decided.

Of course none of these minor annoyances could cover up the real reason she was all out of sorts.

"It must be some kind of mistake," she repeated for the umpteenth time.

"*Shh!*" Rory whispered back, putting a finger to his lips. She made a face at him. He seemed to think the bad guys were running right alongside them with their ears pressed against the side of the wagon. Didn't he know how loud New York could be?

"You *wanted* Dad to be a bad guy," she continued, undeterred. "You're probably making what he did sound worse 'cause you want him to be a traitor or something. You're still mad at him for leaving, so you're making up all this stuff about Dad being Harry Meester. You know what, I think Hex wasn't even in that barn at all! I think you were talking to a cow the whole time!" She crossed her arms defiantly to show she knew she was right.

"Don't be stupid," Rory answered, his voice tired. "Our dad is the infamous Harry Meester, we just have to accept it. He was a bad guy."

"But that was a hundred and fifty years ago," Bridget pointed out. "Is he a god or spirit or something? Wouldn't that make us spirits? I don't feel like a spirit. No one at school had any trouble seeing me when Julie Menendez pantsed me in gym class. Hex has the wrong guy."

"I don't know what Dad is. But I know I saw him on the *Half Moon*. And Verrazano recognized him in my face. So it isn't just Hex I'm listening to. It's *all* the facts."

"They're *stupid* facts." Bridget felt herself choking up. Tears came unbidden to her eyes. "And even if he was this Harry Meester guy, I'm sure he had a reason to do what he did. Maybe he was a double agent. Or maybe there was blackmail.

Or maybe Bucky was really a bad guy and we just don't realize it. Or maybe—"

Rory cut her off. "There are a million maybes, Bridge. Maybe you're right. We're gonna track him down and find out. You're gonna get your wish after all."

"But he could be anywhere! Out to sea, underground, anywhere!" As she made excuses for why they wouldn't be finding their father anytime soon, Bridget realized that she didn't want to see him under these circumstances. She was afraid of what he might say. "We should just follow the necklace and find Olathe. I bet she knows more than Dad!"

"I'm sorry, Bridget."

Suddenly the wagon pulled up short, sending their heads banging into the ceiling again. Light streamed in as the false floor lifted away to reveal Diedrich's concerned face.

"Are you two all right?" he asked.

Bridget gave him her most withering glare. "I may never see straight again!" she announced. She pulled herself unsteadily to her feet, grabbing the papier-mâché version of herself for support. Diedrich helped her from the wagon, then turned back to assist her brother.

"Where are we?" Rory asked as he dropped to the sidewalk. They stood on a quiet street corner. The area felt secluded; not many cars passed by and the cozy street itself ran only six blocks or so before it ended in a small, gated park. Beautiful brownstones and ornate stone apartment buildings lined the sidewalk, with some well-maintained carriage houses mixed in. She spied a street sign that read IRVING PLACE, which would make the small park at the end of the street the exclusive Gramercy Park, for which you had to have a key to enter (which had never sounded very fair to her). All of Irving Place felt as if it hadn't changed in decades, and Bridget found herself wishing she could live on such a beautiful, peaceful street.

Their destination waited directly in front of them, a small brick building on the corner of Irving and 17th Street, red in color with a black wrought-iron fence around the base. On the 17th Street side next to a big bay window, a stone stoop led up to the front door, which had opened to reveal Alexa, Simon at her side.

"Come in! Quick!" she hissed. "We didn't sneak you all the way here to have you be discovered on the sidewalk. Come on!"

Rory ran up the steps, Tucket trotting right behind him. Bridget lifted her paper body and climbed after them. Halfway up the stairs, she saw an old plaque built into the outside wall. It featured a bronzed portrait of a handsome man with unruly hair, surrounded by scenes of people riding horses through the woods and holding muskets. It read: THIS HOUSE WAS ONCE THE HOME OF WASHINGTON IRVING.

So it was with little surprise that Bridget found herself, just moments later, being introduced to the man of the house, the great Washington Irving himself.

"Hello, hello!" Irving said, beaming with delight at his guests. He looked just like his bronze portrait, with his messy hair swept forward onto his forehead. "Wonderful to see you, simply wonderful. I'm happy to be home to accommodate you, as I've only just returned from a voyage deep into the mists, where I discovered a rare plant that enables all who consume it to speak any language they wish. Sadly, I've just eaten the last of it, but it was horrible-tasting, I can assure you! *Waggo uncho licgitum!* That's 'welcome to my home!' in Swahili!"

Rory's eyes narrowed.

"I don't believe you," he said suspiciously.

"Rory!" Bridget was horrified. That was no way to treat a possible benefactor.

Alexa burst out laughing. "Mr. Irving is the God of Tall Tales," she explained, eyes twinkling merrily.

"Indeed I am, indeed I am," Irving admitted, smiling unapologetically. "Certainly you could tell the story of my recent travels another way. You could say I went to the market and bought some string beans from an Italian gentleman who taught me how to say thank you by saying *'grazie!'* But I've already put you to sleep with that version."

"So you don't tell the truth?" Rory asked, not looking happy about that at all.

"Of course I do," Irving replied blithely, unfazed by Rory's rudeness. "I just dress it up a bit. Make it more interesting. The plain old truth is so dull, isn't it? And rarely as 'true' as most people insist."

Bridget knew right then that she'd found a friend.

"I feel the same way," she said fervently, and was rewarded with a huge smile.

"Do you?" Irving said. "Then we will get along fine. Ice cream?"

"Don't mind if I do!" Bridget replied, sweeping past a glowering Rory without glancing at him.

Minutes later, Bridget was happily licking away at a bowl of chocolate ice cream in the kitchen while Rory glowered nearby. Irving sat down next to her with a smile.

"Happy?" he asked.

"Very! I love your house."

Irving exchanged a wry look with Alexa, who had sat

down with an open satchel in front of her, rifling through the contents which consisted of all her old papers from the past two hundred years. She shook her head with a smile before returning to her bag.

"What is it?" Rory asked, suspicious. *The boy can't relax for a minute,* Bridget thought to herself.

"This actually isn't my house at all," Irving admitted.

"What do you mean?" Bridget asked, helping herself to another bite. "I saw the sign outside."

"Ah, the sign." Irving sighed. "That sign is the bane of my existence. I've resided in many places in Manhattan, but never here."

"Then why is there a plaque outside saying you did?" Rory asked. "Isn't this, like, a historical-landmark street and everything?"

"At the end of the nineteenth century, two women lived here," Irving explained. "One was a famous interior designer, the other one of the world's first literary agents. So let's just say they knew something about the power of a good story. They began to tell people that I had lived in their home, to generate publicity for themselves. It didn't matter that my nieces and nephews all wrote in to angrily denounce the tale. They knew I had never set foot in this place. But in the end, the story won.

"Eventually someone stuck that plaque out front, and now everyone thinks I lived here. And what's worse, because they all believe it, now I *have* to live here. Ironic, no? That the great storyteller is trapped by a story. I'm not angry, anymore. Frankly, I'm impressed. Sometimes you just have to tip your cap."

"If you like a good story, you should check out the scorcher in that necklace of theirs," Simon said.

"I'm intrigued," Irving said, his eyebrow raised. But further discussion was interrupted by a cry from the corner.

"I knew it!" Alexa exclaimed as she pulled an ornate card out of her bag. "I knew I heard it somewhere!"

"Whoa, calm down." Simon threw up his hands to ward off the crazy. "Heard what?"

"Harry Meester!"

Bridget glanced at her brother, but he looked away. Alexa didn't notice, too busy with her find. "Look, it's an invite," she said, waving the card. "It was given to me by Jane van Cortlandt and Robert de Vries, back when we were friends."

"You were friends with them?" Simon asked, shocked. "They don't exactly seem like your kind of crowd."

"They were different in those days. More hopeful. But you know how hard it is for the children of the gods. It's tough to hold on to hope when you're trapped between immortality and divinity. I mean, even Nicholas was a hopeless layabout when I met him. He used to spend all his time with Teddy and Martha, drinking and gambling."

"Nicholas was friends with Martha *Jay*!" Simon exclaimed. "She's *horrible*!"

"Yeah, well, now Jane and Robert are horrible, too. But fun at parties, right?" Alexa looked pained. "Sometimes I feel like Martha and I exchanged friends. But I'm nowhere near as fun as she is."

"No, you're not," Simon agreed. "That's part of your charm." Alexa made a face at him.

"What about my dad?" Bridget cut in, exasperated.

"Right," Alexa replied, getting back on track. "It was the last conversation I had with them before we went our separate

ways, that's why I remember it so well. They said they were
going to a party and gave me this invite. I wanted them to stay
away from that crowd. But they didn't listen and ever since
they've been with Martha and her cronies."

"And . . ." Simon encouraged her. She handed the card over.

"Look who hosted the party," she said.

"Harry Meester," Simon read aloud. He passed the card
to Bridget. There it was, in intricate script, her father's other
name.

"I need to talk to them, tonight," Alexa continued. "Maybe
they know something." Simon suddenly started to laugh.
"What?" she asked, annoyed.

"I know where they are tonight," Simon gasped, turning
red with mirth. "But you're not going to like it. It's the start
of the season."

The blood drained from Alexa's face. "No."

"That's nice," Irving said, patting her hand. "You'll have a
wonderful time."

"I think I've got the right outfit," Simon said thoughtfully.
"Maybe something in lime green?" Bridget shuddered at the
thought of the clothes that must hang in that boy's closet.

"It's not fair!" Alexa said, teeth clenching. "I refused to ever
set foot in one of those debasing, inhuman, soul-destroying
carnival freak shows ever again! They go against everything
that's good and clean and worth saving in this world. I can't do
it! I'll never be able to wash the stink off my soul!"

"What is it?" Bridget asked, horrified. Alexa turned to her,
her face in anguish.

"The Debutante Ball!"

THE DEBUTANTE BALL

Well, this is a big disappointment!" Sergeant Kiffer said, staring at the dead body in the alley behind the boarding house.

Fritz didn't reply, spurring Clarence to ride up the stairs of a nearby stoop to get a better look at the corpse. The man certainly fit the description Nicholas and Alexa had given him of the drunk who'd tipped them off to Harry Meester. There was no way to know for sure, of course. The sailor who gave them the tip on where to find this poor fellow had four different names for the guy, none of them Alberto. But too many pieces fit. So, Alberto had been one of Tew's Boys. It made sense. Fritz sighed; this was becoming more and more of a lost cause.

It hadn't been easy, trying to find some trace of Meester or Tew's Boys. No one knew much about the former, and as to the latter, apparently most were shipped out. No one seemed to know how many of Tew's Boys there were, maybe five, maybe twenty, but the one thing everyone could agree on was that they were hard to find. They never stayed long in port, they drank too much, and they always seemed eager to jump on the next ship leaving the harbor. Stories floated about that Captain Kidd had done something horrible to them when he shipwrecked their captain, and Kidd said nothing to deny it. It was noted, at least, that none of Tew's Boys ever worked Kidd's boat.

Fritz had met people who could account for at least two deaths, three if he included the poor body at his feet. He prayed that Rory's dad wasn't one of them.

Hans looked up from where he'd been checking the body's head and throat.

"It looks natural, boss," Hans called up. "I think the drink got him."

"Or his own guilt," Kiffer added.

"Don't be melodramatic." Fritz sighed. "All I know is that the one guy who seemed like he wanted to talk is now gone."

"So what do we do?" Hans asked. "Keep looking?"

"Boss, what about the clan?" Kiffer asked. "We're supposed to be looking after our own people, too, you know. Captain Liv can't cover for us forever."

Fritz sighed. "The fate of the whole city, not just M'Garoth village, hangs in the balance. We can't give up now."

Rory awoke with a start. He'd been dreaming of the park again, only this time the barrier had been covered in snakes. He couldn't even see through to the other side. Finally, one of the snakes had lauched itself at him and he'd been forced to wake up.

He was lying abed in one of Washington Irving's spare rooms. Irving had refused to let him or Bridget leave the house, though Rory had wanted to sneak into the park to check on Soka. Unable to actually do anything productive, Rory had wandered up to this bedroom and fallen asleep. That was during the afternoon; the darkened windows told him that night had since fallen. He sat up, trying to shake the dream. As he took a few deep breaths to steady himself, he noticed the soft strains of music drifting through the door. What was going on?

He hopped out of bed and wandered downstairs. The music was coming from the parlor; Irving appeared to be entertaining some guests. Bridget sat at the base of the stairs, pouting.

"I should be at the Debutante Ball right now," she complained as he sat down next to her. "I could have worn my steel-toe boots and everything. I'd have danced with any boy I wanted, because I'd look so awesome. Then I would have sat on the Debutante throne like a warrior princess, putting the silly girlie-girls in their place with one lift of my eyebrow. Fine, I can't raise my eyebrow right now, even though I practice, like, every day. But I bet at the ball it would come naturally. Instead I'm stuck here listening to Washington and his weirdo friends."

"What's going on in there?" Rory wanted to know. The parlor door was shut, but soft piano drifted through.

"He's having some kind of jam session," Bridget replied. "It's weird. While you were asleep, he tried on Olathe's necklace. And ever since he's been like a crazy person. He said he had a big idea. He called over his oddball friends and they disappeared into that room, to sit around and sing like a bunch of hippies. Some big idea. I should be at the ball!"

"Who's in there with him?" Rory asked, getting up to listen at the door.

"Some weirdo poet, a sad, singing lady, and a bouncy piano guy. I thought he'd bring together a posse, you know, with warriors and guys like that. What do I get? Show tunes!"

The door creaked open and Washington's face poked out.

"We can hear you, you know," he said. "Come on in, children. Let me introduce you to my friends."

Rory and Bridget stepped into the parlor. A merry fire burned in the hearth while three guests gathered around the piano. Washington introduced them.

"This dapper gentleman by the couch is Langston Hughes, God of Poetry. Very big during the Harlem Renaissance, as I'm sure you know. The fine figure of a woman next to him is the famous Billie Holiday, Goddess of the Blues."

"They still play your songs on the radio," Rory said, impressed. "My mom loves you."

"Thank you, honey," Billie said, smiling. "Your mamma has some fine taste."

"And the fellow at the piano is none other than George Gershwin, God of Snappy Tunes."

Gershwin tipped his cap. "An honor to meet ya, kid."

"Why are you all here?" Rory asked.

"We're fightin' back against the tyranny of the men down at City Hall!" Hughes said with a flourish.

"How?" Bridget asked, skeptical. "Are you actually a crack ninja force? Maybe you're working on your theme song before you go on your killing spree. Every ninja force needs a theme song, I guess."

"You don't always need a knife to stab at the heart, little

one," Irving told her. "When I wore that necklace, I was touched by Olathe's story. It needed to be told. The people of Mannahatta are afraid. They're only being fed one story: the tale of Munsee terror. We need to give them something else. A story about love. We need to tear away the frightening mask of the other and show them what lies behind: a beating heart, just like their own."

"And you're going to do this with a piano?" Bridget asked, rolling her eyes.

"We're gonna try, doll," Gershwin said, eyes twinkling. His fingers ran over the keys as fast and light as laughter.

"Oh, we're more than trying," Hughes said confidently. "There won't be a dry eye on the island when we're done."

"But there wasn't a whole story in the necklace," Rory said. "There were only three memories."

"That's enough," Irving said. "We just need a kernel of truth, after all. The rest grows from there, filling out until we have 'The Ballad of Olathe and Buck.' Why don't we show you what we have so far? George?"

Gershwin began to play, a slow but hopeful melody forming under his fingers. Billie Holiday held up the piece of paper given her by Langston Hughes and softly began to sing.

The story that unfolded told of two peoples at war. Billie sang of two lovers from opposite sides who discover that their worlds are not so different after all. The Munsees are accepting; it is Olathe's father who is the obstacle. But their love will not be denied, until Olathe's father turns away from his daughter rather than accept her choice. Buck learns of the Trap and runs to warn Olathe and her people, but the evil adviser has him killed right in front of Olathe. Devastated, she retreats to the woods, preferring to live alone away from the meaningless bickering between the Munsees and the gods. It all means so little compared to her lost love. She leaves her song behind so her father can one day learn the truth and see he was wrong all along about their love.

Through the beautiful music and the haunting words and Billie's deep, rich voice, Rory could *feel* the story. He felt the hope and the love and the anguish and the loss. He felt it as much as if he were wearing the necklace again. By the end, tears fell down his cheeks, and he realized that this song would do more for the Munsees than a hundred knives. People would see themselves in the Munsees, and in the romance of Olathe and Buck they would recognize their own dreams of love. It wouldn't magically make things better, of course. But a little candle in the dark was often all it took to make people wonder what else there is to see.

The next day, "The Ballad of Olathe and Buck" swept through Mannahatta, causing a sensation like few had ever seen. Billie Holiday sang it wherever she could, but soon she was no longer needed to keep the song alive. It sprang up in every tavern, every pub, every parlor and meeting hall across the spirit city within a day. Dutch spirits sang it and Irish spirits and Germans and Jews and African-Americans and Hispanics and Chinese and Koreans and Indians and on and on. That kernel of truth, that feeling of love gone but never truly lost, it slipped into the heart of every spirit who heard it and took up residence there. And soon that kernel of truth began to grow. The fear remained as the rumors ran rampant, but it wasn't the same kind of fear.

Somehow, the Munsees didn't seem quite so alien anymore. After all, they'd been loved by one of their own.

One man in particular was striding along Broadway when he heard the song being sung by an old woman on the street corner. The man stopped to listen, and by the end he was fighting back tears. He ran down a side street, away from the music, from those memories of her. *How did they know?* He thought he'd buried the past. Pushing the pain down deep inside, he struggled to regain control of himself. First all those questions about Meester, now this. The past was refusing to stay past. He didn't think he *would* survive its revival. But could he find a way to stop it now?

Alexa cursed to herself as she adjusted her dress. She couldn't begin to express how much she hated the wretched thing: from the horrible ruffles to the ridiculously huge flower on her shoulder to the weight of the bustle. She looked like the result of an experiment to cross a human with a wedding cake. And the makeup! Oh, the torture that was her makeup! Layer upon layer of foundation and blush and eye shadow and mascara and whatever else girls lather on their faces in an effort to look as inhuman as possible. Alexa felt like she'd been hit in the face with a custard pie and hadn't been allowed to wash up. All in all, between the dress and the makeup, and the shoes (she wasn't going to even think about the twin pillars of pain that were her high heels), Alexa felt at her absolute worst. And that was just how the rest of the children of the gods always made her feel. And now she was about to subject herself to their catty judgments yet again. Wonderful.

Next to her, Simon stood dressed in a bright orange tuxedo with blue stripes. He looked excited and worried all at once, fumbling about in his pocket with one hand while he adjusted his sparkly bow tie with the other.

"Stop fidgeting," Alexa muttered crossly.

"I'm not. I'm just a little on edge. I haven't been to one of these in years."

"Isn't that because your aunt banned you from attending?"

"She's not my aunt!" Simon shot back, glaring. This was a sore subject. "Mrs. Astor is my father's mortal grandson's wife, which makes her absolutely nothing to me. I'm older than her, I'm more stylish than her, and I look way better in orange, believe me. But just because she's the Goddess of Society, she tries to lord it over me every time she sees me. She thinks she's better than me. All the other Astors do, the Colonel and William Waldorf and all of them, just because they're gods and I'm not. I'd be a god, too, if I had ever been mortal! It's not my fault my dad waited until after he was dead to have me!"

Alexa patted Simon's shoulder soothingly.

"Well, there's no reason to see her, Simon. We'll be in and out before she knows we're there."

Simon nodded hesitantly, smoothing his tux with one hand.

"Ready?" she asked him. He nodded, taking a deep breath. "Then let's do this."

Alexa hobbled across 34th Street on her death heels, Simon right behind. Above them loomed the Empire State Building in all its glory; Alexa admired the cool, sleek lines of the skyscraper. But before the tallest building in Manhattan had been built, another famous structure had resided on this block. And it was to the memory of that great institution, accessed by a single door in the center of the Empire State Building's base, that Alexa and Simon were headed. They had just reached the door when they were blocked by a smartly dressed, insolent doorman.

"Are you here for the ball?" he asked, his tone suggesting that he believed it unlikely.

Alexa, already overtaken by nerves, was in no mood.

"Of course, you twit," she replied peevishly. "Why else would I subject myself to these shoes?"

"Alexa van der Donck, escorted by Simon Astor," Simon cut in, bowing slightly. The doorman started at the name, his manner changing completely.

"I am so sorry, Mr. Astor! Please let your dear aunt know that I meant no disrespect! Welcome to the Waldorf-Astoria!"

Simon inclined his head as the two of them swept by.

"She's not my aunt," Simon muttered under his breath as he entered the shrine to the greatness of his last name.

Long considered the emperor of New York City hotels, the Waldorf-Astoria's history was fraught with family drama. In the late nineteenth century, William Waldorf Astor lived next to his aunt Mrs. Astor (who famously went by only her last name) and her son Colonel John Jacob Astor IV. The two branches hated each other with a passion. So William Waldorf had the Waldorf Hotel built on his property next to Mrs. Astor's town house in an effort to drive her crazy. Colonel Astor got him back by persuading his mother to move uptown and then building the Astoria right next to the Waldorf, the newer hotel besting the older one by four stories. The cousins never made up, but money always wins in the end, so the two hotels eventually were combined into one: the Waldorf-Astoria.

Eventually the old hotel was demolished and rebuilt uptown on Park Avenue, but the new Waldorf never quite matched the influence and grandeur of the original. Which was why Mrs. Astor hosted her coming-out balls for the children of the gods *here,* where it all began. Though she only set foot in the Astoria side of the hotel, as some feuds never die.

Alexa's stomach began to ache as Simon led her through the huge atrium, past the bustling spirits checking in and out of the grand hotel.

"I hate this, I hate this, I hate this!" she muttered.

"Don't worry," Simon soothed her. "It will only get worse. We still have to walk Peacock Alley, remember."

Alexa's stomach heaved; she hated being on display, so nothing topped Peacock Alley for pure torture. Originally the alley between the two hotels, Peacock Alley eventually became the precursor to the red carpet, where all the socialites would come to see and be seen. During her mortal days, Mrs. Astor would invite only the "Four Hundred," which were the four hundred people she deemed worth knowing in New York, to her famous parties at the hotel. Now, in Mannahatta, the children of the gods walked the same alley, soaking in the attention as they pretended to matter. But Alexa knew differently. What the Rattle Watch was doing, *that* mattered. Eating cheese on a stick and making fun of some poor girl in an ugly dress behind her back did not matter. And it never would.

"I don't think so," she said emphatically. "We're going in the back way."

Simon looked surprisingly disappointed, but he still led Alexa past the long passage with its throng of reporters toward a small door that led directly into the ballroom. He went to push it open when an imperious voice stopped him in his tracks.

"Halt, intruders!" the voice cried.

Simon turned, and sighed heavily. Alexa followed, her blood turning cold as she laid eyes on the grande dame of the evening, the wicked witch herself, the Goddess of Society, Mrs. Astor.

Mrs. Astor was a short, doughy woman in regal dress; her face dripped disapproval.

"Hello *Caroline*," Simon greeted her, nodding with exaggerated insolence. Mrs. Astor's eyes burned; even Alexa knew you *never* called Mrs. Astor by her first name.

"You are not welcome here, Simon," Mrs. Astor said, staring him down. "Your outburst at the ball of 1915 forced me to permanently ban you, and that ban remains in force. And you, Ms. van der Donck, were never formally introduced to society, so you are not welcome until you are."

"I was around for two hundred years before you were even born," Alexa said, eyes flashing. "Who are you to tell me—"

"I am Mrs. Astor," Mrs. Astor interrupted. "If I say you do not belong, then you do not belong."

Alexa felt a wave of insignificance wash over her. This woman made her feel small and unfit to be seen in polite society. This was Mrs. Astor's divine gift: to bestow or deny belonging. Obviously Simon felt it, too, because he began to stammer.

"You do not tell me what to do!" Simon sputtered. "I am a member of the Rattle Watch!"

"Oh, do be quiet about your little club," Mrs. Astor said, dismissing his words with a raised eyebrow. "No one wants to hear about your childish games. You are and always have been a disgrace to the Astor name."

"I am not a disgrace," Simon insisted. "I could be as powerful as any of you if I wanted."

Alexa blinked, unsure what Simon meant by that. She noticed that the boy was furiously clutching something in his fist, something gold.

"I'm sorry, did you somehow become a god when I wasn't looking?" Mrs. Astor asked, witheringly. Simon didn't respond. "Good evening to you both."

She turned and clapped her hands. Immediately, a dapper man in a smart suit appeared by her side.

"Oscar!" she said to him. "Please escort these interlopers off the premises. We are about to introduce this year's new members of society and I won't have them ruining it."

She spun and marched off into the crowd. Oscar shrugged apologetically.

"I'm sorry to do this, young madam and sir," he said. "But as the God of Maître D's I always have to make my host happy. Please come with me."

He led them down a side hall, back toward the lobby. Simon kept playing with something in his hand while talking to himself. She'd never seen him so worked up.

"I'll show her," he muttered. "She doesn't make the rules . . ."

"Simon, are you all right?" she asked. He didn't answer. Alexa turned to Oscar, ready to beg. "Oscar, please, we just need five minutes to talk to some people who will be at the ball tonight. Jane van Cortlandt or Robert de Vries. We don't want to ruin anything. This is so important, you wouldn't believe it!"

"I regret I cannot help you," Oscar replied smoothly. "Mrs. Astor's instructions were quite explicit. But perhaps someone at the card game in Suite 217 might be of more assistance. Please, have a wonderful evening." His eyes twinkled as he turned to head back swiftly to the ball.

"Card game?" Alexa said, the light dawning. "That's so typical. Come on, Simon!"

She pulled at his arm, causing him to cry out as he dropped what he'd been holding in his hand. He bent down quickly to pick it up, but not before Alexa got a good look at a familiar gold locket. She swiftly yanked him into the corner to whisper furiously in his ear.

"Is that what I think it is?"

"It's just a locket," Simon replied, though he wouldn't look her in the eye.

"Whose locket?"

"I don't know—" Simon began. Alexa cut him off by grabbing his ear. He cried out. "Hey! You promised you'd stop doing that!"

"That's one of the murdered gods' lockets, isn't it?" she said quietly. "You palmed it before Peter could destroy it. Don't bother to deny it, I can read you like a book—the kind of book with lots of pictures and one syllable words."

"I'm not going to wear it," Simon protested. "I just wanted to hold on to it."

"Whose is it?"

"I don't know. Ow!" Simon yelped as Alexa bent his ear almost totally around. "Fine, the God of the Good China. I'm just holding it."

"We're not meant to be gods, Simon," Alexa said sternly. "Give me that locket right now!"

"Why?" Simon whined, twisting under her grasp. "You're

not the boss of me. Anyway, I'm not going to wear it. What do I care about good china?"

Alexa stared at him, weighing the time it would take to beat Simon into giving her the locket and the urgency of their mission. Fortunately for Simon, urgency won out. She pulled him closer, hissing in his face. "You're to give that locket to Peter the minute we get back, and he'll destroy it. Got me?"

"I will next time I see him," Simon promised.

"If you don't, I will twist this ear right off." Alexa gave it a yank for good measure.

"I will! See, I'm putting it in my pocket. I won't even touch it anymore."

"You better," Alexa warned him, releasing his ear. "Come on, we have to crash a card game."

Moments later, they walked down one of the hallways upstairs, past rows of numbered doors. Finally, they stopped at 217, and after a deep breath, Alexa knocked.

"What's the password?" a slurred voice called out from behind the door.

"Wine?" Alexa guessed. She wasn't surprised a bit when the door immediately opened to reveal Robert de Vries, drunk as a skunk.

"Alexa! My word! I never expected this surprise! Look, everyone! Our baby has finally come to her senses and come to join the family!" He turned and fell to the ground face-first, giggling helplessly. Sighing sadly at the state of her old friend, Alexa stepped into the room, Simon immediately behind. The elegant hotel room was filled with familiar faces: Teddy Twiller, Randolph Morris, the infamous Martha Jay, and the other person besides Robert she'd been hoping to see, Jane van

Cortlandt. They all sat around a table, cards in hand, cigars in mouth, and legions of empty bottles scattered everywhere around. It was quite literally the saddest thing Alexa had ever seen. *That could have been me,* she thought. *If not for my father.* The thought of her father made her choke up, and she pushed it away to deal with the situation before her.

"Can I play a hand!" Simon exclaimed excitedly. Alexa put a restraining hand on his arm.

"We're not here to play. We just have a question or two."

"Good ol' Alexa, always all business," Martha said, smirking. "I see that bug up your butt is still thriving."

Simon snorted, attracting a sharp look from Alexa. He smiled weakly.

"It was funny," he muttered, shrugging. Alexa berated him with her eyes, then returned her attention to the poker table.

"I'm not here to fight," she said. "I need your help."

"Then pull up a chair," Randolph offered, smiling hugely as he gestured with his big cigar. "Play a hand, have a drink or ten, enjoy immortality a little!"

Alexa ignored him, focusing on Jane, who stared meekly back at her.

"Jane, please," Alexa said. "We were friends once. I need your help. I just want to know if you recognize this man." She pulled out the picture of Rory's father, but Teddy snatched it away.

"Hey, look, it's ol' Harry Meester! Long time no see! He used to be a barrel of laughs, ol' Harry."

"So you remember him?" Alexa asked, a thrill running through her.

"Sure," Randolph chimed in, puffing smoke in Alexa's direction. She tried desperately not to cough. "He knew how to have a good time. He started hanging out with us . . . wow . . . it's a blur."

"After Nicky left us!" Robert called from the floor, where he still hadn't moved.

"He'd get us booze, smokes, all of it," Teddy said. "He was a really cool guy. He used to hang around that one girl all the time. What was her name? The one who disappeared."

"She didn't disappear, she went to go live in the Bronx on a farm," Robert said.

"I heard she ran off to Queens and lived in a shack in the wilderness," Randolph Morris announced.

"There's no wilderness in Queens, stupid," Robert said from the floor.

"It sure seems like the wilderness to me," Randolph maintained.

"What was her name?" Alexa asked.

"I remember, it was—" Jane quietly started to say, but Martha suddenly cut her off.

"I think you should either grab a drink and play a hand or ride your high horse right on outta here," she declared, her eyes decidedly unfriendly.

"Please, just give me her name," Alexa repeated, staring at Jane.

"You know what?" Martha said, pushing Alexa and Simon toward the door. "I think it's time you left. Bye bye!"

"Please, Jane," Alexa asked Jane intently. "We were close once. You can tell me." Jane glanced away.

"Come on, kid," Simon cried. "Just give us a name."

"Out!" Martha said as she and Randolph pushed them from

the room. "You're not wanted here. Good luck on your wild-goose chase."

"Jane!" Alexa called through the crack in the closing door. "We used to be best friends, remember? We were going to make a difference. Well, this will make a difference. This is important. Please!"

She could see Jane through the rapidly closing slit. Jane looked torn under Alexa's impassioned stare. The rest of them were already going back to their game. Alexa had just about given up when Jane opened her mouth to utter one word before the door closed.

"Abby," she said. Alexa's jaw dropped as the door slammed shut. She'd never expected that name, not in a million years.

"Abby?" Simon asked, not in on Alexa's shock and awe. "Who was she?"

"It all makes sense now," Alexa marveled. "No wonder the Mayor went overboard."

"What are you talking about?" Simon asked peevishly. "Maybe I'll twist *your* ear this time until you tell me what's going on."

"Abby," Alexa explained. "Short for Abigail."

"So?"

"Abigail *Hamilton*, daughter of the Mayor himself. Simon, I think this just got a lot more interesting . . ."

BETHESDA FOUNTAIN

In Washington Heights, right below the George Washington Bridge, stood the Park and Sons Pharmacy, the original of the four Park and Sons Pharmacies that dotted Manhattan. Situated right on the corner, this neighborhood institution had an interesting claim to fame: the present owner and CEO, Ken Park, swore (with his neighbors to back him up) that no one had ever stolen anything from the flagship store, ever, during its entire sixty-year existence. Through three generations of Parks, no one had grabbed, heisted, or run off with a single piece of merchandise. Not even a morning paper. Zilch.

This morning, Ken's teenage son Freddie stood manning the counter, engrossed in a comic book. The power was still out, so Freddie cooled himself with a small fan his dad had brought back from his last trip to Korea. He was so beaten down by the heat that he didn't even bother to look up as the bell above the door tinkled, heralding the entrance of one Corey Deem, twelve-year-old would-be master thief, on a mission to finally be the one to pillage the candy aisle and get away with it.

Corey whistled as he browsed, nonchalant, all the while glancing out the door at his friends, who were whispering and watching with breathless anticipation. Corey sneaked peeks at Freddie over and over again, noting how he never looked up, not once. At last, Corey decided to go for it, quickly snatching a pack of Chuckles, stuffing it in his pocket, and making for the door.

If Rory had been in Corey's shoes, he would have known better, for he would have noticed the old man standing next to Freddie at the counter, staring right at him. The old man had been born Park Mok-Wol, though his customers just called him Mack Park. Mok-Wol had built his pharmacy business up from nothing, and in the process he became a legend. No one could steal from him; he had eyes in the back of his head, people said. Even on the day he died, the tale went, he held off the stroke just long enough to stop a kid from walking off with a paper. Stories about his prowess grew after his death, until finally he ascended to the title of God of Put That Back. And while he attended to *all* his worshippers, no one could blame him if he spent a little more time in the stores that bore his name.

As Corey nervously made for the door, Mok-Wol leaned over to whisper in his great-grandson's ear. At the same time, Mok-Wol tracked Corey's retreat using the eyes on the back of his head. Enough people believed it had to be true that it had, in fact, become true.

"Hey!" Freddie said, not consciously hearing his great-grandfather, but instead noting that familiar feeling that came over him whenever someone was stealing. "Come back here!"

Thrown at how easily he'd been discovered by a man who wasn't even looking at him, Corey broke; he flung the candy behind him as he ran out of the pharmacy in fright. Freddie chuckled softly to himself as he walked around the counter to retrieve the candy from the floor. Little did he know, but his great-grandfather was laughing right along with him.

Corey raced past a man standing outside the door without stopping . . . which did not surprise the man, as he was just as hard to see as Mok-Wol. This man had been wandering the streets for the past day or so, watching the people of this new city he could barely recognize. So many dirty immigrants. So many foreigners who didn't belong here. A burning had begun to flare in his chest. The anger was building, and soon he would need to release it. He pulled a cleaver out from his belt and ran his finger over the edge.

I got to do something about this, the man thought. *It's that boy. Tweed said something big was coming. Something that will shake the city apart if the boy don't do his job. But is that so bad? Maybe the city deserves to be buried under a pile a' rubble. It's been given away to all these drifters, these shifty foreigners. It ain't my city anymore. If I can't have it, no one can. Kill the boy, kill the city. It's that easy.*

The man with the cleaver smiled. Mok-Wol glanced up, catching the man's eye. The god froze at the sight of the killer at the door. The spirit might not be able to take the god's life, but he could make him hurt, and Mok-Wol knew it. The man's smile widened until it screamed of madness, his ruined teeth bursting out of his gums. He faked a throw of his cleaver; Mok-Wol flinched and the man laughed. Mok-Wol turned and ran into the back of the pharmacy. It would be a free day for the little thiefs of Manhattan. *Enjoy it,* the man thought. *There won't be many days left.*

In his dream, Rory flew over the city toward the park. Once again, the blue barrier writhed with snakes, hissing at him to keep back. The frustration built within him; Alexa's news about Olathe's identity made it doubly important that he speak with Soka. He felt the tension rise until he had to scream.

To his surprise, a small circle of snakes was blown back by his shout, like snow off a windshield, and he could peer through to the park. Soka floated right on the other side, peering anxiously at him.

"Soka!" Rory cried, getting as close as he dared. "Are you all right?" Soka nodded. "I know who Olathe is," he continued. "Abigail Hamilton, the Mayor's daughter. No wonder they're trying to keep you from telling me!"

Soka shouted back at him, but her voice sounded far away. "There is more!" she cried faintly. "But no time. Meet me at midday."

"Where?" But an image was already appearing in his head, of an angel rising above a pool of water—he recognized it immediately as Bethesda Fountain. She must be trying to keep the location secret from whoever was fighting to keep them apart by planting the thought directly in his mind. He could only imagine the energy that must have taken, and she looked exhausted by the effort. But Rory frowned. "You told me not to come back."

"We need to risk it! Someone is trying to prevent me from telling you what I have learned. Pretty Nose, you must!"

Suddenly the snakes hissed louder, covering up the open hole and obscuring Soka from Rory's sight. He shouted again and again, but to no avail. Finally, he forced himself to wake up.

He sat up, his face determined. He didn't care what anone said. He was going into that park to meet with Soka. If they wanted to stop him, they'd have to tie him to the bed. She called and he was going to answer.

Rory and Bridget stood next to Bethesda Fountain in Central Park, nervously waiting. The fountain sat in the middle of a circular plaza; one edge opened onto a large pond upon which tourists rowed around in small rented boats. On the opposite side, wide stairs led up to a bridge, and trees flanked them on both sides of the plaza. People milled about everywhere; it was a popular area of park. Bridget glanced to the tree line, where she knew Fritz was watching. He wanted to stay out of sight, just in case. Bridget hoped there'd be no reason for "just in case."

When Rory had woken up from his dream, determined to make his date with Soka, they'd tried to talk him out of it. After all, neither Simon nor Alexa could enter the park with them. But Rory knew Soka needed to tell him something and he would not leave it to anyone else to discover what that something was.

So Alexa and Simon waited unhappily just outside the wall, as did Tucket, while Rory and Bridget kept the date with Soka. Bridget felt acutely uncomfortable out in the open, even though she was in her invulnerable body. She'd weedled and whined until Rory saw how important it was that she wear it—who knew what dangers lurked in the park?—but now she was beginning to regret it. Every time she put on the paper body, she felt a little more strange. That feeling had started up again, the pushing sensation inside that felt as if her soul were somehow trying to burst free. It made her jumpy, and her leg twitched beneath her. Rory gave her an annoyed look and put a hand on her shoulder.

"Stop fidgeting," he said. "You're making me nauseous."

She felt a little sick, too. But she wouldn't complain. Rory's face was excited and nervous; no doubt he couldn't wait to see his *girlfriend* again. What a dork.

Bridget glanced up at the statue perched atop the fountain. The bronze angel gazed mournfully down at the ground. Bridget had always loved the statue, though she couldn't say why. Something about the angel's melancholy face pulled at her heart.

Rory froze beside her.

"Look out there, on the pond."

Bridget turned to stare out across the man-made lake but couldn't tell what Rory was talking about, at least not right away. But then, from among the jumbled throng of rowboats, a long canoe emerged, cutting through the water expertly. A figure paddled with one oar, sinking the paddle on one side, then the other, as the canoe glided toward the lip of the plaza that extended right up to the water's edge. As the canoe came closer, the light fell on the figure's face. Rory's hand grabbed Bridget's elbow as they both realized that this was no Indian girl.

"That's not her," he whispered through clenched teeth.

"Rory, Bridget, get out of there!" Fritz's voice carried from the trees. Bridget glanced over to see the roach racing across the plaza toward them. The world slowed down, as if everything were moving through molasses. Bridget looked back toward the pond, where the Indian had begun to climb out of the boat.

This Munsee was male, and really, really scary-looking. His chest was bare and hair was greased into a Mohawk done up with black raven's feathers. The Munsee had tattoos—just like Tammand's barking dogs—but instead of dogs, his cheeks carried snakes, hissing out at them beneath his eyes.

"We've got to get out of here," Rory whispered. "He's the snake from my dreams. It's a trap."

Seeing them about to bolt, the Munsee raised a hand and shouted some foreign words. Rory immediately froze in place. His eyes grew wide with fright as he struggled to move his limbs. Bridget frantically tugged at him, but he seemed as rooted in place as the angel statue above them.

The Munsee hopped out of the canoe and quickly crossed the plaza. He was smiling, though his snakes appeared even scarier up close.

"What are you waiting for?" Fritz called, almost from their feet. "Run!" But Rory could not budge and Bridget would not leave her brother.

"Soka sends her regards," the Munsee said, and the snakes on his cheeks actually *moved* as he spoke. "Unfortunately, you won't be speaking to her or anyone else ever again, *Sabbeleu*."

With that, he pulled out a bone knife and lunged at Rory, the snakes hissing as he attacked. Without thinking, Bridget leaped into the attacker, knocking him to the side. They both hit the ground hard and rolled up against the fountain. The Munsee's face ended up right by hers, the snakes appearing to almost leap off the skin at her eyes. She scampered away, terrified. The snake Munsee seemed to see her for the first time, and his eyes widened in surprise.

"I can see what you are, demon," he said. "Well, those who tamper with the dark arts should not be surprised at their fate."

He began to chant while making intricate shapes in the air with one hand. Frightened, Bridget tried to push herself to her feet to put some distance between her and the Munsee. But before she could get her legs beneath her, the chanting reached a crescendo and his hand reached out to grab her wrist. A shock ran through her as the paper skin beneath his fingers began to turn black and flake away. One by one, her fingers began to curl, like newspaper in a fire, and her pinkie fell right off her hand. She screamed and pulled away. His hand brushed against her ankle, and her leg began to blacken as well. She started to cry.

"Stop it!" she sobbed, kicking at the Munsee. "Leave me alone!"

"Soon you will trouble the world no longer, demon," the snake Munsee said, smirking. "And now for the *Sabbeleu . . .*"

Suddenly the Munsee's eyes turned white and he began to flail about.

"Come, we must run," a female voice said behind them. "I don't know how long my magic will last."

Bridget felt herself picked up by strong arms, but she didn't bother to see who was rescuing her. Her eyes were glued to her hand, where her four remaining fingers were now blackened and curling. Another fell off and she whimpered at the sight.

"I'm falling apart," she moaned. No one answered her as she was carried out of the plaza into the trees. She saw the snake Munsee writhing on the ground, clutching at his face. The majestic angel statue seemed to watch from above. Then the trees cut off her view and she was left with the sight of another finger falling to the ground, left behind like the shriveled husk of a dead insect.

BRIDGET UNRAVELS

The man with the black eyes sat stiffly behind the desk in his office at the top of one of the tallest buildings in the city. His shades were drawn, as usual, and the flickering fire in the hearth provided the only light in the room.

"I don't understand why you're here, Caesar," he said, every ounce of him suspicious.

The God of Under the Streets shrugged, his fedora held lightly between his long fingers as he sat on the other side of the desk. He looked as if he were applying for a job. But the black-eyed man was not fooled—after all, Caesar Prince was one of the few gods he respected enough to deem an adversary. Prince leaned forward to speak. "You and I both know that the time has come to choose sides. That's what I'm doing. I'm choosing a side."

"*My* side?" the man with the black eyes said, his voice amused. "I find that hard to believe."

"I've been on your side before, Willem," Caesar reminded

him. That was true; at one point Caesar Prince had been a valuable ally.

"That was long ago," the black-eyed man answered. "You've since drifted away on your own, down to your tunnels and your sewers. I don't know what you do down there. And I don't know who you do it for."

"Whatever I do, I do for myself," Caesar replied lightly. "Haven't I always?"

"I ask again, why are you here?"

"I heard a song today. Catchy tune. About a Munsee boy and a girl from Mannahatta and their searing love story. It ends badly; they always do. You heard it yet?"

"It is a nuisance," the black-eyed man snarled. "Nothing more."

"They're fighting back," Caesar said, matter-of-factly. "My Trap is coming down soon, we all know that, and now we're playin' a game of tug-of-war over what happens next. That song is quite a tug. Apparently Hamilton heard it on the street, fell apart, and then locked himself in his office."

"That is quite the . . . overreaction."

"It is indeed." Caesar laughed. "It is indeed. You need to tug back, Willem. If you do it hard enough, I think you'll win. That's why I'm here. At one point the Munsees will find out that I engineered the Trap and they'll want their revenge on me, too. Better to end the threat right at the start."

"What do you propose?" The black-eyed man gave nothing away.

"So many of your opponents are falling ill, aren't they? A bad touch of flu, maybe? All the voices of reason are falling silent, one by one, until only your voice, through Hamilton, of course, will be heard. That's the plan, right? No one to argue when the Trap comes down and the order to fight pops out of the Mayor's mouth. It's a good plan. Except for one stubborn old mule: Peter Stuyvesant. The original thorn in your side. He won't touch anything not cooked by his little lady. So he manages to stay miraculously healthy in the face of so much sickness."

"Why are you telling me this?" the black-eyed man asked.

"There is one other person he'd break bread with, you know. Someone who could hand him a bowl of soup without fear of being denied."

"Who is that?"

Caesar Prince smiled, his teeth glinting in the firelight. "Me."

The small group burst into a clearing by the edge of the park. Rory watched Tammand lay Bridget on the grass while Soka knelt by her side. The two of them had run up from behind Rory and Fritz, and Soka had cast some sort of spell on the Munsee with the snakes on his face. Rory had been shocked to see Tammand, but he had no time to question as the Indian warrior lifted Bridget as if she were a hollow plastic lawn ornament and raced off into the trees as his sister urged them to follow.

"That was a trap," Fritz said as the Munsee siblings looked over Bridget. "Was that your doing?"

"Of course not," Tammand said curtly.

"But, my dreams . . ." Rory began.

"That first time, I reached out to you and you came," Soka explained as she examined Bridget's damaged body. "But then Askook, that's the man who attacked you, blocked me from telling you what I knew. I tried reaching out to you again, but he would never let me through. He must have pretended to be me to lure you here. I'm surprised you listened—did I not tell you not to enter the park?"

"I just wanted to see if you were okay . . ." Rory mumbled.

Tammand snorted. "You are the one who should be counting his blessings. Mother saw in the smoke that you would be at the fountain and sent Soka to warn you. I followed to keep her safe, since I know that Askook is not to be trusted, even if he has the Sachem's ear. Today was filled with luck for you, *Pretty Nose.*"

Soka looked up at Rory.

"Who did this to her?" she asked, her eyes angry.

"That weirdo with the snakes," Rory answered. "You saw him."

"No," Soka said. "Who put her in this prison?"

"The body?" Rory was confused. "We had to do it to save her life. And after she was okay, I let her keep it. As a souvenir."

"A souvenir?" Soka's voice was incredulous.

"I didn't see the harm. But then she started to use the body again, secretly. Since she was invulnerable and everything. I wasn't happy about it, but she convinced me she was all right for this one time only."

"That other man called her a demon," Fritz said. "What did he mean?"

"You are like children!" Tammand's voice dripped with disdain. "You play with things you know nothing about. This is ancient magic. Forbidden magic. Playing with it puts your very soul at risk!"

"We're really sorry about that," Rory said, struggling to keep his temper, though all he wanted to do just then was punch the self-righteous jerk in the face. "But what did that maniac do to my sister?"

"He cast a spell that reverses the magic," Soka said. "Slowly, Bridget's body is disintegrating. Soon her soul will simply fly free."

"I don't want to fly free!" Bridget cried miserably. "I'm really sorry, I didn't mean it."

"Can you do anything to help her?" Fritz asked.

"My mother once told me about a way," Soka said, sounding uncertain. "But I've never actually tried it . . ."

"You have to," Rory urged her. "Please. I'll do anything."

"But I could make things worse," Soka said, fear creeping into her voice. "I could destroy her forever."

"Leave her," Tammand said. Rory shot him a look of utter hatred. "We cannot help her and we will all suffer if we are caught together. Come, Soka! I must get the *Sabbeleu* to Tackapausha."

"Please don't leave me!" Bridget cried, reaching out for Soka with her good hand. Soka seemed paralyzed with indecision. Fritz gave Tammand a look of utter disdain.

"You'd leave her to die?" he said. "Have you no soul?"

Rory felt no hesitation as he stared down at his sister, who was falling apart in front of him. He turned to Soka.

"You've got to try," he said calmly. She looked over with terrified eyes.

"But I could make a mistake," she whispered. "I've never tried anything like this before, with someone's life in my hands . . ."

"You took care of that snake man without a problem," he said, forcing his voice to stay even.

"I know, but that spell had never worked before!" Soka admitted, her eyes filling with tears. "I was as surprised as anyone!"

This shook Rory's confidence, but he had no choice.

"I know you can do it," he said. "You're meant for great things, you told me so yourself. Remember what you said when we met? That you were levelheaded, and that was why you would be a great leader of your people. Forget about the fear, just look inside yourself. Can you do it?"

She stared back at him, eyes terrified, while her brother waited impatiently to leave. Finally, she nodded.

"I think I can," she said.

"Then you have to," he said.

"I will," she said, and the fear in her eyes receded as she decided to do something. Her brother made an angry noise and backed away.

"Stop, Tammand!" she ordered him. "I need your knife and your help."

"I will not be a party to this," he began, but she shushed him with a look.

"You will do as I tell you, or I'll make you regret it!" Soka held out her hand, and finally, Tammand passed her a long knife with a copper blade. He looked angry, but he didn't leave. Instead he joined Rory and Fritz as they watched nervously. As she turned herself over to her magic, Soka's face grew utterly still;

she bowed her head over the knife, muttering words to herself. Suddenly the blade began to glow softly. Soka looked up, her forehead glistening with sweat.

"Here we go," she said, smiling down at Bridget, who gazed back with eyes filled with trust. Then Soka lifted the knife into the air and brought it down onto Bridget's wrist.

"No!" Bridget cried, and Rory felt his face go white. But it was too late. Bridget's hand dropped to the ground, neatly sliced off at the wrist. Soka did not stop to admire her handiwork. She immediately swung the knife again, this time aimed at Bridget's ankle. Bridget cried out as her infected foot fell to the earth. Rory dropped down to her side, cradling her head in his arms. Fritz stared up at Soka, face red with anger.

"What did you do?" he hissed. "You cut off her limbs!"

"I had to, to stop the spell from spreading," she replied, her voice shaking slightly as she inspected the cuts in Bridget's arm and leg. "I think we're all right. I see no further evidence of disintegration."

"I knew you could do it," Rory said as Bridget lay in his arms whimpering.

"It's not over yet," Soka answered him.

"Are you okay, Bridget?" Fritz said softly.

"I don't know," Bridget replied. "I felt something when you cut me. Like something inside me almost broke free. I'm doing everything I can to keep it in me."

"That's your soul," Soka said. "It was never meant to be trapped like this. It is doing its best to escape the prison you've encased it in. That is why this magic is forbidden. It is an unholy state and the soul itself fights against it. We have to plug these holes in you or your soul might break free."

"How do we do that?" Rory asked.

"Tammand, I need some bark from a chestnut tree," Soka said. Tammand glared at her. "Now!" she said. He turned and disappeared into the trees. Without a word, Fritz followed him.

"Can we trust him to come back?" Rory asked. Soka gave him a withering look.

"He is my brother. Of course he will return."

***

Bridget lay still with her eyes closed, fighting to keep her insides intact. It had badly frightened her to learn that the origin of that pressure she'd felt was her actual soul trying to escape. She really had been playing with something she didn't understand. As she struggled to stay whole, an image of Toy sprang into her head. His soul must have been trying to escape for fifty years. How had he held on to it? He'd had holes cut into him by the snow beetle in Tobias's bank, and he'd lost his hand to a Broker. Yet he held on. That thought gave her strength. If he could do it, so could she.

Soka and Rory sat on either side of her. She felt sorry for Rory; every time she tagged along, something bad seemed to happen to her. No wonder he was always telling her to stay home. Next time she would, she promised silently. Once this was all over, she'd march right home to bed and not leave for a week.

"Thank you for this," Rory said to Soka. "You saved her life."

"Thank you for trusting me," Soka said, her eyes lowering. "My own mother doesn't always think I can live up to the standards she sets for me."

"She'll get there," Rory said, smiling. "Moms can be pretty blind sometimes."

"Why did you come back yet again?" Soka asked him. "I told you not to."

"I discovered something about Olathe," he said. He explained about Abigail.

"Tackapausha must have known who Olathe was," Soka said, stunned by this new revelation. "But he told no one, even after. That poor girl . . ."

"What is the deal with that guy with the snakes on his face?" Rory asked.

"Askook," she said, making a face. "He is a tribal elder. He is one of the reasons my mother wanted you away from the park. She has believed for some time that he had a hand in setting the Trap. Before the Trap, he had little power. But since, his magic has grown while others' magic has waned. Mother believes someone is helping him. He would never allow the Trap to be opened, and so it is no surprise he would try to kill any *Sabbeleu* he encounters. But since you are leaving the park, and this time you WILL stay out, he will no longer be a threat to you. You *are* leaving, right? Because sometimes I wonder if your brain was damaged by this great heat."

Bridget stifled a giggle. She liked this girl!

"I'm leaving," Rory promised. "But I will bring this Trap down. Without a war. This has to stop."

"I believe you will," Soka said, smiling slightly. The two of them locked eyes over Bridget's body, and it seemed to Bridget that she no longer existed. It was a little gross. She coughed to break the moment.

"Where's your bro?" she asked Soka, ignoring her own

brother's annoyed look. As if in response, Tammand glided out of the trees, Fritz at his heels. He laid a pile of bark at his sister's feet. Then he wordlessly turned and vanished into the forest. Soka watched him go, her face sad. Fritz coughed, breaking the uncomfortable silence.

"I thought the chestnut was extinct on Manhattan," the roach said, feeling the bark.

"We brought seeds with us when we answered the Mayor's call for a new homeland," Soka explained, turning back to her charge as she gathered the bark into her arms. "We are not so careless with our treasures as some."

Soka placed the bark on Bridget's two stumps. She glanced at Rory's wrist.

"May I borrow your wampum? It will help concentrate the magic."

"Sure," he said, pulling off the purple bracelet. Soka slipped the wampum over one of Bridget's stumps.

"Let's hope this works," Soka muttered. Bridget fervently seconded that thought. Soka closed her eyes and placed her fingers on Bridget's chest. A rush of warmth spread through Bridget's body. She gasped as the warmth turned to fire. A burning yellow poured over her eyes, blocking out her sight. Everything was fire and the only thing she heard was Soka's voice ringing in her ears. She seemed to burn for days and days, until finally the pain subsided. The yellow bled away and she could see again. The fire turned back to warmth, and the pushing inside her ceased. She let out a long sigh as relief flowed through her.

Soka collapsed backward, and Rory leaped forward to steady her. Bridget heard Fritz whistle in awe as Rory knelt down beside her. She was shocked to see tears running down his cheeks.

"Am I all better?" she asked him weakly.

"See for yourself," he answered, smiling through his tears.

She pushed herself up to a seated position and looked down at her wrist. A new hand waved back at her. But this hand was not paper. Instead, it was rough brown wood, as if someone had carved her a new hand from a fallen branch. A glance at her ankle revealed a foot made of the same wood. She was now part papier-mâché and part chestnut tree. A look at her wrist revealed that Rory's wampum bracelet had fused itself into the wood.

"I ruined your bracelet!" she cried. Rory shook his head.

"Don't be stupid. It looks better on you anyway. How do you feel?"

"Better," she replied, running one fake hand over the other.

"Then let's go home," he said.

But it was not that easy. Once they reached the barrier, Bridget could not step through. Something prevented her from leaving. And there could only be one explanation.

"I'm sorry, Bridget," Soka said, her face stricken. "I did not think of this. Your hand and foot are made from the chestnut tree, bound to you by our magic. Those parts of you cannot leave the park, just as we cannot. So long as you are inside that body, I fear you cannot pass the barrier."

"Don't worry. I'll bring back your real body," Rory said. "You can put your soul inside and then we'll *both* leave."

"I'll stay with Bridget," Fritz said. "The watch will help you bring back Bridget's body."

"Stay right here," Rory said to Bridget. "I'll be right back."

"You bet," she said, smiling gamely. "I'll be rooted to the spot like a tree."

Rory rolled his eyes before running through the entrance out onto the sidewalk, disappearing behind the wall. Bridget turned to see if Soka knew any word games to pass the time, when a new voice broke through.

"Here they are," it said. "And as you can see, they are harboring an abomination."

Bridget felt a scream catch in her throat as the Munsee with the snake tattoos stepped into the clearing, followed by a large group of Indians and, last of all, Tammand. Soka gasped beside her.

"I can't believe you did this, Tammand!"

Tammand looked away as the Munsee with the snake tattoos stepped forward, reaching out toward Bridget, who cowered beneath his dead gaze.

"Time to take care of this little demon once and for all."

Bridget waited, wincing . . . but nothing happened. Soka was laughing grimly beside her.

"Stop your chortling, little cousin," Askook spat at her.

"I've altered her body a bit," Soka explained belligerently. "You can't harm her."

Askook's eyes narrowed, making Bridget gulp.

"Oh, I'll be the judge of that."

Rory had just finished filling in Alexa and Simon on the eastern sidewalk by Central Park when Fritz and Clarence scampered out of a hole in the wall.

"What are doing here!" Rory said. "You're supposed to be with Bridget!"

"That snake Munsee has her," Fritz said. Rory felt the blood drain from his face. He turned to run back into the park when he felt someone grab his shoulder.

"Whoa, kiddo," Simon said, holding him back. "Even I know that isn't a good idea."

"But Bridget . . ."

"Hear me out," Fritz said. Rory waited, though inside, his heart was hammering away.

"What happened?" Alexa asked.

"There's a large group of them, led by the snake guy," Fritz said. "They're standing around, trying to figure out what to do with Bridget. And if Rory runs in there, he'll get caught, too."

"We've got to rescue her!" Rory shouted.

"Hold on," Fritz said. "Let me finish. The snake guy tried to do that unraveling trick again, but apparently whatever Soka did with that tree bark made Bridget impervious to his magic spell. They can't harm her. But they *can* harm you. We won't let you do it."

"I don't even know who could go in to rescue her," Alexa said, clearly frustrated. "We're stuck out here! And she's alone."

Rory stared at them for a moment, thinking about how scared her sister would be all alone, then turned away to kneel down by Tucket, putting a hand on the dog's neck.

"Go find my sister," he said to the spirit dog. "Protect her."

Tucket whined, refusing to even look at the park.

"I know you don't like the way it feels when you can't feel the island," Rory said. "But you are my spirit dog, and I need you to help me. Please. She needs someone to look after her."

Rory and Tucket locked eyes for a moment, and Rory tried to communicate how badly he needed this. Finally, Tucket let out a bark, licking Rory's face once. Then the dog leaped to his paws and quickly ran across the sidewalk, disappearing through the entranceway to the park. Rory felt his heart lighten just a bit, knowing the dog would be there to protect his sister.

"That may work out better than you know," Fritz mused. "Those Munsees haven't seen a spirit dog in a hundred and fifty years. It might help Bridget to have one on her side. I'll follow him and see where things stand. Wait here, I'll be back soon."

He raced off into the park. Rory began to pace back and forth while Alexa and Simon watched and waited anxiously.

An hour passed, with agonizing slowness, before Fritz and Clarence reemerged.

"She's okay," he said, and Rory's chest relaxed. "They're not going to harm her."

"Did you talk with her?" Rory asked.

"Yes, and she's fine," Fritz answered. "I think this could work to our advantage. Someone needs to follow Abigail's trail to see what happened to her. I think Bridget will be in the unique position of being able to do just that."

"She can't do it on her own!" Rory cried.

"She has Tucket, she has her paper body, and I believe she will have Soka's help. This might be our best shot to track down the Mayor's daughter."

Rory looked like he wanted to argue, but then he deflated.

"Shouldn't we at least get her the necklace?" he asked.

"That's a funny thing," Fritz said. "I mentioned the necklace before I slipped away and she said she didn't want it. She thought we should get the necklace to the one it was intended for, to Abigail's father. And I think she's right."

"How are we going to do that?" Simon asked.

"We'll have to figure that out, won't we," Fritz answered. He looked thoughtful. "It was impressive, you know, to see Bridget so calm. She's really growing up."

"We aren't leaving her with only a dog, though, are we?" Alexa asked.

"I'll send in one of the boys from my patrol," Fritz continued. "She won't be alone."

Rory nodded, barely listening, praying Bridget would be okay. His heart felt so heavy it had fallen into his shoes. In a strange way, he was the one who felt alone now.

IN THE RAMBLE

Fritz sat astride Clarence, staring down the tunnel deep underneath the Dyckman Street playground. Just around the bend waited M'Garoth village, his home, as well as his wife, Liv. He wished he could go to her and ask for her help, but he knew she would have to say no. She was charged with the protection of their clan, which she took very seriously. The clan had long ago decided to turn its back on Mannahatta, so Liv must as well. Fritz couldn't do that, however. Which left him here outside the gates instead of home with the roach he loved.

"Why can't they see they can't hide from what's coming," Fritz muttered.

He heard a sound and he spun to see Hans scampering down the tunnel.

"They're morons, boss, most of 'em," Hans said. "If they'd bother to risk their necks and take a look topside, they'd see everything isn't happiness and light up there! And when things go bad up there, it always runs down here."

Fritz nodded, his heart heavy. Hans took off his helmet and wiped his sweaty face.

"Do you want to hear my report?" Hans asked. "It's interesting."

Fritz perked up. "You found something."

Hans smiled broadly. "Kiffer and I found something. It wasn't easy, but we finally caught a break . . ."

As Hans gave his report, Fritz felt the fire returning. Here was where he was making a difference, he thought. Once Hans finished, Fritz gave his shoulder a pat.

"Good job, Hans. Good job. Now I have another job for you, if you'll take it. There's a little girl all alone among the Munsees except for a dopey dog. Can you help her out?"

"I'm on it," Hans replied, saluting. Fritz wished all his fellow roaches could be as open as Hans. As he turned his back on his village to return to his duty, he pushed down the sadness. They'd appreciate him in the end, he knew it.

Bridget climbed over the rocks, struggling to keep up with the more sure-footed Munsee warriors surrounding her. Askook stayed close by. She really wished she could kick the sour-faced Munsee in the shin, just to get him back for trying to unravel her. But even though the Munsees were treating her with some respect, she could tell they'd have no problem making her pay if she attacked one of their own. Ahead, Bridget spied Soka being led forward by two guards. Tammand walked close by, but every time he tried to speak to her, Soka turned her head, refusing to even look at him. Even though Bridget was steamed at Tammand, she couldn't help but feel a little sorry for him.

He was so obviously hurt by his sister's anger. Ah well, she thought. Served him right for turning them all over to the enemy, the big poophead.

The forest seemed to get more dense as they pushed farther into a part of Central Park called the Ramble. Originally built to resemble a wilderness where one could wander along winding, secluded paths, the Ramble had never really appealed to Bridget. Not when she had a real wilderness right by her home in Inwood Hill Park. But even to her unknowing eye, *this* Ramble seemed to go much deeper than it had any right to. They'd been walking for hours.

As she stumbled forward, Bridget noticed the Munsees stealing glances at Tucket, padding along happily at her side. They'd been treating the silly pooch with a healthy dose of awe ever since he'd burst into the clearing where Askook's war party was trying to figure out what to do with her. Tucket had knocked her over to cover her with big, sloppy kisses. When she'd finally gotten the huge dog under control, Bridget realized that the mood of the Munsees around her had definitely changed.

A whisper had run through the warriors. *Spirit dog.*

"Where did he come from?" Askook had demanded, towering over her.

"Wampage gave him to Rory," Bridget answered haughtily, not liking his tone. "And I guess Rory sent him to me, because even a great fighter like me needs a friend to keep her company. Tucket likes me better, anyway. Rory doesn't know how to look after dogs, and he never pets Tucket enough. But I'm like a dog wizard. Tucket always listens to me and gives me kisses and sleeps next to me on my bed and everything. If Mom could see him, then she'd make him get down, but she can't, so I get a warm puppy to cuddle with all night long. What's wrong with your face, Mr. Askook? If you keep frowning like that, then you'll stay that way; it's scientifically proven."

Bridget's voice rang with bravado, but inside she was terrified. Askook looked like he wanted to eat her alive and it scared her to death. But she wouldn't let him see it; no, sir.

At the mention of the name, "Wampage" replaced "spirit dog" on the lips of the Munsees.

"You know Wampage?" another Munsee asked. "He still goes on beyond the walls of our prison?"

"He lives up in Inwood, by me," Bridget said, rubbing Tucket's belly to keep the dog from jumping on her again. The sight of her treating the dog so familiarly seemed to shock the Munsees, who muttered among themselves at the sight. "He's pretty mopey all the time, because he misses you guys."

"I doubt that," yet another Munsee said sourly. "Why would he care for those he betrayed?"

"Wampage never betrayed you!" Bridget was indignant. "He is really depressed by the Trap. He's been helping Rory try to bring it down!"

"That's what I've been trying to tell you," Soka cut in, talking to Askook. "You and Tackapausha. But you never listen."

Askook stared intently at Bridget, as if he were trying to read her thoughts. She became uncomfortable and looked away. The snake-faced Munsee turned to his men.

"We will let Tackapausha decide what to do with this foul being," he said. A few of the Munsees nodded, but even more watched how easily Bridget played with Tucket, and muttered uneasily among themselves. As they set of to the Munsee village, these warriors watched her secretly, trying to decide what to think about this new wrinkle.

Hours later, they continued to dive deeper into the Ramble. Bridget sniffed. Was something burning in the distance? She spotted smoke rising above the trees as they finally approached a clearing. Gradually, she heard the sounds of a soft flute playing and voices talking and laughing. A moment later, they stepped out of the forest into the Munsee village.

The clearing stretched out into a circle, much wider than she knew the Ramble could ever hold. This place was a big as a football field, she thought. How could no one know it was there? In the center of the open field stood fifteen or so long, domed buildings of varying sizes set in a rough circle, made of what appeared to be bark hanging from pole frames. A large fire pit sat in the center, unlit. To her left loomed a stone cliff dotted with caves, fires burning in their mouths, sending out the tendrils of smoke Bridget had seen from the forest. Women knelt around the fires, pounding corn and mixing some sort of thick, bubbling soup in pots set over the flames. Men sat among them, chipping at stone arrowheads or carving sticks of wood as they idly chatted. A young man leaned against the cliff, dreamily playing a bone flute, while beside him some younger girls painted animal patterns onto deerskin clothes. Laughing children ran by, chasing a pair of black crows across the clearing. Older men and women with straight, gray-streaked hair gathered around the domed buildings, talking earnestly among themselves. Squirrels scampered around everyone's feet like small dogs, and here and there a Munsee petted one affectionately. Most of the men went shirtless, and their faces and bodies bore all manner of tattoos. The women wore simple skirts and tunics, with necklaces of dried fruit or beans hanging around their necks, and their hair fell in braids over their shoulders. There were perhaps a hundred Munsees in sight and they all stopped what they were doing to stare at the scouting party emerging from the trees.

At first Bridget thought they were all looking at her and she squirmed under the attention. But then she realized that they were fixated on the spirit dog at her feet. The longing on their faces made Bridget's heart hurt. Tucket barked once, breaking the silence, and bedlam broke out.

"Peace, friends!" one woman shouted over the din of questions and demands for explanations. She moved toward the party with quiet grace and authority, and behind her the cacophony eventually subsided. Pouches hung from straps slung over both her shoulders, and beautiful feathers were intertwined in her lush silver hair. Askook sneered at her but made no move to stop the silver-haired woman from approaching Bridget and Tucket. She ignored Bridget, however, and knelt down to run a hand along the tawny dog's soft neck.

"I know you," she whispered to the dog. "This is the second time you have gone beyond for those you love. You are truly a great friend." Tucket barked once, licking the woman happily. She laughed as she rose, turning to face the waiting Munsees of the village.

"I have seen but one of our beloved dogs since the walls of the Blue Abomination sprang from the earth to trap us here. That was this very dog, sent by Wampage from outside to bring me news not one month ago. Yes, Wampage has stayed true to us, as I have told you many times. Others may lie." She nodded at Askook, who stared daggers back at her. "But not I. That one of our dogs walks beside this newcomer girl is a sign, indeed."

"This girl is an abomination, Sooleawa," Askook said, pointing to Bridget. "It matters not what manner of animal accompanies her." Bridget glanced sharply at Soka and Tammand. So this impressive woman was their mother, the medicine woman. Interestingly enough, even though Soka was the prisoner, it was Tammand who would not look at his mother, staring at his feet while Soka stood proud in captivity.

"But she brings hope," Sooleawa continued, undeterred. "When Wampage sent this dog to me, the pup could barely wait to race back out to the world beyond the park, back to where he could feel the land again. But now he stands next to this supposed abomination as docile as can be. Why? Because she brings hope. The tide is turning, friends. The day is coming upon which our exile will end and we will once again feel the land. Did not the very earth shake? Mannahatta searches for us and calls for us to return. We must be ready . . ."

"We will be ready," a man said, stepping out of the largest cave. Everyone quieted, even Sooleawa, at his arrival. He stood tall, taller than any other Munsee Bridget could see, and that was saying something. He wore no tattoos on his face or feathers in his long black hair. Only a pair of tanned leggings and a bright belt of beads wrapped around his waist. The belt looked the twin to the Sachem's belt Rory had taken from Tobais's bank, but the many colors on this belt put Rory's plain white one to shame. Bridget had never seen anything so beautiful. The man walked with power, every step demanding to be obeyed, and the Munsees bowed their heads as he passed.

Emotions warred across many of their faces: love for the man and fear of what he wanted to do. Bridget recognized him from the necklace: this was Tackapausha.

"We will be ready, Sooleawa," Tackapausha said as he approached, "to take our revenge on those who exiled us to this foul land."

"No, that will be our end!" Sooleawa insisted.

"Are we not strong?" the Sachem cried, throwing his arms into the air. "Are we not right? We do not seek to tear down all of Mannahatta. We merely wish to repay the Mayor for all he has done to us. And we merely wish to ask Harry Meester, our *friend,* to explain why he shot down my son in cold blood, even as he raced back to join his people in exile. We do not bring war. We want only justice. And once this Trap falls, justice will be ours!"

Caught up in their leader's speech, some of the Munsees cheered. But Bridget spied more than a few unhappy faces in the crowd. Sooleawa waited for the cheers to die down before cutting in.

"This child brings us this dog as a message of hope, not revenge," she said.

"I agree," Tackapausha said. "Though she is a demon, a trapped soul, unnaturally imprisoned in that body much as we have been in this false paradise, I do believe she brings hope, as you say. Hope for freedom. Hope for a new life. And hope for justice. Hear me! Let the demon walk free!"

Askook shot the Sachem a fierce look, but Tackapausha ignored him. Sooleawa appeared troubled, but she patted Bridget's shoulder to reassure her.

"She is the harbinger of a better day that is almost here,"

the Sachem continued. "So sharpen your spears and practice your bow! Justice is coming!"

Sooleawa leaned in to whisper in Bridget's ear.

"Most of them do not believe this. They are afraid to go against such a mighty warrior. In the old days, there would not even be a thought of war without much discussion by the elders. Tackapausha throws out the rules through sheer force of his personality. But do not worry. Before the Trap is lifted, we will fix this, you and I."

Bridget pulled away to stare back at the medicine woman's intent face, wondering what she'd gotten herself into.

The crowd had dispersed, with Tackapausha not even glancing at Bridget before turning his attention to Soka. Sooleawa and Tammand both whispered fiercely with Tackapausha, with Askook at the Sachem's side arguing right back. After a few minutes, Tackapausha turned and pointed to the caves. Askook marched Soka away. The Munsee girl glanced once at Bridget, her face struggling to remain calm, before she disappeared into the cave. Tackapausha walked away, followed by a small group of warriors including Tammand. Sooleawa shot a look of pure fury at her son—who couldn't meet her eyes—before following the Sachem, continuing her argument as they passed into the trees.

Bridget glanced around; she was all alone with Tucket. No one even looked at her, though they still stole glances at Tucket. She guessed they were taking Tackapausha's order—to let her walk free—seriously. Okay, then, so now what?

"Hello there!" someone called out. She spied a short, portly

Munsee ambling over to greet her. "Demon! Hello!" The man reached her, sweat pouring down his tubby bare chest. He had tattoos of turkeys on his cheeks. Not quite as impressive as dogs or snakes, Bridget decided. His hair had been shaved into a topknot, which hung down the back of his neck. He grinned widely as he wiped the sweat from his forehead.

"Such heat," he said. "It makes my nose itch fiercely. Hair would probably help slow the sweat, but then I wouldn't look so impressive!" He pointed to his head, which looked about as impressive as a honeydew melon. He glanced down at Tucket, who lay panting at Bridget's feet. "He feels it, too. Poor puppy. Let's get you two out of the sun and into the shade."

"I don't mean to be rude," Bridget said. "But who are you?"

"I'm sorry, I thought I said," the man apologized, wiping his forehead again. "My name is Chogan. Sooleawa asked me to look after you while she attends to her daughter. I've been racking my brain, trying to think up things demons might like to do. We could do something evil with a chicken, but unless you've got good hands, they're a devil to catch."

"That's okay," Bridget said, though chasing after a chicken did sound kinda fun. "I'm not really a demon. I'm a preteen!"

"That sounds even worse," Chogan replied, making a face. "Okay, no demon activities. What is left?"

"How about a tour?" Bridget asked, curious about the Munsee village.

"Excellent!" Chogan snapped his fingers, sending beads of sweat flying everywhere. "I know the perfect place to start!"

He led Bridget into one of the caves, where she was soon overpowered by the worst smell in the world.

"What is that?" she asked, gagging. "Who lives here, a troll?"

"This is my cave," Chogan replied stiffly, put off by her reaction. He pointed to the hides hanging from the cave wall. "I work here as a tanner. I make the wonderful clothes my people wear. Unfortunately, the smell comes with the territory. I cure the hides here and then hang them out back. But if my occupation offends you . . ."

"No, no!" she insisted, even as Tucket began to whine beside her. She fought down the urge to throw up, not that there was anything inside her hollow shell to come up. "It's very interesting."

"I know!" Chogan announced, mollified. "Come, I'll show you where we use the urine to make the hides supple and easy to work."

"You know what?" Bridget said, backing up. "I'm a little hungry."

"Demons eat?" Chogan asked, surprised.

"Yes, we do." Bridget improvised. "We actually eat fresh air. And I'd love to grab a snack. Can we?"

Chogan shrugged and led her back outside. Bridget sighed, glad to have dodged the urine bullet.

As they walked through the village, everyone they passed made certain not to look at either Bridget or Tucket. But she felt their eyes all the same. All the while Chogan explained the layout of the settlement.

"These are the wigwams," he said, pointing to the bark-covered domes. "I don't live in one, since I have my cave, but many do. See the three larger houses?" Bridget nodded as she spied some longer wigwams in the center of the field near the big fire. "Those are the longhouses. There are three, one for each clan."

"So there are really only three families here?" Bridget asked. "That doesn't sound like much."

"Clans are a little larger than simple families," Chogan explained, smiling. "There have always been three, throughout our history. The Wolf, the Turtle, and the Turkey. You belong to your mother's clan, not your father's, so a father and son would live in different longhouses once the son had his own family."

"Which clan are you?" Bridget asked, glancing sidelong at the turkeys on Chogan's cheeks.

"Turtle," Chogan replied blithely, and Bridget lost the bet with herself. "Like Sooleawa and her children. Penhawitz was Turtle, too. Tackapausha, Penhawitz's son, belongs to the Wolf Clan like his mother. You see?"

Chogan led her out of the clearing, into the trees. They walked a few feet before emerging into another clearing, this one filled with tall stalks.

"Corn!" Bridget cried at the sight of the ears hanging from the tall green stalks.

"And beans and squash," Chogan said, pointing out the other vegetables curled around the base of the maize. The beans grew on vines that wrapped around the cornstalks, while the squash and pumpkins filled the spaces on the ground in between. He wiped his forehead again, this time with a corn husk he pulled off the nearest ear. "We call them the Three Sisters. We grow them together, as they support each other. The cornstalks support the bean vines, the beans keep the soil rich, and the squash send out roots to keep out the weeds while shading the ground to keep it moist during the driest of summers. Like the one we're suffering through now."

"Do you guys make mazes in the fall?" Bridget asked, thinking of the corn maze her mother took them to in Westchester every October. "I bet this one is even better than the one in Peekskill! The kids must be lost for days! I've even got a name for you! The Maize Maze! How awesome is that?"

"No, we don't make mazes," Chogan replied, crinkling his nose at her strange ideas. "Life is hard enough already. Where is Wopi? He's supposed to be watching out for animals. Some deer will wander by and eat all the squash!"

"So all you guys eat are veggies? That's the most disgusting thing I ever heard!"

"Most of the men hunt," Chogan explained. "We have a second camp half a day's walk north in the Ravine by the Loch, which is the only real river in this place. There the men venture out to track game in the North Woods, and also to fish in the Loch."

Bridget cocked her head. "What's that sound?"

Tucket's ears perked up as the sound of laughter drifted by. He let out a howl and ran into the woods.

"Tucket, where are you going?" Bridget cried.

"He just hears the game, that's all," Chogan replied. "I guess we found out where Wopi went, huh? There is another clearing nearby where the we play sports."

"Let's run and catch up, then!" Bridget took off after her dog. She heard Chogan sigh behind her.

"No need to run, it's only twenty paces away," he complained before lumbering after her.

Bridget followed Tucket through the brush, bursting out

onto a new field, where the dog pulled up, tail wagging, to watch the game under way.

The field was set up in a way similar to football, with goal-posts on each end, though there was no crossbar to connect the two posts. To Bridget's surprise, one team seemed to be made up entirely of girls; the other was all boys. An old woman sat on the sidelines, a row of sticks at her feet. Probably keeping score, Bridget guessed. The kids were so wrapped up in their game that they didn't notice the visitors on the sidelines immediately, giving the girl a chance to watch them play.

There seemed to be different rules for the boys and the girls. The boys could only kick the ball toward the goal or one another, while the girls could run with it and pass it back and forth. Bridget didn't like different rules for different people, but she had to admit it looked fun. The boys tried to knock the ball out of the girls' hands, but they didn't try to tackle. The girls, however, often brought a boy running with the ball down to the ground. Bridget imagined how easily she'd tackle that boy; she'd be queen of the ball field. She smiled at the thought.

"It's called Pahsaheman," Chogan said, stepping up next to her. He leaned over to put his hands on his knees, trying to catch his breath after running after the girl and her dog. "I'm in no shape to play it now, but I used to be fairly good."

"I bet I could pick it up real quick," Bridget said. "Does Soka play?"

"She is one of the best," Chogan replied. "I'm sure the girls' team misses her out there."

One of the boys leaped to the side to avoid a tackle and kicked the ball square through the posts. His team erupted into cheers. The girls grumbled, clapping hands while encouraging one another as they prepared to exact their revenge. It made Bridget's heart ache for her days playing soccer at camp, or shooting hoops with Rory down at the courts. She wanted to join in, to play with the others. It looked so fun.

And that was when they noticed her. The players froze, a hush falling over them as they spied the visitor and the spirit dog. Bridget decided to make the first move, stepping forward with her hand raised in hello.

"Hi! I'm Bridget. And this is Tucket. He's a spirit dog, you know. I'm just a girl, not a demon, by the way. Can I . . . can I play?"

They greeted her with stony silence. As she glanced around, she saw a whole bunch of different emotions on their faces: fear, worry—interest, even. But no one said a word. Finally, the old woman stepped forward.

"Perhaps next time, young one," she said, not unsympathetically. "This game is almost through."

Some of the kids nodded, though Bridget thought she heard the word *demon* float by. It made her unbearably sad. All she wanted to do was play. Chogan took her arm.

"We should go," he said softly, his eyes kind.

"We do need someone to take Soka's spot," one of the Munsee girls piped up suddenly. "They are truly killing us out there."

Bridget felt a wave of gratitude wash over her as the Munsee girl smiled at her. An argument broke out behind the girl over the invitation. Some of the other girls seemed to agree, while the rest most certainly did not. It was the same with the boys; some said yes, some no. Bridget realized that she'd mess up their game if she joined in, so she declined. But she'd never forget the girl who'd spoken up. As she walked away with Chogan at her side and Tucket right behind, she felt renewed hope that their people would one day live together. She'd make it happen. She'd just have to speak up.

THE DOCKS

After sending Tucket to his sister, Rory had followed Alexa and Simon back to Washington Irving's house. But upon turning onto Irving Place, they were shocked to find the entire residence surrounded; a group of the green-skinned Brokers of Tobias patrolled the sidewalk. Rory felt sick; they'd been discovered.

They quickly retreated before they could be noticed, heading south toward the Stuyvesant farmhouse. They'd just reached the outskirts of the farm when Fritz had overtaken them with news. Hans had found a sailor down at the docks who had information about Harry Meester. Rory's stomach did a somersault as he realized they might be getting closer to his dad. They left right away, heading downtown to meet this mystery sailor, finally ending up on Pearl Street, hurrying toward a large warehouse.

But now Rory was confused. The street they were walking down was a good three long blocks from the East River—docks tended to be near water, in his experience. So why were they headed toward a large, completely landlocked building?

Alexa patiently explained it to him.

"The island has changed a lot over the centuries," she said. "When my father first came here in the seventeenth century, Manhattan was much thinner, especially down here toward the southern tip. As the years passed, people wanted more land, but there wasn't any more to be had down here. So they made some from scratch. They extended the island out into the river, dumping dirt and stones in the water to create a new shoreline, much wider than before. They'd even sink old ships into the areas they were filling in to stabilize the landfill. So over the years, Pearl Street, which used to be the shore, became one block from the river, then two, then three."

"But the ships still sail into the same docks," Simon said, taking up the tale. "Spirits are really set in their ways, if you haven't noticed. So the docks remain here on Pearl Street, even though there hasn't been any water nearby in three hundred years."

"Keep an eye out for anything odd and don't attract any attention," Alexa warned them all. "We don't want to be noticed." She led them into the warehouse, and what Rory saw inside took his breath away.

It was as if someone had crammed every ship that ever existed into one place. A large pool of water extended before him, into which stretched a multitude of wooden piers from a dock that ran the length of the wall through which Rory had entered. Though the warehouse was much bigger on the inside than appeared possible from the outside, it could barely contain all the ships in its harbor. The boats bobbed gently in their slips, so close to one another that their sides scraped. Rory stepped onto the long wooden dock that stretched into the distance on either side of him. Looking up, he could just see the ceiling far above, the wooden planks of the warehouse roof barely visible by the yellow light of the many lamps hanging from posts that thrust up from the dock.

The docks were filled with people: hawkers selling food and supplies, women of questionable character, dockhands seeing to the ships, and, of course, sailors in every manner of dress from the past four hundred years. They intermingled in a loud orchestra of chaos. But Fritz, sitting on Alexa's shoulder, appeared to know just where to go, and Rory and Simon followed them into the mass of people.

They weaved in and out of the throng, heading toward a row of rickety shacks built up against the wall of the warehouse. One building had a lodgings sign above the door, and it was into this so-called hotel that Alexa and Fritz disappeared, bidding Simon and Rory to wait.

"Who is this guy we're meeting, anyway?" Rory asked as they stood staring out at the ships.

"Just some old sailor," Simon replied absently. His eyes had lit upon a commotion farther down the dock. A crowd of people had gathered around something outside a tavern. Simon inched forward, trying to see. Rory held back, but then a loud shout emitted from the throng brought Simon hurrying over to see what was what, leaving Rory alone. Rory watched as Simon burrowed into the crowd, disappearing from view. He thought about staying put, but then another cry erupted and he decided he had to make sure Simon didn't get himself into trouble.

Forcing his way, Rory muscled into the center of the crowd, just in time to see Simon sit on the ground in front of a black man in a colorful outfit that rivaled Simon's own. They had dice on a strange board in front of them and Simon was placing some gold pieces on the ground. Something about the man tugged at Rory's memory, but he couldn't quite place it. Worried, he quickly knelt down by Simon.

"What are you doing?" Rory hissed in Simon's ear. "We're supposed *not* to be attracting any notice!"

Simon shrugged, unconcerned. "This will only take a second. I'm great at this game. I'm gonna win this guy's shirt. Look how cool it is!"

Staring at the other man's bright red shirt threatened to burn holes in Rory's eyes; he pulled at Simon's shoulder.

"We don't have time to play with dice," he said. "We've got to stay focused, here!"

"Quit your talking," the other man said, looking irritated. "What's your bet?"

"Calm down—Hendrick, is it?" Simon picked up the dice to look them over. "You keep pushing me and I'll think this game isn't on the up-and-up."

"Would I rob you?" Hendrick appeared offended at the very thought.

"It's not that I don't trust you," Simon said airily. "But you *are* a pirate."

"Fair enough." Hendrick flashed Rory a smile, which unsettled the boy. *Where have I seen him before?* he thought. Hendrick opened a button on his shirt to fan his face with the collar, and Rory spied a flash of a tattoo on his chest.

It hit him all at once: the smile, the tattoo, all of it.

"You tried to kidnap me!" Rory cried. "At that tavern the other day! I barely fought you off! You're a kidnapper!"

Hendrick stood up as the crowd began to rumble.

"Now, those are some hard words, boy. I never kidnapped anyone. What do you think I am?"

Simon stood up next Rory. "We think you're a pirate."

"A pirate, yes, but a kidnapper? Please." People began to drift away, not wanting to get mixed up in a fight. Hendrick shot Rory an angry look. "You're messing with my gold, boy."

"You messed with my life!"

"Hey, you got away, didn't you?" Hendrick spat. "With the help of that magic bear or whatever it was. And now you've scared away my day's take. So we're even, okay? Beat it!"

"How can you call that even!" Rory cried. "I got lost in those tunnels! I was almost run over by a subway train. You owe me!"

"I don't owe you nothing except a knock for costing me money," Hendrick replied. He balled his fists and Rory belatedly realized that he was picking a fight with a pirate, and that wasn't the best path to a long, pain-free life.

Suddenly a loud laugh boomed behind them, making Hendrick jump in his boots. Strolling through the thinning crowd came an older man, dressed expensively in seventeenth century clothing, with hose from his knee to his boots and a white wig atop his head. He slapped Hendrick on the back, so hard it almost knocked the smaller man clear across the dock.

"Don't be such a grinch!" the man announced. "You owe this boy an apology. Say you're sorry!"

"I'm the one who lost money," Hendrick replied, his voice sullen now. The man in the wig winked at Rory.

"Hendrick . . ." the man warned, his voice tinged with laughter, though his eyes flashed angrily. "Never let it be said that Captain Kidd's men kidnap children, especially his first mate!"

Rory had to keep from staring. This was the famous Captain Kidd, the great pirate and privateer? The man who had apparently marooned Thomas Tew and left Rory's father for dead?

"Hendrick," Kidd continued, still scolding his first mate. "Go on. Say you're sorry you tried to kidnap him and sentence him to a life of hard labor far out to sea!"

"I'm sorry I tried to kidnap you and sentence you to a life of hard labor far out to sea," Hendrick muttered, looking everywhere but at Rory.

"So there you have it," Kidd said, smiling broadly. "An apology. Not enough for the pain you endured, I'm sure, but it's something."

"Simon! What are you two doing!" an angry voice called out behind them. It was Alexa, sticking her head out of the hotel window. Simon flinched and grabbed Rory's shoulder to go. Kidd smirked.

"I see your mother calls." He winked, then frowned. "You look familiar, boy . . ."

"Gotta go, sorry!" Simon pulled Rory away from the pirate as quickly as he could. Rory glanced back. Captain Kidd was already walking away, his chastised first mate in tow. Kidd glanced back at him, his eyes narrow, and Rory quickly turned his eyes forward again.

Alexa was yelling at Simon.

"You call that not being noticed!" she said, giving Simon a hateful glare. "I could kill you! Come on, we finally found the guy. Let's see what he knows and then get out of here!"

She led them into the hotel. The inside of the building wasn't much nicer than the outside. Rotted stairs led up to rooms in the back, while the lobby was dark, musty, and empty. An old woman manned a desk where one could check in, and behind her was a small room with tables for meals. A man sat at the only occupied table, his forehead resting on his dinner plate. Fritz stood by the plate, shaking his head at the sight, while Sergeant Kiffer stood on the other side, arms crossed. Alexa nodded toward the prone man.

"That's him. It's taken us this long to rouse him from his stupor, and now it looks like he's fallen right back into it. One thing, Rory." She leaned over to give him her complete attention. "Apparently Hans and Kiffer were only able to get this guy to talk because of you."

"Me?" Rory was confused.

"Hans was becoming desperate, so he started mentioning up and down he docks that Meester's son was looking for him. And that's when this man approached them. I just thought you should know that. Come on."

They walked up to the man and Alexa jostled his shoulder.

"Hey, Farhad, wake up," she said loudly. "You've got company." The man groaned but did not stir. "I think he may have drunk too much."

"Really?" Simon's voice dripped with sarcasm. "I thought he was just sleepy."

"Why is he like this?" Rory asked.

"Because this is what drunkards do." Farhad's voice rose up from his plate, though his head didn't move. "We drink. A lot. And we say things we should not."

"Just tell us what you know and we'll leave you to your

cups," Fritz said, his voice ringing with disapproval. Farhad's head rose up from his plate. His face was beet red, and puffy, with a long vein-riddled nose poking out of his thick curly beard. The outline of the plate had imprinted itself on his forehead. Rory would not have been able to take this man seriously if not for his haunted eyes, which spoke of some ancient pain that never stopped aching.

"You do look like him, a little bit," Farhad said. Rory felt a shock run through him. "I knew your father, boy. We sailed together, long ago, with Captain Tew. Until Tew met his fate on that damned piece of rock out in the mists and we were left adrift, the twelve of us."

"What happened?" Rory asked. "What did Kidd do?"

"We swore an oath out there, clinging to that piece of plank," Farhad said. "An oath that has haunted us ever since. I cannot speak of it, on pain of my soul. I sailed with your father many times, on many voyages out into the mist. We both changed our names as often as we changed shirts, which is to say not as often as we should have. He was Ronald Flint and Michael Lee and Otto Kruger and Isaac Weinstein and Jean-Paul LaRoche and so many others. I won't bore you with my many names, as I can barely remember who I am now, let alone last year or last century. I do remember one voyage—I don't recall the name of the ship, though I believe it's been a good sixty years since that boat was lost forever to the outer reaches. On this one voyage I was Raheem something-or-other, and your father was Peter Hennessy. He liked that one, I remember. Not surprised he went back to it. Good man, your dad. Good friend. Are you all right, boy?"

Tears were running down Rory's face. He quickly wiped his

cheeks clean and sniffed away his pain. He didn't care, he told himself. He didn't care that he hadn't seen his father in eight and a half years, that he'd never had a chance to know him, while this red-faced, booze-drenched mess spent years, *decades,* with the man.

"I'm fine," he replied finally, gathering himself. Alexa put a hand on his shoulder, but he shrugged it off before her attempts at comfort made him cry again.

"Do you know where he is now?" Fritz asked the man.

"I haven't seen him since he stopped sailing fifteen years ago," Farhad said, shaking his head. "A few of us have passed on, you know. Usually the drink devours us. Our oath is heavy and weighs upon our soul. The drink is all that can soothe us. Just the other day, one of my old companions passed of it."

"He was the one who told us to look for Harry Meester," Alexa said.

"Oh, Alberto," Farhad said, shaking his head sadly. "Just doing that much must have cost him. No wonder he drank himself into oblivion."

"I don't understand any of this," Rory said. "What happened back then to do this to you?"

"You will have to ask your father when you find him," Farhad said. "I know I cannot tell you or I will surely follow Alberto to the grave."

"Can you give us any idea where Meester might be now?" Fritz asked. "Rory thinks he saw him on the *Half Moon* a month or so ago."

"Really?" Farhad whistled, his head swaying from drink. "Now, that is desperation. No one signs on to that ship unless he has no other choice."

"Isn't there anything you can tell us that might help us find my dad?" Rory asked. "Anything at all?"

"Well, maybe one thing." Farhad's voice was slurring.

"What?" Rory bent down to look Farhad in the eye and force him to answer. Farhad smiled slightly.

"You really do look like him, you know that?" he said softly.

"Please help me," Rory begged him.

"Well . . ." Farhad took a deep breath, steadying himself for a moment. "Your father had a routine, something he had to do every time we shipped out. Somehow, he got the captains of whatever vessels we signed on with to agree, I don't know how. Most sailors would never set foot on that island, it is one of our strongest superstitions. But your father never cared about that. See, when you sail out into the mist, there are two final pieces of New York you pass before you disappear into the fog. Two islands: Hoffman, which has remained desolate for a hundred years, and Swinburne, the last dry land before the mists."

"I know Swinburne Island," Simon exclaimed, and Alexa nodded agreement. "That's where the convent is!"

"Yes." Farhad didn't look away from Rory. "We don't go onto the island because the nuns put a curse on any men who dare set foot on their soil. Your nether regions shrivel up and fall off. Don't laugh!" This was to Alexa, who had let out a scoffing chuckle. "I've met men who knew men who talked with men it's happened to. You couldn't get any sailor to go anywhere near that cursed beach, not for a million dollars. But your father was different, Rory. Things like that never touched him.

"Somehow, your dad talked every captain we ever sailed with into dropping anchor near the island so he could take the skiff and row himself up to the little dock that poked out of that deserted, fog-drenched beach. There he'd disappear into the depths of the island for a few hours, then reappear, row back to our ship, and we'd sail off again. I never knew how he convinced the captains to do it . . . the sailors were never happy about it, I can tell you. But your dad always managed to work it out. So time and time again, he'd get his shore leave on Swinburne Island."

"Why did he go there?" Rory asked.

"The way he looked forward to it, the way he appeared both at peace and unbearably sad when he returned, it could only mean one thing. There was a woman he loved in that convent. I asked him and he didn't deny it."

"Did he tell you her name?" Alexa asked. Farhad shook his head.

"He wouldn't speak of her at all. But I do think that if anyone knows where your father is, it will be that woman on Swinburne. If not her, then no one, and your father is gone for good like I always feared."

With that, Farhad's head fell gently forward to rest on the table and he would speak no more.

16

SWINBURNE ISLAND

Peter Stuyvesant nibbled at a small biscuit his wife had baked him as he rested beneath his pear tree on the corner of 13th and 3rd. He was taking no chances; he knew poison when he saw it, and Whitman and the others were definitely poisoned. Although they were already improving—they were gods, after all—it would be days before his fellow council members would be up and around. Until then, Peter had to shoulder all of the load himself.

And the load was getting heavier. The rumors about a Munsee assassin roaming free had been replaced by actual sightings of bands of Munsees, causing general mayhem throughout Mannahatta. Peter knew they weren't Munsees, of course. Probably hooligans in war paint and feathers, he figured. But it spooked people, and when people got spooked, they panicked. And when they panicked, well, that's when people got hurt.

Folks didn't scare so easily back in his day, he thought sourly to himself. *We had real courage, back then,* he thought. All these namby-pamby new gods just didn't have any stomach. So he had to run around, keeping the peace and reminding people that just because some underworld thug put on a headdress, it didn't mean the city was under attack.

"Mind if I join you?" Peter looked up in surprise to see Caesar Prince smiling down at him.

"I haven't seen you in a while," Peter told Caesar, relaxing. "I thought you'd fallen down a hole through the center of the earth."

"Nope," Prince said, settling beneath the tree beside Peter. "Just biding my time."

"I could use you, you know," Peter told him. "Everyone else is sick as dogs. Poison, you know."

"Doesn't surprise me," Caesar said. "Something big's coming and you know Kieft would want the big guns out of the way."

"I know it," Peter said, preening slightly at being called a big gun. "You don't get the same caliber of god anymore. God of Parking Meters? God of Text Messages? God of Co-op Boards? That last man is a real weasel, by the way. They're just not the same."

"I'll help all I can," Caesar promised. He pulled out a large sandwich. Peter sniffed the air; it smelled like pastrami on rye.

"Is that Mr. Katz's pastrami?" The God of Delicatessens made a mean sandwich.

"No, I made it myself. You can't trust anyone, you know?"

Peter looked longingly at the big, bursting sandwich, and then glanced down at his sad little biscuit. Caesar was right; you couldn't trust anyone. But he'd known Prince for so long. And he was so hungry for anything but his wife's cooking.

Caesar noticed Peter's sidelong glances and smiled.

"Want a bite?"

The small boat rocked violently beneath Rory. Even though the skies were clear, the wind whipped the waves into whitecaps that threatened to overwhelm the small vessel. A particularly large wave sent them careening up and down, prompting a cry of pure terror from the galley.

"I thought you said it wasn't out in open water!" Simon cried, huddled miserably in the bottom of the boat. Alexa shrugged from her place by the tiller, smiling apologetically as she wiped spray from her eyes.

"I know you." Her lip twitched as she struggled not to smile at Simon's distress. "You're a big baby about boats."

"If I sink, I'm not strong enough to will my way to shore!" Simon shot back, ducking as another wave crashed overhead. "I'm not a god, remember!"

"And you never will be," Alexa replied, which seemed to Rory to be a strangely obvious statement. But Simon nodded glumly and looked away. Fritz glanced over at them from his place near the stern, shaking his head before returning his gaze to the ocean. Rory stood at the bow of the tiny vessel, clinging to the mast. Even though he'd never been on a real boat before—somehow the Circle Line just didn't count—he wasn't scared. He felt at home on the boat, moving with it as it fought the waves. The wind sent spray flying into his eyes, but he didn't flinch. Maybe his dad was out there staring down the sea, too. He'd never felt this connected to the old man.

Swinburne Island proved to be way past Staten Island, almost out to sea. Alexa hadn't wanted to hire a boat down at the docks because of the number of people who would witness the transaction, so instead she rustled up an old two-person sail-boat her father had owned. They'd all piled into the boat and pushed out into the river from an old pier by Battery Park. As they sailed away, Rory had thought he'd seen someone step out of the shadows beneath the pier to watch them, but he blinked and whoever it was was gone. He must have been imagining things, he hoped. Still, he kept a watch behind them, and at one point he thought he saw another sail in the distance. But when he went to point it out to the others, it was gone and it never returned. Neither did Rory's peace of mind.

The voyage quickly grew more dangerous as they drifted out into choppier waters. Now the waves tossed them about as they sailed under the great Verrazano-Narrows Bridge, which connected Brooklyn to Staten Island (thinking of its grouchy namesake made Rory smile). Beyond the bridge lay the open sea. Mist clung to the horizon, covering the distant water in fog.

"I can't see anything out there," Rory shouted over the wind. "Will the mist clear up later in the day?"

"The mist never clears up," Alexa replied. "It's always been there and it always will be. It's the last great frontier. Great mariners sail into its murky depths in search of the secret islands where, supposedly, strange hermits hold caskets of treasure. Others hunt great whales the size of ocean liners. And the bravest souls of all search for the lost gods, who left never to return."

"Lost gods?" Rory had never heard of any lost gods.

"Not all the gods who no longer grace Mannahatta faded away with the passing of mortal memory," Alexa explained.

"Some tired of their days trapped by their blood and set sail for new lands out in the mist."

"Like Europe?" Rory asked.

"There is no Europe out there," Fritz said, his eyes distant. "No other side. Just mist, forever and ever."

"That's where Wampage went!" Rory suddenly understood his friend's parting words. "He's looking for his old leader."

"Many great gods went off into the mist," Alexa said. "Henry Hudson, Peter Minuet, Adriaen Block. Most of the first gods left before they could be bound to the land, or so my dad told me."

"What do you mean, bound to the land?" Rory asked.

"I'm not sure, myself," Alexa said. "My father mentioned it once and then refused to speak of it again. Something happened in the early days to send many of the first gods off into the mists. None of the other gods who were there will speak of it, either. Maybe it's something they're ashamed of."

"Whatever it is, it's long past now," Simon said. "No use worrying about it. You couldn't pay me enough gold to get me to sail off into those mists. There's no treasure, no heaven, on the other side. I don't think there's anything out there but water. Endless water." He shuddered at the thought, his hand playing with something in his pocket. Alexa shot him a sharp look, and Simon started, before pulling out an old penknife from his pocket with a shrug. Alexa pursed her lips and returned to steering the boat.

Rory stared out at the wall of mist slowly approaching, feeling his heart stir. His father had sailed out into that fog. Rory wondered what he had discovered out there. Maybe when he found him, the elder Hennessy would tell all his stories. Or maybe Rory would sail out there himself, one day, and find out firsthand.

Or maybe he'd find out now, he thought as the mist loomed larger and larger before them.

"Are we going in there?" Rory asked.

"No!" Simon said with conviction.

"The convent sits on an island at the edge of the mist," Alexa explained. "There are two islands there, Hoffman and Swinburne. Swinburne houses the convent, and as Farhad mentioned, Hoffman is empty."

"Are they part of Mannahatta?" Rory asked. "Is that how you all can set foot on it?"

"Actually, no," Alexa said. "The two islands were created by mortals only a hundred and fifty years ago. Because they were new, the boroughs agreed to make them neutral ground. Women from all five boroughs live in the convent. And Hoffman is the site of all official dealings between the borough leaders. See, that's Hoffman Island there."

A small hump of land rose up out of the water before them. As they floated closer, Rory could see trees and a few abandoned buildings. The whole place appeared deserted.

"They meet there?" Rory asked, incredulous. "It looks like no one's been there in decades."

"Longer," Simon said. "Borough mayors don't like to leave their cushy offices. The five boroughs haven't officially met in almost a hundred years."

They were now almost past the island. Alexa let out a cry and pointed into the mist.

"Thar she blows!"

"It's not a whale, you silly girl," Simon muttered. His face was growing white as he contemplated the new island in the distance gradually appearing out of the mist that now surrounded them.

"Nervous?" Alexa needled him.

"No!" Simon shot back.

"It's just superstition, you know," she continued, teasing him. "You won't really lose your nether regions."

"I know that. Leave me alone!"

Rory tried not to laugh at Simon's worried face. The older boy didn't look as confident as he tried to sound. Rory turned his attention instead to the island rising before them. This island was covered in mist, making it difficult to pick out many features. He could barely make out what looked like trees poking out of the fog. As the headed toward the island, he spied what appeared to be a small dock jutting out of the fog. Alexa guided the boat through the undulating sea up to the side of the dock, where Rory leaped out and tied them up. Alexa brought down the sail and nimbly hopped off the deck onto the dock; Fritz climbed out after her. Simon, however, had to be coaxed from his seat like a scared puppy.

"Don't be such a baby," Alexa scolded him. "Look at Rory; he's fine."

"He's mortal, maybe it doesn't affect him."

"Get out of the boat, Simon, before I make the curse come true myself!"

Muttering resentfully, Simon gingerly climbed out of the boat and stepped onto dry land. A relieved smile spread over his face.

"I knew it! Stupid superstition!" He sounded quite disdainful now that he'd survived unscathed. "Those sailors are so gullible. Let's go find this woman your dad's so fond of, Rory!"

If any of them had turned around as they hurried down the dock, they would have spied a small white sail approaching, gradually getting bigger. But none of them did.

The small party made their way carefully up a rocky path away from the dock into the trees. Mist hung from the branches, cloaking everything in fog. They bunched together so as not to lose one another.

"How big is this island?" Rory whispered to Alexa.

"Not big enough to get lost in," she whispered back. "But I can't seem to find the convent! It's all fog!"

"What are you talking about?" Rory said, pointing to the left, where he could see something in the distance. "Isn't that it over there?"

Sure enough, out of the mist rose a tall white steeple. Alexa gave Rory a strange look as they drew nearer, and Simon muttered "How did I miss that?" under his breath. As they approached, a large convent gradually emerged, seeming to take shape from the fog itself. White walls spread in each direction, disappearing into the mist. The tall steeple loomed above a large wooden door. As they came nearer to the door, a bell began to toll.

"I guess they know we're here," Alexa said. She marched up to the door and knocked. After a moment the door creaked open to reveal a woman in a long gray robe.

"Go away," she said. "You are not wanted."

She began to close the door, but Alexa put out a hand to stop it.

"We have traveled far," she said. "We seek one of your nuns—"

"No!" the woman said sternly. "The nuns are not to be disturbed. As official greeter, only I can speak with outsiders. And I use that privilege only to tell you all to go away!"

"Interesting use of the word *greeter*, eh?," Simon whispered to Rory.

"Wait!" Rory said before the woman could close the door again. He wasn't about to be turned away this easily. "I'm looking for a friend of my father. My father used to visit this place all the time! They say I look like him. Don't you recognize me?"

The woman shook her head and seemed ready to turn them away when another voice came from behind her.

"Let them enter."

The nun at the door quickly glanced over her shoulder, nodded reluctantly, and stepped aside, waving them into the convent. Inside, another woman awaited them in the soaring foyer, dressed in a simple habit of light blue. She seemed too youthful to carry much authority, but the first nun bowed her head.

"Where shall I take them, Mother?"

"*I* will take them to my study," the younger woman said, her voice kind but firm. She nodded slightly to the newcomers. "I am the abbess here. Normally, we would not admit strangers. But we do not live in normal times. Come with me."

"Wait," Rory said, stepping forward. "I'm looking for someone. A sailor—"

"All in good time," the abbess said, cutting him off. "Please, come."

The abbess led them through the stone entrance hall toward a long hallway. The ceiling rose majestically, a sky of stone far above their heads. No one was around and the halls were eerily silent. Their footsteps rang loudly as they walked through the empty passage. Finally, they reached a small wooden door, which the abbess opened.

"There is a small dining chamber through here where you may wait. Sister Patience will be by with refreshments. I cannot speak to all of you, I am afraid. Only the Light."

Rory gasped as the others exchanged shocked glances. Fritz stepped forward.

"How do you know what he is . . . ?" he asked.

"How can I not?" the abbess asked. "Only a Light could have seen the convent in the mist. And he is the only mortal human among you. So it is with him I must speak."

She stepped aside to let the others enter the dining room. They turned to look back at Rory with worry as the abbess closed the door and locked it.

"Not that I don't trust them," she said with a smile. "But that fellow in the loud puffy shirt seems a bit shifty to me. Shall we?"

The abbess led Rory down the stone hallway to another wooden door. She opened it with a long metal key, holding the door for Rory to step through. She followed him through, letting the door close behind them with a loud click, leaving the hallway empty and still.

Sister Hope hurried through the main hall toward the front door. Sister Patience usually handled the entrance to the outside world, but she was off getting food and wine for the visitors. She would never admit it, of course, but Sister Hope had always wanted to be the door opener. She couldn't see why Sister Patience was the only one allowed to greet outsiders. Just because Sister Hope had come here to contemplate the great beyond for all eternity shouldn't mean she couldn't enjoy a bit of conversation now and again.

So when the knock resounded through the halls, she had rushed to get the door before anyone could beat her to it. And her tenacity was rewarded when, upon opening the door, she was greeted by a man stepping out of the fog, smiling sweetly.

"Hello, young miss," the man said, doffing his cap. "Sorry to bother you. Friends of mine came before me to visit and I was hoping to catch up."

As he came closer, Sister Hope revised her initial impression. This was not a nice man; no, not at all. A heavily greased mustache hung down limpy on his upper lip, while his gaunt face and beady eyes made him look like a zombie.

"I'm sorry . . ." she stammered, wishing Sister Patience, or anyone at all, would come. "We don't allow visitors . . . you shouldn't even be able to find us . . ."

"But your lovely bell led me right here." He smiled, a mouth full of rotten teeth staring back at her. "And my friends are inside, right? So why don't you run and fetch them for me, would ya?"

Uncertain, Sister Hope glanced behind her to see if anyone else was coming to help. Unfortunately, the hallway was empty. She turned back to her visitor, who stepped up to her.

"I'm sorry, if you could just wait—"

Her voice cut off suddenly, and she fell to the ground.

"Sorry, darling," Bill the Butcher said, bending over to wipe his cleaver on the nun's habit. "I really don't have all day."

He straightened and ran down the hall, keeping an ear out for voices drifting through this monument to silence.

Rory glanced around the study as the abbess moved past him toward her desk. The small room looked lived in, with folders and books stacked everywhere. The main desk was barely visible under the mountains of paper. The walls held towering bookshelves in every direction. A big comfy-looking chair sat in front of the desk, and it was in this that the abbess indicated Rory should sit. She settled behind her desk and gazed thoughtfully at him, her fingers tapping her chin.

"What are you looking at?" Rory asked nervously.

"I think you know," the abbess replied. "You're not the spitting image of him, of course, but the likeness is there. What's your name?"

"Rory Hennessy," he replied, off balance.

"So you knew him as Peter Hennessy, correct?" The abbess smiled. "He always did like that name."

"Who are you!" Rory demanded.

"I'm the abbess of this convent. I established it long ago, for many reasons, not least of which was to give the daughters of the gods a place where they could ponder the mists in peace. The mists remind us that there is more out there than ourselves. Much more than we can ever understand. We may be immortal, but we are as lost as you mortals in many ways."

"So you started an abbey to look at fog?"

The abbess laughed. "Among other things. Myself, I've

always been a healer. It is my way of making up for who I used to be. This convent allows me time to study my craft. And, of course, it was a convenient escape."

"Escape from what?"

The abbess smiled again, this time with a slight twinge of bitterness. "From your father."

Rory shivered. He was so close. "So you know him? Who he is? Where he is? What he is?"

"So many questions. I don't have all the answers. We are such old friends, but even I don't know all his secrets. Even as he made certain to visit before every voyage, there were always holes in his past he never bothered to fill in for me. Such a sad man. But, then again, sad people tend to flock to me, I'm afraid.

"And then he disappeared for a little while. I thought he'd passed on. But then he reappeared, about eight years ago, only this time he was shipping out on the worst boat imaginable. The ghost ship, the *Half Moon*. He was truly lost to despair. It was heartbreaking to see."

"I don't understand," Rory said. "What was wrong with him?"

"That is up to him to explain, not I," the abbess said. "I wish I could tell you your father is a paragon of virtue. But in many ways, he is a weak, weak man. He has hurt so many people, including myself, and he runs rather than answer for his actions. I pray for him to find strength, but I fear that prayer is in vain. Perhaps my prayers have been answered in you, instead."

"Why won't you just tell me what you *do* know?" Rory cried. "At least tell me his real name!"

"I don't know it," the abbess admitted. "He never told me. Perhaps it *is* Peter Hennessy. It wouldn't surprise me one bit."

"None of this is helping," Rory complained, slumping in his chair. "I guess you didn't know him that well."

The abbess leaned back, sighing. "Perhaps not. I loved him too much to know him."

Rory started. "Did you . . . date?"

"We were together for a while." The abbess stared out at nothing, her face wistful. "I would have done anything for him. His name was Morgan when I first met him. Morgan Green. That is the name I call him in my head. I fell for him immediately. He had such a way about him, so kind and wise. I had made many mistakes in my past and been around some rough men, so I appreciated his gentle manner. I didn't know at the time how prone he was to flight. He loved me in his way, but never enough, and finally, he left me. I pursued him for a while, a good hundred years I'd say, through at least four different identities, but he could never give me what I wanted. So eventually I retreated here to found my abbey, and he would visit on his way out to sea. I knew he was running from something, for he made me promise never to reveal any of his names, especially Harry Meester. I see by your face that you know that one. I helped him all I could, for I could not stop loving him, and I still do. We became great friends. But he could never truly love me. That he reserved for your mother."

"Come on," Rory said, disbelieving. "He left her alone with two kids to feed. How is that love?"

"Like I said, he is a weak man. But I could tell by his face on that day eight years ago. He was leaving his true love behind, and it killed him."

"Then why did he do it!" Rory cried.

"You will have to ask him that," the abbess replied. "I don't have the answer. We were very close, but I never knew much about him. I cannot tell you why he did the things he did. I can only tell you where he is now."

"Where is that?" Rory asked, overwhelmed.

"Headed due east. The ghost ship is heading out to sea once again. He passed by here not three days ago. The *Half Moon* is not in good shape, so you might be able to catch him if you can find yourself a fast ship. But you'll have to be quick to—"

A cry in the hall interrupted her, followed by a crash. The abbess sprang to her feet. Rory felt fear gnaw its way into his belly.

"Maybe you shouldn't go out there," he warned her.

"You remain here," she said. "I'll be right back."

Rory couldn't bear the thought of waiting, so he followed the abbess out into the hall. They heard yelling and cries for help. The abbess began to run, until she spied something ahead. Her hand flew to her mouth in shock. Peering around her, Rory saw a body on the ground; it was a nun, barely moving.

"Sister Patience!" the abbess cried, running forward.

"Wait!" Rory whispered, following her carefully. His heart pounded as he came nearer. The nun lay in front of the door to the room where his friends waited. But there wasn't much of a door left. It had been hacked to pieces. Yelling and crying came from inside the room. Rory peered around the door frame.

Inside, he was greeted by a chaotic sight. Alexa clung to the back of a hulking man, who waved his knives back and forth, trying to slice everything that moved. It was Bill the Butcher,

Rory realized with a sick feeling in his stomach. Somehow the killer had found him. Simon sat quivering in the corner, a cleaver buried an inch from his head, half his hair sliced off onto the floor. As Rory watched, Bill threw Alexa off his back, sending her slamming into the stone wall; she fell in a senseless heap. Fritz's tiny form raced in front of her, tossing firecrackers at Bill's feet to no avail. Bill raised his cleaver.

"Where is he?" he bellowed.

"We'll never tell you anything!" Fritz cried, tossing another firecracker. Bill roared and brought the cleaver down toward the defiant battle roach.

"NO!" Rory cried. But he needn't have worried; Fritz easily leaped aside, missing the blade by a hairbreadth. Rory's cry had given Bill a new target, however: him.

"There you are, boy." Bill smiled. Rory blanched at his sickly grin. "I've been looking for you."

"You will not touch him, ruffian," the abbess announced, stepping in front of Rory. Bill began to laugh.

"You're gonna stop me? A little girl like you?" He stepped forward with cleaver held high, ready to cut her down where she stood. The abbess did not flinch.

"Sisters!" she cried, stepping aside. "Defend our house!"

A group of nuns raced by her into the room, rushing Bill. With a cry, he disappeared under a sea of habits as more and more nuns poured in to subdue the intruder. The abbess turned to Rory.

"Run! Quickly! We can't hold him forever. Find your father! Tell him Mary Burton still thinks of him! Go!"

Rory ran forward and helped up Alexa, who was still shaken

from her meeting with the wall. He turned to Simon, yanking the frightened boy to his feet.

"Come on!" Rory yelled, spurring them to action. Behind them, with a Herculean effort, Bill roared to his feet, tossing off nuns as if they were leaves.

"You're not goin' nowhere, Rory Hennessy!" He lunged forward with his cleaver in hand. Rory watched him come, unable to move. The cleaver descended, heading directly for his neck. But it never landed there.

Thwack.

The abbess staggered back into him, the cleaver sticking out of her chest. She'd leaped in front of Rory and taken the blow meant for him. She slid to the ground, staring up at Rory.

"Go . . ." she whispered, and her eyes closed as she went still. The nuns stood still for a moment, stunned, and then they roared into action, pummeling Bill into the ground until he disappeared under a flurry of habits. The abbess's last word still hung in the air. *Go.*

Terrified, Rory ran for it, followed by Alexa and Simon, the former carrying Fritz in her hand. They raced through the stone halls of the convent and out the front door into the fog, swerving around the mist-shrouded trees as they made their way toward the dock. Finally, they reached the boat, which had been joined by a second vessel tied up right beside it. Rory ran up to the second boat and ripped the sail right off the mast with strength born of terror. Anything to make sure Bill could not follow.

They piled into their boat and pushed off the dock as Alexa quickly hoisted the sail. The wind picked up and they had begun to move away from the shore when a scream of pure fury shook them all to the bone.

Bill burst out of the trees to race down the dock, a hulking mess of a man barreling toward them with unstoppable force. He bled from numerous wounds, but he did not slow. Reaching the end of the dock, he launched through the air at the boat, grabbing at the mast. He just missed, but he managed to wrap his hand around one of the lines as he flew by, and the weight of his falling body brought the boat dangerously close to capsizing as he splashed into the ocean.

"He's going to kill us all!" Simon cried, pulling out a knife to hack at the rope.

"No, Simon!" Alexa cried, trying to stop him, but Simon's fear could not be contained. He severed line after line, sending the entire sail fluttering into the sea. Letting go of his rope, Bill tried to swim toward the boat, but it became obvious that he did not know how. His fury turned to fear as the waves began to crash over him, pushing him under. He struggled to stay afloat, cursing at Rory, safe in the boat, but the cause was a losing one, and finally, Bill the Butcher sank beneath the waves.

They all fell back against the side of the boat, exhausted. Glancing back, Rory noticed that the current had pulled the boat far from Swinburne Island, dragging them deeper into the mist. Alexa stared daggers at Simon.

"All you had to do was cut the one line he was tangled up in," she said angrily. "Why did you have to cut them all?"

"I didn't want him to get me—I mean, us," Simon muttered, his face still ashen.

"You are such a coward!" she shouted back. Simon didn't

answer, sitting miserably at the bottom of the boat. Fritz put up a calming hand.

"Let's simmer down," he said. "We need to figure out what to do now."

"Well, we've got no sail and we've got no oars and the current is taking us away from land," Alexa said, counting their troubles off on her hand. "If we try to swim, we'll most likely be dragged to the bottom of the ocean. So in reality we've got one option: float."

And float they did, out into the mist.

Hours seemed to pass as they drifted through the thick fog. Finally, Rory lost his temper.

"*CRAP!*" he shouted into the void. Alexa snorted.

"Feel better?" she asked.

"AHOY THERE!" a voice called out from the mist. Rory exchanged shocked looks with his fellow castaways.

"HELLO!" he shouted back. The others joined him in shouting, until a ship came gliding out of the fog. ADVENTURE GALLEY it read on the bow. A familiar face leaned out over the rail; it was Captain Kidd himself. His eyes twinkled as he called down to them.

"Need a hand?"

NORTHWARD BOUND

Night had fallen over the Munsee village. Bridget sat cross-legged at the mouth of Chogan's cave, slowly petting Tucket's soft fur as he lay at her feet. She stared up at the stars, so brilliant in the moonless sky. It was the sky of a world without electricity, and its beauty awed her. Around her, fires crackled in the other caves, as did the large fire pit in the center of the village. Chogan had mentioned that during times of feasting, there was dancing around the fire pit, but there would be no dancing tonight. A hushed murmer of conversation floated by from the Munsees sitting around the fires, and she knew they spoke about her.

A council was under way inside one of the longhouses that would decide Soka's fate. Earlier, while Bridget had watched from a distance, some of Tackapausha's loyal warriors had marched Soka into the longhouse. Then a voice had whispered Bridget's name from behind her, making her almost jump out of her paper skin. It was Askook, sneaking up to watch his people getting ready for the trial.

"I see you worry, demon," he had hissed, the snake tattoos on his cheeks writhing. "You should worry for yourself. Your very soul is in danger. It drips out of you. Drip drip. I would very much like to drink it up."

Askook had grinned, and his smile dripped madness.

"You're a sicko!" Bridget said, shuddering as she backed away. "How can everyone not see that?"

"Maybe they do and they don't care," Askook had said, shrugging. "I tell Tackapausha how to make his dream of revenge come true. He does not care about the rest." He stepped forward, prompting Bridget to stagger back. "I shall make you my special project. There must be some way to open you up like a nut. Soka is not so powerful with the magical arts. I would like to cut you open and see what happens to your soul. Will it stay trapped in here with us? Will it fly away? Can I imprison it in something a bit sturdier than that paper body you wear? Or should I just devour it? We will find out together, you and I."

"You stay away from me!" Bridget cried as the snake-tattood man took another dangerous step toward her. Suddenly Askook looked past her.

"The council begins and I must join in," he said. He gave her a nasty smile. "I am watching you. I can see you wherever you go. Perhaps I will just crack you open like an oyster and eat you whole. We will see."

It had taken hours for Bridget to stop shivering. Even now, she kept thinking she could see Askook's face leering out at her from the shadows. She needed to get out of here, she decided.

"It sickens me to see what our elder council has become," Chogan said, stepping up beside her to poke the fire emphatically with a stick, sending embers flying through the air like lightning bugs. Tucket's head reared up to stalk this new prey, snapping at the tiny fires as they floated by. "We used to be governed by many equal voices. Your people learned much of their democracy from us, after all. It worked so well: Penhawitz was sachem, overseeing the day-to-day needs of the tribe, and Tackapausha was war leader, leading the hunt and all things war. But then Tackapausha had to seize control, forcing his own father out for being short on revenge. It was a disgrace! There is a reason we separate the defense of the tribe from the government; they require very different men, with very different strengths. But now we just have the one sachem, and our whole world is out of balance."

"What happened to Penhawitz, anyway?"

"He left," Chogan said, clearly frustrated. "No one knows where he went. We've heard of sightings from everywhere from the Ravine to Seneca Village."

"What's Seneca Village? Another Indian settlement?"

"No, it's a newcomer town a little ways north of here. We often trade with them. It's filled with the spirits of your people. After all, we Munsees weren't the only ones locked up in this Trap."

"What do you mean? I thought only the Munsees were caught in here."

"Oh no," Chogan said. "Any spirit inside the park when the blue barrier rose up was trapped. Many of the giant beasts that used to roam this land in ancient times had wandered down to the park, attracted by the new wilderness. They, too, are in here with us—plaguing us. And some of your people, the Mayor's own subjects, were living here when the Trap was sprung. Seneca Village was home to many of them; they reside there still, unable to leave, just like the rest of us. Your mayor didn't only hurt us; he hurt his own people."

A new voice piped up from the area of their ankles.

"There you are! You are harder to find than my helmet when I'm late! I've been searching all day! Finally, I had to set my homing device to 'paper.' Not easy."

Looking down, Bridget spied a familiar sight: a roach making its way across the ground. Tucket turned his attention away from the flying embers with a happy yip, eager to play with this new toy. The roach lifted his arm and sprayed the dog on the snout, sending Tucket away with a whine.

"Take that, you big brute!" the roach said.

"Hans!" Bridget said, delighted.

"Sorry about that," the roach said, continuing toward Bridget, leaving the dog sneezing in its wake. "It's just pheromones; they won't hurt him. I developed them to keep him from smelling us when we trailed Rory." The roach reached up to lift off his helmet, revealing a youthful, smiling face.

"It's a Wemetaken'is! One of the little people!" Chogan sat up in excitement.

"Hey!" Hans warned him. "I'm no little person, okay, Captain Sweatstain? I'm a battle roach."

"What are you doing here?" Bridget asked.

"Fritz sent me to look after you. Though you look like you're doing all right so far . . ."

"That will change." Sooleawa stepped into the firelight, Soka behind her. Soka looked chastised, and she held her mother's hand tightly. "Even now, Tackapausha is thinking of ways to use you, Bridget, to get to your brother. That is why he is giving you the illusion of freedom; it keeps you here in the village."

"Well, I don't think I want to stay here anymore," Bridget said. "Not with that Askook creep sneaking around. What happened with you, Soka? Are you all right?"

Soka nodded, then looked to her mother. Sooleawa's eyes burned in the firelight.

"They are deliberating on her punishment now. It was only through my influence that I was able to convince them to let me take her to wash. Foolish. Do they truly think I will stand by while they banish my daughter, my beloved Sokanon?" Her eyes flashed in the firelight.

"Mother, I will face my fate. I am not afraid," Soka said quietly.

"*I* am afraid!" Sooleawa exclaimed. "Afraid of what that worm Askook will do when no one is watching. I must stay here, to be the voice of reason to counter Tackapausha's drive for revenge. But you, Bridget, you can take my daughter and go after the woman you came to find. Not only is she Hamilton's daughter, but Tackapausha loved her as his own. She might be the only one who could talk sense into him. The hope is slim, but it is all we have."

"I don't want to leave you, Mother," Soka said. Sooleawa cupped her chin with one hand.

"I am fine," she said, smiling at her daughter. "Head north, toward the Great Hill, and see if you can find any trace of her. Seneca is the gateway to the north; you would do well to try to pick up her trail there."

"Don't worry, Soka," Bridget assured the Munsee girl. "This won't take too long. Central Park is only so big, right?"

Sooleawa, Soka, and Chogan all shook their heads at this with a smile.

"You have no idea," Soka said.

Less than an hour later, Bridget and her companions sneaked away from the Munsee village under the cover of night. As they made their way through the shadowy forest, gradually leaving the flickering fires of the settlement behind, Bridget caught a glimpse of Soka's face in the starlight. The Munsee girl was crying silently in the dark.

"It'll be okay," Bridget whispered. "We'll be back before you know it and everyone will see you were right. I promise."

"I hope so," Soka replied, wiping her eyes. "I never wanted to hurt my people. And now they want to kick me out."

"Rory will bring down the Trap and make everything all right," Bridget promised. "You'll see. He can do anything. Anyway, no one wants to kick you out. Just Tackapausha, and that Askook weirdo. And Abigail will set them straight. We're all good, okay?"

"Okay." Soka sniffed, then set her shoulders. "Then let's move quickly. We want to get there soon, before my people realize we're missing. Mother promised to leave a false trail that leads south toward the fountain, so that should grant us a little time."

"I think we better keep the chatter down, then, so we don't spoil all her hard work by being loudmouths," Hans said from his spot in Bridget's pocket. "Let's keep our focus on the trail so no one trips and flattens a poor battle roach who's just along for the ride, okay?"

Soka picked up the pace, leading Bridget and Tucket through

the trees as quickly as she dared. Bridget was glad she had a paper body; if she'd been flesh and blood, she'd be wheezing like an old lady. Soka didn't seem to feel the effects; she kept soldiering on, her face stone.

They continued to make their way north, passing the Great Lawn on their right. Bridget opened her mouth to ask why they didn't try running through that open field rather than falling over themselves in the dense trees, but then a giant shadow swooped across the meadow, dropping down from above to grab something before flying off. Bridget's mouth remained open in surprise as Soka gave her an amused glance.

"Giant owl," Soka whispered. "Feeding on a deer, I believe. Just keep to the trees and don't act too deerlike, and you should be fine."

Soka led onward. Eventually, they left the Great Lawn behind, and finally, Soka pulled up by a small group of bushes around a huge elm. She pushed them aside to reveal a hollow hidden from the trail.

"We'll spend the rest of the night here," she announced, climbing on hands and knees into the brush. Bridget dropped down to follow her, wincing as the branches scraped her paper skin. She hoped she wasn't leaving behind any wood shavings. Once Tucket climbed into the hollow, Soka let the bushes fall back, hiding them from sight in their tiny hole at the base of the tree.

"Do the others know about this spot?" Hans asked, stretching after his confinement to Bridget's pocket.

"No, this is my place," Soka replied. "I come here to think sometimes. Preparing to be a medicine woman takes a lot of hard thinking."

As if to prove it, Soka leaned back against the tree and closed her eyes. She seemed so serious it made Bridget sad. She missed the twinkle-eyed girl she'd first met. She bet Rory would restore that twinkle, a thought that made Bridget smile. Maybe they'd get married and have little half-serious/half-twinkly babies. *Eww.* She'd gone too far in her daydreaming and grossed herself out.

She closed her eyes, though she knew she wouldn't really sleep. Maybe she'd keep one eye open, for giant owls. This park was far more dangerous than she'd ever imagined.

SENECA VILLAGE

Askook knelt down in the dirt beneath the tall chestnut trees not far from the Munsee village. He didn't expect to be stumbled upon, but it would not harm him if someone were to happen by. The eerie sight of what he was about to do would only help his dangerous reputation. After all, without fear, where would he be?

Most of Tackapausha's warriors had headed south, following a path Askook suspected to be false. Probably laid by that witch, Sooleawa. He'd often wondered how she'd managed to hold onto her magic after being cut off from the land. Their people's powers came from the island itself, and most of the other Munsees had diminished since the Trap had denied them the source of their magic. Before, even that fat fool Chogan had been able to turn into a blackbird now and again. But since the Trap, Tackapausha himself could barely do basic magic, and that was with the help of his War Leader's belt. Yet somehow Sooleawa and her daughter managed to call on an impressive amount of power. Maybe after the coming slaughter, Askook would save the medicine woman for some pointed questions. He ran his finger over the blade of the knife in his hand. He looked forward to that conversation.

The Trap could not deny him his power, however. He felt around with his mind. There it was—the hole in the Trap made just for him. Kieft had promised to give him power in exchange for his help, and the black-eyed god had not disappointed him, burrowing a hole in the barrier surrounding the park for his exclusive use. Askook drew magic through the hole and guided it into the flint knife in his hand. Time to find out what Soka and the demon girl were up to.

Once the knife was glowing, he opened the sack at his side, pulling out a squirming rabbit. A quick slice later, a small pool of blood gathered at his feet, infused with the magic from the blade. Tossing aside the hare's still body, Askook peered intently into the red pool, searching. And gradually, familiar forms began to take shape. Soka and the demon girl lay hidden in a hollow, somewhere north of the Ramble. He had an idea of where they were going, a thought that caused a slow grin to spread across his eager face. This was going to be fun . . .

The night had passed uneventfully, though Bridget thought she had heard a shout at one point, somewhere in the distance. But no one came by their hidden spot. Finally, the sky brightened as the morning light trickled down through the trees above, sending little leaf-shaped shadows dancing across the ground. Somewhere, a rooster crowed, a sound Bridget had only heard on television. Soka roused herself, as did Hans, who couldn't find his helmet for a moment and panicked before realizing he'd been leaning against it the whole time. Springing to his feet, Tucket went to work licking Bridget's arm.

"I'm already awake, doofus." She laughed.

"Everyone ready?" Soka asked. "We need to be careful at Seneca Village, in case Tackapausha sent scouts this way. Come on."

She led them out of the brush and back onto the path. As they walked under the trees, which glowed softly in the early morning light, Soka told Bridget and Hans the story of Seneca Village. Settled by free blacks in the early nineteenth century in then-rural upper Manhattan, Seneca soon became home as well to Irish, Germans, and other European immigrants, making the small village one of the few places at the time where blacks and whites lived together in peace. The village had its own school, its own churches, and its own farms, the different races mixing together peacefully in a way unheard of throughout the rest of the United States. It wasn't to last, however, as the city officials downtown began to eye their land for the new park they were planning. The citizens of Seneca Village were evicted by Manhattan City Hall, and their home of the past third of a century was razed to make way for Central Park. The memory of Seneca Village remained, however, as did the spirits of many of the inhabitants, so when the Trap to imprison the Munsees was sprung, the unlucky souls in Seneca found themselves trapped as well. But they made the best of it, living out their lives as they had done before, farming the land, working together in peace, and welcoming all who showed up at their doorstep.

They reached the tree line; Seneca lay just ahead. Hans decided to stay out of sight; no reason for attracting undue attention. Once he was well situated in Bridget's pocket, they stepped out of the trees and Bridget caught her first glimpse of Seneca Village.

The small town was nestled under a tall mound of stone Soka referred to as Summit Rock. Well-kept clapboard houses lined a few dirt streets, one of which contained a group of children playing some kind of stickball. She could see small plots of land behind the houses where crops were laid out in neat rows, while small pens held pigs, goats, and chickens. The town was bustling as it awoke, with people out and about bidding good morning to their neighbors as they went about their errands. Bridget spied people of many different nationalities and races, and everyone seemed on friendly terms. A bell rang from the steeple of a church in the center of the small town. All in all, it seemed like a nice place to live.

A small commotion on the porch of a house nearby alerted them that they had been noticed. A tall black man in a smart, old-fashioned suit and wide-brimmed hat waved at them, smiling widely.

"Soka! Mighty good to see you! It's been a long time!"

"Yes, it has, Mayor Williams," Soka replied, a little of the sparkle returning to her eyes at the warmth of her welcome as she led them to meet the mayor. "Bridget, this is Mayor Williams."

"You can call me Andy," Mayor Williams replied, shaking Bridget's hand briskly. He laughed as Tucket tried to jump up on him, and gave the great dog a brisk pat on the head. "This brute is a high-spirited pup, ain't he. Is this your dog, Bridget?"

"I guess," Bridget replied. "His name is Tucket."

"Strong name for a strong dog," Mayor Williams said.

"Are you here to trade, Soka? We've gotten some goods from the soldiers at Fort Clinton just last week, if you want to take a gander."

"Actually, we're looking for information," Soka said as Mayor Williams walked them toward the center of town. People watched as they passed, but they didn't seem overly interested. They obviously had visitors here all the time. "I'm looking for a woman who passed through here about a hundred and fifty years ago."

"My word!" Mayor Williams cocked his head. "You don't mess around. That's quite some time ago."

"Her name was Abigail!" Bridget jumped in. "Or Olathe. Do you remember her?"

Mayor Williams's eyes suddenly went blank and he looked away. "Why, no. Sorry, I never heard of her."

Soka and Bridget exchanged glances. Something strange was going on here.

"Really?" Bridget said. "Because you sure do look like you remember something."

"Sorry," Mayor Williams said, still not looking at them. "It was quite some time ago."

"Mayor Williams, you are acting odd," Soka said. "Is something wrong?"

"No," Mayor Williams replied, making a big show of shaking his head. "Just sorry I couldn't help you."

"Andy," Bridget said, her voice dripping with camaraderie as she lightly punched him in the arm. "Andy, Andy, Andy. Come on, it's us. Your old friend Soka and your new, bestest friend, Bridget. You can tell us anything."

"I'm telling you everthing I know," Mayor Williams said.

He turned to an old woman sewing on the porch nearby. "Georgia? Ever heard of a lady called Abigail? Or Olathe, for that matter?"

"No, sir," Georgia replied promptly, then went back to her yarn. Mayor Williams turned to others passing by and asked them the same question; they all quickly answered no, as if they'd been rehearsed.

"I'm sorry," Mayor Williams said finally. "We just don't remember her."

"I certainly can see that," Soka replied sarcastically.

"Well, good luck to you, Soka," Mayor Williams said, turning away. "It's time for church, so I will have to take my leave. Enjoy the rest of this fine morning!"

He hurried off, joining the group of villagers making their way down the street. Most of them poured into a large church in the center of town, the source of the tolling bell, but some made their way into another, simpler church next door, while the rest crossed the street to yet a third church.

"That's a lot of churches," Bridget observed. "You'd think they'd be too Goody Two-shoes to lie."

"What was with him, anyway?" Hans asked, popping out of Bridget's pocket.

"He's trying to protect a friend," someone said behind them. They spun around and came face-to-face with the most handsome teenager Bridget had ever seen. *If this guy were on the Disney Channel, he'd be up on my wall,* she thought. He had dusky skin, curly hair, and blue, almond-shaped eyes. He was the very definition of the word *hunk,* and the way he stood there, so cocky and sure of himself, Bridget could tell he knew it. Beside her, Soka shifted nervously, suddenly unsure of herself.

"How do you know?" Bridget asked the boy, since Soka didn't seem capable of talking.

"Because I was there when he and the whole town promised to your uncle Penhawitz not to tell anyone about Olathe or that he was searching for her," he said.

"Penhawitz is behind this?" Soka asked. "I didn't know he was looking for Olathe."

"Well, he and Mayor Andy are old friends," the boy said, smiling at Soka. "He used to come around here all the time. Once, a few decades back, he beat off a crazed mastodon who was terrorizing the town and they've been grateful ever since."

"What's a mastodon?" Bridget asked, her imagination running wild.

"Giant elephant with huge tusks," the boy told her. "They mostly stay up on the Great Hill, where they live, but sometimes an avalanche or the like will send them stampeding into more civilized lands."

"Awesome!" Bridget said, hoping she'd get to see a mastodon someday.

"Anyway, when Penhawitz showed up a little over a year ago," the boy continued, "Seneca Village was more than happy to cover his tracks. I guess he was afraid of who might come looking for him."

"But I'm his niece!" Soka protested.

"No one was to know," the boy said, shrugging. "Sorry."

"So why are you telling us this?" Soka asked. "Aren't you breaking your promise, Mr. . . . ?"

"Finn Lee," the boy said, inclining his head. "Blame my grandfather. He saw the commotion from his window, and once

he heard your name and who you were looking for, he sent me
to invite you to meet him. Come on, he'll explain everything."

Finn led them to his house, a small shack the size of Bridget's apartment. Inside, the shack was darkened by the closed
shutters, with only small slices of light cutting up the shadows.
The place reminded Bridget of an old antiques store, and not
the upscale kind. Furs hung on the walls, lanterns lay in a heap
on the floor, and old muskets were piled up in the corner. Beside a rickety old table, an old man sat in an overstuffed chair.
He wheezed as he watched the two girls with the dog step into
his house. His grandson rushed to his side, but the old man
waved him off.

"I'm fine, I'm fine," he muttered in a thick French accent.
"Leave me be, boy. So you're Soka. I've heard a lot about you
from your uncle. And who is your companion?"

"Hello, sir," Bridget said, bowing extravagantly. "My name
is Bridget and that is my dog, Tucket. Don't worry, he's house-
trained. Or at least, he was in my house. And this . . ."

"What's that in your pocket?" the old man cried suddenly,
his voice cracking. "A foul insect!"

"Wait, wait, don't panic!" Hans said, pulling off his helmet as he climbed out of Bridget's pocket. "I'm just a battle
roach."

The old man shuddered. "You'll have to excuse me. I've got
a thing about insects. No offense, little one."

"It's understandable," Hans replied. "I wig myself out
sometimes."

"Is that everyone?" the man asked, looking around. "Don't
lie to me. I may look broken down, but my eyes are keen. I am
merely injured, sorely injured, and I may never recover."

"That's not true, Granddad," Finn assured him, but the old man waved him off.

"I don't lie to myself, either. The wound I took would have killed most men, so I count myself lucky to have surived at all. Let it not be said that Pierre Duchamp is easily felled!"

"What hurt you?" Bridget asked, fascinated.

"One of the most dangerous of creatures to be found in the high reaches of the Great Hill," Pierre declared. "The giant squirrel!"

Bridget fought back a giggle. Pierre's eyes narrowed.

"You think I am lying? You think something as puny as a coyote or bear did this to me? It was a giant squirrel, I swear it."

"I'm sorry, I didn't think there were such things as giant squirrels," Bridget said, fighting down the laughter.

"There is a wealth of such creatures atop the Great Hill! Giant bears and cougars and wolves and spiders and mastodons and snow beetles and, of course, squirrels. It is no laughing matter. It takes great bravery to climb the Great Hill without a dozen warriors at your side."

"What exactly is going on here, anyway?" Soka asked. "Who are you and where is my uncle?"

"Who am I?" Pierre asked. "In my mortal life, I was a trapper. I came to these shores to hunt for beaver pelts. There wasn't a beaver who could hear me coming, I promise you this. Nor a human, for that matter! I would come to this city back when it was New Amsterdam, and there were actual animals in the surrounding wilderness to trap. The beavers are all gone now, sadly, but I stayed, and have since called Mannahatta my home. I was visiting McGown's Tavern up by the pass with some of my fellow trapper spirits when the Great Trap was sprung. I have been stuck here ever since, of course. I came to Seneca, met a beautiful African princess of a woman, and built her this house. She's where Finn gets his good looks. Well, her and his dad, who was a half-Italian, half-Chinese farmer. Of course he knows it. Don't shake your head, Finn. You are a good boy, but you are too pretty for your own good. Where was I?"

"You built this house . . ." Finn said, not fazed by his grandfather's words.

"Yes. And after my wife fell to a sinkhole in the Ravine, I spent most of my days here. A little over a year ago, Penhawitz showed up, searching for poor Olathe's trail. He didn't think she was still alive, of course, but he was interested in what secrets Olathe had been seeking. The trail was a hundred and fifty years cold, but that didn't bother him. He asked around everywhere before I heard what he was looking for and decided to help him. It was the least I could for the memory of that poor girl."

"You knew Abigail, too?" Bridget asked, leaning in.

"Course I did," Pierre exclaimed. "Who do you think it was who led her north when she came to Seneca Village looking for a guide in the weeks after the Trap was sprung? I didn't tell anyone at the time, since why was it their business? She asked for secrecy, just as Penhawitz did a hundred and fifty years later, and I gave it to both of them."

"Then why are you telling us?" Soka asked.

"Because I know Penhawitz loves you," the old man said. "He'd want you to know."

"Where did you take Abigail?" Hans asked.

"North, to the Great Hill. Nasty business, the Great Hill.

Steep and wild and covered in snow. Giant animals out for blood behind every rock and up every tree. And the weather! It'd be bright sun one minute and then blizzard the next. A man could get lost forever on that terrible mountain, or eaten alive, or worse. But she wanted to follow someone's trail—she never did tell me whose—so I led her up the mountain, picked up the trail and followed it to the mouth of a cave. But out of nowhere a fierce blizzard blew up, almost as if someone had left behind some magic to keep people away from that cave and we'd triggered it. I couldn't see two feet in front of me. Olathe and I became separated in the storm and I couldn't find her or the cave in the blinding snow. I wandered through the white for hours until the storm passed, and by then I was shocked to discover I was halfway back down the mountain. I tried to re-trace my steps to find Olathe, but I could find no trace of her, or that cave. It was as if they both had been erased completely from the mountain. I never saw her again."

"She survived the storm," Bridget said, hopping in excitement. "And she saw what was in that cave!"

"How could you possibly know that?" Pierre exclaimed, leaning forward.

Bridget explained about how Abigail had discovered the cave only to be chased by someone across the park, leaving behind her wampum necklace to tell the tale. Pierre's eyes filled with tears at the story.

"I had hoped, but I never knew . . ." Pierre whispered. "I have to confess, I asked Finn to bring you to me so I could warn you away from following Olathe's trail. I believed whatever signs remained of her or that cave had been lost long ago. I only agreed to take Penhawitz to the mountain because I felt like I owed the girl one last attempt to find her final resting place. But that ended in this damned injury."

"Because of the giant squirrel," Bridget said, still skeptical.

"Don't mock! I led Penhawitz up that mountain just as I did Olathe so many years before. The trail was long cold, of course, but I remembered certain features, like the dragon rock and the craggly tree. Finn knows, I've told him all about it. But I couldn't find the ruby icefall. It was the last thing I remembered before the blizzard swallowed me up: a wall of red-colored rock covered in a sheet of ice, under which flowed an eternal waterfall. It was the most beautiful thing I'd ever seen. But I couldn't find it again. So we were stopped at a fork in the trail, sitting in the snow trying to figure out what to do next, when we were attacked by a vicious giant squirrel. Penhawitz saved me, fighting the animal off before it could eat me whole, but I was sorely injured. He helped me back down the mountain, leaving me at McGown's Tavern. Then he set off again. And that's the last time I saw him. I came home to recuperate, though it's been slow going this past year. And now you're here."

"Can you show us the trail on a map?" Soka asked excitedly.

"I could, but I won't," Pierre replied firmly. "Even if Olathe truly did survive the blizzard, who says you will? And how will you find her trail when I, one of the best trackers in the park, could not uncover it? No, I will not send two girls out to die."

"We're going whether you help us or not," Bridget said firmly. "She's too important for us to turn back now."

"I won't be a party to putting you in such danger." He sounded so certain that Bridget's spirits sank.

"I'll take them." Finn stepped forward. "I've heard your

story enough to know the way up the Great Hill. I've been north with you up to its base, many times."

"You think you can find a trail I couldn't, boy?" Pierre asked, his eyes flashing.

"Probably not." Finn smiled at Soka. "But these ladies seem determined. I'd rather be there to help if I could. Such pretty faces need to be protected from harm."

Soka blushed and Bridget realized that the boy was flirting with her. With Soka! Rory's almost girlfriend! That just wasn't right!

"I'm stronger than I look," she said, stepping between Soka and Finn. "Just give me the directions and we'll be out of your hair."

"No, if you must go, then I will send Finn with you," Pierre decided. "But when you find what I found—nothing—he'll escort you right off that mountain again. It's too dangerous up there to linger in a vain hope to find what I know is gone forever."

"Thank you for this, Finn," Soka said, her eyes smiling for the first time since Askook had stepped out of the trees by the fountain. Finn grinned right back and Bridget gritted her teeth. Rory was off saving the world and there was no one to look after his almost girlfriend. Bridget would have to make sure this pretty boy didn't steal Soka's heart. Sensing Bridget's mood, Tucket growled at Finn, who took a step back from the bristling animal. Bridget gave the dog a pat.

"Good boy. Hold that thought."

19

INTO THE MIST

Sly Jimmy had come up in the world. He adjusted his top hat and spun his shiny new knife in his hand. Ever since he'd hooked up with Boss Tweed, life had been gravy. Tweed had first come to Jimmy about sending his gang, the B'wry Boys, out on little missions of mayhem. Dressed as Indians, they laid waste to all kinds of places across the island: taverns and houses and shops and the like. They were a regular Munsee crime wave. Jimmy didn't know why Tweed wanted people to think Indians were busting up stuff, but so long as Jimmy and his boys were paid, they were glad to slather on the war paint and whoop it up all over town.

The other talent Jimmy possessed besides a knack for mischief was a sense for who was in charge. Boss Tweed was the most powerful god on the streets, sending his boys out on crime sprees while putting on a veneer of respectability with his place on the Council of Twelve. God of Rabble Politics, he called himself. More like the God of Two Faces. Jimmy had been a smart cookie to hitch his wagon to the ambitious god, and so far it had paid dividends, and how. Just a month earlier he'd been hanging out on street corners looking to mug passing strangers. Now he was summoned to the boss's office for a very special meeting all by himself, without his boys. This could only mean big things. He smiled to himself. Really big things.

Sly Jimmy easily navigated the back alleys of Five Points, heading toward Tweed's office. The most crime-ridden slum of the nineteenth century, Five Points had long ago been paved over and made respectable. But hidden in the alleys and side streets of the new neighborhood lay the dives and dens of old gang-infested New York. If a fellow wasn't careful, he'd have his throat slit before he could say Jack Robinson. Jimmy spun the knife in his hand, not too worried; he was a careful sort of fellow.

Jimmy reached the old pub where Boss Tweed held court, making his way through to the back room, where Tweed awaited him. He pushed through the door without knocking, swaggering as he prepared to give an insolent hello. Instead, he was shocked to find a knife at his own throat. Terrified, he spied Tweed sitting at his desk, his big, full beard twitching with amusement.

"Haven't you heard of knocking, boy?" Tweed said merrily, though his eyes didn't smile one bit. Jimmy felt the knife pull away from his throat and he spun to face his attacker. He recognized the boy in front of him; his name was Sammy "Two Blade" Liu since he always carried a pair of knives. He was a member of the Four Brothers Tong, one of the many mortal enemies of the B'wry Boys, and Jimmy opened his mouth to challenge him to a fight. But then he noticed Sammy's eyes; they spun in their sockets like pinwheels. Jimmy staggered back away as he realized that Sammy was possessesd.

"Have a seat, Jimmy," Sammy said, but the voice wasn't Sammy's; it was deeper and much, much older. Truly scared now, Jimmy sat heavily in a chair in front of Tweed's desk. Sammy sat across from him, his eyes still rolling around.

"Who are you?" Jimmy demanded.

"That's not important, Jimmy, you know that," Tweed admonished him. "What's important is that our friend here has a job for you and your merry band of Indians."

"What job?" Jimmy didn't know if he wanted to do a job for this scary creature, but something told him he didn't have much of a choice.

"You've done your work well, Jimmy," the voice inside Sammy congratulated him. "People are more frightened of the Munsees than they've been in more than a century. And now that Mr. Stuyvesant has gone ill . . ."

"I get ya," Jimmy said. "People are saying that the only ones left to protect us from the Munsees are the Mayor and Mr. Kieft. Even though not everyone likes it, beggin' your pardon."

"Why would I be offended?" the voice inside Sammy said. "So everything is going to plan, that foolish song notwithstanding."

"I hate that song," Jimmy said. "It gets stuck in your head and never leaves. And who cares if somebody fell in love with a dirty Indian? Some people fall in love with goats, or so I heard."

"That's the spirit," the voice in Sammy said. "We need more of that around here."

"I told Mr.—" Tweed glanced at Sammy, stopping himself. "I told our friend here about how much you want to help."

"Here is what I need," the voice in Sammy said. "I need one final act of terror to set the stage for the big show. I need a murder."

"A murder?" Jimmy shrugged. "Is that all? Who do you want me to kill?"

"It's not who, so much as how," the voice in Sammy continued. "I need you and your friends to be Munsees for the night, as you do so well. And as Munsees, you'll ransack the house and kill whoever is inside. But most of all, I need you to kill one person, and I need you to make it messy. I want the entire city in an outrage."

"Who?" Jimmy asked, eyes gleaming. Maybe he could work with this guy after all.

"Nicholas Stuyvesant."

Rory wiped the spray from his eyes, peering intently into the black mist that surrounded him. He believed that they'd been sailing for over a day, though the fog made it impossible to tell day from night. Lanterns glowed along the deck, sending faint tendrils of light floating out into the fog, but nothing could pierce the dark beyond the bow. He felt like their ship was the only one in the whole world. How were they going to find his dad in this mess?

"I think your friend up there has a death wish," said a voice behind him. Rory turned to see Captain Kidd strolling across the foredeck toward him, pointing to the mast. Fritz was up at the top, in the crow's nest, staring out into the black.

"He's just keeping a lookout," Rory replied. "I wanted to go up there, but he wouldn't let me. He said he'd do it for me."

"He looks out for you, doesn't he," Kidd said. Rory nodded. He didn't know where he'd be without Fritz.

"How can you tell we're going the right way?" Rory asked.

"I've been sailing into the mist for centuries, boy," Kidd said, smiling. He always seemed to smile. "I know as well as anyone how to make my way. You asked me to find the *Half Moon,* and we will find it."

"What if we miss them in the fog?" That was Rory's biggest worry, seeing as they couldn't see ten feet in front of the boat. But Kidd simply smiled wider.

"Don't you worry," he said, his bared teeth glinting in the lamplight. "I know how to find ships in the open water. Some might call that my specialty."

Alexa stepped out onto the deck from below. Kidd bowed.

"I trust your quarters are sufficient?" he said, winking at her. Alexa blushed.

"I'm fine bunking with the guys," she said. "I don't need special treatment."

"Nonsense," Kidd replied. "When a lady seeks adventure on the *Adventure Galley,* we strive to make it a comfortable journey. Now, if you'll excuse me, I need to make certain my helmsman hasn't fallen asleep at the tiller again. That's one of the difficulties with all this cold mist: all the lads seek out rum to warm their bones. Excuse me."

He bowed to Alexa, deeply, and strode off down the deck toward the rear of the ship. Alexa joined Rory at the bow, watching the pirate captain disappear into the stern.

"He's a charmer," she said, shaking her head.

"He's a pirate," Rory answered her. "Aren't they all charmers?"

"Most pirates were dirty killers and rapists," she said with a wry smile. "But I guess mortals remember pirates a bit differently."

"I'm not sure if I trust Kidd," Rory said.

"I don't trust any of them." Alexa turned to stare out at the darkness. "They're pirates. And Kidd is the worst of them, I bet. But beggars can't be choosers, and so long as we keep up our guard, we've got a chance."

She sighed, gazing out into nothing.

"Something wrong?" Rory asked, hesitant.

"Simon's in my quarters, sitting on the floor, mumbling under his breath. He's been cracking under the strain and I don't know what to do about it. And you . . . you look like you want to punch somebody, all the time."

"No, I don't!"

"Yes, you do." Alexa turned to him, smiling sadly. "Not that I blame you. But I feel like I'm failing you all. If Nicholas were here, things would be going so much more smoothly. I'm not really meant to lead people, I think. I'm a number two. I helped my father, then I helped Nicholas. But now . . . I'm in over my head and I'm afraid someone is going to pay."

"That's crazy," Rory said firmly. "You've been great. Look where we are! We're almost at the end. We've almost caught up to my dad. And you've held us together. I don't think Nicholas could have done a better job than that."

"That's very nice of you to say." Alexa patted his hand. "Of course we're on a pirate ship surrounded by criminals we can't

trust, but still, I see your general point. I just . . . I can see
you burning with this anger, and it really worries me. I don't
know what you'll do. We need you, Rory, more than anything,
and that means you need to keep your head. Tell me you'll
do that."

Rory took a deep breath.

"I will, I promise," he said. But could he keep that promise?
Until he came face-to-face with his father, he wouldn't know
for sure.

They sailed onward into the unchanging mist, hours passing
with no sign of the *Half Moon*. Rory and Alexa checked in on
Simon, who still hadn't left his bunk. The older boy started
when they barged in, stuffing something into his pocket while
a guilty look spread across his face.

"What was that?" Alexa demanded.

"Nothing." Simon tried to look innocent but failed spec-
tacularly.

Alexa looked suspicious but didn't press. "Why don't you
come up to the deck with me. Some air will do you good."

"No thanks." Simon waved her off. "I hate the mist. I'd
rather be down here trying to forget what we're sailing into."
His face was green.

"Suit yourself." Alexa looked worried, but she didn't press
the issue. She and Rory returned topside, where Captain Kidd
was waiting for them.

"May I borrow the young master for a moment, dear?" Kidd
patted Rory on the shoulder.

"Why?" Alexa said, clearly not trusting the pirate.

"I'd appreciate it if you'd indulge an old sea dog like myself. I just want to speak with him."

Alexa glanced at Rory, who shrugged.

"Where am I gonna go?" he asked, and Alexa couldn't really argue with that. So Rory followed Kidd belowdecks, down a claustrophobic corridor, past the first mate's room, where Alexa was staying (Hendrick, who couldn't seem to catch a break, was sleeping below with the crew). Through the slats in the boards he walked on, Rory spied the room below where ammunition was stored: gunpowder and cannonballs for the dozens of cannons that poked out of each side of the *Adventure Galley*. Nearby, oars lined the walls, waiting to be dipped into the water in case of a sea battle. One of the sailors, who went by the unlikely name of Hugh Parrot, had explained to Rory that having oars gave the ship more maneuverability during those deadly fights, which often meant the difference between victory and sinking to the bottom of the ocean. Rory hoped he never had to see any of the oars or cannons in action.

Kidd reached the door to his cabin and invited Rory inside. Stepping into the large room, the boy had to admit he was impressed. Everything was gold: the paint on the walls, the furniture, even the rug. A large dining-room table sat in the middle of the room, which Kidd explained he used to entertain rich captives he kidnapped. A large cabinet stood behind the table, filled with expensive plates and goblets. The dinnerware was tightly lashed to the shelves, but Rory wondered if they'd survive a big storm. A half-open door to the side led into a similarly opulent bedroom, with what appeared to be a four-poster bed, whose sheets, Rory was not shocked to see, were also colored a bright gold. Windows lined the back of the dining room, looking out the stern of the ship. Stepping up to glance outside, he could see their wake disappear into the fog. Kidd leaned forward beside him to stare out at the water.

"I didn't begin my life at sea as a pirate, you know," he said. Rory glanced over, but the man was still looking out into the distance. "I was hired by the good people of New York to *chase* pirates. And any French ships I might come across, of course. The King of England himself put money into my campaign. A privateer, they called me. I did very well. I shared the loot with the crown and the colony, and everyone was happy. I was a respected member of the community. I even helped build Trinity Church! And then . . . things began to go poorly for me."

"I grew up hearing all about your treasure," Rory said, glancing about the gold-infused cabin. "It doesn't look like you did too badly."

"It's all relative, my boy," Kidd said, repressing a smile. "Poorly from a respectability standpoint, at least. I lost most of my loyal crew to the British navy, who in those days would often sail right up to your ship on the open sea and take many of your ablest men by force to work their own sails. I replaced them as best I could, but most of the new men were old pirates with no loyalty to anyone but themselves. So when I began to have trouble finding French ships to plunder, they began to rumble. Mutiny was in the air. It came to a head when I happened upon a rich ship loaded with gold and silk and silver. They had French passes but an English captain. I knew it was a mistake, but my crew would have set me adrift in the middle of the ocean if I had refused them the spoils. So we took everything and sank the ship and thus did I truly became a pirate."

"So what you're telling me is that you're really not that bad a guy," Rory said. Kidd laughed.

"Yes, that's what I'm saying." He strode over to the small bar near the table to pour himself a drink. "I'd offer you some, but your fierce friend Alexa might run me through for corrupting a youth."

"Probably," Rory answered absently. A growing sense of discomfort was rising up in his belly. This was going somewhere and he had a feeling he wouldn't like the destination. Kidd took a long drink and set the glass down with a satisfied sigh.

"Rum, a pirate's best friend. Washes away all the guilt."

"What are you guilty about?"

"I finally placed you," Kidd said casually, refilling his glass. "You look just like one of Tew's Boys. Their leader; at least I always believed him to be. An ancestor, I suppose?"

Rory froze. "What are you talking about?"

"Come now," Kidd said, smiling. "I can see the way you look at me. What have you heard? That I hunted poor Thomas Tew down and murdered his crew and left him for dead? Such tales."

"That isn't what you did?"

"Goodness no. Tew hunted *me* down. He was tired of the competition. I fought him off, finally sinking his ship and leaving him on an island to rot." Kidd's eyes flashed and Rory saw a little of the hard pirate under the roguish charm. "But don't worry. I have nothing but respect for you. After all, you are a Light."

Rory suddenly felt like he was going to throw up, but he refused to give in to it.

"I don't know what you're talking about," he said, bluffing furiously.

"Don't you?" Kidd laughed before taking a smaller sip of rum. "There have been rumors lately, about a Light who survived infanthood. That Light is you, is it not? There was a time, hundreds and hundreds of years ago, when your kind was more common. The walls between Mannahatta and Manhattan were thinner then, I guess. I even knew one of you when I was mortal. He was my first galley cook, John Tenpin, and he'd rave about what he'd seen. And some of his mates would whisper about spying these crazy things as well, once John pointed them out. After a while no one would speak with him for fear of what he'd make them see. It's a difficult life, being a Light. But no one knows that better than you do, am I right?"

Rory felt out of control. "What are you going to do?" he asked quietly. "Give me over to Kieft?"

"Oh no," Kidd replied, waving his drink in the air. "I despise the man, always have. If you are on some noble journey to take him down a peg, I am all for it. But as for my help . . . here is where it gets tricky."

"You promised!" Desperation made Rory bold. "You said you'd help me because Hendrick tried to kidnap me. You said we'd work something out."

"We *are* working something out," Kidd replied, smiling with cold eyes. "What you ask of me now, sailing after a ghost ship, putting my entire crew at risk for no gain, that is far more than you get for simply being the victim of one of Hendrick's little schemes. I need something more."

"Why did you wait until now to tell me this?" Rory asked.

"Because I know how to bargain!" Kidd laughed. "Out in the middle of the ocean is a hard place to refuse an offer. Now, will I throw you overboard and let you sink to your death if you refuse me? Maybe. I've done it before. But if you say yes, then I will consider our bargain struck and I will help you all that I can."

"How do I know I can trust you?" Rory asked.

"Because I will give you what you want first," Kidd said. "I will continue to sail this ship in the direction you choose, until we find what you are looking for."

"Then what?"

"Then, one day, I will arrive at your door. You will pack up your things and come with me on a long sea voyage. More than that, I will not say."

"When . . ."

"Not now. Not tomorrow. Maybe not even next year. The time is not right yet. The world is too out of whack. But one day I will arrive and call your debt due. And you will come with me to see what only a Light can see. Do we have a deal?"

Rory stared back at the old sea captain, wondering if he could trust him. But in the end, what choice did he have?

"I agree."

"Shake." Kidd stepped forward, spitting on his hand. Rory spat on his hand as well and they shook. As their hands pumped, a shock ran up Rory's arm and through his body. Kidd's satisfied smile made him sick to his stomach.

"Feel that? That means it's a sealed deal. Now let's go find that ship."

Alexa had questions for Rory when he rejoined her on deck after his meeting with Kidd, but he didn't feel like sharing. He felt like an idiot. He should have seen this shakedown coming. The man was a pirate after all. What had he just signed up for?

He stared out at the mist. Something in the air had changed. One of the sailors noticed it, too, and gave him a look.

"Storm's comin'," the sailor said. "And it's gonna be a big one . . ."

HOWLS IN THE
DISTANCE

Bridget and her companions decided to leave Seneca Village while everyone was still at church. Bridget wore a backpack Pierre had given her, which he stuffed with heavy jackets for the climb up the Great Hill (not that *she* needed one). Hans did an emergency check of his armor's heating system, and after almost melting his eyebrows off, he pronounced everything shipshape. As she turned to say good-bye to Pierre, Bridget saw tears in his eyes. He gave her shoulder a squeeze.

"Good luck," he said. "And if you do ever find Abigail, tell her I'm sorry."

Bridget didn't know what to say, so she gave the old trapper a hug. She hoped the old man found some peace here in his shack filled with lost memories.

They passed out of the village quickly, heading into the trees to the north. Finn took the lead, with Soka right beside him. Bridget walked a bit behind, Hans in her pocket and Tucket by her side. Soka laughed at something Finn said, and Bridget grumbled.

"Stupid boy."

"I hope not," Hans said, overhearing. "At least, I hope he has some sense of direction."

"Look at him, talking to her like that." Bridget was disgusted. Finn said something else stupid that Soka didn't realize wasn't funny, and the Munsee girl laughed. "Maybe he's a sorcerer or something, bewitching her."

"Or maybe he's just a really good-looking guy," Hans said. "I mean, I'm secure enough to say that he is a tasty treat of a dude."

"She's not supposed to be laughing at his jokes. She's supposed to be laughing at Rory's jokes!"

"Well, Rory better speak up, because he's kinda hard to hear from so far away," Hans said. His eyes widened. "Oh. Oh, wait, I see. You think Soka and Rory are going to be an item? Maybe he'd have a chance if Finn weren't around. But sorry, girl, your brother just can't compete with all that."

"Rory's gonna save her people!"

"Look at that guy's biceps! Rory could part the Hudson and lead the Munsees to the promised land, but he just ain't got the guns."

Bridget stewed as they hiked on, growing more and more agitated with every shared moment between Soka and Finn. She had to calm herself down, so she concentrated on looking around. She could see the large reservoir that lay in the middle of the northern part of the park through the trees, and now and again, mortals would jog by one of the paths before disappearing again. But it seemed to take far longer to hike up past the reservoir than it should, and she only saw a few people when she knew a lot more should be out and about. She couldn't wrap her head around how big the spirit world was compared to the Central Park she knew. But judging by how they'd been hiking, she could guess that most of the time they walked through a place where most mortals could not go.

"What are you hoping to find up on the mountain, anyway?" Finn asked Soka as they walked ahead of Bridget and Tucket. "If this Abigail girl escaped as you say she did, then how do you expect to find her by returning to the Great Hill?"

"If you must know," Bridget said, inserting herself into the conversation, "in her last memory in the necklace, Abigail said she left something in the cave, which was supposed to help her find it again. Like a homing beacon."

"How will that help *us* find *her*?" Finn asked, his beautiful face confused. At least he didn't look too bright, Bridget thought with some satisfaction. But Soka was nodding.

"That puzzled me, too," Soka replied. "But when I asked my mother, she mentioned a trick she taught Abigail long ago. You take a piece of wampum and you split it in half directly down the middle. They have to be perfect halves or it won't work. Then the two halves remember each other, and they'll call out to each other no matter how far apart they may be. I wouldn't be surprised if Abigail tried this trick—left behind half a piece of wampum in this cave and kept the other. The nice thing for us is that it will work in reverse: we can use the half in the cave to find Abigail, so long as she still holds that other piece of wampum."

"That's pretty clever," Finn said admiringly. "Of course a tiny piece of wampum won't be easy to find among all that treasure."

"Treasure?" Bridget asked suspiciously. "Who said anything about treasure?"

"Calm down, little one." Finn laughed, making Bridget want to plant her steel toe in a very bad place. "Grandfather always talked about the treasure that was supposed to be in the cave. We would try to guess what it could be, but, of course, we never knew."

"I bet it's something good!" Hans declared. "If ol' Kieft went to all that trouble to sneak it in the park right before he turned it into the world's largest safety-deposit box, I bet it's something really important."

"Like gold?" Finn asked. "I always thought it would be gold."

"That doesn't seem big enough," Hans replied as Bridget rolled her eyes at the pretty boy's lack of imagination. "Maybe evidence of his black magic? Eyeballs in jars, bags of stolen brains, that sort of thing?"

"Eww!" Bridget shuddered. "I hope not. Maybe there are a bunch of really cool weapons with magical powers that he had to hide away because they were the only things that could hurt him or even kill him. Maybe there's a big sword and I'll pull it out of the floor and then I'll be the new mayor of Mannahatta!"

Hans gave her an amused glance. "Or maybe not."

"We can only guess," Soka said. "Hopefully, whatever we find in Kieft's cave will help us. But remember, our search is for Abigail, not treasure. So don't let our attention wander."

"Of course," Finn said. "I was just curious."

I bet you were, Bridget thought. She'd have to watch this boy closely. He was not to be trusted.

. . .

Askook, who had been watching Soka's party hike northward with amusement, decided to send his mind ahead, to see what fun he could stir up. Animals were his specialty. There was nothing like a pack of dangerous animals prowling outside the village to keep the Munsees afraid and eager to follow. Were there any suitably deadly beasts ahead? Casting about, he felt a flutter of minds racing through the forest directly in his victims' path. *Oh yes,* he thought with an evil grin. *This will do just fine.*

The afternoon passed as Bridget and her companions made their way north. Finally, they left the reservoir behind and approached some dense woodlands. They stopped for a bit to rest before entering the trees, and after a moment Hans piped up.

"I think we're being followed," he said.

"What?" Finn looked skeptical, glancing behind them. "I haven't noticed anything."

"That's because you've been too busy preening like a peacock in spring," Hans replied, prompting Finn to scowl at him. Even his scowls looked pretty, Bridget thought sourly. "I turned on a special audio transmitter in my helmet that I normally use to find my way in the darkest of underground tunnels. I thought I'd keep an ear out, you know. And I've picked up something very strange. The mortals go in and out as they slip back and forth between our world and theirs, but there is also a consistent sound out there, a movement through the brush about a half hour behind us. Someone's tracking us."

"Askook!" Soka cried. "I knew he wouldn't let us leave."

"It could be an animal," Finn replied. "Or maybe a friend who's bringing something you left behind?"

"No matter who, or what, it is, we should try to lose him," Hans said.

"We can run in zigzags!" Bridget suggested. "That should confuse him!"

"Or we can just take to the water," Soka suggested. "Our hunting camp isn't far from here on the banks of the Loch. If we can get there before Askook, or whoever's behind us, we can grab both the canoes and paddle north through the Ravine, leaving him behind."

"Perfect!" Finn said, smiling widely. "You are such a quick thinker, Soka. I swear you're ready to be the medicine woman now. You have no reason to doubt yourself!"

Soka had already told him about her hopes and dreams? Bridget was aghast. The next step was holding hands! She stepped between the two.

"So where is this camp?" she asked.

"Not far," Soka replied, still smiling at Finn. "I'll take you there, come on."

They swiftly moved through the denser forest that engulfed this part of the park. Outcroppings of rock rose up on either side as they made their way down into the Ravine. Eventually, Bridget could hear the sound of running water. They burst out of the trees onto the banks of a swiftly moving stream. The sound of water gushing over the rocks as the sun shone overhead through the dense ceiling of leaves unexpectedly soothed Bridget's soul. She knelt down, placing her hand under the water, watching as the stream rushed over her skin. Her fingers looked like sticks floating in the river. For the first time since

Soka had healed her, Bridget missed her real body. She would have liked to have felt the cool water on her hand. A splash broke her concentration as Tucket leaped into the stream, biting at a fish. She laughed; the dog looked so happy.

Suddenly Soka gasped behind her. "What happened to the camp!"

Bridget quickly sprang to her feet, hurrying after Soka and Finn. She rounded a small bend, almost stumbling into them as they surveyed the remains of what must have been the Munsee hunting camp.

A group of small tents lay along the riverbank nestled beneath a rock outcropping. They'd been torn to pieces—spears, food, and hides strewn everywhere. It was as if a tornado had hit the area. Finn crouched down by the nearest disaster.

"These are claw marks," he said. He straightend quickly, his face panicked. "We need to go."

"Why?" Bridget asked. Before Finn could answer, a howl rang out in the distance. Tucket perked up, a low growl forming in his throat. He'd already begun to grow larger, Bridget noticed. She swallowed as she looked in every direction for some sign of the source of the howl. Another howl followed the first, than a third. Tucket's growl was louder now, rumbling from his muzzle like a passing subway train.

"That doesn't sound good," Hans said, climbing up onto her shoulder.

"Everyone move into the stream," Finn said, already inching that way as he scanned the trees. "They don't love water."

"Who doesn't love water?" Bridget asked, looking around in a panic. A final howl, practically in her ear, answered her, which was their last warning before the beasts were upon them.

A gray blur leaped from the stone outcropping above, right toward Soka. Another blur, this one tawny, intercepted it, wrestling the creature to the ground. Tucket had grown to the size of a small pony, and he used his size to keep the attacking animal on the ground.

"Coyotes!" Soka cried, moving toward the river while pulling out her knife. Another coyote joined the first, attacking Tucket from behind. Tucket reached around with his jaws and pulled the animal right off him. The coyotes were the size of lions, and saliva dripped from their snarling teeth as they circled the giant dog. A third coyote loped into view, coming at Tucket from a third side. That was enough for Bridget.

"What are you doing, Bridget!" Hans yelled in her ear.

"Hold on!" she cried. He clutched onto her hair for dear life as she ran right at the nearest coyote. She grabbed it by the neck and threw it to the ground, where it immediately sprang back up to snap at her leg. Its teeth sank into her paper skin, and she used the animal's momentary confusion to punch it in the muzzle. It released her with a whine and momentarily backed off.

"Take that, you bully!" she taunted it. But before she could celebrate, another coyote hit her from behind, sending her tumbling to the ground.

Spinning on her back, she came face-to-face with the slobbery jaws of the enraged creature. It snapped at her face, again and again, trying to get at her neck. She could barely hold it off.

"I've got it!" Hans cried from behind her ear. Suddenly a loud bang exploded right in the coyote's mouth, sending it flying. Bridget saw stars for a moment.

"You could have warned me you were throwing a firecracker!" she cried.

"Sorry, no time!" Hans replied. "Another one!"

She whirled to see another coyote join the group, trying to bring Tucket down. Grown still larger, to the size of a bear, he swiped angrily at the coyotes nipping at his flanks. Two of the coyotes sported arrows in their sides—courtesty of Soka, Bridget guessed—but they weren't slowing down.

"What is with these things!" she cried in frustration.

"They've been whipped up into a frenzy," Soka yelled from her spot knee-deep in the river, where she was reloading her bow. She loosed another arrow at a coyote that was leaping at Tucket's head. "We've got to get out of here."

"I've got boats!" Finn called, paddling down the stream toward them. He was seated in a dugout canoe, pulling another one behind him. "Get in, Soka!"

Soka grabbed the other canoe and pulled herself aboard. Bridget yelled at them.

"We can't leave Tucket!"

"He'll come if you do!" Soka cried back. She sent another arrow flying into an attacking coyote who was just about to hit Bridget from behind.

"Let's go! There are too many to fight," Hans cried in her ear. Bridget ran forward and scattered the two coyotes hanging from Tucket's flank.

"Tucket, come!" she yelled, and turned to race toward the waiting canoes. Suddenly a coyote sprang out of nowhere to sink its teeth into her neck, pulling her down. She hit the ground, batting at the animal frantically. She could feel something pushing against her neck from the inside; the paper wasn't as thick there, and the coyote's teeth threatened to tear through. So far she'd been able to survive some small punctures in her paper body, but what would happen if she split open? Would her soul escape? Terrified, she thrashed around, but the coyote would not let go. She heard something begin to tear and the pushing inside grew unbearable as her soul strove to break free . . .

Suddenly she heard a thud and the beast shuddered, losing its grip on her throat as it fell to the side. Her hand sprang to her neck. Her fingers ran over the rough paper, checking for rips. She felt some rough grooves where the teeth had dug in, but no holes. She shuddered at her close call; she wasn't as invulnerable as she thought. Sitting up, she looked over at the coyote, which lay dead at her side. Its head had been crushed by a large rock.

"It just fell from the outcropping onto the wolf's head!" Hans breathed from beside her head. "Somebody up there likes you!"

Glancing up, she saw a small cliff looming above the riverbank. Could the rock have just fallen like that, dislodged by Tucket's thrashing? Was she that lucky? She hoped that luck held.

"Bridget, come on!" Soka cried from the canoe. Bridget hopped to her feet, Hans still hanging from her hair. She ran to the water, hitting it with a splash; the stream was surprisingly swift. She pushed forward, struggling to keep her balance on the slippery rocks of the streambed, finally reaching the side of the canoe. Soka held out her hand and pulled her aboard as Finn reached over from his canoe with a steadying hand to keep them from capsizing. Turning back to the shore, Bridget was able to see the full picture. There were at least ten coyotes rushing over the ruins of the Munsee camp at poor Tucket, nipping at every side of the giant dog as they tried to bring him down.

"Tucket, COME!" Bridget screamed, and this time Tucket turned to look at her. Seeing that she was safe, he barreled through the predators, kicking and biting until they fell back. He reached the river and gave a mighty leap through the air right at Finn's canoe.

"*NO!*" Finn cried, realizing that the giant dog would crush both him and his boat. He threw up his hands. But Tucket was shrinking in midair. He landed, normal size, in the bow of the boat with a yelp. Finn sighed with relief, then grabbed a paddle.

"Let's go!" he yelled back, and began to guide his canoe downstream. Soka grabbed the paddle of their canoe and followed suit, pulling the oar through water on one side and then the other, picking up speed as they left the decimated Munsee camp behind. The coyotes ran alongside the stream, keeping up for a while, but soon the canoes became caught in the pull of the water and they swiftly moved forward down the Loch, leaving their attackers behind. Finally, only the howls of the frustrated beasts remained, until even these, too, faded into the background of the forest.

"Is everyone all right?" Finn called back.

"Sure," Bridget replied sarcastically. "I mean, I just fought off a bunch of crazy killing machines with my bare hands while you went and got boats! I'm just peachy!"

"Hey, we needed these canoes to escape, Bridget," Soka reminded her gently. "Be nice."

"Fine." Bridget pouted. "Thanks for the awesome boats."

"You're welcome," Finn called back, fighting sarcasm with sincerity. "Thanks for fighting off the killing machines with your bare hands."

"My pleasure," Bridget muttered, sinking down into the floor of the canoe.

"Well, at least we left a little present behind for whoever is following us," Soka said. "A whole pack of angry coyotes!" Bridget nodded, gradually calming herself down. They'd escaped, that was all that mattered, she told herself. They were still on the path.

Soka continued paddling, her oar moving from side to side with smooth, practiced motions. No one spoke; the hum of the forest around them begged for their silence. The air was alive with sound—birds chirping, frogs croaking, the buzz of insects along the shore—the music of the woodlands overpowering Bridget's adrenaline and reminding her that they were safe again, at least for the time being.

After a while she propped her chin on the edge of the canoe to watch the trees pass peacefully by. Ahead, she spied Tucket doing the same, and she smiled to see the dog's tongue wagging happily as they glided down the river. He'd earned this moment of rest. Bridget turned her gaze back to the scenery, which took her breath away. Soka had called the Ravine the most beautiful place in the park, and as Bridget stared up at the cliffs on either side, covered in beautiful beds of wildflowers, she could see why. She wondered if the Ravine was this beautiful in mortal Central Park. Probably not. But even if it was just a fraction as breathtaking, it would be the most peaceful spot on Manhattan.

• • •

They were still paddling down the Loch as golden light began to creep through the canopy of leaves, telling them that the day was near an end. Finally, just as the twilight crept in, Finn guided his canoe to the shore and Soka followed suit.

"There are a few waterfalls ahead, so we need to head back to the trail, but we're not far from the edge of the Ravine, so it will be a short journey from here," Finn told them, hopping out to pull the canoe onto the bank. Bridget helped Soka do the same, and they stashed the canoes in beneath the trees, covered in branches.

"Night's falling," Soka said. "How far are we from the path up the Great Hill?"

"We have to come at it from the north," Finn replied. "It will probably be better if we camp here and then climb in the morning."

"Camp out here?" Bridget asked, looking around at the wild surrounding them. "What if there are more coyotes? Or giant squirrels? We'll be sitting ducks."

"We can always spend the night at McGown's Tavern," Soka suggested.

"Well . . . well . . . that's not such a good idea," Finn stuttered. Bridget didn't understand why he was so flustered all of a sudden, and by the look of her, Soka didn't understand, either.

"Why not?" Soka asked. "It's unlikely any of my people have ventured this far north in search of me—not yet, anyway. We'll be careful to stay inconspicuous."

"Yes, well, it's out of the way. We'd have to go an hour's walk east, which is in the wrong direction entirely. And the customers . . . they're a bit rough. Old soldiers and trappers and politicians and other unsavory types. We'd be better off camping here."

"That doesn't make any sense at all," Bridget said, putting her hands on her hips. "It's better to spend the night away from animals that are trying to eat us, even if that means a little walk and some weird guys at the bar."

"She's right," Hans said. "Anyway, your grandfather mentioned that he parted ways with Penhawitz there. Maybe someone there knows where the old Sachem went."

"Fine." Finn gave in angrily. "We'll go to the tavern, if it's so important to you."

He stomped away, not waiting for the others to follow. Soka glanced at Bridget and shrugged before setting off after him.

"What got into him?" Hans asked from Bridget's shoulder.

"Maybe he's got a big bar tab or something," Bridget guessed before following the others into the darkening forest, Tucket at her heels.

A NIGHT AT
McGOWN'S

Nicholas woke up suddenly. The room was dark and still. Did he have a bad dream? He turned over to see Lincoln asleep on the other bed. Everything seemed to be fine. So what had awakened him?

A creaking inside the room startled him. He looked sharply to see the door opening slowly to admit a shadow of a man. Nicholas froze, watching the intruder entering his room and knowing in his heart that he'd come to kill them both. Nicholas's pulse began to race as the shadow crept over to him and reached for his neck . . .

Nicholas's hand shot up to grab the man's wrist, and he leaped forward to drive the intruder to the floor. A muffled cry came from beneath him as he landed atop the would-be killer.

"It's not what you think!" the figure cried. "I'm a friend! A friend! You've got the wrong Jimmy!"

"Wasssgoingon?" Lincoln muttered sleepily, sitting up. Nicholas pulled back to see whom he'd tackled. To his great surprise, Jimmy Walker, aide to the mayor, stared back at him, eyes wide.

"What are you doing in here?" Nicholas asked suspiciously. "Lincoln, light a candle."

"No!" Walker hissed. "They'll see it!"

"Who'll see it?" Lincoln asked, eyes narrowing.

"Look out the window," Walker whispered. "Now!"

Nicholas pushed himself to his feet, wincing as the pain of his injured stomach flared up. He clutched his belly as he staggered over to the window. Gazing out at his parents' lawn, he didn't see anything at first. Limping up beside him, Lincoln let out a gasp.

"Look!" Lincoln said softly. Nicholas peered closer and then he saw it: dark shapes moving slowly across the lawn toward the farmhouse. As they came close, he could make out feathers and a flash of war paint.

"B'wry Boys," Walker said from behind them. "Dressed as Munsees—like they've been doing all week. But this time they've got murder on the mind. *Yours*."

"How do you know this?" Nicholas said, turning back to the man on the floor.

"Because I'm supposed to be opening the front door," Walker admitted. "I made a copy of your mother's key the last time when I paid you a visit. Kieft instructed me to let Sly Jimmy and his B'wry Boys in so they can do what they do. They'll be at the door in a minute, so we don't have much time."

"Why are you helping us, then?" Lincoln whispered, confused.

"Because I'm tired of all this!" Walker said, gritting his teeth. "Kieft wants a war, and I don't like wars! Wars are bad for business! There's no time for dancing and singing and all the good things in life. There's rationing and shortages and death! What a party killer!

"Besides, I know the Mayor wouldn't want this. He's made a whole mess of mistakes, but he respects Peter. He wouldn't agree to this if he knew. But Kieft keeps things from the Mayor all the time. I think he sees that Alexander is being slowly consumed with regret. I hate to see it! Such a waste when he could be having a good time! I won't let your death be another of those regrets. I won't! So come on, I've got some horses out back. We can sneak away with none the wiser."

"But the house . . ." Nicholas muttered. Thankfully, his father was down at the hospital, still laid up with the awful sickness going around, and his mother was with him. Kieft had probably planned it that way, knowing that Peter Stuyvesant was too powerful to be taken down so crudely. But the farmhouse where he'd grown up . . . he couldn't leave it. He glanced at Lincoln.

"You know I'm the first one to jump into a fight," Lincoln told him solemnly. "But even I know there are too many of them. It's just a house."

"Come on, you're wasting time!" Walker warned them, walking to the door. Nicholas glanced back out the window. The fake Munsees were already climbing onto the porch, no doubt waiting for Walker to let them inside. He sighed, his heart aching. He'd make Kieft pay for this, he thought. Then he turned back to Walker.

"Let's go."

They staggered out of the room and down the stairs, Walker supporting Nicholas as they ran. As they hobbled out the back door to the stables, they could hear the B'wry Boys beginning to beat on the front door. A crash sounded as something flew through the front window. When they reached the horses Walker had waiting, a smell of smoke began to drift by on the wind.

Nicholas shot Lincoln a look of horror. "They're burning it down!" he cried, fighting tears.

"We'll get them back!" Lincoln assured him. "If it's the last thing we do."

"Hurry, it won't take them long to check back here," Walker said, climbing aboard one of the horses. Lincoln and Nicholas followed suit and they galloped away, over the side and down to the street to safety. Behind them, the wonderful farmhouse where Nicholas had spent the last four hundred years burned brightly in the night. Nicholas could not watch, but he knew the sight would be with him always.

⁂

They heard McGown's Tavern before they saw it. Night had fallen and the weary travelers had to make their way by starlight. They'd passed out of the trees onto one of Central Park's paved paths, but Manhattan still suffered under the blackout, so the streetlamps were all dark. Bridget spied the shadowy buildings of the city in the distance, just over the trees. She wondered how her brother's search was going. And their mother, was she still okay? Bridget had to hope so. There was nothing she could do for them now.

Distant sounds of music and laughter floated by on the wind

as they approached the hill that marked McGown's Pass. Finn explained that the pass had been used to hold back the British as General Washington retreated with his men from their defeat at the Battle of Brooklyn. The British claimed the pass—and all of New York—once Washington was well away, and they built forts nearby overlooking the rivers on either side. Eventually, the British would be defeated, and the patriots would triumphantly take back the city. Through it all, McGown's Tavern had survived, untouched by war or occupation, faithfully serving travelers on their way north. It even survived Central Park; the tavern remained at the same spot at the top of the hill into the twentieth century, becoming a favorite haunt of Tammany Hall politicians, before finally being demolished in the early teens.

Its memory was very much alive, however, judging by the merriment coming from atop the hill. At last, Bridget and her companions reached the hilltop where the tavern waited, a warm light in the dark. Lanterns hung outside, welcoming travelers. A stable stood nearby, filled with horses waiting for their masters to finish hobnobbing and head home to their beds. Smoke drifted out of the chimney, promising a blazing fire within. The thought of a nice seat by the fire seemed very pleasant to Bridget. She found herself getting excited as they reached the door and pushed through.

Inside, McGown's Tavern was jumping with the boisterous energy of its customers. Long tables stretched out along the big fireplace, filled with loudly talking—and in some cases singing—guests. And what guests! Soldiers from both sides of the Revolution sat on opposite ends of one table, redcoats near the door, browncoats by the fire. A group of Civil War soldiers took up the corner of another table, eagerly drinking away. Some well-to-do farmers sat eating their porridge next to a pair of nuns who were gingerly sipping wine. And standing by the bar, singing loudly, were three men in old-fashioned tuxedo tails and top hats—Bridget later learned they were corrupt politicians from the turn of the last century who'd died one snowy New Year's Eve when the horse-drawn sleigh they were riding slid into the lake.

Behind the bar, a woman in a wool dress and apron rushed about, filling cups and passing plates of food from the back kitchen out to her serving maids. She brightened when she spied Finn standing in the doorway.

"Finn Lee!" she cried, and the singing politicians stopped long enough to shout hello. "How is your dear grandfather?"

"He's getting better, thank you," he said, stepping up to the bar. He turned to the nuns, who smiled up at him. "And thank you, Sisters, for your help with his leg. He told me that you saved him, sure as I'm standing here." The nuns blushed and waved him off. Bridget had to admit, the boy knew how to work a room. Finn turned back to the woman behind the bar. "Catherine, do you have room for my friends and me?"

"Of course!" Catherine exclaimed, pointing to three chairs in the corner. "Sally will be by to see what you'll be having. That is if Megan or Molly don't beat her to it." She winked. Finn looked away, as if embarrassed, and led Bridget and Soka (but mostly Soka, Bridget noticed) over to the table. Hans popped his head out of Bridget's pocket.

"What do they have? Pie?"

"Stay out of sight," Bridget told him. "We're not supposed to be memorable."

"Really?" Hans said. "I noticed that Finn just slips into a room like a ninja, doesn't he?"

"You know what I mean," Bridget said.

"Well, I can't sit in your pocket all night, I'll suffocate," Hans said. "I'm going outside for a moment to breathe some fresh air while I can. I'll be back." He dropped down to the floor and raced toward the door. He just narrowly missed being stepped on by one of the serving maids, who gave a stamp as the battle roach passed by. She stepped up to their table.

"Did you see that?" she asked. "Little vermin get bolder every year." She turned to Finn. "Hello, Finn. It's so nice to see you around these parts again." Finn smiled slightly and nodded. Another serving girl stopped by.

"I bet he's happier to see *me*, right, Finn?" she said. The third serving girl popped by as well.

"I think we all know who he likes best, right, Finn?" She winked as Finn turned red. Catherine bellowed over from the bar.

"Leave him be, girls! There will be time enough for courtin' when the place is closed for the night!"

The girls frowned, batting their eyes at Finn. Soka turned to the handsome guide, her eyes narrowing.

"You know all these girls?" she asked evenly. Finn blanched.

"Not really. I mean, I do!" he hastily added as the girls shrieked with indignation. "But it's not . . . I'm not . . . I told you we shouldn't have come." He sank back in his chair, defeated. Bridget smirked; no wonder he'd wanted to keep Soka away from this place. He'd dated everyone in here. He was a man-tramp.

"How's your grandfather?" the first girl asked as the others moved away now that they realized there'd be no courting tonight.

"He's getting better, Sally, thanks," Finn replied, not looking her in the eye.

"Did he ever find out what happened to his Indian friend?"

"You mean Penhawitz?" Soka asked, her interest caught.

"I guess. The two of them stopped here on their way out to the Great Hill, and a day later, your granddad showed up alone with his leg a complete mess. I guess he parted with his Indian friend on the road after they survived the squirrel attack. I'd wondered what ever happened to the Munsee fellow. He seemed nice."

"Penhawitz didn't stop in here, then?" Soka asked. "I was hoping to find news of him."

"Sorry, miss," Sally said. "I haven't seen him." She gave Soka a second, sharper look, her eyes going from the Munsee girl to Finn and back. "And try to remember your place in line, honey. Last." She walked away as the other girls gave Soka mean looks from the bar.

"Well, I'm looking forward to a good night's sleep!" Finn declared, desperately trying to change the topic. "I'll be happy knowing that that Askook guy isn't right behind us."

"Why?" Bridget asked innocently. "Did you two used to date?" Soka erupted into laughter and Bridget joined her while Finn looked on, red-faced.

"There's nothing wrong with knowing a few lasses," he said.

"It is true, you are a comely man," Soka replied. "I don't fault you. If I looked as fine as you, I'd probably be unable to walk into a tavern without being accosted by an ex-dalliance, either. Or three."

Finn pursed his lips, looking away as his face turned red. Bridget suddenly felt a whole lot better about Rory's chances.

She sat back in her chair, listening in on some of the conversations around her. One was quickly becoming quite heated. Two groups of soldiers, from different eras, to judge by their uniforms, began to argue by the fire.

"At least we saw combat!" one solder said.

"That was a retreat," another soldier across the fireplace replied. "Washington was on the run. It's not called 'seeing combat' if you run away."

"You never even fired a single shot," the first soldier said. "You built all the pretty forts and cannons and then the British never even showed up!"

"Hey, we were ready!" the second soldier said. "It was the War of 1812, right? It's not our fault we were so good that we finished it up in twelve months. It took you Revolution boys years!"

"And still we almost beat you!" a British soldier called out, and his mates cheered, clinking glasses.

"'Almost' only counts in horseshoes and cannonballs!" the Revolutionary soldier shot back. "Cannonballs these boys never got around to firing!"

"I'll show you cannonballs!" the other American solder cried, reaching for a musket.

"That's enough!" Catherine shouted, stomping between the two groups. "Ned, you know the rules. I think you need to take your friends home for the night."

"He started it," the one called Ned said, but Catherine

would have none of it. She watched over the soldiers from the War of 1812 as they gathered their muskets and staggered sheepishly outside.

The evening passed quickly, with Finn trying not to talk to the serving girls and Bridget thoroughly enjoying his discomfort. When it came time to hit the sack, Finn seemed relieved to be leaving the common room. The few rooms of the tavern were filled, so Catherine agreed to let them sleep in the stable. They headed outside, and Bridget spied Hans lying beneath a bush beside the front door, his helmet under his head, fast asleep. She nudged him awake to tell him where they were sleeping, but he only murmured and turned over. She decided to let him rest and followed the others into the stable.

A few horses still stamped in their stalls. A ladder led up to the loft, and Finn seemed to know exactly where to go, which caused Soka to raise an eyebrow; he shrugged sheepishly before climbing up. Soka and Bridget followed, and Bridget waved good night to Tucket, who curled up at the base of the ladder, as they all turned in for the night.

THE SQUALL

The wind had picked up greatly around the *Adventure Galley*, sending the sails flapping. Shouts rose from the sailors as they scurried around, securing the lashings. Kidd emerged from below and shot them a grim smile.

"Squall," he said. "You should get below—"

He hadn't even finished his sentence when a violent gust of wind slammed into the ship, sending them reeling. Rory was flung from his feet, landing heavily on the deck. Alexa had somehow kept her footing, but she flailed about for something to hold on to. Rain began to fall through the darkening mist— first a drizzle, then quickly a downpour. Within moments, Rory was soaked to the bone.

Alexa stumbled to the railing, which she clung to tightly. Rory crawled over to her side, thrusting an arm around the rail to hold on.

"Are you okay?" she shouted. Alexa had to yell to be heard over the wind.

"I'm fine," he answered, wiping water from his face. The sailors raced to and fro, battening down anything loose. Kidd ordered his men to bring down the sails so the wind wouldn't capsize them. The ship began to rock violently as the waves swelled larger and larger, and the rain beat down harder. Rory had visions of it breaking into pieces before sinking to the bottom of the sea.

"Let's get belowdecks," Alexa yelled in his ear, pointing to the open hatch. Rory wasn't so sure he wanted to be down in the bowels of the ship as it was tossed about like a toy, but he started to crawl toward the door. A huge wave broke over them, drenching them. Rory spat out salt water.

"Where did this come from?" he screamed back at Alexa.

"My father used to tell me these squalls could kick up out of nowhere," she yelled back, barely audible over the roaring wind. "Come on!"

"Where's Fritz?" he yelled back. "Did you see him come down?" She shook her head, fear coming over her face. They both peered at the crow's nest far above, almost invisible through the sheets of rain. Another wave crashed over the side of the ship and Rory reached out for the rail to keep from being swept overboard.

"He's still up there!" he screamed. "He'll never make it down in this! What do we do?"

"We can't do anything! If we try to climb up the mast in this, we'll get blown away like a feather!"

Her face showed that she agonized over the decision, but she was firm. Rory, however, would not give up.

"Maybe one of the sailors can help us?" He glanced around

but every hand was busy trying to hold the ship together. Pirates clung to the rigging, trying to fight the wind as they finished tying up the sails. There was no one to help them.

"I'll go," he said finally.

"What! No! That's suicide. Come on, we have to get you
to safety." She crawled up to him and began to pull him toward
the hatch. He yanked himself away.

"I have to! He's saved my life over and over. I can't leave
him!"

"You don't even know if he's alive up there. You're too important to risk. I'll go."

She looked terrified but resolute. Rory would not let her risk
her life for him. He was tired of everyone taking the bullet for
him. Fritz was his friend and he needed him. Rory waited for
the next wave to break over them and then leaped to his feet.
He raced across the deck, past a soaked Captain Kidd, who
was still giving orders.

"Hey!" Kidd cried as he saw Rory run past. "Where are you
going? I told you to get below!"

Rory ignored the pirate captain, launching himself at the
mast. He had just enough time to get a good hold of the rigging before the next wave hit. He spat out more salt water,
shook his eyes clear, and began to climb.

The higher he climbed, the harder the wind beat at him. The
rigging was slick with rainwater, and he had to fight to keep
his grip. He couldn't look back, because he knew he'd freeze
with fear, so he gritted his teeth and reached out for the next
handhold. Slowly he rose up the mast, fighting to stay on.

"Hold on, Rory, it's a big one!" he heard Alexa cry behind

him, and he had just enough time to wrap his arms in the rigging before the huge wave hit.

The entire ship leaned to starboard under the force of the wall of water. Rory went blind for a moment as the water poured over him, blocking out all his senses. He felt his arms weaken as the force of the wave threatened to pull him off the mast. But somehow, when the water cleared, he still hung from the rigging. The ship, however, had tilted almost sideways. He was hanging mere feet above the sea, perpendicular to the mast, and for a second he thought for sure they would capsize. Somehow, thankfully, the ship slowly righted itself, and he fell back against the mast. He went to pull out his arm from the rigging and resume his climb when he hit a snag.

He couldn't budge.

The rope from the rigging had wrapped itself around his arms, pinning him to the mast. He couldn't move them even an inch. Terrified, he finally looked back down at the deck. Alexa was clinging to the mast, trying to climb after him. She looked as frightened as he felt. He watched as she realized why he wasn't moving. But before she could pull herself up, someone ran through the door from down below. It was Simon, and he was . . . *laughing*.

Where was the moping, scared boy who wouldn't leave his stateroom? This Simon nimbly raced across the wet deck, waving up at Rory. He reached the base of the mast and yelled up.

"You look like a trussed turkey! Need a hand?"

Rory could only nod. Simon turned back to an equally stunned Alexa and gave her a thumbs-up. Then he leaped onto the rigging and swiftly pulled himself up. Alexa shouted another warning and Rory ducked his head as a wave beat down on them. Looking back at Simon, he was shocked to see the older boy spitting a stream of salt water into the air like he'd just come up from a dip in his bathtub. Simon grinned up at him, and quickly climbed to Rory's side.

"Ouch," he said. "Looks painful."

"Simon! What is wrong with you?"

Simon's eyes flashed as he grinned from ear to ear.

"Wrong? There's nothing wrong. In fact, I'd say that everything is finally right! Let's get you untangled, shall we? Then we can enjoy this magnificent storm from ground level."

"Wait! Fritz is up there. I'm afraid it may be too late—"

"Well, let's see, shall we? Hang tight until I get back!"

With that, Simon scampered up the rigging like a spider monkey, giving no thought to the driving wind and rain. He reached the crow's nest and disappeared inside. Rory's heart froze as he waited. Finally, Simon leaned over and gave him an okay sign. Rory felt like a huge weight had lifted. Fritz was all right.

Simon slid down the mast as if it were a fireman's pole, stopping himself when he reached Rory.

"He's A-OK. He was wedged in the corner, which was why he didn't fall out. Lucky sucker. I've got him in my pocket. Now let's see to you!"

Simon dangled from the mast by one hand as he rifled around his belt. Rory was sure the boy would fall, but he somehow kept his grip. Finally, Simon pulled out a knife.

"Hold on!" he said brightly. "Wouldn't want to lose you now, eh?"

He reached over and sawed at the rigging above Rory's hands. The wind had ripped open Simon's shirt, and Rory thought he saw a flash of something gold around his neck. Before he could look closer, the ropes came free and he had to cling quickly to keep from falling.

"Come on!" Simon cried, sliding down the rest of the mast. Rory followed more carefully, but thankfully the largest of the waves had passed. He hit the deck with a thud and collapsed. Alexa ran over and began to smack him on the shoulder.

"You idiot! You could have died up there! Where would we have been without you? That was the most selfish, stupid, thickheaded—"

"Hold a moment, Alexa." A weak voice rose from Simon's hand. It was Fritz, white-faced but alive.

"Fritz!" Rory and Alexa both rushed to lean over the battle roach, who spoke up at them, his voice shaking.

"Rory, everything Alexa is saying is correct. You can't risk yourself like that, you're too important."

"But—" Rory began.

"Wait, let me finish. It was stupid, but I thank you anyway. And you especially, Simon. Both of you saved my life. I owe you both a debt I can never repay. Thank you."

Rory's eyes welled up and even Simon looked gratified and surprised. Alexa quickly broke that spell by turning on her fellow Rattle Watcher.

"What *was* that, Simon? What is going on! One moment you're too afraid to even leave your room, then the next you're climbing up that mast like an acrobat! You better explain yourself, and fast!"

Simon opened his mouth to speak, but before he could answer, a shout interrupted them.

"Man overboard!"

They all spun around to stare over the side. The rain had slackened, but the storm wasn't over yet. Wind still lifted the waves into heady peaks and valleys. They scanned the dark water for any sign of life; at first there seemed to be nothing out there. Then Rory saw it, a few yards out. A small canoe, capsized, and a man clinging its side. Hope and fear simultaneously ran through him. Could it be . . . ?

The man waved at the ship, allaying Rory's fear for the moment. The sailors tossed a line over the side. Soon the man was lying on the deck gasping for air. Rory ran to his side, and his throat tightened as his hope was confirmed. The man saw him, his eyes widening.

"Rory . . ."

"Hello, Wampage," Rory said, tears pouring down his cheeks. "Am I glad to see you."

The storm had passed, leaving the *Adventure Galley* in still waters. So calm, in fact, that they weren't moving at all. The wind had completely died down, leaving them becalmed. Wampage dried himself off on the deck as Rory and his friends gathered around him. Rory quickly explained their mission, which Wampage took in impassively.

"You have had a difficult path," he said finally. "And I fear it is not getting any easier. A great storm is coming."

"I know," Simon said brightly. "And it was awesome!"

"Not that small thing that just blew by," Wampage continued. "That was but a hint of what is coming. I rode here with the true storm at my back, and I fear we will not be able to beat it back home."

"What kind of storm are we talking about?" Alexa asked.

"I believe it is the catastrophe we were warned of, the island's last, greatest effort to shake the Trap off its back. The earthquake was but a nuisance compared to what approaches."

"How can you know that?" Fritz asked.

"How can I not?" Wampage sighed and said no more. Rory couldn't bear it any longer.

"Did you find that god you were looking for?" he asked. Wampage glanced over at him and smiled sadly.

"Kishelamakank? Yes," he said. "I found him. On an island far from here. He had been living there for years and years. And he had been expecting me. He had food and drink waiting for me when I paddled into his harbor. He lived simply, but happily, or so it seemed. But he was very weak. He has been almost forgotten. He had just enough strength left to know I was coming, and that a storm would rise soon after. We spoke of many things, most of which I keep in my heart, but when our talk turned to our people, he had a command for me: I was to return home and help our people through this storm. For it comes to tear us all apart. Our time has run out, Rory. We must open the Trap, or we will perish."

They stood there for a moment, stunned into silence. Finally, Simon turned to the others.

"Well, that's a bummer," he said.

"Where is Kish . . . um . . . Kish . . . ?" Rory began.

"Kishelamakank?" Wampage said for him, smiling slightly.

"Where is he now?" Rory finished.

"He is gone." Wampage looked away. "Memory could no longer sustain him. He had been waiting for me—to warn me. He faded, leaving behind a gift. It was a sad day for my people."

"What did he leave you?" Simon asked, and Alexa elbowed him for his rudeness.

"A single bead of bright blue wampum," Wampage answered him. "The rarest kind. It contains his final breath. With that breath he told all of our lost stories. I will spend the voyage listening to them, absorbing them so that they will survive in me. If we make it back before the storm, that is."

"How far back is that storm?" Alexa asked.

"Half a day. We must turn back now."

"No!" Rory cried, startling them all. They turned to stare at him. "We're out here for a reason. To find my father. We can't go back without him. We've barely even tried!"

"It's too dangerous," Wampage said. "You cannot risk it."

Captain Kidd walked up. "Am I interrupting?" he said. "Glad to see you're all right, savage."

"Don't call him a savage," Alexa snarled. Kidd smiled.

"Sorry. Old habits die hard. We have to decide what to do. I overheard you talking about a storm bigger than the one we just lived through. If that is true, we need to head back toward the mainland."

"If you do that, our deal is null and void," Rory said darkly. The others gave him anxious looks but he would not budge. "I came out here to find my father. The storm isn't here, yet. Wampage says we've got half a day. I can't go back yet, not when there's still a chance we could catch him."

"Rory, you're not—" Alexa started, but Kidd put up a hand.

"It is your decision, Rory," he said. "Everyone's lives are in your hands. Are you certain you want to go on?"

Rory nodded. Kidd bowed slightly.

"Then we break out the oars," he said.

Hours passed as they rowed the ship farther into the mist. Everyone was tense, as many of the sailors had overheard Wampage's warnings. Alexa wasn't speaking to Rory, she was so angry. Simon seemed unconcerned, flitting about, trying to learn how to sail and failing horribly. Rory wondered what was going on with him, but he was too wrapped up in the search for his father's ship to think much on it now. Wampage lay on the deck, staring up, lost in thought. Rory stood at the bow, staring into the fog, desperately searching for sails in the mist.

"How long are you going to give this?" Fritz asked from his place on Rory's shoulder. "What if his ship got caught up in the storm and sank? What if they never came this way after all? There are so many what-ifs here, Rory. Are you willing to bet all our lives on them?"

Rory didn't want to hear this.

"Everyone's been saying 'Talk to Harry Meester!' So that's what we're going to do."

"Even if it kills us?"

Rory's throat was so tight he couldn't speak. The bow of the ship blurred as he blinked angrily. Fritz shook his head, eyes filled with compassion.

"Rory, come on. You and I both know that you're not doing this for anyone but yourself. . . . But it's not too late. You need to let go."

Rory looked away, wiping a tear from his eye. His hand came away wetter than he expected. It was starting to rain. "I'm sorry, Fritz," he said, ashamed.

"Keep your apologies for when you need them," Fritz said. "For now, let's just go home."

Rory nodded, his hair moving slightly as the wind finally picked up. A happy cry came from behind him as the sailors realized they no longer had to row. But before they could truly celebrate, the wind exploded into a gale, rocking the ship. Rory reached out and grabbed Fritz, to keep him from falling. The roach yelled up at him.

"It's here!"

Rain began to fall, faster and faster. With a sick feeling, Rory realized that Fritz was right; the storm was here and it was too late. Fear swept over him as the wind pushed him back. Had he doomed them all? He ran back to the stern, where his friends waited with Captain Kidd.

"Turn her around!" he yelled.

"It's too late," Kidd screamed back. "We'll never out-run her."

Rory's heart sank as he looked around at his friends.

"I'm so sorry," he said hopelessly. Alexa sighed but said nothing.

"I'm not worried," Simon announced. "What's a little wind?"

As if in answer, a huge gust of hurricane-strength winds thrust the ship sideways. They all had to scramble to keep from being blown over the side. Rory knew that this time they wouldn't ride out the storm. This time they'd be battered to pieces. And it was all his fault.

In the midst of all this terrified confusion, Wampage calmly lifted himself off the ground. His eyes were flowing, but his face was determined.

"I am sorry, Kishelamakank," he said, reaching out his hand. "I will remember what I can."

He opened his hand, and inside lay a brilliant blue bead. It began to glow brightly, and Rory realized that he could hear words on the wind. They were the lilting syllables of a beautiful language, filled with music and light, and it made his heart glad to hear it. Wampage lifted his hand toward the sails, and they filled under the force of those beautiful words.

"Hold on," the Munsee warrior warned them. He turned to Captain Kidd, who was staring at him with his mouth open. "Steer us home."

Kidd's face changed as the realization dawned over him. He ran back to his helmsmen.

"Steer us west! If you let that rudder budge, I will cut you in half!"

The words on the wind rose as the sails billowed. There was a large shudder as the *Adventure Galley* lurched forward. Alexa turned to Rory, awe on her face.

"Those are the stories of his people," she said.

"Well, they're saving our hides," Simon replied. Sure enough, the ship was moving forward now, faster and faster, as the tales of Kishelamakank drove them on. Wampage held the bead aloft, sending his people's voices into the sails, all the while muttering under his breath. Rory stepped up beside him to hear what the warrior was saying. Wampage was repeating the same mantra over and over again.

"I will remember. I will remember. I will remember. I will remember."

On and on, he recited those words as the ship broke free of the rain and raced westward, leaving the storm behind. The wind still blew all around them, but it was a good, clean wind. A wind that guided them home.

ATOP THE
GREAT HILL

The dim light of dawn crept through the cracks of the roof of the stable. Bridget lay serenely on her back, listening to the birds and insects gradually waking up outside. So she was beyond startled when a voice whispered right in her ear.

"There's someone outside!" Hans hissed.

Bridget bolted straight up. Beside her, Soka and Finn were sitting up, rubbing their eyes. She stared down the ladder at Tucket, who stood staring at the doors to the stable, growling in the back of his throat. Soka quickly climbed down, staring out through the slats of the stable door.

"I don't see anything," she whispered back. Bridget followed her down, carrying her backpack. She peered out at the tavern through the door; it stood still in the gray, early morning light. The grass glistened with dew, and no one stirred. Finn stepped up next to her, placing his eye to the opening between doors.

"It looks quiet out there to me," he said.

"I saw something, in the bushes," Hans insisted. "I couldn't quite make it out, but it was definitely a person—who didn't want to be seen."

Bridget glanced back at Soka. "Sounds like Askook to me."

"How are we going to get past him?" Soka asked, raising her arms helplessly.

"Will you keep it down, some people's heads hurt!" a voice called from the back of the stable.

Startled, they all hurried back to check on who was in the stable with them. Two men lay in the last stall, next to one of the horses. Bridget recognized them as the soldiers Catherine had kicked out the night before.

"It's too early for all this talking," one of them was saying.

"I thought you were going home," Soka accused them.

"We meant to," the other man said. "But we didn't quite make it. I'm Ned Peacock, first sergeant, State Militia. This is Private Kindernook."

"Tom," the other man said. Ned gave him a look.

"When you're on duty, you are Private Kindernook!"

"What duty?" Private Kindernook shot back wearily. "No one ever attacked."

"That's just bad luck, that is!" Sergeant Peacock replied haughtily. "We could have taken 'em if they'd tried!" He pushed himself to his feet, staggering over to his horse. "Now saddle up and keep quiet."

"Sir," Bridget said deferentially. "Would you mind doing us a favor? We think someone is lurking out there . . ."

"Yes, see, we've been followed by someone—" Soka said, but the sergeant cut her off, indignant.

"Citizens being threatened! Women not free to walk the woods! Sounds like the British to me!"

Before anyone could contradict the soldier, Finn stepped forward with a nod. "You've guessed it, sir," he said, eyes shifting left and right. "The British are right on our tail."

"By golly, you must come with us!" Sergeant Peacock declared. "We can assail them from the blockhouse! We've got cannons and muskets and the works! Oh boy, action at last!"

"How many are there?" Private Kindernook looked frightened. "I haven't really been keeping up with my cannon training. It's just the two of us in the little fort, you see, and I'm in charge of cannons."

"You'll pick it up as you go!" Sergeant Peacock assured his subordinate, who turned green at the prospect.

"You know, even helping us escape would be a setback to the British," Finn said, giving the girls a look that begged not to be trapped in a little fort with these two, waiting for the nonexistent enemy to storm the walls.

"That's true." Bridget backed him up. "Just taking us to the north side of the Great Hill would be a deadly blow to the Brits."

"That sounds good," Private Kindernook said hopefully. "You hear that, Sergeant? A deadly blow!"

"I guess," Sergeant Peacock said suspiciously. "I'd rather blow them to pieces in a gun battle."

"But this avoids the loss of life while still crippling the British war effort," Finn argued.

"Then mount up!" Sergeant Peacock ordered. "I hope your hound can keep up with our horses! You take the two young ladies, Kindernook, and I'll have the handsome lad!"

Finn looked like he wanted to protest about being stuck with the sergeant, but there was no time to argue. Soka smiled slyly at Bridget as Finn pulled himself up behind the sergeant on his horse.

"Serves him right," she said, whatever that meant. Bridget and Soka climbed up behind Kindernook atop his steed.

"Hold on tight," he warned them. "The sergeant likes to ride fast."

They trotted up to the front door, Tucket following on the ground. Peacock counted to three then shouted, "NOW!" He urged his horse forward, bursting through the stable door like a battering ram, making Finn squeal like a frightened old woman. Kindernook followed, galloping past the sleepy tavern, down the hill, and away.

They quickly left McGown's Tavern in their dust. Bridget laughed with joy as the horses galloped full speed down the hill and through the pass. Tucket sped along behind, easily keeping up. The soldiers from the War of 1812 might never have seen action, but they certainly weren't rusty at horse racing.

They galloped along a path through the woods, passing a fort on their left. Kindernook shouted that it was Fort Fish, a War of 1812 fort that had long since been torn down in the mortal world. The whole area seemed to be teeming with soldiers from all eras, but these soldiers' little fort—blockhouse number one—was the farthest out, and the smallest. It wasn't much, the private shouted, but it was home.

They soon left all the fortifications behind as they raced into the North Woods. The trees streamed past as they galloped by; there was no way anyone could keep up on foot, Bridget thought happily. She decided to revise her initial dislike of horses; riding them really fast was awesome. The morning brightened around them, the natural world coming to life as they passed. Finally, the horses slowed to a trot as they approached the head of a long trail that led up the side of a steep cliff, which loomed over them, its top disappearing into a cloud bank high above.

Finn dismounted and the girls followed suit.

"We'll take it from here," Finn said, saluting. Sergeant Peacock saluted back, crisply.

"How bad a blow to the British would you say this is?" he asked hopefully.

"They may never recover," Finn replied. Peacock beamed. Kindernook waved good-bye as the two of them turned their horses to trot back home to their little fort in the woods. Soon Bridget and her companions were alone.

"Quick thinking about the British," Soka said to Finn, nodding with approval. Finn smiled, turning to Bridget for her approval.

"Yeah, you said it right before I did," Bridget added, not wanting to give him the satisfaction of knowing she was impressed with his quick thinking. Finn stuck his tongue out at her playfully before turning to face the trail.

"Let's break out the coats," he said. "It's about to get really cold."

Askook was growing testy and tired of the game. The Trap would soon be falling, and he didn't have the luxury of playing with his toys any longer. Time to end his sport, for good. He knew what awaited them atop the Great Hill. It would not be at all what they're expecting. The climb itelf could very well kill them, of course. But just in case they survived the ascent, he cast his mind ahead to make certain the guardian was awake. He sensed the mad haze of the guardian's mind, poking it to get it good and angry. If they reached his master's hiding place, they would find a nasty, and most certainly fatal, surprise waiting for them . . .

The steep path up the Great Hill was as treacherous as it was long. For hours they climbed, up the rocky path that wound around the mountain. Bridget knew there couldn't be such a high mountain in her Central Park, so she had to be deep in the spirit realm, deeper than she'd been so far. The air grew colder as they climbed higher and higher, and soon snow began to fall softly, making the path even more treacherous.

"Stay near me!" Finn called back, bundled up in his heavy coat. Soka and Bridget made certain to keep up, and Tucket trotted behind, licking at the flakes as they landed on his nose. The wind picked up the higher they rose, which, coupled with the ice-covered stone beneath their feet, made the trail all the more dangerous. At one point, Bridget took a quick peek over the side, and it took her breath away how high they had risen. She could make out trees down below, but she couldn't see the buildings of New York in the distance. Instead, a blue glow covered the horizon, cutting off the world beyond.

Presently, they came to a fork in the path. Finn pondered both ways for a moment, glancing up the side of the icy cliff. Finally, he pointed excitedly.

"The dragon rock!" he yelled over the wind. Bridget could just make out a primitive drawing of a winged lizard on one of the outcroppings.

"Who drew that?" she asked.

"I don't know," he replied. "It's lost to history."

They continued to climb. At one point, Finn pulled them back against the wall as a giant condor flew right past them, searching the ground in the distance for prey. Bridget shuddered to see the great bird swoop by so close, glad the falling snow made them hard to see.

Soon they reached another fork, but this time Finn didn't even pause, heading to the right while wordlessly pointing to a scrawny tree halfway up the path, hanging out over the edge of the trail. The snow was falling faster now, sticking to Bridget's eyelashes and making it hard to see. She moved closer to Soka, who stopped to brush off Bridget's face.

"Better?" Soka asked. Bridget nodded gratefully. But she could feel her paper limbs starting to freeze up. She had no blood to keep her insides warm. If she stayed out in the cold too long, she'd freeze solid. She thought about saying something, but she didn't want to slow down now. They couldn't be far, she thought. How high could a little mountain in Central Park be, anyway?

Various sounds on the wind alerted them to the animals on the prowl, but thankfully they stayed away. The snow was piling up over their ankles now, making it harder to walk. If they didn't find this cave soon, they'd have to turn back. Finally, they reached a fork with four paths heading in different directions: two went back down, one continued to twist around the way they had been walking, and the last led directly up the side of the mountain at a steep incline. Here Finn stopped, perplexed.

"This is the spot Granddad always had trouble with," he

said. "The way he remembered it, he and Abigail made their way up that steep incline. But he told me when he tried to retrace his steps after the blizzard, there was a dead end up there, with nowhere to go. So he tried all the other paths to no avail. He looked everywhere for the ruby icefall, but he could never find it."

"Great," Bridget yelled, bending her arms to keep them from stiffening up. "So what do we do?"

"Well, we know it's a dead end up there," Finn said, pointing to the steep path. "And it's probably not down. So we'll follow the same path we're on."

"No, wait!" Soka stopped him. "Let's try the steep path first."

"Why?" Finn asked. "We can't stay up here forever; we'll freeze!"

"Because I trust your grandfather's memory. What else do we have?"

Finn looked at her, uncertain, then nodded.

"Fine," he said. "But we have to move fast. It's pure luck nothing has found us out here, and our luck won't last forever."

Soka nodded, then turned to climb the steep path. Bridget followed, willing her bendy-bits not to freeze. Hans poked his head out of her pocket, his teeth chattering.

"I think my heater is starting to cut out!" he cried. "It was never meant for such cold! If I die, don't let the dog eat me!"

"Oh, don't be so negative," Bridget said as Tucket happily climbed past her. He seemed to be the only one unaffected by the cold. The luxury that comes with a thick coat, she thought.

They climbed and climbed, and the path became almost

vertical. Finally, they dropped to their hands and knees, pulling themselves up the final few feet to a plateau. Finn had to push Tucket's bottom to get the dog over the hump. They reached the ledge, looked around, and felt their spirits fall.

In front of them loomed a wall of ice and snow, completely cutting off their way forward. It was a dead end.

"I knew it!" Finn cried, kicking the ice with his boot. "I told you this was a mistake."

"It was the only way worth trying," Soka said, her face sad.

"There's nothing here but ice, ice, and more ice," Finn replied, sinking to the ground. Bridget approached the wall, touching it lightly. Hans leaned out, his face intent.

"Wait a second," he said, putting his helmet back on. "I'm picking something up. On the other side of this wall. It sounds like falling water." His voice grew excited. "Remember what Pierre said? The ruby icefall? A waterfall under the ice. I think I hear it!"

"So we *are* here!" Bridget cried.

"Wait, I'm picking something else up. It sounds like . . . breathing?" Hans pulled off his helmet and stared up at Bridget, perplexed. "I think there's someone on the other side of this wall."

"Who? Abigail?" Bridget could barely contain her excitement. She backed up in order to stare at the top of the wall above. Finn and Soka turned to watch her as Hans cautioned her from her pocket.

"We don't know who it is," he said. "I think we should wait and—"

"HELLO!" Bridget screamed as loud as she could. "IS THAT YOU, ABIGAIL?" Her cry echoed through the pass, bouncing off the icy walls into the distance. Finn ran up, his face furious.

"What are you doing, you stupid child?" he cried.

"Hans heard someone on the other side of the wall!" Bridget told him excitedly. This didn't seem to get Finn quite as amped as she'd expected. Instead, his face grew white.

"Someone . . . or something?" he asked, backing away while staring up at the wall in terror. Soka glanced up and she, too, went pale. Tucket began to bark furiously at something above them, and Bridget slowly turned to see what they were looking at. Her stomach dropped as a huge shadow fell on them, cast by something standing atop the wall. Hans threw on his helmet, adjusted something inside to see better, then screamed.

"BEAR!" he cried, just as the shadow fell upon them with a roar.

It was a huge bear, the size of an elephant, at least, and they were just able to leap out of the way before it barreled past. It hit Bridget with a heavy swipe of its paw, sending her careening into the wall. She slid to the ground with a thud. She didn't feel any pain, but she could see the beast had cut a chunk of paper off her shoulder. Hans lay at her feet, stunned. She looked to the path, where all she could see was the back of the bellowing bear. Then Finn ran into view, pulling Soka behind a rock for cover. The bear started to turn toward them, but then it stopped, staring at something just out of Bridget's sight. A growl rumbled through the ledge, making the very rocks shake. Slowly, Bridget pulled herself to the side to see what the bear was looking at. Her breath caught in her throat. She never imagined he could get that big!

Tucket had grown. Really GROWN! He had puffed up to the size of a woolly mammoth, towering over them like a creature from another planet. There was barely enough room for both giant animals on the ledge, and Bridget knew that soon one would have to fall. She could only hope that it would be her Tucket who survived. Tucket reared his head back and howled, once, sending icicles crashing to the floor around them. The bear roared back, shaking the very mountain with his challenge. And then, at once, they charged, meeting in the middle of the ledge with a mighty crash that seemed to make the world shudder.

Bridget could barely comprehend the battle she was witnessing. It was too big for her to fully take in. She quickly ran to the far corner of the ledge, knowing that if she stayed she'd be buried in no time. Finn and Soka joined her, their faces as terrified as she knew hers to be as they clung to one another.

Tucket and the bear clashed, again and again, swiping and biting with huge jaws and claws the size of crane shovels. The mountain quivered with each mighty blow, but neither would give an inch. The snow fell harder, making it difficult to see, and soon Bridget could barely make out shadows in the white, crashing into each other, tearing each other apart. On and on they fought, neither giving way. At one point, the sun peeked through the snow, and Bridget's heart broke to see the blood pouring down Tucket's beautiful tawny fur. But the great bear bled, too, from many wounds, and it seemed as though they'd keep fighting forever.

But then it happened; Tucket slipped, and the bear did not hesitate. He thrust one mighty paw across Tucket's head, sending the dog crashing into the wall. Debris began to rain from the peak above, and Bridget and her friends had to dodge the falling rocks. Tucket whined, barely moving, as the bear reared back to roar in triumph before one last, fatal swipe.

"NOOOOO!" Bridget cried, and Soka had to hold her from running in front of the blow. Soka glanced up at the top of the wall and her eyes widened. She yelled down at Hans, who had just staggered to his feet.

"Can you toss one of your firecrackers up there?"

"I'd need to get closer and the wall's too slippery to climb. You'll have to throw me."

Finn stepped forward.

"I'll do it!" he said, picking up the roach. Hans gave the order and Finn reared back and threw with all his strength, sending the small insect warrior soaring through the air. Up the battle roach flew, and for a moment it appeared as if he'd reach the top of the wall. But the roach began to slow far short of safety. Instead, once he reached the apex of his flight, Hans threw a tiny firecracker, the miniature missile arcing toward a large icicle swaying up above. Then the battle roach fell, fast, crashing into the rocks at Tucket's feet.

For a moment nothing happened, and the bear lifted its paw for the deathblow. But just as the paw descended, a small explosion went off up above and the large icicle fell loose, whistling through the air as it dropped to impale the bear right through the jaw and send him crashing to the ground. The bear began to thrash, crashing into the wall again and again over the injured bodies of the brave spirit dog and the spunky battle roach. At last, the bear fell forward right through the ice, breaking it apart. An avalanche of ice and stone tumbled forward over its dead body—over Tucket and Hans, too—until they all disappeared completely under the rubble. The last few rocks tumbled forward down the path to the trail below, and then all was still. The great bear was dead.

Bridget rushed forward with a cry. She tore at the rocks with her bare hands. Soka tried to stop her, but she wouldn't listen. She kept digging and digging, until finally she heard a whine. Following the sound, she tossed aside the rubble until she came across the gigantic bear paw. Nestled underneath, protected by the curved palm of the dead beast, lay Tucket and Hans.

She pulled Tucket out, sobbing without tears. He had shrunk to the size he'd been when she'd first met him, barely larger than a puppy. He was covered in scratches from his battle, and his beautiful coat was matted with blood. But he still breathed, and she sat by his side, petting him and whispering that everything would be all right.

"Good dog," she breathed into his ear. "You're a good, good dog."

Meanwhile, Soka knelt down next to the prone battle roach, gently pulling off his helmet.

"He's unconscious," she said. "And it looks like one of his arms is crushed. But we won't know how injured he is until he wakes up. If he wakes up . . ."

Bridget's heart ached at the sight of her injured friends. She didn't even react when Finn let out a shout from the other side of the fallen wall.

"It's here! The cave! The ruby icefall. All of it! There must have been an avalanche that sealed it off during that blizzard Granddad talked about. Come on, the cave's warm inside!"

Bridget lifted Tucket into her arms and carried him over the rubble. On the other side, a beautiful sight greeted her. The entire wall along the path glittered ruby red, like a dazzling gemstone. She realized that the red came from the stone, but the glittering came from the ice that encased it. Behind the ice, water trickled down the stone in a steady stream. The effect was of a magical curtain giving her a glimpse into another world. She passed by in silence, the ruby icefall stealing her voice away.

Farther down the path she came upon the cave, which loomed before her like an open airplane hangar. As she entered, she realized from the mess that the bear had been living in it. She wondered what it had done to whatever secrets Kieft had left there.

But the cave was empty, save for some bones in the corner and giant mounds of manure everywhere. Finn, however, had already found a way farther inside, and he led them to the thin crack in the far wall.

"This is it," Finn said, smiling from excitement. "The old man never found it, but I did."

Soka smiled, though her eyes seemed tired. She glanced down at Tucket and Hans. "But was it worth the fight?" she wondered.

"Can I take Tucket in first?" Bridget asked. "He deserves to see the secret before anyone else. I'll even close my eyes."

Finn hesitated, but Soka nodded gently.

"After you," she said. Bridget stepped forward with Tucket in her arms, her eyes screwed shut. Finally, she stopped.

"Impressed, Tucket?" she asked. "Can I look now?" With that, she opened her eyes.

She felt like weeping. The room was empty.

But it hadn't always been so. There were clues to what had once filled the cave—Finn found a single gold piece, which he bit into and pronounced real, and Soka discovered a single piece of parchment.

"This is a Munsee spell," she said. "My mother always thought Kieft was stealing Munsee magic. Who knows how many of these parchments Kieft stored in here? All of our knowledge . . . we've lost so much of it since we've been trapped! Think of what we'd regain!"

"Well, it's gone now," Finn said, kicking a pebble in frustration. "Someone must have moved it all."

"What about Abigail's token?" Bridget asked. "That's what we're here for, right?"

"If it was wrapped up in Kieft's treasure, then it's probably gone, too," Hans said sourly. Discouraged, Bridget sat against the wall with Tucket in her arms. Soka knelt down beside her.

"It's okay," she began, taking Bridget's hand, but she stopped midsentence, her eyes puzzled. She lifted Bridget's arm. "Your wrist is so hot it's practically on fire, Bridget."

"What?" Bridget wished she could feel something through her paper skin. She looked down at her wrist, noticing the purple wampum melted into the bark. "The bracelet! There must be wampum near me!"

Soka nodded hopefully. She took Bridget's wrist and began passing it over the floor. Finally, she stopped over a flat rock set flush with the dirt on the cave floor, indistinguishable from the rest of the cave. "Here it is, whatever it is." Soka quickly lifted up the rock. Underneath lay a dirty brown pouch, cracked with age. Pulling it open, Soka upended it over her palm—and out dropped half of a single purple wampum bead.

"I can feel it," Soka exclaimed, face flushed with excitement. "It's calling us south! She left a final arrow pointing to her. If we follow it, we find her!"

"Well, we better get going," Bridget said, standing up. "We don't want to be any later than we already are!"

REVELATIONS

The *Adventure Galley* flew through the mist, moving blindly at a ridiculous speed powered by the stories in Wampage's bead. Rory wondered what would happen if they hit something, and from the look on Kidd's face, the pirate captain was worried, too.

Hours passed tensely, with only the words pouring forth from the wampum breaking the wall of wind that surrounded them. Though he didn't speak the language, Rory found himself understanding many of the tales—they bypassed his ears and went directly into his memory. Glancing around, he noticed not only his friends, but many of the sailors as well, listening intently. Some of the stories Rory picked up were familiar; he guessed that Wampage had told him those tales when he was a baby. A few of them flew by him before he could hear them. But most of them caught inside, and he would remember them always. It felt like a bigger gift than the escape, though he couldn't explain why. He promised himself that he would pass these stories on, not only to the Munsees, but to anyone who would listen. That would be his way of thanking Wampage for his sacrifice.

Finally, the words sputtered out as the last tale flew up into the sails and the ship began to slow. By now, the normal wind had picked up and they began sailing under natural power. Wampage put the bead of wampum into a pouch at his waist, his face stone. Rory stepped up to him.

"I'm so sorry." Rory didn't know if he could touch Wampage's arm, so he just stood there awkwardly at the Munsee's side. "This is all my fault. I was too stubborn . . ."

Wampage sighed. "Perhaps Kishelamakank meant for his stories to be let loose among all these strangers. Perhaps they will take root with them and spread through the city when we return, binding my people to yours. Either way, there is nothing we can do now but sail on."

"Something's ahead, Captain!" The cry came down from the crow's nest, interrupting them. Rory ran to the bow, peering intently through the fog. Suddenly a dark shape formed out of the mist, its indistinct features sharpening as they approached. It was a ship. Rory's heart leaped. *Could it be?* As they sailed closer, he could make out more details: the rotting hull, the tattered sails . . . it was the *Half Moon* all right. Rory could hardly breathe as he realized that this was it. Alexa stepped up beside him, shaking her head in disbelief.

"You are a lucky guy, Rory," she said. "We're all pretty lucky today."

They sailed up alongside the listing ship. Rory wondered how the thing ever sailed in such awful condition. He was nervous to set foot on the thing. But he would.

A shout carried across the water.

"Ahoy!" the voice cried. "Do not come aboard! We'll come to you!"

A pair of men were climbing down the hull into a small skiff. The little boat pushed off, and the men inside rowed the short distance between the ships. They bounced into the *Adventure Galley* with a clang and one of them called up.

"Permission to come aboard?"

"Granted," Kidd yelled back, though he motioned to his men to pull their pistols and cutlasses in case of an attack. The two men climbed up the ladder and stepped onto the deck. And there he was, striding up to Kidd, not a day older than in his picture. Rory's father, in the flesh.

Alexa's hand tightened on Rory's shoulder. Should he walk up? He knew he should, but instead he held back. He didn't know what to say to the man. Rory's father was clearly in charge, stepping up to Captain Kidd to shake his hand.

"I don't know if you remember me, Captain," Mr. Hennessy was saying. "My name is Ronald Flint. I was one of Tew's Boys, if you recall." Kidd glanced sharply at Rory; the captain had recognized Rory's father right away. "My associate and I are the only ones who could come over to your vessel. The rest are damned souls, sad to say, and they can't leave the ship."

"What are you doing sailing on a ghost ship, anyway?" Kidd asked.

"It's a bit mournful at times, I won't lie to you," Mr. Hennessy admitted. "But since the *Half Moon* is a cursed ship, no one in their right mind would ever try to sail alongside and board her. So if you can take the depression of hanging out with cursed people with their constant moaning and the like, there are certain perks to joining the crew, especially if you don't want to be found. If you get my drift."

Kidd nodded, one marked man to another.

"Now, however, a big storm is coming and the *Half Moon* is about to head homeward yet again to warn the city of its impending doom," Mr. Hennessy continued. "She will show up right before the storm, which means those of us who aren't damned won't get much of a chance to reach shore before we're battered to pieces. So if you wouldn't mind, we'd like to sail the rest of the way with you. We'd rather not get torn apart by what's coming—at least not yet."

Kidd nodded. He laid out the terms of service, which they agreed to, then welcomed them aboard. Kidd left them to Hendrick, and walked over to Rory.

"Are you going to talk to him or just stand there?" he asked.

Rory shrugged, hanging back. He had no idea what to say. His father wasn't a real person. He was a picture, a memory, a legend. What do you say to someone like that? Rory held back and watched, unable to decide what to do.

Wampage, however, was creeping forward, a confused look on his face. At first, Rory thought his friend was headed toward Mr. Hennessy, but instead Wampage circled toward his father's companion. A tall fellow in a wide hat that covered his face in shadow, the man wasn't looking their way. But Wampage seemed to be fascinated by him. He stepped closer and finally the other man heard him, turning toward the sound. Wampage fell back, shocked.

"You . . ."

The man took off his hat to reveal wide, awed eyes. His

cheeks bore tattoos of snarling dogs, the twins of Tammand's. Rory knew that face; he had seen it before . . .

"You're out!" the man cried. "Are they free? Are our people free?" Wampage couldn't reply, having difficulty finding his voice.

"What's going on?" Simon whispered to Rory. "Who *is* that guy?"

"I don't believe it," Alexa said, understanding blossoming across her face. Rory turned to Simon, who was still a step behind.

"His name is Buckongahelas," he said, wonder creeping into his voice. "And he's supposed to be dead."

Kidd invited Mr. Hennessy and Buckongahelas, who insisted they call him Buck, into his dining room, where Rory, Alexa, Simon, Fritz, and Wampage joined them. Mr. Hennessy kept shooting glances at Rory, obviously wondering why he looked familiar, but Rory did not introduce himself. He still didn't know what he should say to his long-absent dad, so he settled on staring a hole into the man.

Mr. Hennessy nodded at Wampage. "Hey, you. Long time no see. How you stayed out of the Trap is one story I'd like to hear."

"Later, Harry Meester," Wampage said curtly.

"Harry Meester." Mr. Hennessy rolled the name around on his tongue. "Been a long time since I've been called that. A *long* time."

"Is that your real name?" Alexa asked.

"Of course not." Mr. Hennessy winked at her. "Names are like jackets. They're something for people to grab onto when you're running. That's so easy to wiggle out of. The perfect thing to leave dangling uselessly in their hand as you hightail it down the road. People think names pin you down, but it's the other way around. Your name pins them down and no mistake."

"Sounds like years of experience talking," Kidd said drily.

"More than you know," Mr. Hennessy replied, giving him a faint smile. He shrugged at Wampage, who stared, stone-faced, at him. "You never liked me, did you, Wampage. Didn't trust me."

"I was right not to," Wampage replied. "You are a liar."

"But not a murderer." Mr. Hennessy pointed to Buck, who was sitting uncomfortably at his side. "That counts for something, right?"

"What happened?" Alexa asked. "Witnesses watched you shoot Buck in cold blood!"

"Yeah, well . . ." Now Mr. Hennessy looked uncomfortable. "Why is this kid burning a hole in my head?" He pointed right at Rory, who looked away. "You look a little familiar. Do I know your mother or something?"

"Something like that," Rory replied. Mr. Hennessy gave him a sharp look.

Buck spoke up. "I didn't know you were free, Wampage. I am sorry. I would have sought you out. I have done everything wrong." His face ached with sadness.

"Start at the beginning," Wampage instructed him, his eyes softening for his old friend.

"Well, like most things, it began with Kieft," Mr. Hennessy jumped in. "I don't mind telling you that because if that old goat ever catches up with me, this particular story will be way down on the list of secrets he'll make me wish I never knew.

Not that I don't wish that already. Anyway, Kieft wanted to get rid of the Munsees. He'd hated them for a long, long time, and he knew that having them around was a threat to his power. They had access to magic he couldn't match, at least not then. So he dreamed up the Trap, with some help, of course."

"Did you help?" Wampage asked, his voice dangerously soft.

"No, no, that was far beyond me," Mr. Hennessy quickly assured him. "I had nothing to do with it. But when it came to putting his plan to action . . . Kieft always had a way of making certain I play along with his games. No matter how I might want to throw in my chips and go home, he'd always make sure I was in for the next hand. And that time was no different."

Rory's stomach twisted as he listened. Alexa put her hand over his, flashing him an empathetic smile. *What does she know*, Rory thought. Her dad had been one of the good guys, *the* good guy. His dad . . . he wanted to cry.

"How long had you worked for Kieft?" Fritz wanted to know. Mr. Hennessy shot him a look.

"It's better for all of us if you don't know the answer to that question. Not meaning to be rude, but there it is. Anyway, Kieft had this great plan to gather up all the Munsees in Central Park and trap them there. There was just one problem: he needed the Mayor's help. And Mayor Hamilton loved the Munsees. He was good friends with Tackapausha himself. They'd often let their children play together. Which blinded both of them to what was going on between Buck here and sweet little Abigail."

Mr. Hennessy's eyes grew soft.

"She was the brightest little kid," he said, smiling. Buck stared down at his hands, not looking at anyone. "She did not deserve any of what I did to her. I am truly sorry for any pain I caused that poor child. It will haunt me till the end of my long days."

"What did you do to her, exactly?" Fritz asked.

"Well, Hamilton and Tackapausha may have been blind to their children's growing love for each other, but Kieft wasn't. And there lay his chance. So he instructed me to help the two of them fan the embers of their love into a flame. Which I did, not that it took much."

"I loved her the minute I met her," Buck said, his voice overflowing with sadness. "There were no barriers to our love among my people, especially since Hamilton was such a friend to us. But Abigail knew that her father would not approve. She was his joy, and he would not give her over to a *savage*, no matter how many meals he shared with my father."

"Now, you don't know that, Buck," Mr. Hennessy said. "Alexander really liked you. Who knows what may have happened without Kieft. As it was, Kieft forced me to tell Hamilton tall tales of how barbaric the mating rituals were among the savages, and on and on. Awful things that no right-thinking man would ever believe. But Hamilton was blinded by his worries for his daughter. I went back and forth, planting ideas in both Buck and Abigail that their fathers would never let them live together. He had me tell Abigail that her father was ready to lock her up rather than let her marry a savage. So she ran to the Munsees.

"Then I went with Kieft to see the Mayor and told him a bald-faced lie. I said that Abigail was renouncing him as her father. She was being adopted by Tackapausha and would be one of the Munsees, throwing away her past. She wanted to be Munsee only, forever. I told him lie after lie after lie—how Tackapausha urged Abigail to curse her father's name, how Buck had three other wives—things no one else would ever believe. But Hamilton was already despondent, so he swallowed them all. Mayor Hamilton turned to Kieft and authorized the Trap right then and there."

"We should have known," Buck said. "We should have wondered why he was so upset that his own daughter had come to live with us. But my father believed that one had nothing to do with the other. Hamilton was still a good man, decent, and he wouldn't turn against us."

"By this point, I was hurtin'," Mr. Hennessy said. "I liked both these kids and I knew what was coming. I wanted to warn them, but I was so scared of what Kieft would do to me. He's done awful things before, to me and mine, and I couldn't bear it. I was weak, and that shame will stay with me always.

"But when the day of the Trap arrived, I hatched a little plan of my own. I knew I couldn't stop the Trap, but I wanted to save Buck and Abigail. So I convinced Buck to travel to City Hall and plead with the Mayor to reconsider his opposition to the marriage—just to get the boy out of the park. Hamilton was already taking care of his own—he'd sent men to take Abigail from the Munsee camp the night before to bring her back home. But things didn't work out that way. For one thing, Abigail was nowhere to be found when the Mayor's man arrived at the Munsee camp."

Rory glanced at Alexa, who nodded back. That was the night Abigail had followed Kieft. If not for that, she would have been carried off before the Trap was sprung and everything would have been different.

"And Buck . . ." Mr. Hennessy was saying.

"It did not go well with the Mayor," Buck finished, his face dark. "He had no forgiveness in his heart."

"But I knew that," Mr. Hennessy said. "I just wanted Buck out of the park. But Kieft, who was there with Hamilton as usual in those days, made it a point to tell Buck about the Trap, just to make certain he ran back to his people. Kieft didn't want a happily married Buck and Abigail bouncing around the island, reminding everyone that maybe the Munsees weren't so unlike us after all.

"Then Kieft pulled me aside and told me to go after the boy and kill him, in front of the Munsees. To make certain no one ever forgives, he said. And it was here I reached my limit. I had done so many things for Kieft, things I would never tell a soul. And as the years passed, the burden grew heavier and heavier. But *this* . . . ? Murdering a friend, a boy I watched grow up? I couldn't do it. So I followed Buck back to his people, and just as the Trap was being sprung, I shot him in the back, to wound him while making him appear dead."

"Why?" Alexa asked. "Why not just run?"

"Kieft wanted Buck dead," Mr. Hennessy told her. "If he knew that Buck was alive somewhere, nothing would stop him from hunting the poor boy down and destroying both him and me. I had to do it."

"A shot in the back is a dangerous gamble," Kidd said. "Weren't you afraid you'd kill him?"

"I know a good healer," Mr. Hennessy said. "Let's leave it at that."

Alexa nudged Rory and whispered, "The abbess!" into his ear. *Of course*, Rory thought. *It all comes together.*

"But it didn't go perfectly," Mr. Hennessy continued. "As Buck fell, I saw Abigail standing next to Tackapausha at the edge of the park, and both of them were devastated. I'll always remember that look on Abigial's face. It haunts me to this day. Then the blue light flew up and they were gone. Buck and I holed up until he was healed, and then we snuck down to the dock, hopped aboard the first ship leaving port, and sailed away. We later heard that Abigail had died, which broke our hearts all over again."

"I sent in a squirrel, when I was on my first shore leave," Buck said. "I didn't want any of my people to know I was alive. I was ashamed. I could do nothing for them, so I felt it was better if they thought I was dead. The squirrel came back with news that it was true. My Olathe was dead. Once I knew that, there was no reason for me to ever step foot on the shore again."

"Yep, we've been running ever since," Mr Hennessy said. "Keeping out of sight."

"Keeping out of sight?" Fritz asked. "Was that business with Tew's Boys keeping out of sight?"

Mr. Hennessy's eyes went dark. "That was a mistake." He glared at Kidd. "You'd sunk our ship, Captain. I understand your reasons, but that still left me and ten other men clinging to a couple of planks for weeks. I thought I was going to sink to the bottom of the sea. So I told the other men some things I shouldn't have. Secrets that I certainly would never tell anyone normally, including you lot, so don't bother to ask. I should have kept my mouth shut, just let it die with me. But I didn't. And those secrets were far too dangerous to get out, so I had to use a bit of Munsee magic I'd picked up over the years to prevent anyone from telling any tales. This protected them as much as me, believe me. Some things we'd all be better off not knowing. I only meant for it to be a simple bind, but I'm not really much for magic and I did it all wrong. I made the spell far too strong. It weighed on their souls like anchors dragging them down. And they could never be free. I ruined the lives of ten men that day, and I will forever be ashamed of it. So much to answer for . . ."

No one spoke as her stared off into nothing. Finally, he let out a long breath.

"Anyway," he said, "that's how we ended up here. And now we've been found out, so I don't know what's going to happen. I'm pretty curious, I have to admit. But for now, would you all mind giving me a moment?"

"For what?" Fritz asked.

Mr. Hennessy looked right at Rory.

"I'd like to speak to my son."

Rory and his father stared at each other across the table. The others had left them alone, but for a while neither of them spoke. Finally, Mr. Hennessy nodded.

"You've got your mother's nose. And from what Kidd just told me about you coming after me, her stubborn refusal to quit. She could argue a point forever. Usually, I'd just give in. Easier to say 'yes, dear' than keep fighting."

Rory didn't answer.

"How's Bridget?" Mr. Hennessy continued uncomfortably. "What kind of girl is she? Smart? Pretty? Quick on her feet like her old man?"

"She's good," Rory said finally. "She's all those things."

"I always knew she'd be like her dad. You could see it in her, even when she was a baby."

"What about me?" Rory asked. "What did you see in me?" Mr. Hennessy sighed.

"I saw a lot of your mother. We should all be more like her." He paused, steadying his breathing. Rory was shocked to realize his father was barely holding on.

"I can't believe it's you," his father said finally. "You, of all people. My son, the Light. How did you find me?"

"The abbess told me you were sailing this way," Rory said, his thoughts awhirl.

"You saw Mary? I'm glad she sent you after me."

"She was murdered." Rory wanted to shock his father. But Mr. Hennessy shrugged.

"I doubt that. She's a goddess, you know, and they aren't easy to kill. The Goddess of Remorse. You can see why we'd be such good friends."

"Why did you leave?" Rory blurted out, the tears running down his face. "Why?"

"I'm so sorry for what I did to you, to your sister, to your poor mother . . ." Mr. Hennessy wiped away a tear. "I was weak. I met your mother and I fell in love. I thought I could hide on the mainland for a while. Buck was doing fine and didn't need me by his side every minute of every day. And I thought, if I stayed up in Inwood, the furthest corner of the island, then maybe I could live at least one lifetime in peace. But then . . . one morning, I saw him. A battle roach, waving at me from the baseboard. I recognized the markings . . . he was a M'Garoth, one of the Mayor's own guard. I'd been discovered! I panicked, and ran for the docks, hopping on the first ship out of port. I told myself I did it for the good of my family. If Kieft discovered me with a family, he'd have killed the whole lot of you just to teach me a lesson. I couldn't chance it. At least, with me gone . . . maybe you'd have a chance at a normal life."

"Normal?" Rory cried. "Normal? The only reason I'm even alive is because Wampage repressed my abilities. Mom works every moment of every day to keep food on the table—we never see her anymore. And now . . . now it feels like everyone is trying to get me."

"Rory, I never wanted . . ." Mr. Hennessy began, despondent, but Rory wasn't done yet.

"You could have protected me," he said angrily. "Kieft has been searching for me since I was born, to kill me. You could have watched out for me instead of leaving me to face Mannahatta on my own."

"I'm sorry," his father said miserably. "I didn't know. I swear, I didn't know . . ."

"Would you have stayed if you did know?" Rory asked. Mr. Hennessy looked shocked at the question. Slowly, he nodded.

"I'd like to think I would have," he said.

"I guess we'll never know," Rory answered bitterly. They lapsed into silence, neither looking at the other. What was left to say?

Rory approached Alexa's room, noticing that the door was ajar. He could hear her talking quietly but urgently to Simon.

"I saw those plates, Simon. There is no way they could have survived that storm. No way. That floor should have been littered with broken china. Instead, there they all sat, a perfect set. Of *good* china. How do you explain that?"

"Alexa," Simon began, "these are just well-made plates. They're only a notch below a Flora Danica—" He stopped himself as he realized he'd said too much.

"Flora Danica?" Alexa cried. "How do you even know what that means? I can't believe this. Take it off, right now!"

"But—" Simon cut off as he noticed Rory standing in the doorway. He eagerly latched onto Rory's presence in order to change the subject.

"How'd it go?" he asked.

Rory didn't answer. He stumbled over to the bed and collapsed at its foot. Her argument put on hold, Alexa sat down next to him.

"You did it, Rory," she said. "Finding Buck alive changes everything. Tackapausha has to listen to his son. We've got a real chance to avert war."

"I know," Rory said miserably. "It feels really good." He began to cry. Simon shot Alexa a helpless look then punched Rory lightly on the arm.

"Cheer up there, soldier!" he said with false brightness. "Welcome to the disappointing dad club! You should come to the meetings. We serve punch. Get it?"

Rory only cried harder. Alexa enveloped him in her arms.

"It's okay, Rory. It's okay."

She comforted him as Simon looked on awkwardly. After a moment the tears dried up. Now a new worry rose in his heart. What was he going to tell Bridget?

UNDER THE ANGEL

After trekking back down the mountain, Bridget and her companions decided they needed a ride, since their little homing wampum was leading them far to the south. So they followed the trail right to Sergeant Peacock and Private Kindernook's little fort. The two soldiers happily lent their horses to the cause against the British, with the warning that if let free, the horses would return north to their owners. Thanking them profusely, Finn and Soka climbed atop one steed, while Bridget cradled Tucket in her arms on the other. Hans had finally woken up, groggy and in pain from his injured arm, but he refused to take off his armor to look at his injuries. Bridget placed him in the saddlebag, where he lay muttering ideas for new inventions to himself to keep his mind off the pain.

They took off, galloping away at full speed. Bridget's horse didn't need much guiding; it seemed happy to follow its friend. Soka held the wampum, so Bridget just concentrated on holding on to Tucket without falling off.

They raced south, passing through the North Woods and

the Ravine, outracing the coyotes that still milled about the river, finally bursting out onto the Great Lawn. They galloped past the hordes of sunbathers, scattering a flock of wild turkeys that gobbled unseen and unheard in their midst. They made their way around the Ramble along the edge of the park, and still the bead led them on, skirting the boaters' pond and finally pulling up at a trot to Bethesda Plaza.

"The pull is strongest right here," Soka called, dismounting. The rest of them followed, gazing around the crowded plaza. Soka began to scan the plaza for clues of Abigail's whereabouts; Bridget stepped forward to follow, guiding her horse, when Finn sidled up beside her.

"You don't like me," he said.

"You don't know that!" Bridget replied, too startled by his bluntness to come up with anything better.

"I've heard enough about Rory Hennessy on this trip to see where you stand. I know you think I'm trying to steal your brother's girl. You probably think I'm some kind of rogue, with a woman at every tavern."

"Yeah," Bridget agreed. "That's pretty much it."

"I can't help the way I look," Finn said, his handsome features making a perfect pout. "I can't help that women act the way they do around me. Most of them are just silly girls, you know. Nothing like Soka. Or you, for that matter."

"Hey!" Bridget exclaimed. "Watch yourself!"

"I'm only saying that you are a strong person," Finn said, putting his hands up with an ingratiating smile. His eyes softened. "And Soka . . . Soka is like no one I've ever known. Adventurous, smart, not afraid to fight for what she believes in. How can I not fall in love? I know, I know . . . according to you, she's meant for your brother. And who knows, maybe that will all work out just the way you want it to. To hear Soka talk about him, he practically walks on water. And if that's what she wants, then I will step aside. But I won't give up without even trying. Surely, you can understand that."

He looked over at Soka, who was tugging thoughtfully on her braid as she searched around the edge of the plaza. A look of longing passed over his face and for the first time Bridget felt sorry for the guy. But then loyalty took over and she scowled.

"I know what this is," she informed him haughtily. "You're trying to trick me into helping you. Well, it won't work! We're on different teams, mister! I'm on Team Rory and you're on Team Pretty Boy!"

"Well, I had to try," Finn said, shaking his head with a rueful smile.

"Let's just find Abigail, and no more being tricky!" Bridget said.

Leading the horse, she jogged over to join Soka's search. Bridget hoped Abigail wasn't buried under the flagstones . . . that would be a heartbreaking end. Bridget sighed. She'd thought this was supposed to be the easy part.

She stepped back, taking in all of Bethesda Plaza. She couldn't believe she'd just been here two days earlier—it felt like a lifetime ago that Askook had attempted to destroy her. She glanced up at the angel in the fountain—the angel still gazed mournfully at the ground, same as always.

She froze, staring at the statue. How could she not have seen it before? It was right there in the bronze features, in front of her this whole time. Soka stepped up next to her.

"What is it?" the Munsee girl asked. She followed Bridget's

gaze and her jaw dropped. "She looks just like—" Soka gasped. Dropping the reins, Bridget ran forward, climbing into the fountain. Soka followed, the two of them splashing as they raced toward the statue.

"What is it?" Finn called from the edge of the fountain, where he was now holding both horses. "What did you find?"

Bridget reached the base of the pedestal and stared upward. She pointed excitedly.

"Look!" she cried. "In her hand! It's a bead!"

Sure enough, a small bronze bead lay clutched in the outstretched hand of the statue.

"I can't believe it," Soka breathed.

Bridget's eyes shone with vindication. "Abigail is the angel in Bethesda Fountain!"

"*Mon Dieu,* you're right!" a voice said from behind them, drenched in a thick French accent. Spinning, they came face-to-face with Pierre Duchamp, limping out of the trees. "You found her!

"Granddad!" Finn cried. "What are you doing here?"

"I am with Penhawitz! He lies injured, just beyond the trees. He came to me soon after you left with the news that he'd picked up Abigail's trail again. You were too far north to send word, so we decided to follow it south ourselves. Earlier today, we were waylaid by coyotes, not far from here. I came to the pond for some water, never guessing that the object of our hundred-year search waited here, hidden under our very noses!"

"Penhawitz is injured!" Soka cried. "We must go to him."

"Of course," Pierre agreed. "But first, I must know. If you found Abigail, you must have found the cave!"

"We did, Grandfather!" Finn told him excitedly. "It was

hidden behind a huge sheet of ice. We had to fight off a great bear to reach it. Both the dog and the battle roach were sorely injured."

"But you entered the cave?" Pierre's eyes glinted. Bridget suddenly didn't like the look on the old man's face. Soka seemed to notice it as well. She warily stepped forward, feet splashing in the pool.

"How far is my uncle?" she asked. "Are his injuries grave?"

"He will be fine," Pierre assured her. "What did you find? What treasure did Kieft hide away?"

"Take me to Penhawitz."

"Of course. But you must tell me: what did you find?"

"We will talk all about it once I see to my uncle," Soka said, her face stone.

"Why are you playing games with me?" Pierre asked, his brow furrowing in irritation. "What did you find in the cave?"

Finn looked puzzled at Soka's reluctance, so he jumped in. "It was amazing, Grandfather—"

"Finn!" Soka cut him off. "Don't say another word."

"Why are you acting like this?" Finn asked. "He deserves to know—"

"I'm not so sure about that," Soka replied. "Something's not right here."

"Unbelievable!" Pierre cried. He suddenly pulled out a pistol and trained it on Soka. "Is this how you want it? You are just like your uncle."

"Grandfather!" Finn cried, shocked. "What are you doing?"

"I am finishing what I started a century and a half ago, boy." Pierre waved the gun in the air. "Where is my treasure!"

"How old is that pistol?" Soka asked calmly. "It looks more

elderly than you are." Bridget noticed that the gun in Pierre's hand looked pitted and worn, like an ancient relic you hang on the wall. "Can you even shoot that thing?"

Pierre sneered and fired once in the air. The retort rang through the plaza as a huge cloud of smoke drifted from the barrel. "Old, yes. Useless, no. And if you even take one step toward me, paper girl, the next bullet goes right between Soka's eyes."

"You're a horrible man!" Bridget cried. "How could you stick Abigail in that statue for all these years?"

"She did that herself," Pierre said. "She had a piece of parchment in her hand when I caught up with her here, at the fountain. She warned me that she had a spell that would help her escape from me, and from everyone, until her father came to get her. Deluded girl, thinking her daddy would ever come. Before I could stop her, she read the spell off the page, and it fused her with that statue up there. I've often wondered if that was the escape she had in mind. I don't think she was too familiar with that spell. I'm fairly sure she must have found it in Kieft's cave. Part of the treasure you're going to bring to me."

"Did you lie to me about everything?" Finn asked, his face ashen.

"No, no. I guided her up that mountain, just as she asked. And we were separated by the blizzard. But I found her again, a day later, wandering down the path. She almost told me what she'd found in Kieft's cave, but something in my eager manner must have tipped her off that I wanted the treasure for myself, because she suddenly stopped and refused to speak further. When I tried to persuade her more forcefully, she escaped me and I followed her across the park, until I caught up just in time to witness her little statue trick. I tried going back to the Great Hill, but I couldn't find the cave. I took Penhawitz up there, hoping that his Munsee magic would lead me to the spoils. But nothing . . . until you came along."

"Is my uncle even with you?" Soka asked.

"Oh yes," Pierre assured her. "Though he has had better days. Our trip up the mountain ended with him suspecting me, so I struck him before he could strike me. He gave me this limp, but surprise was on my side and I have him in my power now."

"I knew there wasn't any giant squirrel!" Bridget cried.

"Take me to my uncle," Soka commanded.

"Tell me about the treasure or I'll shoot you," Pierre said coldly, aiming at Soka. Soka put up her hands.

"I will tell you," she said. "But first I want to know that Penhawitz is all right. If it were your kin, you would do the same."

Pierre glanced at his grandson, who was staring back at him in horror. A look of pain flashed across the old man's face. He waved his gun at them. "Get out of the fountain. I will take you to see him. And then you will tell me all about Kieft's treasure and this whole ordeal will be over before you know it . . ."

Pierre made them release the horses, so Soka put Hans carefully in one of her pouches while Bridget carried Tucket in her arms. Pierre took them away from the plaza, down a little path that led under a small bridge.

Once they were underneath, he pushed on some of the stones, which moved to the side to reveal a little room. Inside the room, blinking in the light, sat a bound and gagged Munsee with long, flowing hair.

"Uncle!" Soka cried, running to his side. Finn crouched down beside her, leaving Bridget standing next to the old man with the gun. He wasn't even looking at her as he trained the gun on Soka.

"Now tell me what I want to know."

Suddenly something slammed into Bridget, hard, lifting her up with Tucket still in her arms and carrying her away. She heard Pierre's shouts in the distance, but they quickly faded as something swiftly carried her into the trees. She struggled, but the grip around her was ironclad. Tucket tried to nip at whoever held her, but the injured dog couldn't reach far enough. Finally, she was deposited beneath a tree, where she spun around to face her kidnapper. Her jaw dropped as she came face-to-face with the last person she ever expected to see.

"Toy."

Askook stood up from his place under the chestnut trees. He no longer had any time for games, with the Trap on the verge of opening. He'd worked toward this day for decades, whispering Kieft's words into Tackapausha's ear, until the war leader turned sachem was ready to lead his people to destruction. Time to watch as his efforts finally paid off.

He kicked dirt over the pool of blood at his feet to hide any trace of his presence. He'd watched Soka's party from this spot the entire time, never leaving the outskirts of the Munsee village. He'd known all along that they'd find nothing in Kieft's cave. Askook had moved his master's things long ago, after discovering that the old trapper, Pierre, had led Abigail up the mountain. He'd decided to play with Pierre's mind, gradually pushing the old man to madness over the years with dreams of fabulous riches. That little game had definitely bore fruit today; he had no doubt that the old trapper would take care of things in a satisfactory manner. Pierre was a hairbreadth from snapping completely; someone was going to get hurt. Hopefully, all of them.

As for the demon girl's miraculous escape, Askook couldn't care less. There was nothing she could do now. There was never anything she could do, to be honest. Askook's plans were too well laid. The only thing that could stop Tackapausha was a knife in the gut, an end that hopefully awaited him on the other side of the barrier. There would be no freeing Abigail from her bronze prison, a prison Askook had always known she lay trapped within since that day long ago when he watched from the trees as she recited one of his master's spells to escape Pierre's hungry pursuit. No, there would be nothing ahead for any of them but blood. He could already taste it. As he walked away from the red-soaked earth under the chestnut trees, he practically shook from excitement. It would be a good day, indeed.

Bridget sat against the tree, staring at Toy. The poor paper boy had deteriorated even further since she'd seen him last. The stump where his hand had been was tattered and filthy, his skin was cracked and yellowed from fire and weather, and she could spy a depression in his shirt from the hole she knew had been poked open in his chest. She had no idea how he kept it together, and her heart broke at the thought of what he must be going through.

"We'll get Soka to fix you up," she said, patting Toy's hand. "She fixed me, see?" She held up her bark fingers. "She's a miracle worker. Would you like that?" Toy didn't respond, staring back at her impassively as usual. "How did you find me?"

"He followed you!" said a voice from the grass beside her. Looking down, she was surprised to see the familiar form of a huge roach, clinging to the back of a trotting rat she knew to be Clarence.

"Sergeant Kiffer, it's so good to see you!" she cried. The battle roach pulled off his helmet, revealing his tiny head.

"Good to see you, too," Kiffer replied. "It's been a long couple of days, let me tell you. And riding this stupid rat didn't make it any easier!" He clumsily dismounted Clarence, who sidled away, just as glad to be free of his rider as Kiffer was to be on solid ground. Kiffer brushed off his armor. "I don't know how Fritz puts up with you, rodent! You're a terror!"

Clarence just looked away, curling up in a ball by Bridget's feet.

"What are you doing here?" Bridget asked.

"Looking for you," Kiffer replied. "Fritz gave me Clarence and told me to track you guys down. But instead of your trail, I found myself following *his* by mistake!" He pointed to Toy, who stood by, silent, impassively watching Bridget. "We passed by some town, up toward a river, where I almost caught up with you! Wolves were attacking you, and one almost got you, until this guy, here, dropped a rock on its head."

"That was you!" Bridget gasped.

"I tried to call out, but you guys hopped into those canoes and sped off down the river. So I followed Toy, figuring that he'd lead me to you. Which he did, when he snuck up to some tavern at the crack of dawn. And then I saw you, kicking down that door of the stable and riding off like a crazy person! You didn't make this easy, Bridget!"

Bridget turned to Toy, her mouth dropping open. "That was you outside the Tavern, Jason? Why?"

"Why do you think?" Kiffer answered for the mute paper boy. "The kid keeps protecting you. I think he's got a crush."

"We ran from you," Bridget said to Toy, sadness settling over her face. "And all you wanted to do was help."

"You're a lucky girl!" Kiffer said, shaking his head in admiration. "He wanted to help so bad, when you rode off on those horses he started to run. And I mean *run*! He never slowed down for a second. We were exhausted chasing after him, and Clarence is no easy ride! My butt is killing me! He ran after you all the way to that big mountain, getting there just when you were coming back down the trail, and he ran after you down south to the fountain. This time he was finally able to help, and thankfully, you're all right."

"But my friends!" Bridget cried. "Pierre has them! I have to go help them."

"I'm not letting you go in there with only this paper guy to get your back!" Kiffer said. "Fritz would have my armor! Clarence, go tell Fritz what happened here. Tell him to bring reinforcements."

Immediately the rat was off like a shot, racing into the trees toward the exit to the street. Once Clarence was out of sight, Bridget turned back to Kiffer and Toy, her face deadly serious.

"We don't have time to wait for backup," she said fiercely. "We've got some rescuing to do and we've got to do it now."

THE STORM APPROACHES

Alexander Hamilton leaned back in his comfortable leather chair, staring out the big windows that made up two of the four walls of his corner office in City Hall. He found it soothing to take in the Brooklyn Bridge majestically rising above the East River in the distance, as impressive now as it had been a hundred years earlier. Clouds were racing in from the sea. A storm was coming, and the afternoon sun was now completely hidden away, leaving the bridge's beautiful brick towers in shadow. Such storms he was forced to weather . . . he wished he could just cross that bridge into Brooklyn, leaving behind the mess he'd made here in Mannahatta. But his blood prohibited it, keeping him here in Mannahatta to face his sins. There would be no hiding from what he'd done.

The Trap was falling; he'd be a fool to ignore it. Kieft had said as much to him earlier that day. Hamilton had always fancied himself able to keep one step ahead of the black-eyed god. He knew Kieft's nature was to seek power, but he also knew that without Hamilton, the old god would have nothing. No one would accept the black-eyed man as the mayor of Mannahatta. They feared what he would do with it. Hamilton was the one with the title and the real power. Or so he'd always thought . . .

But now the Trap was about to fall, which Kieft had promised would never happen. And the Munsees waited on the other side, waited for *him*. Not Kieft, who had pushed the Trap on him so many years ago; not Burr, who'd thought it up; not Prince, who engineered it; but him, Alexander Hamilton, the Munsees' greatest supporter before they tried to steal his daughter from him. It didn't seem right after all he'd suffered . . .

Kieft now argued that they had to strike first, to attack the moment the Trap fell. Munsee and god cannot live together; this had been proven long ago. Their age-old struggle must be stopped before it could begin again. And that would mean Hamilton had to strike hard and fast, ending the threat at the outset.

This made sense to the Mayor. Even as a small guilty voice inside whispered that Hamilton deserved to suffer for what he'd done, a louder voice argued that Tackapausha had made his own bed, by encouraging Buck to take Abigail away from her own father. At least the Munsees should have watched over Abigail once she'd been inadvertently trapped along with them, instead of allowing her to perish. Tackapausha's sins were no fewer than Hamilton's own, and he had no call to hold a grudge.

Thoughts of Abigail ran through his head, opening old wounds long scabbed over. That blasted song seemed to be everywhere these days, giving strength to Hamilton's guilty voice and slicing his heart with each note. He'd forgotten how much Abigail had loved Buckongahelas, how happy he'd made her.

He'd been impressed with Buck as well, before he'd learned that the boy's true plans involved stealing his daughter away. But did any of it matter, when all was said and done? His worries, his furious attempts to keep her close, any of it? He lost her anyway, in the end. He lost her forever.

A knock on the door interrupted his thoughts. Hamilton had just enough time to gather himself before Jimmy Walker stuck his head in.

"Someone to see you, sir," he said, and disappeared before Hamilton could tell him to turn the visitors away.

Nicholas Stuyvesant stepped into the room, followed by a limping Lincoln Douglass.

"Sorry to disturb you, sir," Nicholas said. Hamilton was taken aback. Kieft had told him the boy was dead.

"I'm happy to see you survived the attack on your father's farm," Hamilton said, keeping his surprise off his face. "But I'm very busy, so I'm afraid I can't—"

"I have something for you," Nicholas said. "It's a gift. From your daughter."

Hamilton felt a shock run through him. His voice rumbled with anger. "Now see here, that is in very poor taste indeed . . ."

Lincoln stepped forward and pulled something out of his pocket. Hamilton's heart almost stopped as he beheld a beautiful necklace made of wampum. Somehow he knew instantly: he was supposed to wear this. Lincoln dropped it on his desk and the two children of the gods silently left his office, closing the door behind them. With shaking hands, Hamilton reached out to take the necklace, unable to resist its call. He lifted it over his head and around his neck, and soon the tears began to flow in earnest as everything he thought he knew came crashing down around him . . .

———————〜〜〜/\/\〜〜〜———————

The *Adventure Galley* reached the dock in the late afternoon. Rory had avoided his father during the rest of the voyage, opting instead to stand at the stern, scanning the mist for signs of the storm. They seemed to have outraced it, for now. But he knew that they didn't have much time.

Captain Kidd bid them farewell with a pointed look at Rory. Rory knew that the pirate captain would not forget his debt. One day he would have to deal with that, but one crisis at a time, Rory decided. Right now he had to bring down the Trap before the storm arrived and blew them all to pieces.

Rory and his friends stood on the dock, Buck and Mr. Hennessy at their side, as they tried to figure out what to do. Fritz took note of all the sailors disappearing into the crowd.

"They'll be telling their friends about their voyage and the storm that's coming," he said.

"So we'd better move fast," Alexa said. "We need to get Buckongahelas to the place where Tackapausha will be when the Trap falls."

"That'll be Columbus Circle," Mr. Hennessy said. "Where he thought he saw his son die."

"Are you sure?" Fritz asked.

"Yes," Buck answered. "My father will want to pay his respects to the dead before searching out the Mayor. That is where we need to be when the Trap falls."

A commotion at their feet caught their attention. A familiar rat ran up to their feet.

"Clarence!" Fritz cried, climbing down to the ground. "Am I glad to see you! Where's Sergeant Kiffer?"

Clarence began to chitter, and Fritz listened intently.

"Toy! You found Toy!" Fritz was astounded. "Bridget is okay! She's with Toy and Sergeant Kiffer. They're going to do some sort of rescue mission; apparently it's a long story. And then Bridget is going to try to release . . ." Fritz lifted his head to the others, his jaw dropping. "To release Abigail from her prison," he finished in awe. "Bridget was right all along. Abigail is still alive."

A gasp behind them signaled that the others had heard.

"Saints preserve us," Mr. Hennessy said. "Can it really be?"

"Olathe," Buck breathed, overcome.

Everyone who had known Abigail Hamilton was frozen with shock, so Alexa immediately took charge.

"This changes everything. We have to tell the Mayor. Wampage, do you still have the belt hidden in Inwood Hill Park? Good. Race up and grab it. We'll meet you at Columbus Circle, at the park's main entrance."

"I'll go back to the park," Rory said.

"No!" Alexa shook her head firmly. "It's too dangerous for you. Fritz will go alone. He and Bridget will tell the Munsees that Buck is alive. Simon, you go let Nicholas know what's going on. He'll get word to the Mayor. I'll stay with Rory. We'll all meet up at the Circle."

Buck glanced up in a daze.

"I will see her again?"

"Yes, old friend," Mr. Hennessy clapped him on the shoulder. "I guess we all will."

"Thank you," Buck said to Rory's dad. "I know I have

cursed you for making me live on without her. But now . . .
thank you."

"It was the least I could do," Mr. Hennessy replied. Rory
could see his father was touched. Mr. Hennessy turned to the
rest of them. "So what do I do?"

"Stay with your son," Fritz said. "He needs you."

As Simon ran off in one direction, Wampage in another,
and Fritz in a third, Rory wondered if that was true. Did he
need his father? Looking into the sad eyes of the man from the
picture, he had to admit, he had no clue.

As the storm clouds gathered in the distance, the word began
to spread: *the Trap was falling*. From the docks outward, the
news bounced from spirit to spirit, god to god, covering the
island in a matter of hours. Some were angry and terrified that
their old adversaries were about to return. Others felt peace
wash over them as they realized that the decades of guilt were
almost at an end. A few understood that the real test was just
beginning. And everyone heard that it was all going to begin at
Columbus Circle. And so, little by little, they began to gather
there, to see it through.

Kieft heard the rumors and he smiled with the knowledge
that his plans were working so well. The minute he'd sensed
the storm coming, he'd sent word to his ally in the Munsee
camp. Once Tackapausha learned that the Trap was about to
fall, Kieft knew the Sachem would not disappoint him.

The sky darkened as Tackapausha gathered his people to him. Askook stood at his side, his snake-ridden face impassive. Tackapausha, on the other hand, appeared to be a man possessed.

"Our time is at hand!" he cried, and many of his warriors cheered. The rest of the Munsees muttered uneasily, their hope for a release from this prison warring with their misgivings with what was to come. Sooleawa couldn't blame them. She scanned the trees one last time; no Soka, no Abigail, no one. No one was coming. She was a pebble in the stream now, and she could not turn aside the flood.

"We must head south. The Trap is falling, as foretold by the demon, and now it is time for our revenge."

"But the demon told us other things as well," Chogan cried out, the tanner's voice carrying across the crowd. "She warned us against this obsession with revenge."

"If those who wronged us lie prone on the ground when we emerge, then there is no need for revenge," Tackapausha told him. But Sooleawa could tell that the Sachem did not want things to end so easily. He'd been hurting for a century and a half; someone had to pay for that pain. Her son, Tammand, stood near the Sachem, watching his leader with shining eyes. How had she lost him? He hadn't even been born when the Mayor betrayed them. Was such intense hate so easily passed on? Sooleawa could not see how this would end happily for her people. She would just have to hope Soka survived to pick up the pieces.

Tackapausha gave the word and the entire Munsee nation began to move south. They'd be at the entrance to the world outside in an hour. What happened after that, Sooleawa could not foresee.

———————

Bridget and her friends approached the bridge, staying safely within the trees. Sergent Kiffer rode upon her shoulder, while Toy mutely walked a step behind. She didn't know what to expect from the paper boy; she hoped he'd help when the time came. Tucket had recovered enough to limp at her side. She planned to make certain the tawny dog didn't get involved with this rescue attempt. He'd done enough already.

The sky was darkening above them and the wind began to pick up as they reached the bridge, staying out of sight. They could hear Pierre muttering to himself under the arch. He was probably halfway down the passage, where he could see in both directions. So there'd be no sneaking up on him. What to do? Stumped, she glanced down at Sergeant Kiffer, who stood staring up at her, awaiting orders. With his helmet on, he looked terrifyingly huge. An image flashed in her mind, the memory of meeting Pierre in his dank little shack—and the way he'd reacted when he first spied Hans. An idea presented itself, and she began to smile.

A few minutes later, she stepped out onto the path, right where Pierre could see her.

"Hi, Pierre!" she called out. Pierre spun around, eyes wild, training his pistol on her.

"You!" he exclaimed, taking a step toward her. *Not enough,* she thought. She needed him closer.

"I give up," she said, the wind whipping her paper hair in

every direction as if she were Medusa. She must truly look like a demon, she thought. "You've got all my friends, so you win! I'll tell you the truth."

"The truth?" he asked, taking another step toward her. "And what is the truth?"

"The cave was full of Kieft's treasure."

"I already know that!" Pierre took another step toward her. *Almost,* she thought. He gestured wildly with his gun. "Why didn't you tell me that in the first place?"

"Why would we want to share with you?" she asked, goading him further. "You weren't smart enough to find it on your own. Why should we give you any? You don't deserve it."

"Don't deserve it!" Pierre took another step, coming out from under the bridge into the open air. "I suffered for that treasure! That is my treasure. And you won't take it from me."

He took his last step, pointing the gun at her. But he never got the chance to fire.

"Geronimo!" Sergeant Kiffer yelled as he dropped from the edge of the bridge directly onto Pierre's astonished face. And the freak-out she'd witnessed in Pierre's shack at the sight of Hans paled in comparision to the dance of horror that unfolded when the huge roach landed on the old trapper's forehead.

"GET IT OFF ME GET IT OFF ME GET IT OFF ME!" Pierre screamed, clutching at his face in sheer terror. He ran in crazed circles, shaking his head violently, trying to dislodge the huge roach from his head. But Kiffer had grabbed hold of his hair and his ears. The battle roach was not giving in. He rode Pierre's forehead like it was a rodeo bull.

"You're mine, you little weasel!" Sergeant Kiffer cried as he held on. "I ain't going nowhere!" And despite Pierre's frantic attempts, Kiffer's words held true.

Bridget tore herself away from the sight and ran under the bridge. She threw open the hidden door as Toy reached her side, and together they tore at the bonds that held their friends.

"Thank you, Bridget!" Soka cried, climbing to her feet. Finn followed, helping the old Sachem Penhawitz find his balance. "We owe you our lives."

Bridget blushed with pleasure. "Let's get out of here."

They turned to leave the bridge, where Pierre still struggled with Kiffer. Rain had begun to fall as the wind picked up. A particularly strong gust hit them, knocking Kiffer right off the trapper and into the bushes. Pierre staggered, but did not fall, turning to face his former prisoners, still clutching his ancient gun.

"No!" he cried, gesturing wildly with his pistol. "You will not keep me from my treasure! I've waited too long!"

He trained his gun on the first person he saw through the rain, who happened to be Soka. A look of fear came over Finn's face and he raced toward his grandfather.

"Grandfather, don't hurt her!" he cried. Just as Finn reached the gun, his hand pushing the barrel of the pistol into the air, Pierre pulled the trigger. But the old pistol, wet from the rain, finally gave in to its advanced age, and instead of firing a bullet into the sky, it exploded into a million pieces, covering both Pierre and Finn in shrapnel. They fell to the ground in a tangled heap, smoke drifting lazily above them as the boom of the gun's self-destruction echoed into the distance.

With a cry, Soka ran to the two prone bodies, falling to her knees at their sides. Pierre was groaning, the old man crying as he clutched his smoldering, ruined hand in pain. But Finn was in far worse shape, his chest a mess of burns and blood.

"That was so stupid!" Soka scolded him, her eyes filling with tears at the sight of Finn's broken body.

"I couldn't let him hurt you." Finn smiled weakly, and then dissolved into a fit of coughing. "Not you, Soka. Not you." He shuddered once, his eyes opening wide, and then he went still.

"He saved me," Soka whispered, crying in the rain. "Oh, Finn. I'm so sorry."

"It's over, Soka," Penhawitz said, his hand on his niece's shoulder. "We must go. His sacrifice must not be in vain."

"Finn." Pierre was whimpering. "I never meant to . . . why did you get in the way!"

"Will you watch him?" Soka asked Sergeant Kiffer, wiping her eyes. "You and Hans. I don't think he'll give you much trouble."

"Of course," Kiffer promised. "You can count on us."

Soka turned to Bridget and the others, her face stone.

"Come," she said. "We must find my mother. She will know what to do about Abigail."

Bridget and Penhawitz nodded, and they took off down the path, leaving the man whose greed had caused such misery broken by the ruination of his schemes.

AT THE GATE

When they reached Columbus Circle, Alexa guided Rory and his father to the large shopping mall across from the entrance to the park.

"You'll see why," she said cryptically, and she urged them to hunker down in the doorway of one of the stores. A jewelry store, it seemed closed for the day, with its lights dim and door bolted shut. Rory stared out across the traffic circle toward the park, past the little plaza in the middle, with its towering pedestal at the top of which stood a statue of Christopher Columbus himself. The rain was picking up, and steam rose from distant trees, making the park look like a rain forest during monsoon season. Across from them, the main entrance to Central Park, called Merchant's Gate, lay at the end of a paved semicircle that dipped in from the street. Another statue stood here to welcome visitors to the park, perched atop a grand pedestal decorated with sculptures of barely clothed Roman sprites. This golden statue, a warrior woman guiding a team of ferocious horses, seemed poised to leap off the monument in attack. This seemed a fitting place to make a last stand, Rory decided.

As he watched, people began streaming into the circle, heading for the plaza in the center. At least Rory thought at first that they were people. But then strange feelings began to rush through him. He felt optimistic and sad and invincible and righteous and nostaligic and clever, all at the same time. He wanted to invest some money and rescue a kitten and play point guard for the Knicks. The feelings overwhelmed him, and he fell back heavily against the door to the jewelry store. Alexa gave him a pitying look.

"Those are gods you're seeing out there in the rain," she said. "You know how it feels to be in the presence of one of them, right? Now imagine hundreds of them, all in the same place. If you were out there in the middle of all of them, you'd be a bloody mess, believe me. Mortals weren't meant to be around that much divinity. I'm hoping that once you put on the Sachem's belt, you'll be buffered, but until then, we'll stay out of the way. I think you'll find that your fellow mortals will be staying away as well, though they won't know why."

Sure enough, the flow of cars around the traffic circle had ceased. No one was walking down the sidewalk in front of the mall, either. They must have known instinctively to stay away. From now on, it was only to be the gods and the Munsees. And Rory.

"We shouldn't be here," Mr. Hennessy muttered next to him as more and more gods entered the circle, spilling out onto the now-empty street. Glancing around the rapidly filling roundabout, Rory sympathized with his father, even as he settled into the corner of the doorway to wait for Wampage and the belt. The sooner he turned that key and got out of there, the better.

The rain had intensified, driving in every direction, as Bridget and her companions caught up to the Munsees. The Indians had just arrived at Merchant's Gate, gathering around the spot where they would soon be able to reenter the world. Tackapausha stood apart, surrounded by his warriors, Tammand among them. But Sooleawa saw them first, and she came running with a happy cry.

"Penhawitz! Brother! You are safe!" She threw herself into her brother's arms. A whisper ran through the crowd at the sight of their old sachem.

"Father," Tackapausha said, walking over through the downpour to greet the former Sachem. "I am glad to see you have rejoined your people. Though your company could be better. A fugitive and a demon." He nodded at Soka and Bridget, then noticed Toy standing mutely behind them. His eyes widened. "I'm sorry, two demons! They seem to be multiplying."

"I have come to beg you to turn from your path," Penhawitz said, shouting above the rising gale that surrounded them as he addressed the crowd. "My people, we have all suffered. We have every right to desire revenge. But at what cost? When the Trap falls, we will feel the land again. The hole in our hearts that has plagued us for so long will be filled at last. We will be whole, as we were before! Tackapausha wishes to throw that away. His revenge? It can only destroy us. It is suicide."

"It is justice," Tackapausha insisted. "They have treated us like dogs to be penned up. Will we let that go unanswered?"

"We have lived here in the park for over a hundred and fifty years," Penhawitz reminded him. "This is our home. It will be the heart of our nation. If the newcomers try to take it from us, they will suffer for it. That will be our revenge—we will prosper."

"It was here, you know," Tackapausha said, raindrops dripping off his hand as he pointed toward the Circle. "Right on the other side of that gate, Meester shot my son. I cannot forgive that. When the Trap falls, there will be more of the same. More senseless murder. The newcomers will think they can do what they will to us. They will come under the cover of night and murder our children! That is who they are. Murderers of children. There is only one way to speak to such people—in the language of blood!"

The group of young warriors around Tackapausha, Tammand included, cheered. Some of the other Munsees held back, fear and hope warring across their faces.

Bridget could stand it no more. She called out, "What about Abigail!"

Tackapausha turned to her. "Olathe is gone, demon."

"No, she's trapped in the angel at Bethesda Fountain."

"Olathe is alive?" Chogan asked, eyes wide as he pushed himself to the fore. Penhawitz nodded and Chogan's jaw dropped.

"So is Buckongahelas," a new voice called out. Fritz rode into view at their feet. "I've seen him." A whisper ran through the Munsees.

"I don't know who you are, little one, but I saw him die," Tackapausha inisisted, eyes flashing. "Why do you defile the memory of my son with these lies?"

Fritz explained about Harry Meester's plan to save Buck.

Bridget's heart leaped—Rory had found their father! Soon she would meet him. She didn't know if she was excited or scared. Probably both. But first they had to get out of this mess, which didn't seem too promising as Tackapausha's eyes were narrowing in disbelief.

"This is what they stoop to!" he announced to his people. "Attempting to buy us off with false hope! Is there nothing they won't lie about?" Many of the Munsees looked angry as well; no one trusted the news they had just heard. Bridget sighed. Some things were just too unbelievable.

"At least let us release Olathe so we can return her to her people," Sooleawa said.

"Is that such a good idea?" Askook said, stepping up to his sachem's side. "After all, right now she is a hostage, but the minute we hand her over, she loses all value."

"You are wise, Askook," Tackapausha said, nodding.

"Are you crazy?" Bridget yelled, stamping her foot, sending wet mud flying in all directions.

"If you won't release her from the fountain, then I will," Soka said defiantly.

"I'm sorry, I cannot allow that," Tackapausha replied. He nodded toward his nearest warriors, who immediately encircled Bridget and her companions, including Chogan and Sooleawa. "It is better if you remain here under guard until it is over."

He turned and walked away, straight and tall, as if the rain that pelted down upon them did not touch him at all.

Once he and Askook were out of sight, Sooleawa turned to her daughter. "It has to be up to you, now. I will cause a distraction. You must free Olathe and return her to her father."

Soka took a deep breath and nodded.

"I'll head back to the other side of the wall," Fritz said. "They need to know what's going on in here."

"Good, then I'll cause a disturbance," Sooleawa said to her daughter. "And you, and Bridget, and the silent one will make a break for the trees. You don't have much time, so you must be swift. Understand?"

Soka nodded and Sooleawa smiled at her daughter, kissing the top of her head. "Get ready to run." She reached into her pouch and pulled out a thick substance. She rubbed it on her forehead, muttering under her breath. Then, suddenly, she disappeared. Almost immediately, a cry went up among their guards.

"Sooleawa is gone!" the one nearest Bridget cried. A voice called out clear across the path on the other side of the line of Munsees, who now cast about in confusion for the source of the commotion.

"You cannot hold Sooleawa!"

Bridget concentrated on the spot where the voice came from, and to her horror, she could see the faint outline of the medicine woman, made from the falling raindrops as they bounced off Sooleawa's invisible shoulders. The rain made it impossible to be truly unseen. The guards immediately saw Sooleawa's outline in the rain as well, and they ran toward her. For a moment the rest of Bridget's group were unwatched.

Penhawitz whispered to them. "Run!"

Bridget, Soka, and Toy immediately made a break for it, crashing into the brush. The warrior princess needed to be saved, Bridget thought as they raced north toward the plaza, and she would not let her down.

OLD MAGIC UNDONE

Nicholas stood uncomfortably in the rain, trying not to worry. He and Lincoln had arrived at Columbus Circle to find a multitude of gods already waiting. Word had gotten around, apparently, that the Trap was falling and they were here to see it for themselves. Nicholas tried to gauge the mood of the crowd; fear was in the air and they teetered on the edge. They would follow the Mayor, Nicholas thought. There was no one else left standing. But what would the Mayor do?

Hamilton didn't even look at them as he spoke with various gods. Nicholas couldn't tell if Abigail's necklace had changed Hamilton's mind. He wished the Mayor would give some sign of his intentions . . .

"Nicholas! Lincoln! Hello!" Nicholas turned to see Simon running up to them. For some reason he was carrying a stack of plates, which Nicholas recognized.

"Why are you carting around my mother's china?" he asked, bewildered. Simon started, staring down at the plates as if he'd never seen them before.

"I don't know . . ." he said, confused. "I went to your house to get you, but the whole place was a burned shell. Some guy named Diedrich told me that the house went up in flames, and Burr was one of the casualties. I don't believe that for a second, by the way. There was nothing more I could do, so I ran here."

"With my mother's plates . . ." Nicholas's eyes narrowed, and suddenly he pushed Simon, hard. The Astor boy lost control of the china and plates flew through the air, but somehow, miraculously, he managed to catch each one. Nicholas jabbed a finger in his chest. "You put on the locket, didn't you!"

Simon tried to protest, but Lincoln reached out and pulled open Simon's puffy shirt. The gold locket hung there, plain as day. Simon quickly pulled his shirt closed and looked around to see if anyone had noticed.

"Are you crazy?" he said. "What if someone saw?"

"Take it off, right now," Nicholas ordered.

"I'll take it off later," Simon promised. "It's too dangerous now, someone might notice."

A commotion on the other side of the plaza alerted them to a new arrival. Alexa marched up through the driving rain, a strange man by her side. The Mayor caught sight of the man and froze, his face turning white.

"You!" he cried. "But you're dead!"

"Hello, Alexander," the Munsee said, his eyes burning at the sight of the Mayor.

"Buckongahelas!" Hamilton breathed. "How can this be? It is a miracle. Where have you been all this time?"

"I am not here to catch up, Hamilton," Buckongahelas said, his eyes cold. "I am here to see my wife."

"They told me she still lived," Hamilton said, in shock. "It seems too good to be true."

"Perhaps it *is* too good to be true. We will find out together."

"I—" Hamilton started to say something, then stopped himself. "I guess we will," he finished lamely. Nicholas sighed. The Mayor had been so close to an apology, but he'd backed away. He still didn't know what the Mayor would do once the Trap fell. He'd have to wait and hope, along with everyone else.

Rory watched from his place in front of the jewelry store, unable to see much through the rain.

"I think I see the Mayor," he said to his father. "Maybe you should go talk to him. Confess and everything."

"Rory," Mr. Hennessy said. Rory turned to see that his father was staring at him with haunted eyes. "I want you to know something. I love you. I love your sister, too. And I love your mother. But there are things in my past—horrible secrets—that will not leave me be. I try to outrun them, but I can only keep a step ahead if I never stop. And I won't drag you or your mother or sister into this with me. It's too much."

"So what are you saying?" Rory asked, dreading where this conversation was going. His father pushed himself to his feet.

"You're safer without me. You all are. Every minute I stay means I get closer to being discovered."

"By who?" Rory asked. "I don't understand."

"I love you, Rory," his father said. "I hope I see you again one day. Good-bye."

With that, Rory's father backed away, disappearing down

Eighth Avenue. Once again, Rory was alone. It didn't hurt any less this time around.

Sly Jimmy stood on the outskirts of Columbus Circle, watching the crowds. He'd come to see bloodshed, and he hoped he wouldn't be disappointed. He'd been keeping a low profile since the screwup at the Stuyvesant farm, but he hoped Kieft would somehow forget about him if he stayed out of sight long enough.

Unfortunately, that wish proved overly optimistic.

"Hello, Jimmy," a voice breathed in his ear. Jimmy fell back, terrified. A possessed little girl stood before him, her eyes going crazy in their sockets.

"I can explain about the farm," Jimmy stammered.

"Save it," Kieft's voice said. "You may redeem yourself today. Have you seen the Munsee gentleman standing near the Mayor?"

"Yeah," Jimmy said. He'd been shaken to see an actual Munsee free from the Trap. He hoped the brave didn't try to pay him back for giving his people a bad name.

"I would most appreciate it if that man were to not survive the hour. Can you do that for me?"

"Yes!" Sly Jimmy promised eagerly. "I won't fail you again!"

"I know," Kieft's voice said. "Or you will not live to fail me thrice."

The rain was falling in sheets by the time Bridget and her companions approached Bethesda Fountain. The plaza was empty, any visitors driven to shelter by the worsening storm. They stopped under the trees, though the leaves offered no protection from the water pouring from the angry sky. Soka gazed out at the statue, swaying in place as she muttered to herself in her own language. Finally, she gasped.

"I can see it!" she declared. "A web wrapped all around the statue, trailing down to the fountain in three spots, like the pegs of a tent. If I can release those three points, she should be free."

"Nothing to it!" Bridget said brightly. "Right?"

Soka nodded, swallowing. She stepped out into the plaza, pushing her soaking hair away from her face as she concentrated on the statue. Bridget urged Tucket to follow, which the wet dog reluctantly did. But Bridget held back, turning to Toy.

"Jason?" she said awkwardly. "I just want to say . . . You've been a really good friend. You saved me and I'll always be grateful. But do you think you can help me one more time? My brother is in a lot of danger. He needs you a lot more than I do. Can you do this one thing for me and go help him?"

Toy slowly nodded. The paper boy turned to go, but Bridget strode over and gave him a big hug. She hoped their papier-mâché wasn't so soggy it stuck them together, but she was willing to risk it. She pulled back, and for the first time, she could see Toy's soul in his eyes. He was trying to say something, she realized. His father, Burr, had taken out his paper tongue to keep Jason from giving Burr away, and ever since, the paper boy had been mute. But he wanted to speak to her now.

"An oo," he said finally, and her heart ached. *Thank you.*

"Thank you, too, Jason. I'll see you later, I promise."

Toy nodded once, then ran off into the trees. Bridget watched him disappear into the rain with a heavy heart, then turned back toward the plaza to finish what she'd started.

Soka was bent over the fountain's edge, Tucket by her side. Bridget could barely see her through the wall of water crashing down on them. Lightning flashed in the distance, making her jump. If this storm was really going to get as bad as Fritz said it might, then they had to move quickly. A mist had risen around them, driven up by the rain, and the angel rose above it like a true creature of heaven. Bridget almost felt sorry for bringing it back to earth. Almost . . .

Bridget ran to Soka's side. The Munsee girl was still muttering as she ran her fingers along something invisible in front of her. Bridget leaned in to see what was going on.

Zip!

An arrow whizzed by Soka's cheek, making Bridget jump. But Soka didn't even flinch.

"Stop it, Tammand," she said, not turning from her task. "If you want to hit me, then hit me. Don't insult me with these near misses." Bridget spun around to see Soka's brother warily approaching them, Chepi on his shoulder. He had another arrow cocked in the bow. His face was stone.

"I can't let you do this, Soka," he called out over the wind. "We need her as a hostage. If you set her free, you could doom us all."

"That's ridiculous," Soka answered, not glancing back at him. "Returning her to her people can only help us."

"You heard Tackapausha say how important it was that she remain a hostage," Tammand continued. "When Askook showed me your trail, I knew I had to follow. I don't want you hurt, Soka, so I won't tell anyone if you just come back with me now. But I can't let you do this."

"You're not going to shoot me," Soka informed him. "You're my brother."

"Maybe I will," he replied, sending another arrow whispering by her cheek. In a flash he notched another arrow. "You're my family, but I can't let you gamble with the lives of our people."

"We're not scared of you!" Bridget said. "You're a bully, just like your snake-faced buddy!"

"You can't stop me, Tammand," Soka declared.

Tammand looked miserable. "I'm sorry, Soka. I love you, but our people come first."

He let loose another arrow, and this one flew straight at Soka.

Bridget reacted quicker than she ever thought possible. She launched herself at Soka, pulling the girl to the ground just as the arrow reached the space where her heart had been moments before. The arrow flew on, bouncing off the fountain's pedestal, to land in the water with a splash. Soka was speechless with fury, pushing herself to her feet.

"You are no longer my brother, Tammand," she said, her eyes burning. "I don't know what you are anymore. But you are not my brother."

"I'm sorry, Soka," Tammand said softly, his face pained. "But you never listen."

Bridget raced across the plaza and tackled the Munsee youth to the ground. Tucket limped over, growling, and sat right by Tammand's head. Bridget adjusted her grip to keep Tammand from getting up, but the Munsee wasn't resisting. He seemed to know that his chance had passed. And lines were now drawn that could never be undone. She'd feel for him if he hadn't almost killed his own sister. She turned around to yell back at Soka.

"Finish it!"

Soka nodded, and ran back to the fountain. Bridget lay back and stared up at the rain, watching the gray sky flash with lightning and thunder. The storm was getting worse and they were running out of time.

A happy yell caught her attention. Soka had moved on to another corner of the fountain. And already, the angel was starting to sag, listing toward the ground. A frightened thought occurred to Bridget, which was confirmed once the second tie was undone and the statue leaned even farther toward the ground.

"Tucket, watch him!" she ordered the dog as she jumped to her feet. She began to run toward the fountain as Soka, who hadn't been looking up as she worked, concentrated on the last tie.

"Wait!" Bridget yelled, but the wind had picked up so much that she couldn't be heard over its roar. She ran more quickly, just as Soka stood up in triumph. Soka looked up, flushed with success, but her excited expression soon changed to panic as she realized what was happening. The statue, with no invisible binds to hold it, was falling.

Bridget kicked it up a notch as the statue seemed to fall through the air in slow motion. It cleared the pillar it had stood atop for over a hundred years and dropped toward the shallow pool below. Bridget leaped into the pool, wading frantically through the shallow water. As she watched, the statue began to move, as if waking up. Bridget jumped through the air, sliding beneath the angel just before it hit the ground.

The statue lay in her lap, faceup. Only it wasn't a statue anymore. The wings had broken off midfall to land on either side of them. But the woman who had worn them for years and years of captivity was now free, slowly stirring in Bridget's lap as her bronze skin faded to pink flesh. The angel's head, which had looked down for decades, lifted up to gaze at Bridget. The mouth long closed moved once again.

"Who are you?" the woman asked weakly, her voice scratchy from disuse.

"I'm Bridget, Abigail," Bridget said, smiling through the rain. "Welcome back."

29

THE EYE OF THE STORM

The number of gods in the plaza was growing quickly. Fear still sent ripples through the crowd as they stared across the road at the park, but Nicholas had hope that maybe they'd keep their composure when the time came to face the Munsees.

"If we stay calm, we'll be fine," Nicholas advised the Mayor, who didn't appear to be even listening as he kept his nervous eyes trained on the park. "Buckongahelas will talk to his father and hopefully we can nip any fighting in the bud."

"You will be shot down before the savage has time to take a step," a new voice interjected. The crowd fell back as Willem Kieft walked up, Tobias and Boss Tweed at his heels. "Tackapausha does not care for forgiveness. He lusts only for revenge."

"You don't know that," Nicholas insisted.

"Do you remember how you died?" Kieft asked Hamilton, ignoring Nicholas. "Out on that godforsaken cliff across the river, dueling pistol in your hand, facing Aaron Burr, a man who hated you more than anything? You didn't want bloodshed then, either, did you? So what did you do?"

"I fired into the air," Hamilton muttered, his eyes pained. Kieft shook his head at the fragility of honor.

"Leaving Burr to calmly shoot you down like a wounded dog. Will you repeat your mistake here? Will you fire into the air when faced with someone who hates you that much? Tackapausha will not hesitate to cut you down where you stand." Kieft turned to address the rest of the crowd. "We created this Trap for a reason. This is not a question of right and wrong. This is about fantasy and reality. The fantasy is that the Munsees will reemerge, see that we didn't kill one of their own the way they'd believed, and then forgive us for locking them away for a century—promising to live with us side by side in harmony until the end of days. We all know that will not happen. The reality is that we will fight, they will fight, we will die, they will die, and blood will run through these streets again. We cannot live together, that has been proven again and again. We took this island from them, yes, and it no longer matters if it was right or wrong. It happened. And Mannahatta has been ours alone for a hundred and fifty years. Now the savages want to take it back for themselves. Well, I say that they don't belong here anymore. We do. Under their watch, this island was practically deserted; under ours, it has blossomed into the greatest city in the world. That makes this land ours and ours alone. And I, for one, refuse to give it up!"

To Nicholas's horror, heads were nodding throughout the crowd behind Kieft. The old god sounded so matter-of-fact, so reasonable, while talking about trampling a people into the ground, that Nicholas had to shake his head in horrified admiration. But he could not let the man go unanswered.

"You are a liar, Mr. Kieft!" he exclaimed, leaping up the steps that led to the base of the pedestal. "You speak of fear and war as if they are the natural order of things. You talk about the past as if it had to happen that way. You are wrong. We created our past, *with* the Munsees. Together, we made every war, every watchful peace, every sneak attack, every truce. Together we can agree to change."

"Words won't stop the bloodshed, Nicholas," Kieft said scornfully.

"Why not?" Nicholas shot back. "I grew up hearing about how things used to be, and I used to curse my father for every memory he forced upon me. But now I know how lucky I was. Because if we ignore the past, then we hand it over to people like you, Mr. Kieft. If we refuse to look backward, we let you write the histories. We let you tell us what is possible and what isn't. We let you convince us that the Munsees were savages who had to be exterminated for the good of the city. And how can we say any different? What do we know? Well, unfortunately for you, I grew up with the past in my ear every day, and I have not ignored it. We had a chance a century and a half ago to turn a new page with the Munsees and put away the hatred and mistrust in the name of peace. Instead, we bottled them up like a frightened child who refuses to face his mistakes. Well, now we're at that crossroads again. We can fight out of fear, or we can move on as one and see what kind of world we make together. Someone has to take the first step; it might as well be us. What say you, Mayor?"

Everyone looked to Mayor Hamilton. It would all be on him now.

As Rory watched the commotion, he spied Alexa walking toward him. She glanced around in confusion.

"Where's your father?"

Before he could explain, Wampage came gliding up, carrying a leather bag.

"It appears that I am just in time," he said, handing over the bag. He glanced out at the crowd. "We are too exposed here. We need to move, perhaps inside this glass structure." He pointed to the mall behind them. He glanced over his shoulder at the trees swaying in the storm. "To think I will soon be with my people again," he said wistfully. Rory put a hand on his shoulder.

"You should go," he told the Munsee. "To be there when the Trap falls. Alexa can keep watch. You deserve to see their faces when they emerge a free people again."

Wampage gave him a look of profound gratitude and swiftly ran toward the crowd. Alexa smiled.

"Nicely done," she said.

The intensity of the storm made it hard to hear, but Rory thought he heard a creaking behind him. Before he could turn, a loud thump sounded at his side. He spun to see Alexa slumped on the floor, blood streaming from her head. He opened his mouth to shout for help, but an arm flew out around his neck, cutting off his air. It pulled him back, through the now-open door to the jewelry store. Another hand reached out and slammed the door shut, kicking over a display case to keep anyone from coming in. Rory was flung into the corner, where the impact of his landing sent the leather bag flying. He scrambled to his knees, looking up to see who had attacked him. A familiar hulk of a man stood before him, clothing in tatters, staring impassively down at him.

"You're dead!" Rory cried, fear shooting through him.

"I know," Bill the Butcher replied, running a finger over a rusty cleaver. "That's what makes this so easy."

Rory could see no one through the glass windows of the store; they were watching the park. Alexa was slumped right outside, unconscious. Rory had a brief wild hope that his father would come back, but he knew that was a pipe dream. He was alone, with a killer, and there was no one to save him.

"You're not supposed to hurt me!" Rory cried as Bill took a step toward him.

"That was before," Bill said, smiling with delight at his new freedom. "Before I realized that this city is a lost cause. Everything I fought for, to keep the island pure—it's all come to nothing. This city ain't nothin' but foreign, and I can't save it. I know that now. It's beyond my trusty cleavers. But this storm . . . this storm is a godsend. It'll wash everyone away, all the filth, so the city can start fresh and clean. That's why I have to kill you, Rory. So you can't turn that key and ruin my beautiful storm."

Bill the Butcher advanced on Rory, who cast about wildly for a way to escape. He was cornered, without any weapons, and there was no way he could overpower the crazed man before him. He looked into the killer's eyes and he knew that hope was dead. This was it. Bill's shadow covered Rory's face and he braced himself for the inevitable blow . . .

Crash!

Something came flying through the window, sending shattered glass in every direction. Bill glanced back, surprised, and Rory used the momentary distraction to scramble out of the corner. To his considerable surprise, a familiar form pulled itself up from the floor, covered in broken glass.

"Toy?" he said out loud, dumbfounded. Bill whirled back around to see that his prey had crawled away. Rory stumbled to his feet and ran as the crazed killer chased him, totally ignoring the paper boy who'd just come hurtling through the window. That proved to be his mistake.

Toy launched himself through the air, landing on Bill's back. He clawed at the man's face, making him cry out in pain. Rory stood there, dumbly watching the struggle, until a familiar rat leaped through the broken window to land at his feet.

"Where's the belt?" Fritz cried up at him from his place on Clarence's back.

Good question. Rory scanned the floor, looking for the leather bag. Bill was banging into various display cases, sending jewelry and jagged glass flying everwhere in an effort to dislodge the paper boy. Rory shielded himself as best he could, but soon little cuts covered his hands and face. The scattered merchandise made it harder for him to find the bag, but he dug through the debris frantically, refusing to give up.

Fritz grabbed a handful of firecrackers from his armor and began throwing them at the hulking killer. The explosions sent Bill reeling backward, Toy still attached to his neck. Bill stopped himself and glanced around, eyes coming to rest on a particularly large display case. He launched himself at the case, spinning onto his back so that Toy would land first. They

crashed into the case with so much force that the entire structure flattened like a pancake, rings and necklaces bursting into
the air like candy from a broken piñata.

Toy's legs now hung in tatters below his waist. But his arm
would not loose its grip on Bill's neck. Rory quickly resumed
his search. There wasn't much time left, he could tell. Some
people were coming, he could see through the window, but
they wouldn't be in time. Toy was almost finished, and Fritz's
firecrackers didn't have much effect on the man besides herd-
ing him away from Rory. It was now or never.

That's when Rory saw the bag, poking out from under a
collapsed display case. He raced to pull it from beneath the
glass and metal. Tearing it open, he was greeted by blinding
white—the belt. Now he had to finish the job.

He pulled out the belt and wrapped it around his waist. All
at once the world became sharper. Staring out at the plaza, he
could see colors swirling. Fear, anger, hope, aggression—they
all churned through the gods waiting to greet the Munsees. He
was completely lost in what he saw until Fritz again caught his
attention.

"Toy's done for. Finish it!"

Rory turned around to see Toy's grip slacken and his devastated body slip to the floor, where it lay motionless. Bill the
Butcher was blinking, dazed from the fight, and Rory quickly
rifled through his pockets to take advantage of the last distraction he was likely to get. Where was it . . . there! His hand
closed around the lock and he pulled it free of his jacket. His
other hand went to the key around his neck.

But it was too late. Bill shook off his confusion and focused
in on Rory. There was no time for anything, not even a fire-

cracker, as the big man stomped across the ruins of the jewelry store, arm outstretched, ready to choke the life from the last Light in Mannahatta.

"Hey, you!"

Bill glanced around at the unfamiliar voice. A shot rang out and he staggered back before falling to his knees. He fell forward like a tree, landing with a crash on the glass-covered floor, where he moved no more.

Caesar Prince stood in the doorway, a smoking gun in his hand. He walked forward, calmly felt around the dead man's back, and pulled out a glowing bullet. The truth dawned on Rory: this was another soul pistol, like the one Hex had once used on Bridget.

Caesar stared at the glowing bullet thoughtfully and put it in his pocket. Rory stepped forward.

"Caesar, I'm so glad you . . ."

Rory trailed off as the God of Under the Streets turned to look at him with pitiless eyes. Then his supposed friend and bene-factor pulled out a copper spear, much like the one Wampage carried, and hurled that spear right into Rory's belly.

"No!" Fritz screamed, rushing to Rory's side as he fell.

"Quickly, Rory," Caesar said, calmly staring down at the stricken boy. "You have an instant to save the world, for now and to come." With that cryptic statement, he turned and strode out of the store, disappearing into the storm.

Rory wondered if he was dying. But there was no pain. In fact, the feelings he'd received when he put on the belt grew even stronger. Looking down at his stomach, he was shocked to see the spear was sticking right out of the belt. The wampum had saved his life.

"What was he talking about?" Fritz asked, anger coloring his voice. "You could have died. Why . . . ?"

Suddenly Rory gasped. The belt began to melt.

It was as if someone had thrown it into a fire. The beads lost their shape as they oozed off the strings that held them together. The brilliant white faded, turning to burned black. The last hope to bring down the Trap and free the Munsees was falling to pieces around him and he couldn't do anything about it.

Caesar had doomed them all.

AN INSTANT TO
SAVE THE WORLD

The wind had now risen to hurricane strength, knocking down trees and blowing down anything not made of granite. The beautiful stained-glass windows at the Bowery Mission burst into a million pieces under the force of the gale. Fire hydrants were torn from the sidewalks and anyone foolish enough to be caught out in the storm was blown down the street. Lightning struck again and again—if the power hadn't been out already, it never would have survived the attack.

But light did return to the city, in the form of the many fires that sprang up everywhere. Fire engines raced through the howling wind, struggling to get to the flames, but most of them were blown clear across the road into the sides of buildings. The entire city was under attack, and its inhabitants fled like rats down into the basements, where they huddled together, flinching at every loud noise that filtered in from above, waiting in fear either for the storm to pass or the end of days, whichever came first.

The wind blew the glass through the air of the store like deadly dust, and Rory ducked behind his arm to avoid being blinded. The glow of the belt had almost faded, as had any hope he'd had of ending this. The last display case teetered under the gale, finally falling on top of the dead spirit on the floor. Rory turned aside to avoid the new barrage of glass, and his eyes came to rest on Toy.

The poor creature lay splayed out on the floor, limbs in tatters. He was dying for nothing, Rory thought hopelessly, and an immense sadness washed over him. Then, to his surprise, Toy's body moved. At first he thought it was the wind, but Toy's head rolled over to show that the paper boy's eyes were open and staring right at Rory.

Toy's eyes seemed to plead with him, begging him not to make it all for nothing. And that prompted Rory take another look at his belt. It was fading, melting, dissolving . . . but it wasn't gone yet. Quickly, Caesar had said. He had but an instant. Was this what the old god meant? An instant before the belt melted away into nothing?

His father would give up; the thought rose up inside him. His father would run. His father would find a place to hide and wait out the storm, ready to pick up the pieces once it was over.

"I'm not my father," Rory snarled. He fought the wind to grab the key from around his neck. The lock still lay in his other hand. The glow was almost gone from the Sachem's belt, so it was now or never. He thrust the key into the lock, said a prayer to whichever god might listen, and gave it a turn. But the key protested, not wanting to move. Rory screamed into the wind as he strained, putting everything he had into his twist, digging deep inside as he willed the key to turn. Finally, up sprang a familiar warmth that spread through him like wildfire, coursing through his veins. He could see the truth, all of it, for one blazing moment. Then the key turned.

A soft sigh flew from his mouth as he fell back, exhausted. But the sigh didn't fade. The wind carried it out toward the park. It was no longer his sigh, it was everywhere, as if the island itself were expressing relief. The island itself was finally whole again.

Rory climbed to his knees and stared out at the park. The blue glow that he could usually see only from a distance was now growing brighter by the second, until he could barely look at the park. Turning away, he noticed that Toy's head was facing the back of the store. The paper boy's mouth was moving soundlessly as he stared at the flickering blue reflection in the glass that littered the floor. Rory crawled across the floor to his side, lifting the paper body in his arms. He turned Toy's ruined face toward the park, toward the light that now threatened to overwhelm them. Toy's mouth opened in astonishment as his eyes drank it all in. His mouth formed the unspoken words: *It's beautiful.*

Tears were running down Rory's cheeks, mixing with the rain, as he silently agreed. It was beautiful. So beautiful. It enveloped them in one last, all-encompassing blue blanket of light. And then it faded, slowly, until it was gone forever. Toy's body slumped and Rory knew that he, too, was gone forever. But his cracked paper lips were turned upward in an unfamiliar, but unmistakable smile.

OLD WOUNDS

The storm subsided, the wind dying down as the rain slackened. Nicholas shook himself alert, still awed by the beautiful light that had washed over them all. The death throes of the Trap had been breathtaking. But now there was still work to do.

Kieft still waited, watching to see what happened next. Would Tackapausha step out of the park first? Or would it be Abigail? Buck moved ahead of the crowd, his eyes filled with the hope of just that possibility.

Suddenly, there was a commotion behind him and Nicholas spied a boy in a stovepipe hat running toward Buck's back with a bared knife. Nicholas was too far away to do anything, he realized with horror; he could only watch helplessly as the boy sprang at Buck, stabbing the knife down toward a spot directly between the unwitting Munsee's shoulder blades—

Thwack!

From out of nowhere, an arrow appeared in the boy's shoulder, prompting him to drop his knife in pain. Buck realized his danger and spun around, but the injured boy was already disappearing into the crowd. Before anyone could chase the would-be assassin, a voice rang out from the entrance to the park.

"It cannot be—"

They all turned back toward the park, where a man had appeared, striding out of the trees with his bow in hand. The man's eyes were shocked, even as he fit another arrow into his bowstring. Nicholas knew him of old—it was Tackapausha, free at last.

Hundreds of Munsee warriors poured out of the entrance behind their sachem, fanning out to take positions behind benches and trees. They appeared ready to fight. The gods around him took a step back, muttering to themselves. Many of them pulled out pistols and swords. *Great,* Nicholas thought. They'd come this far just to kill one another.

Buckongahelas took a step forward, a tearful smile flowing across his face. "Father! You've come home."

"It is you who has come home," Tackapausha replied, his face still disbelieving. "I do not know how it is possible, but I am beyond joyful to see you again, my son."

"Where is my daughter?" the Mayor demanded, striding forward. Tackapausha turned away from his son, his face becoming stone at the sound of the Mayor's voice.

"I am surprised to see you here, Hamilton," the Sachem said. "I would have thought you were hiding in a cellar somewhere."

The gods grumbled among themselves at the Sachem's haughty tone. It was as if they'd forgotten who had put whom in a cage, Nicholas thought.

"I was told she still lived," Hamilton said.

"Is it true?" Buck asked his father, who nodded. "Where is she?"

"My business here is not finished yet," Tackapausha answered.

"I demand that you return her to me!" Hamilton shouted.

"There will be no demands!" Tackapausha declared. "Only justice. All through the long years of our captivity, I continued to promise my people that one thing: justice. There were many architects of our prison, I know this. But you, Hamilton, you were the great betrayer. You took everything from me! And now I want the same from you."

"What are you talking about?" Hamilton asked warily.

"I demand your life. That is justice."

"My people, this insult cannot be borne!" Kieft cried, lifting his pistol. The gods followed him, training their weapons on the Indians at the gate. "If you threaten our mayor, you threaten us all."

Nicholas had to admire the way Kieft incited the crowd. When the fighting began, people would remember only Tackapausha's demands, not Kieft's fanning of the flames. The Munsees reacted in kind, brandishing their weapons. Hamilton shook his head.

"You're mad, Tackapausha, if you think I'll let you take my life."

"I knew you'd be a coward," Tackapausha said. "Your people's lives are on your head."

"Father, please, don't do this," Buck said, stepping forward, but the Sachem refused to hear him.

"Let's all just calm down a minute!" Nicholas called out, but no one listened. Hamilton pulled out a gun.

"You're the one who is keeping my daughter from me. You're the one making unreasonable demands. Look around you. I have ten times as many people behind me. It will be a slaughter if you try to fight."

"We will make a good accounting of ourselves, I promise you," Tackapausha said fiercely. Weapons pointed in every direction as the battle waited only upon a single first shot to explode.

"Hey, poopheads! Chill out! You're worse than the boys in my class, and they eat paste!"

A familiar girl ran right between Tackapausha and Hamilton, followed by a large dog.

"You should be ashamed of yourselves!" Bridget scolded them. For a second both the Sachem and the Mayor seemed taken aback by this paper girl in their midst, but Tackapausha quickly rallied.

"You have no say in this, demon," he informed her haughtily.

"*I* don't," she replied in the same tone, pointing toward the park, where a figure was emerging. "But she does."

Buck was already eagerly running past the girl toward the trees, and the look on his face brought tears to Nicholas's eyes.

"Abby . . ." he whispered. He joyfully reached the tired-looking girl in a dirty dress who was laughing at the sight of her love. They kissed, clutching at each other fiercely.

"Abigail." Hamilton's voice came out anguished as he lowered his gun hand. He reached out to his daughter, tears rising in his eyes.

"Hello, Father," Abigail said, her voice cold as she turned toward him. "I waited for you. I thought you would come for me."

"I couldn't," Hamilton stammered. "The Trap . . ."

"I waited a hundred and fifty years for you to come, and you never did," Abigail said. "I love you, Father, but for what you've done . . . I can never forgive you."

Hamilton seemed to deflate in front of everyone.

"You're right," he muttered. A murmur ran through the crowd. Tackpausha looked taken aback. "Justice is required. You may have your revenge, Tackapausha. There is nothing left to me, anyway. Just try to forgive my people. Too many lives have been ruined already. Let mine be the last taken. But let's not call it an execution, for both our sakes. Let's call it a duel."

Hamilton raised his gun and fired into the air. Tackapausha lifted his bow, the arrow aimed right at Hamilton's heart. But his hand shook. Abruptly, he dropped the bow to his side.

"I will not kill you today," he said. "It is our first day of freedom and I will not stain it with blood . . . even your blood." He raised his voice to address the gods. "We are returning to our home. The park is ours; newcomers are not welcome in our home. We have neither forgiven nor have we forgotten. But today . . . Today we enjoy the passing of the storm."

He turned and strode into the park without looking back. Taken off guard at the abrupt shift from the edge of war to peace, the Munsees slowly followed their sachem back to their home. Nicholas could tell by their faces that, indeed, nothing had been forgiven. He sighed, the tension finally seeping out of him as the Munsees disappeared into the trees. At least war had been averted for now.

Turning, Nicholas noticed that Kieft was already starting to move away, followed by Boss Tweed and Tobias, among others.

Though some of the gods looked relieved, others appeared both angry and fearful. Kieft's work had been done too well, he thought. It was apparent that not all of Mannahatta welcomed the Munsees back. This peace was fragile, and it would not take much to shatter it into a million pieces.

But for now, the storm had passed.

AFTER THE STORM

Rory hadn't moved from his spot in the store. He watched as the Munsees and the gods almost came to blows, then he breathed a sigh of relief when he saw them avert disaster. It had all worked out. He glanced down at Toy. Well, almost.

When he looked back up again, someone was standing there.

"Your nice nose is all ruined," Soka said, smiling softly.

"It's just blood," Rory replied. "I'll heal. So you're free."

"Thanks to you."

"I just did my part," he said, too exhausted to brag.

"Well, my people are going back into the park. But I'll be back to see you, I promise. Or you could visit me. Tacka-pausha has forbidden newcomers, but I'm not afraid to break the rules."

"No, you're not," Rory replied. The two of them stared at each other, unsure what to say next. A lot had happened in the past week and Rory felt different. Soka looked different as well;

sadder, wiser, and somehow more beautiful. He felt a million miles away from this otherworldy Indian girl.

"The demon is dead," Soka said finally, breaking the silence as she noticed Toy for the first time.

"He saved my life," Rory said, a mild reproach in his voice.

"Then he was no demon."

"Where's your brother?" he asked, looking around for the disapproving face of Tammand. Soka's eyes darkened.

"I do not care. He is not who I had hoped he'd be."

"Family hardly ever is," Rory said ruefully.

"Do not let Bridget hear you say that," Soka replied, smiling. She put a hand on Rory's face, sending a shiver down his spine. "I will see you soon, Rory Hennessy. I promise."

With that, she left to rejoin her people. Rory watched her go with a sad feeling in his heart and he didn't know why.

"Rory!"

Rory spun to see Bridget standing there, her face all smiles as he reached in to envelop her in the biggest hug ever given, and he held it for what felt like forever.

Askook felt the call in his head, demanding his presence. It led him to the deserted City Hall, down the winding corridors he knew from the time before the Trap, into an area of the building he'd never seen before. Judging by the age and rottenness of the wall hangings, and all the dust on the floor, no one had come this way in a long time. Finally, the call led him to a large oak door crisscrossed with forbidding iron bars. He pushed it open with a large creak. Standing on the other side was Willem Kieft.

The ancient god's black, black eyes bore into Askook, the force of his stare bringing his wayward servant to his knees.

"I'm sorry." Askook began to shake. "In the end, he would not fight. It was not my fault!"

"I'm not going to kill you, Askook," Kieft said softly. "Not today. Did you move my things?"

"Of course," Askook replied, getting himself under control. "They will be safe until you come to claim them. But what can we do now? There was no war."

Kieft smiled. "I'm going to enlighten you, Askook. This was not a setback. It is an overture for the last act I always knew was coming. I wished the Munsees dead, certainly, for your people's magic brings certain snags to my ultimate plan. But I can, as they say, roll with the punches. The most important part of my plan lagged behind schedule. But at the last minute, I received some unexpected help from an old friend. I wished the Mayor could have fallen, but his life doesn't matter in the end. New sides have been chosen and I no longer need him. The march to the last battle proceeds apace and I will win, of that I have no doubt. Why don't you come look at this."

Kieft stepped over to a large cabinet that took up an entire wall in the dingy little room. Askook stood next to his master, but not too close, as Kieft reached out and flung open the door. Askook began to chuckle bitterly.

"I will never doubt you again," he said.

"Of course you won't," Kieft replied. A smile finally made an appearance on the old god's face, which was reflected in the hundreds of shiny new knives that hung in the long cabinet. Each one capable of ending a god's life.

"You could slit every god's throat at once with these." Askook marveled.

"I won't be slitting anyone's throat," Kieft said. "After all, they would see me coming. But there will be blood. More blood than you could possibly imagine. Soon we will be floating in it."

Askook took in the sight of those shiny blades and his heart settled. There would be no triumphing over all this death. This war would end all wars. And judging from Kieft's smile, the ancient god had no doubt who would win.

The sun had broken through the clouds as the remnants of the great storm moved on. Cars began to make their way cautiously around the traffic circle, and tourists were emerging from their hiding places inside the nearest buildings. There was some damage visible from the wind and lightning, with many downed streetlamps and broken glass littering the streets, but all in all, a sense of relief permeated the air. In the aftermath of the storm, the heat had broken. The city was returning to normal, slowly but surely.

The Rattle Watch sat in the center of the plaza on the steps leading up to the pedestal. Sergeant Kiffer and Hans had returned from the park, where'd they let Pierre go to bury his grandson. The old man was broken, they reasoned, and not a threat anymore. Hans's arm was completely useless, but he didn't appear depressed. Instead, the battle roach began to outline plans for a bionic arm, excitedly sketching it with his good arm in the dirt at their feet. Rory lay back, staring up at the blue sky, while Nicholas, Lincoln, and Alexa argued with

Simon, trying to get him to remove his locket. Finally, they broke Simon down.

"I can't!" he admitted. "It won't come off. I tried earlier today, when I found myself thinking about china patterns. It's horrible! What do I care about dishes? I eat off my lap most of the time! But now I can hear their prayers. 'Please don't break' is the one I get the most, followed closely by 'please don't ask me to use it.' It's driving me crazy!"

"There has to be some way to get it off you," Nicholas said while Alexa smiled behind her hand. She had a bandage wrapped around her forehead, but otherwise she seemed all right. "We'll find it, I promise."

"Good." Simon sighed, his head in his hands. "Godhood sucks."

Bridget sat on the other side of Nicholas, Toy's body at her feet. She smoothed his paper hair with her own paper hand, sadness written across her face.

"He was a real hero," she said. "He saved us all so many times. Right back to the first time he refused to turn the key. I hope he's at peace now."

Fritz stood on the other side of Toy's body, his helmet under his arm.

"I'm sure he is," he said softly. "You deserved so much better, Jason. But you did us all proud in the end."

A tear ran down his cheek.

"We should bury him," Bridget said, turning to Rory.

"We will, in the park," Rory replied.

"Good." Bridget sat back and sighed. "I wish I could have seen Dad. Do you think he'll come back to see me?"

Her shoulders slumped. Fritz climbed up next to her.

"He sailed into the mist a thousand times," Fritz said, his voice certain. "And he always came back. Many sailors haven't. There are hundreds of islands out there, many of them very livable, from what I've heard. He could have easily stayed away forever. But he always came back. You'll see him again, I promise it. And maybe then you'll get the rest of your answers."

Rory nodded, though he wasn't sure if he believed it.

"We can't get too comfortable," Nicholas warned them all. "I don't think Kieft is done."

"But my job is over, right?" Rory asked. "I opened the Trap."

"Turning that key didn't stop you from being a Light, Rory," Alexa told him. "You're still very much a part of Mannahatta and we need you. The belt might be gone, but you still have valuable powers."

Rory didn't want to mention the strange feelings that had been running through him ever since Caesar had melted the belt off his body. Every once in a while the world looked and felt like it had when he was wearing the belt, even though the belt was no more. But then the feeling would go away. He didn't know what to make of it.

"I'll help if I can," he said while Bridget leaped to her feet.

"Of course we'll help, in any way you need!" she exclaimed. "We're in the Rattle Watch, right? That's our job! To protect the innocent and weak and short and ugly!"

"Something like that." Nicholas laughed.

Rory stood up.

"We need to get you back to your real body, Bridget," he said. "It's waiting for you at Washington Irving's house.

But first, I think we should lay Toy to rest. Anyone coming with me?"

"Of course we are," Nicholas said. "He was practically one of us."

"I'm dying to see what the park looks like," Simon said. "It's been locked away since before I was born."

"Let's go, then." Alexa hopped to her feet and reached down to lift Toy up in her arms."

Together, they crossed the street, passing below the statue of the gilded lady and into the park. The sun slowly dried up the pools of rainwater, and soon the only remains of the great storm lay in memory. But that memory lived on long after the day, though it shifted and grew until not even those who'd lived through it could agree on what had happened exactly. Their outlandish stories were never particularly close to the truth. It didn't matter. All that mattered was that they remembered.

EPILOGUE

Mrs. Hennessy was feeling ragged. Both her children had been ill for a few days now, and she had taken off from work to care for them, which didn't please her boss at the law firm. Mr. Corgin had very little patience for her family responsibilities, constantly reminding her that there were plenty of young up-and-comers willing to work all hours for a chance at her job. He might be bluffing, since she knew she was no slouch, but then again, he might not. And since they'd been sick, Rory and Bridget both seemed . . . odd to her. They didn't laugh as loud or complain as often or argue as vehemently as they should have. Something was going on with them, and, as usual, she had no idea what it was.

The doorbell rang. Mrs. Hennessy had been sitting, exhausted, at the kitchen table, having finally coaxed her children to sleep. She forced herself to her feet and shuffled over to the door. Mrs. Mallon, a middle-aged woman with bright red hair who had moved in next door the day before, stood on the other side, a big pot in her hand.

"Here you go, dear, for the children!" she said. Mrs. Hennessy took the pot being offered her with a tired but thankful smile and carried it inside. Mrs. Mallon followed her in, closing the door behind her.

"It's chicken noodle," she said. "It's simple, but it works. You should have some yourself."

"I'm sure it's wonderful, Mrs. Mallon," Mrs. Hennessy assured her, placing the pot on the stove. "Maybe I'll try it. It's only that my stomach has been so crazy lately I haven't been able to eat more than some crackers . . ."

"I wonder why that is," Mrs. Mallon said, pretending to think. "Oh yes, your two sick children and your pressure-cooker job. That's enough to turn anyone's appetite. But this one is much gentler on the digestion. You could eat with no worries."

"I'll think about it," Mrs. Hennessy said, grateful for the sympathy. "I've just been overtaxed. Actually, would you mind if I cut short our visit today? I'm feeling a bit tired."

"Sure, of course," Mrs. Mallon said, reaching to give her a hug. Even though she liked the other woman, Mrs. Hennessy still felt a wave of nausea hit her as she put her arms around Mrs. Mallon. The woman let off a slight scent of decay, like rotting leaves. Mrs. Hennessy hid her reaction as always and patted the other woman on the shoulder. Mrs. Mallon couldn't help how she smelled.

"Thank you."

"No thanks necessary. It's what anyone would do in my place. And please, call me Mary."

Mrs. Hennessy nodded as Mary Mallon turned and left, leaving her alone with her children sleeping in the next room.

A moment later she absently grabbed a spoon. She slid the large pot across the countertop, lifting off the lid. It certainly looked tasty. Even though she still felt queasy, she wanted to eat something, to keep up her strength. No harm in a taste, she decided. She dipped her spoon in, taking a big spoonful of Mrs. Mallon's gift and swallowing it down. It was so good, she wanted more. She took another large mouthful. So good, she thought. She hoped she'd leave something for her kids. She leaned over the pot on her counter, drinking directly from the cookware. *This is more like it,* she thought. *I feel better already . . .*

⮐ ACKNOWLEDGMENTS ⮐

FIRST OF ALL, THE BIGGEST OF THANKS to my editor Julie Strauss-Gabel. This was not the easiest book to write, and it took a bit longer than expected to finish, and her patience and fortitude were taxed to the limit. She deserves a vacation (a real one, not one where she has to read my manuscript by the pool). Thanks to my agent, David Dunton, for his wisdom and support (and to his son, Noah, for taking a gander at an early draft). Thanks to the folks at Dutton for their enthusiasm and hard work. Thanks to my friends and family, especially my wife, Kristina, who had to put up with my late night disappearances into my office to work on the evening's pages. And a special thanks to all the independent booksellers, bloggers, and librarians out there who championed *Gods of Manhattan*. You are the backbone of any success I've had.